Praise for TJ Alexander and

A Lady for All Seasons

"*A Lady for All Seasons* is the queer, trans Regency romance I desperately needed. Elegant prose meets messy Shakespearean romantic entanglements, threaded with hilarious witticisms, resulting in a book that few will be able to read in more than one sitting."

–Lindz McLeod, author of *The Unlikely Pursuit of Mary Bennet*

"Intoxicatingly delicious–Alexander's wonderful characters feel so real."

–Megan Frampton, author of *The Scot's Seduction*

"Alexander brings trans and queer joy to the Regency era with deft depth, romance, and fun."

–Emma R. Alban, *USA Today* bestselling author of *Don't Want You Like a Best Friend*

"TJ Alexander genuinely does not miss for me."

–Dahlia Adler, Smart Bitches Trashy Books

"TJ Alexander [is] a welcome and exciting voice in historical fiction."

–Adriana Herrera, *USA Today* bestselling author of *An Island Princess Starts a Scandal*

"Alexander's writing is lovely, and their characters are incredibly carefully drawn."

—Martha Waters, author of *To Love and to Loathe*

"TJ Alexander builds the heat between their unforgettable heroes with an achingly slow sweetness while giving tropey historical hijinks the most sumptuous queer flair."

—Joanna Lowell, author of *A Shore Thing*

TJ Alexander

A Lady for All Seasons

TJ Alexander is the author of *Chef's Kiss, Chef's Choice, Second Chances in New Port Stephen, Triple Sec,* and *A Gentleman's Gentleman.* They received their MA in writing and publishing from Emerson College, and they live in New York City with their wife and various houseplants.

ALSO BY TJ ALEXANDER

A Gentleman's Gentleman

Triple Sec

Second Chances in New Port Stephen

Chef's Choice

Chef's Kiss

A Lady for All Seasons

A Lady for All Seasons

TJ Alexander

Vintage Books
A Division of Penguin Random House LLC
New York

A VINTAGE BOOKS ORIGINAL 2026

Published by Vintage Books, a division of Penguin Random House LLC,
1745 Broadway, New York, NY 10019.

Vintage and colophon are registered trademarks of
Penguin Random House LLC.

Cataloging-in-Publication Data is on file with the Library of Congress.

Vintage Trade Paperback ISBN: 979-8-217-00728-8
eBook ISBN: 979-8-217-00729-5

Book design by Steven Walker

penguinrandomhouse.com | vintagebooks.com

Printed in the United States of America
2nd Printing

The authorized representative in the EU for product safety and compliance is Penguin Random House Ireland, Morrison Chambers, 32 Nassau Street, Dublin DO2 YH68, Ireland, https://eu-contact.penguin.ie.

To Lauren, for the spark, and Kaila, for the dance.
And for all who come after me.

A Lady for All Seasons

Chapter 1

July 1820

It was a damp and dreary afternoon near the end of the London season in the year the regent had become King. After six months of rule, even the densest members of the ton were finally referring to His Majesty correctly on the first try. All of London—and, indeed, the empire—found itself at a turning point, but as is usual in such circumstances, hardly anyone understood what was happening in the moment. Some people had more pressing matters to consider.

For example, all the social machinations and maneuverings of a midsummer picnic.

Verbena Montrose surveyed the scene. The hostess had outdone herself. On a patch of flat grass, footmen had erected canopies to provide protection from the intermittent drizzle, and low tables were being laid with cold roast chicken and platters of minuscule foodstuffs. Turkish rugs were unfurled and goose-down pillows arranged so those who wished could recline. Some distance away, beneath their own canopy, a string quartet was tuning their instruments. Everywhere one looked, glasses of cold lemonade and champagne were being offered on silver salvers by liveried servants in powdered wigs.

To Verbena, this was all on par with watching armies prepare for an onslaught. A social event such as this may not involve the same amount of bloodshed, but in her mind, it was war all the same. When one was searching for a husband as she was, there was no sense in pretending society was anything else.

"Everyone! Shall we play a game before we eat?" their hostess called over the faint murmur of the gathering crowd.

Verbena turned to regard the handsome woman of middle age. Her mind supplied all the relevant facts without hesitation: the dowager countess, Lady Croydon. Recently out of mourning. Very rich, and very eager to return to society.

The lady sipped at her glass of wine and gestured to a knot of young bucks. "Find something we can use as a blindfold," she directed.

While the men tried to locate an extra cravat that someone swore had been brought for just this purpose, Verbena exchanged amiable greetings with her mutual acquaintances. There was an earl whose daughter was rumored to have run off to Spain to become a nun; a lady who had almost certainly poisoned her first husband so she might marry her second; the twins who had a gambling habit and laudanum addiction, respectively; and three Howe sisters who, Verbena knew for a fact, were all in love with the same man, who in turn was in love with a butcher's daughter from Kent.

Verbena knew these things because she had made it her business to know. The trick was to take in all conversation, no matter how boring, and piece it together with all the other conversations she had absorbed. Whereas others might see pointless chatter, with all the bits and baubles combined, she was able to form a complete picture. It was during one of these interminable chats, where Verbena was politely listening to one guest talk about the weather (unseasonably cool), that she heard the eldest Howe sister mention "a most unnatural death."

Her ears attuned to this instantly, being a student of the macabre and well-versed in broadside stories of murderous intrigue. It was an interest that Verbena often hid in polite company, unladylike as it was, so the opportunity to hear some tawdry tidbit was a welcome one.

"That is the title?" the conversation partner asked.

"Yes, Flora Witcombe's latest," Miss Howe insisted, "is the most amusing collection of poems yet. By far my favorite, even better than her first!"

Poetry. Bah. Verbena would gain more by listening to someone speak about the weather. At least then, the speaker might divulge some future plans that could be stymied or helped along by rain or sun. If the murder was a mere metaphor, what was the point?

"Aha!" Lady Croydon waved the white strip of silk someone had finally procured. "Now we may begin." She looked over her guests, her eyes alighting upon Verbena. Not for the first time, Verbena cursed her bright red hair, which often made her stand out in a crowd. She tried to tuck the fashionably errant wisps back under her bonnet, but it was too late. "Shall you be 'it' in our first round of blindman's bluff, Miss Montrose?" their hostess asked.

"It would bring me great pleasure," Verbena lied. She shut her parasol and leaned it against a nearby tree, as many of the other ladies had already done.

"Careful, dear," warned Lady Croydon as she fastened the silk around Verbena's head. "In a game like this, who knows where one's hands will alight?" Several gentlemen chuckled.

Verbena was very glad for the blindfold. It allowed her to roll her eyes without being seen.

"Over here, Miss Montrose!" A high-pitched voice dissolved into giggles, joined by the titters of a dozen other guests. Verbena could hear clumsy feet scampering in the opposite direction quite clearly, but she feigned confusion with a pleasant smile. It was important to be a good sport, no matter how much one would rather be elsewhere.

"Dear me," she murmured, arms outstretched. "I'm hopeless at this! How am I supposed to catch anyone?"

Someone to the left whispered something Verbena could not quite make out, but the recipient of the remark snickered cruelly. Verbena's head whipped in that direction. If someone had something to say about her, she very much wished to know who had said it. She made for the perpetrator, marching quickly and changing course as she heard dainty shoes shuffling along the grass.

"Ah, no!" cried her prey.

Verbena knew well the sound of skirts being lifted in preparation for running. When one had played as many rounds of blindman's bluff at picnics as she had, it was impossible not to.

She struck with assured deftness, catching hold of a soft arm. "Now I've got you." Verbena lifted her blindfold in triumph.

Her captive was Miss Landsbury, second daughter of the Cheshire Landsburys. A middling family of no real consequence. Her cheeks were aflame, and not, Verbena suspected, from their playful exertions. The girl knew she had been caught gossiping, and she had no choice but to weather Verbena's hard stare.

"Good showing, Miss Montrose," she said, attempting to reclaim her dignity by standing taller. "You give yourself too little credit. You make a wonderful 'it' after all."

"The trick is to listen and stay as quiet as possible," Verbena said. She gave Miss Landsbury's arm a shake to drive home her meaning. "A bit of advice I hope will serve you well, now that you are . . . 'it.'" She held the blindfold aloft on the crook of one finger.

Miss Landsbury took it with a sullen sneer that did her no favors. Verbena noticed Lady Croydon whisper something to one of the twins while holding out her glass for a servant to refill. Society could not countenance a slip in a lady's feminine facade.

Verbena's smile widened. Silly girls with no head for strategy should not play for such high stakes against a more experienced player.

Still, the encounter disturbed Verbena. She thought it over as she collected her parasol in case the rain began again. There was little doubt in her mind that Miss Landsbury had made some remark about Verbena's recent difficulties in finding a husband. That she felt free to do so without repercussion was troubling.

In truth, word of her father's financial state had spread despite Verbena's efforts to stem the tide. A household could not release a flock of footmen and three chambermaids from employment while neglecting to hire replacements without some comment. Even second daughters from Cheshire now knew Mr. Lewis Montrose had been bilked out of his fortune by scoundrels and charlatans. His creditors were being held at bay with promises of some future windfall, which was to say, Verbena's future marriage.

If Verbena ever managed to find a suitable husband, of course.

"Ah, Miss Montrose!"

Verbena shook herself from her dour thoughts as a gentleman approached from across the lawn. It was Lord Newham, a pale man of forty-some years with a distinct lack of chin. He possessed a wife twenty years his junior and a hat in dire need of brushing.

"My lord." Verbena dropped a curtsy. "Do you wish to join our game?" She gestured to the blindfolded Miss Landsbury, who was currently headed directly for an elm.

"No, no," said the baron. "I was hoping to have a word with you."

Verbena could hardly refuse the polite request, surrounded as she was by curious eyes. "Of course."

Parasol raised above her head, she allowed the baron to escort her some distance away so they could speak privately, although Verbena did keep an eye on the game. After all, one couldn't miss the chance to watch Miss Landsbury walk face-first into a tree with an undignified yelp.

The baron appeared distracted, though not by Miss Landsbury's folly. He looked at the sky, the ground, the flower beds—everywhere but Verbena. "Lovely day," he said as if by rote.

"Yes, isn't it perfect?" This was a lie, of course, but one the English collectively indulged in anytime they found themselves at a party in the open air. Verbena hoped the damp grass would not seep through her soft shoes; her feet were already quite chilled. "And how fares Lady Newham?" The baron's wife was heavy with their third child, or so people said. She was not present at the picnic, so the rumor seemed likely.

"Oh, she . . . " The baron trailed off, waving a hand through the air as if his wife's health was of no consequence. "But what of you? Have you formed any attachments this season?"

Verbena controlled her face into a pleasant, blank mask. It

was extremely forward of Newham to ask if she had any suitors, but some people did not have the gift of subtlety. She elected to ignore the rudeness; the baron might have an unattached nephew or cousin, and perhaps his impertinent question was only in service of making a match.

"I have fostered many excellent friendships"–another lie; most of these people were awful bores–"but I am not entertaining a suit at the moment, if that is what you mean."

Not for lack of trying. Her family's dire financial situation and her subsequent nonexistent dowry made it difficult to attract a proposal.

"Capital, capital." In addition to his hat, the baron's shave also needed tending. Whoever had done the job had left several bristles where his chin should be. "I wonder, then, if you might entertain a proposal of my own."

"And what is that, my lord?" asked Verbena. While she still held out hope for an unattached nephew in the wings, the hairs on the back of her neck prickled in warning. She glanced about to see if anyone could overhear, but all the other guests were still absorbed in the game.

"I think we could come to quite a beneficial arrangement," the baron murmured, more to Verbena's décolletage rather than her entire person.

Verbena felt a flush of anger overtake her. It straightened her spine and sharpened her mind. Already her thoughts were in motion, not in a distressed whirl, but in the focused way a cobra might stalk a mouse. Despite his wealth and title, Newham was not immune to the whispers of the ton. She had heard tidbits here and there of his private dealings; it was not difficult for her to piece them together to create a vivid tapestry. He thought her fit for nothing more than a clandestine romp? She would prove him wrong.

"Lord Newham," she said with ice in her tone, "I am certain I misheard you. Surely a man of your stature could not say what I erroneously believe you said."

"Now, don't be coy." His upper lip twitched with mirth as he leaned in closer. Verbena leaned away, gripping her parasol handle. "I would be very kind to you, yes, very kind. Two pounds a month, perhaps, and the use of some rooms where we might meet thrice a week or so."

Verbena reminded herself that beating a baron with a parasol in the middle of a picnic was not the polite thing to do. Not to mention, the parasol would hardly inflict the desired amount of damage. Her true weapon was information, and she possessed that in droves.

She forced a smile to her lips.

"My lord, I would rather perish," she said cheerfully.

"Three pounds, then. Not a bad deal for a girl who can't procure the affections of a husband," Newham drawled.

She drew herself up to her full height. "This is not a negotiation, sir. My quibble is not with the price; it is with your person, which is abhorrent to me."

The horror of spending time in the baron's private company aside, Verbena knew what happened to women who agreed to similar arrangements. She could hardly escape such knowledge, as devoted as she was to reading the news of the day, from the most opaque political dealings to the tawdriest tales of the criminal underworld—and, yes, stories of girls in untenable situations. High-class or low, they tended to be tossed out on the street on the man's fickle whim—usually with child, always with a black mark on their reputation. Better for women skilled in those arts to be their own masters and ply their expert trade on their own terms, in her view. But of course, that was not what men like the baron sought.

Lord Newham's amused smirk fell into a scowl. "Think it over carefully before you rebuff me," he hissed. "By now, all of London knows your dire situation. You're lucky to have caught my interest at all. Do you imagine Lady Croydon might extend future invitations to you if I told her that you've already offered yourself to me?"

"Do you imagine Lady Croydon will believe that once I tell her how you allow your brothers to lay with your wife?"

That shut his foul mouth. His lips pursed, his cheeks flaming a ludicrous red.

"I noticed," Verbena said, all innocence, "that Admiral Newham was in town about nine months before your last child was born, was he not? And your youngest brother–was he not seen escorting Lady Newham in the park several months ago? I excel at arithmetic, you know." She fixed her steely gaze on the baron. "Society will forgive a man his vices. They will even encourage them. But they will never respect a cuckold, and a willing one at that."

It was entirely possible he and Lady Newham had resorted to using the brothers to produce an heir if Lord Newham was unable to produce one himself, but the reason behind the arrangement was none of Verbena's concern. It was the result that would cause a scandal. Was it unfair for her to use such a thing against him? Perhaps, but it was equally unfair of him to threaten her as he had. Cobras, when taunted, attack. A creature cannot be faulted for doing what is in its nature.

Newham quivered with rage. His hands balled into fists at his sides. Verbena noted all this coolly.

"Strike me in view of everyone," she said, "and see which of us receives their sympathy. Who knows? You might even win me a husband."

"Vixen," Newham said under his breath. "*Witch.*"

Verbena cleared her throat, speaking loudly enough that the other guests might hear her. "Farewell, baron. A pity you must leave the festivities so early. Give my love to your wife."

Puffing like an overworked cart horse, Lord Newham could only sketch the shallowest of bows before storming off across the lawn. Verbena watched him disappear over a hill with a sort of grim satisfaction.

She meant to rejoin the game, but as she turned to inspect the state of play, she was arrested by a cloud of perfume draped in taffeta.

"Miss Montrose," said the cloud, "what was all that about?"

The cloud took the shape of Miss Diedre Hollyhock, a lovely if unrelenting girl destined to be an old maid at twenty-six. Despite being perfectly pleasant, if no great beauty, she had never married. She served as a harsh reminder to all the younger women of their circle that if they didn't find husbands, they would be consigned to a lifetime of spinsterhood. Despite this state of affairs, Miss Hollyhock was a jolly presence at parties, always eager to collect bits of gossip. One could see from the glint in her eyes that she meant to dig some out of Verbena.

"All about what, Miss Hollyhock?" Verbena parried.

"Lord Newham left rather abruptly, I noticed," Miss Hollyhock said. "Your conversation was not the cause of any distress, was it?"

"Oh, nothing of the kind." Verbena laughed. "Idle chitchat. We remarked upon the weather, mostly."

While Verbena enjoyed Miss Hollyhock's company, she was not what one might call a bosom friend. Confidantes were a risk that Verbena did not dare take. From the moment she'd made her debut, Verbena had been acutely aware of how quickly a so-called trusted friend could reveal herself a turncoat if it meant even the most meager increase in her own standing. She remembered with a pang her dearest childhood friend, Winifred Stassel, who had once betrayed her before a pivotal ball.

Miss Hollyhock eyed Verbena closely. "Perhaps you might recall what His Lordship said in more detail later. Oh!" Her gaze went to something over Verbena's shoulder that caused her eyes to widen. "We'll speak later. I must return to the game."

"I'll accompany–" Verbena began to say, but Miss Hollyhock fled faster than she could utter a response. How odd.

Verbena turned, curious as to what had made Miss Hollyhock rush away, and was confronted with the unwelcome sight of an extremely tall, thin viscount with a smattering of white hair on his head. He was standing much too close to her.

"Lord Merven," she said with all the politeness she could muster. While she normally considered all conversation vital to her aims, Verbena had great difficulty understanding how this man's could be anything but useless. Lord Merven talked of nothing but his hobby of cataloging snails; he was well-known for haranguing a captive audience on the subject. Snails were, of course, one of god's creations, and Verbena had no quarrel with them, but she had more important things to do than learn about viscous shell dwellers.

Lady Croydon's picnic was one of the last opportunities to circulate for the season, after all. A few more outings, perhaps a ball, and it would all be over.

"Miss Montrose, have you ever heard of the left-hand spiraled snail?" Lord Merven asked in lieu of a greeting. He clasped his hands behind his back with the air of a philosopher settling in for a long lecture.

Verbena made a sound of regret. "My lord, excuse me, I really must–"

She picked up her skirts, but Lord Merven began speaking again in his steady, dull monotone.

"Lefties, we call them in my circle," he said. "Exceedingly rare. Find a good lefty and I assure you, the London Society of Mollusks will be in an uproar. Well, what do you suppose I found amongst my letters just this week?"

Verbena resigned herself to her fate. There was no escaping Merven and his snails. If she broke away while he was still conversing, her rudeness would no doubt tarnish her already not-so-sterling reputation. The man was a viscount, after all. Snails notwithstanding.

"I couldn't begin to guess," she said miserably.

"A note from a chap in Leeds–Leeds!–saying he had discovered such a lefty in his employer's garden, and would I like to have a look at it. Now, he included some sketches of the snail in question–nothing too detailed, mind. He's not a professional. He only knows of the Society of Mollusks and my own interest in the matter because his cousin served aboard the same ship as my half brother. Do you know my half brother?"

Verbena opened her mouth to say she had not yet had the pleasure, but Lord Merven carried on without her input, telling the meandering story of who served aboard the HMS *Larkspur* and when and in what capacity. As hard as Verbena tried to follow the narrative, she could feel her eyes glazing over. The spirit could only suffer so much.

"Pardon me," a voice with a soft Scottish brogue said from behind her, "but did either of you see that pack of snails over by the bushes? Terribly interesting."

Verbena turned to find a lanky man with a kind face and a kinder smile. He wore a curious pair of spectacles with one clear lens and the other blacked out. She did not know him at all, which would have been worrisome–she'd thought she knew everyone worth knowing–if she were not so relieved by his sudden appearance.

"What!" cried Lord Merven. He bustled away to inspect the bushes without even a farewell.

Verbena watched him go with wide eyes. She'd never before seen the man dispatched with such alacrity. Or at all.

The stranger continued in the face of her surprised silence. "Apologies for the interruption. You looked like you might appreciate a reprieve."

It was improper for him to speak to her without having been introduced by a mutual friend first, yet there were worse improprieties. Verbena wondered what sort of man he could be. He was wearing a coat expertly cut to his trim form, but in a shade of taupe that hadn't been in fashion for several seasons. His tawny hair, too, was arranged in a sweep that young bucks had been enamored with three years ago. He was in no way shabby, but he did appear out of place. Verbena chalked this up to the fact that he was Scottish, and was, obviously, not currently in Scotland.

"His Lordship is harmless," Verbena said once she found her tongue. "But yes, his conversation is somewhat . . . challenging." She glanced toward the bushes, where Merven had crouched to examine its contents. "*Are* there snails over there, or did you invent a reason for Lord Merven to investigate?"

"Oh, on my honor, there's at least a dozen! I'd never lie about snails." He shot her a boyish grin. "It's fortunate I noticed them on my way over."

"Exceedingly fortunate," Verbena said. She looked over at the rest of the party, still engaged in blindman's bluff. If anyone noticed her speaking to a strange man, no one had protested, likely assuming that Lord Merven had done his duty and conducted a proper introduction. Since that was not the case, and they were already exchanging words, she felt it necessary to get through the niceties herself. "I don't believe we've been introduced. Miss Verbena Montrose." She gave him a small nod of her chin, not wanting to draw any attention with a handshake or elaborate curtsy.

"Mr. Miles Montague McDonald," said he, inclining his head in return.

"McDonald–of the Edinburgh McDonalds?" she inquired. Her heart rose on a crested wave of hope.

"Erm, no. The Peeblewick McDonalds." He grimaced and tossed his hair from his eyes. Well, his single visible eye. Hazel, Verbena noted out of habit. "We're not the most well-known branch."

"Of course. Peeblewick," Verbena said as if everyone knew the place. "It is lovely to meet you. Any friend of Lady Croydon is a friend of mine." This was laying it on a bit thick, but Verbena could be forgiven. Compared to the other men she'd encountered today, Miles McDonald was a prize, even if he didn't belong to the more famed, well-off family of McDonalds.

"That's very kind of you," said Mr. McDonald, "but I'm not so much a friend of Lady Croydon as a distant acquaintance. My mother was a friend of a friend of hers, which is how I managed an invitation. I've not met her before." He frowned. "Well, I've not met anyone. Not here, anyway. Of course I've met other people in other places." His nervous laugh was charming in its own way. "I've just arrived in London, you see." The Scots accent became more pronounced. "If I'm honest, I only noticed those snails because I was dawdling. I'm really not sure how to go about this. I don't suppose you could point out Lady Croydon to me?"

Verbena was moved by his helplessness. He was clearly unused to the vicious games of London society; no gentleman who'd grown up in its ranks would ever admit to only barely rating an invitation to a picnic, or that their family tree was anything less than impressive. Perhaps his naïveté could be an asset to her.

"By all means," she said, "allow me to introduce you."

"Wonderful!" He gave her his arm, and together they walked across the lawn. The game of bluff was over now and the repast was served. Lady Croydon was ushering her guests into the shade of the tents, newly filled wineglass in hand. She laughed at something someone said as Verbena closed her parasol, stowing it among the others.

Good. The lady was in excellent humor, which would make the job easier.

Verbena cleared her throat. "Pardon me, Lady Croydon, but I owe you an apology," she said.

The conversation died down as the lady examined Verbena. "Oh? Whatever for, Miss Montrose?" Her eyes moved to the man at Verbena's side, meandering up and down his long form, lingering on his eyeglasses. Verbena hoped she did not find them too strange, nor too distasteful. They were, after all, the mark of a clerk.

"I'm afraid I've delayed Mr. Miles Montague McDonald, who I gather is a son of your dear friend. Instead of greeting you promptly as he'd planned, he gallantly saved me from a beetle. The dreadful thing was crawling up my skirts like a devil, and he batted it away for me."

Mr. McDonald gave Verbena a startled look, which Verbena ignored. "I did?" he said.

"You did," she echoed, smiling at him encouragingly. She knew what she was doing, and he didn't. It was rather the usual state of affairs for a woman of her talents.

He nodded at Lady Croydon, wide-eyed. "I did."

It was a small, silly lie, but an important one. It would raise him up a bit in the hostess's estimation, and, most pressingly, it established Verbena as the object of his notice, just in case Mr. McDonald proved of interest to any unattached ladies.

"Mr. McDonald! Yes, of course." Lady Croydon greeted him

like an old friend and not the distant acquaintance he actually was. The lady was very malleable when in her cups, and she'd drunk at least four glasses by Verbena's count. She was likely erring on the side of friendliness, thinking she had simply misplaced the memory of this guest in the whirl of the party. "Finally, a little excitement injected into our dreary lives. Behold the hero of the hour! Beetles are such awful pests." She clasped his hands warmly in hers.

"Oh, they're not so bad," he said. "I can think of worse."

The assembled guests laughed like this was the height of wit, leaving Mr. McDonald looking quite confused. The man really was too darling.

"Well, I'll let you two chat," Verbena said as she obligingly peeled away from Mr. McDonald's side. If she stayed on him like a limpet, people would begin to talk. As with most things, a delicate balance was required.

She was about to investigate the egg sandwiches when the perfumed cloud returned to her side.

"Here, Miss Montrose, drink this," said Miss Hollyhock as she pressed a cup of lemonade into her hand. "You look absolutely parched after your harrowing experience." Her eyes roved knowingly over Miles McDonald's form. Luckily, he was turned away.

Verbena drew Miss Hollyhock to a less occupied corner of the sumptuous tent so they could speak in close conference. "I was only doing a kindness," she said, "something you might consider trying every so often. How could you leave me to Lord Merven like that? I might have expired from boredom had I not been rescued." Her tone was playful, though she had been rather inconvenienced.

"I am sorry to have abandoned you." Miss Hollyhock had the grace to look ashamed as she sipped from her own cup. "Father invited Lord Merven to dinner last week. You have no idea how little I care to hear another word on snails."

That eked some sympathy from Verbena. She tossed her head, another red curl escaping her bonnet. "Understandable."

"That reminds me," Miss Hollyhock said. "Have you recalled your conversation with Lord Newham at all? I do wonder why he had to leave so soon after his arrival."

Verbena hesitated. She knew what Miss Hollyhock was implying—that if Verbena truly wished for them to help each other, she would give Miss Hollyhock fair warning about the baron's proclivities and how he might be dispatched—but distrust held her tongue. In the end, she could only muster the vaguest of words: "I suppose he must be worried for his dear wife. I would, if I were in his position. Perhaps something I said reminded him of her condition."

"I see." Miss Hollyhock sipped her lemonade with one eye on Verbena, then inclined her head in Miles McDonald's direction. "Have you heard much about this gentleman?" He was laughing at something Lady Croydon was saying in her animated way. "I gather he's new in town. Very interesting background."

Verbena lifted one finely sculpted eyebrow. "Really?"

"I do hope your friendship with him begins and ends with that masterful introduction. He's—well, you see—" Miss Hollyhock leaned in as if divulging a secret of the Crown. "He arrived in a hackney."

Verbena's heart sank. "Oh?"

Miss Hollyhock scrunched her nose apologetically. "You wouldn't have noticed, what with Lord Merven monopolizing your attention."

A certain veneer of wealth was expected in London society. To appear in a rented hack instead of a proper carriage was a social blunder tantamount to sneezing on the king. Verbena was lucky to have been offered a seat in the Howe coach to this picnic, as her father had sold the family carriage early in the season. As an unattached lady, she had the excuse of being escorted, thus avoiding the shameful alternative.

Arriving in a hack meant that Miles McDonald was terribly poor. Worse, he did not know enough to hide that fact.

She watched him at a distance, awkwardly accepting a cup of punch, his thin smile aimed at everyone in the vicinity. The outmoded fashions he wore, his lack of survival instinct, it all added up to one thing: he was not a good prospect.

"I know. It's such a disappointment." Miss Hollyhock sighed. "He's rather handsome, for a Scot. Even with the–" She gestured to her own face, presumably indicating the eyeglasses.

"I suppose." Looks were not important to Verbena; that was reserved for finances. She could not marry a man who would be unable to support her–or her wretched parents, for that matter. The resulting poverty would be the same as if she remained unattached, so what would be the point?

"They say his parents have both died, leaving him as the sole heir to nothing." Miss Hollyhock looped her arm in Verbena's and led her to sit on a pile of pillows, where they could graze among the platters of fresh berries and petit fours. "Does he really think he will find an English wife when he has nothing to offer her but his looks?"

Verbena grimaced in sympathy for the man even as she selected a miniature strawberry tart. They were in similar boats, it seemed, both searching for a port.

Ah, well. Back to the start, then.

"What is the world coming to? Today it's an impoverished gentleman Highlander," Miss Hollyhock continued, "tomorrow it's a tailor who's to become a gentleman. It's all topsy-turvy."

Verbena had not yet heard of this latter example, but no reason to let Miss Hollyhock know that. "Oh, yes, the tailor. You're too right. What was that man's surname? I believe it started with an H?"

"No, no. It's one of the Charbonneau brothers." Miss Hollyhock raised her brows meaningfully. "People are saying this very day he is taking ownership of the house in Bloomsbury previously owned by Lord Eden. What sort of windfall would account for that, I wonder?" She paused. "Didn't a Charbonneau brother figure in one of your amusing misadventures?"

Verbena once more schooled her face into impassivity. She now knew the man Miss Hollyhock meant: Étienne, her onetime accomplice. Last season, she'd gone on the ride of her life in a bid to help a duke's daughter, one Belinda Greene, elope with her secret lover, a man called Chesterfield. It was a long story, and one she often told at parties—leaving out any of the incriminating details, of course. As far as the ton was aware, she and Étienne had been the guests of Lord Eden, a keen horseman who'd taken them for an innocent midnight jaunt with Verbena's maid acting as chaperone. They'd been chased by the enraged duke, who'd mistaken them for the lovers, who were actually escaping via another road.

If Verbena never saw another dueling pistol in her life, it would be too soon.

Mr. and Mrs. Chesterfield were now happily married, and often invited Verbena to tea. But what had happened to her friend Étienne since that fateful night? A lot, apparently, not all of it mentioned in their irregular correspondence. Although now that Verbena thought of it, his last missive had said that her next letter to him should be sent to a new address in Bloomsbury. A fine time for the man to choose modesty! Did he not know that all details of such news should be furnished to her without delay?

"I believe the man's name was Charbonneau, though I cannot recall his Christian name," she managed to say. "I only knew him in passing." A lie, but a necessary one.

"Well, it's the youngest one who is being installed in Bloomsbury. My father gets all his togs from their shop," Miss Hollyhock prattled on. "A little place in Savile Row. Do you know it?"

The wheels in Verbena's mind clicked at a fair pace. "Was there not some commotion in Savile Row but a day or two ago? I remember someone mentioning it." She had filed it away, thinking to ask Étienne about it in her next letter to him, but had not yet gotten around to doing so. Husband hunting was an all-consuming business. Her correspondence had suffered.

"Oh, yes," Miss Hollyhock said. "Some terrible row with a customer at the very shop. Perhaps the two are connected. Imagine, a gentleman tailor rising above his station, attending the same balls as the men he's dressed. How droll! If someone didn't like the cut of a coat, he'd hear about it at the buffet table."

"Yes. Very amusing." Verbena chewed on her lip. She doubted that was the reason behind the altercation, but Miss Hollyhock was right about one thing. These two facts—Étienne's sudden good fortune and the scene at his shop—could not be a coincidence.

"Or perhaps he is rising above his station in other ways," Miss Hollyhock remarked, "hence the shouting match in the street. If he has any intelligence, he will try to procure a wife of stature to climb the social ladder. Very likely he has pressed his suit with a woman of the ton. Probably an angry father desired to remind him of his place."

Verbena bit her tongue. If Miss Hollyhock had spent an evening in a carriage with the man, as Verbena had, she would understand Étienne possessed no interest in the fairer sex. His entire manner was always courteous and proper, yet spoke of something Verbena could only describe as unlike other men—and not just because he was French.

If he had engaged in a public shouting match, it was not over some girl. It was much more likely to have been caused by a love affair of a different kind. Something more Achillean, she'd wager . . .

Verbena's breath caught. Oh, dear.

If her instincts were correct, Étienne was poised on the knife's edge of ruin.

She had to get to Bloomsbury this instant. Verbena was no slouch at putting clues together, but it was only a matter of time before someone else arrived at the truth.

She stood abruptly. "I'm feeling terribly faint," she said to Miss Hollyhock.

"Shall I have someone fetch you a drop of something fortifying? Brandy, perhaps?" Miss Hollyhock asked.

"I think I must get home and lie down." Already she was walking backward out of the tent. "Do give Lady Croydon my regrets, would you?"

Without waiting for Miss Hollyhock's agreement, Verbena snapped up her parasol and made her exit from the picnic grounds as quickly as she could without attracting notice.

Chapter 2

Bloomsbury, while not as coveted an address as other parts of the city, was still an enviable locale. Verbena's father always said that if the neighborhood could only excise its infestation of poets, it would be as tony as Mayfair itself.

Verbena didn't much mind poets; in fact, she counted two—the Chesterfields—as her close friends, though she personally didn't indulge in poetry very often. It simply didn't interest her. Now, however, as she bustled through the twisting Bloomsbury streets, she could not avoid the genre. Chapbooks and pamphlets were available on every corner, hawked by grubby boys in battered caps. "The latest from Peacock!" they cried. "Fresh odes from Shelley! The newest Flora Witcombe!"

Verbena hurried past them all, careful not to so much as glance at their wares. She could see why the erstwhile Lord Eden had favored the place as his city home. Eccentric types often gravitated to such streets.

At last, she turned a corner and spotted the house. It was easy to find in the long row of lookalikes; a dogcart was parked out front, overflowing with crates and bolts of fabric. Workmen were moving trunks into the home with lumbering slowness.

That gave Verbena pause. She had hoped she would be able to speak to Étienne in private. A glance up and down the busy thoroughfare did not immediately show any familiar faces, but that meant nothing. In a city like London, all it took was one person who might recognize her. What would the ton say if she, already an unaccompanied lady, was seen calling upon a bachelor?

In matters of life and death, etiquette must be ignored. She would have to go around the back.

The trick to slipping into places where one wasn't supposed to be, Verbena had recently learned, was to pretend that one belonged there. It was a skill she'd honed entering parties and soirees to which she had not technically been invited–oversights, surely. She clutched her parasol in one tight fist and lifted her head high as she walked past the house. A few of the workmen stopped to tip their hats, and she nodded to them pleasantly.

Just a lone woman, meandering around the block of houses and through the mews. Nothing to see here.

One small hop over a low fence and Verbena was in the back garden. At least, it would have been a small hop if Verbena were wearing something other than her petticoat and walking gown. Her slippered foot hovered in the air, nearly catching the wrought iron loops that made up the barrier, but she managed to clear it with only a little flailing. Once that was done, she stood upright and smoothed her clothing back into order.

No one had seen, thank god. Onward.

The servants' door was blessedly unlocked, and she let herself inside cautiously. There was no one in the kitchen; the only sounds were the thump of crates in the front hall and workmen calling to each other. Verbena did not hear a French accent directing them, so she left her parasol in a corner and crept up the back stairs.

It was not difficult to locate the master's bedroom. She merely followed the sound of weeping.

The door was open a crack, and through it Verbena spied Étienne Charbonneau flung face down on a chaise covered in a white sheet. The man's slight shoulders were wracked with sobs, and his black curls were in terrible disarray.

Verbena opened the door further and cleared her throat to announce her presence.

"If you are a robber," Étienne said into the cushions, his thick accent muffled, "help yourself to whatever you wish. I only ask that you murder me before you depart so that I may be free of this heartache."

Verbena smiled fondly. "Very well. Shall I oblige you with a pistol or a knife?"

Étienne's head shot up. His dark eyes were very pretty despite their tears. "Mademoiselle Montrose!" He wiped his face with a handkerchief that seemed to appear from nowhere. "I–I thought you were someone else."

"I daresay you did."

Étienne stood, looking as welcoming as a host can with red eyes and a shiny nose. He beckoned her forward. "Come in, come in. Apologies for the state of–well, everything. You are my very first houseguest, mademoiselle."

"Please, call me Verbena." She entered the bedroom and removed her lemon-colored kid gloves. "In my view, once you're tossed about a carriage together like a couple of coins in a purse, Christian names will suffice."

"Of course. Verbena." Étienne clasped her hands in his. "I am delighted to see you."

"And *I* must congratulate you on your newfound success." Verbena squeezed his slim hands in hers. "How wonderful that I am the first to do so. I expect you'll have droves of callers soon enough."

"I did not consider that. I will need to buy chairs. Will you not sit?" He gestured to the chaise, where damp spots from his tears still marked the protective cloth.

Verbena sat well away from the wetness, smoothing her skirts as she did so. Étienne sat next to her, closer than was proper, but it hardly mattered given his proclivities.

As a woman well-versed in the news of the day, Verbena had heard every sort of rumor under the sun, most of which dealt with the bedroom habits of the well-heeled. Verbena hadn't batted an eye at the idea of a man making love to another man since Winifred Stassel had explained the concept to her at age thirteen–all in service to better understand a piece of gossip involving an infamous baron who had since fled to the Continent. No one among her set was truly shocked by such things, though they might feign to be; sodomy was even somewhat fashionable among a certain set of hedonist artistic types. The lower classes, of course, could be brought up on charges if anyone cared to make a fuss, but gentlemen were largely exempt from those dangers.

Morals and laws, Verbena reasoned, were mostly for show, a set of rules that applied only to some and only when it was convenient to those with power.

Which is all to say, while she had no qualms about Étienne's nature, it made his situation all the more pressing.

"What a wonderful property you have here," she said. She cast her assessing gaze along the crown moldings and fine carpets. "Forgive me, but everyone in town is wondering how you could afford it, you know." Miss Hollyhock was not everyone, but Verbena was confident that more would follow.

"Including yourself?" Étienne asked with a smile.

She gave him a playful slap on the arm. "That would be the height of impertinence! I merely wanted to tell you, as a friend, that people are talking."

"Yes, they do that." Étienne regarded her with his warm eyes. "I do not mind telling you: there was no purchase. It was a gift from our mutual friend, the previous owner."

"Was it?" She allowed her countenance to show how impressed she was. "Lord Eden was exceedingly generous." She had heard that he'd abandoned the Eden estate but not the reason for doing so, though she would wager it might've had something to do with an Achillean attachment of his own. He never *had* married, as far as she knew.

Étienne sighed. "I told Christopher I did not need such a large house of my own, but he insisted. He even furnished me with a tidy sum to cover the expenses such a property incurs, taxes and staff and such." He ran a hand through his curls, mussing them further. "Better this than to sell it off to some dour vicomte, he said, whilst he is living abroad. He knew how dearly I wished for a place of my own. My older brothers, I love them, but our rooms above the shop are . . . a challenge to share."

"I can imagine," Verbena said with great diplomacy. "This house affords you so much more space. And freedom." She let the word hang in the air.

"Yes. So many rooms." Tears welled at the corners of Étienne's eyes once more. He ducked his head as if he could hide them. "All of them empty, save for myself."

Verbena placed a sympathetic hand on his arm. "Your brothers did not wish to reside here with you?"

Étienne shook his head. "I had planned . . ." He gave a mirthless laugh. "It does not matter now. All my plans are ruined." He turned to her with a tight smile. "Please ignore me, Verbena. I am only made maudlin from such a tiring day."

Verbena hadn't expected him to confess outright, and she couldn't blame him. It was not a simple thing, saying aloud what one had so closely guarded for so long. There would be a certain kindness in doing it for him—not to mention expediency.

She put aside delicacy for the moment, saying, "My friend, I can see you have suffered a terrible heartbreak. And I want you to know he is a fool."

Those dark, damp eyes widened. "He—? I do not understand what you mean."

"It is obvious that you meant to share this good fortune"—she gestured at the grand room—"with your lover, whoever he is. Yet when you offered it to him, there was an argument. I assume he is wealthy?"

"He comes from a long line of successful merchants, yes," Étienne said.

"Ah. Then he is the kind of man who would kick like a mule at a tailor rising above his station. He let his pride, not his sense, guide his tongue. I imagine he said some dreadful things to you."

"He did," Étienne croaked. "He was a beast. All those years together, pah! Gone in an instant. But—how did you know about Bernard?"

Bernard. There were three Bernards in Verbena's recollection.

One was currently abroad; one was nearly ninety years of age. Étienne's former lover must then be—well, it did not matter, she reminded herself. Her ability to tease out the truth would do Étienne no good.

"My dear Étienne." Verbena placed a hand on his cheek. "Your shop is patronized by some of the most incorrigible gossips in London—young gentlemen," she said. "Rumors of the argument between you and Bernard reached me, though I don't think his name has come up as of yet. That works in your favor. Or his, to be more accurate."

Étienne's pale visage flamed to match his eyes. "And you are not shocked by this?" he asked. "By the company I keep?"

She gave his cheek a pat, then let her hand fall away. "A man loving another man is hardly worth my notice—although others may not feel similarly," she said as gently as she could.

Étienne stared at the thick Persian carpet beneath their feet. "I see."

"That is why I came here," Verbena said. "If I managed to put the pieces together, it's only a matter of time before even the dullest blades in high society do, too. And dull blades cause the most damage. I do not want to see you come to harm."

There was also the matter of saving her own skin, but Verbena had the good sense to describe Étienne's problem first before offering him the solution. Perhaps it was self-centered, but really, could anyone blame a girl for wanting to secure her own future?

"I will be ruined," Étienne whispered as he arrived at the intended realization. "My family, my shop, my good name. I will lose it all."

"Unless." Verbena stuck a single finger in the air. "We outmaneuver the rumors."

He gave her a strange look. "What is it you mean?"

This part required all of Verbena's tact. She cleared her throat and held her head high. "I don't suppose you've heard of my own family's difficulties?"

Étienne wrinkled his nose in apparent embarrassment. "I am sorry, my friend, but in my line of work, it is impossible not to hear the idle chatter of so-called gentlemen."

"No need to apologize. It saves me the explanation." An explanation that would be chock-full of choice words regarding her father's lack of business sense. "Suffice to say, I find myself in an awkward position as well." She paused. "I require a husband, Étienne."

Étienne had the air of a man confused by a rapid change in subject, but was too polite to shift the conversation back to his own worries. "I am afraid I know of no one suitable, now that Lord Eden has left our shores. There was a fourth son of the Earl of Stockton, but his taste in hats . . ." He gave a disapproving shake of his head.

Verbena sighed. This was not how she had envisioned this moment as a little girl. In those childish daydreams, she was the one receiving the proposal, for one thing. For another, the imagined man sitting opposite desired her.

Of course, a man who desired her would likely want to possess her like a new cart horse, so maybe this wasn't *all* bad. Best to get on with it.

"Étienne," she said, "I mean to marry *you*."

Chapter 3

"Me?" Étienne squeaked. "You wish to marry *me*?"

"Yes," Verbena said. "If you would consent to such an arrangement."

Étienne sketched a line between them with his hand. "An arrangement? As in, une farce? Not . . . ?" His face took on an uncomfortable cast.

Verbena had thought through the entire thing on the walk to Bloomsbury. Now she allowed the plan to unfurl like a flag in the breeze. "We would not be as husband and wife to each other in actuality, no. I would live here with you, but you would be free to conduct any affairs you wished with a reasonable amount of discretion. In return, I could do as I pleased. We might attend certain events together to keep up appearances, but that would be the extent of our union. Really, it would be more agreeable than most marriages I know."

The more she spoke on it aloud, the more appealing it became. Verbena had never expected to marry for love; such a thing was so rare as to be unheard-of (except in the case of her friends, the Chesterfields, but poets were different sorts of people). And at this late date, with her future hanging in the balance, a false marriage to a pleasant, handsome, well-dressed, financially viable man was better than her alternatives. She wouldn't even need to bear children, a prospect that had inspired only ambivalence in her since she was old enough to understand the mechanics of the thing.

"A marriage in name only?" Étienne asked, as if the concept was new to him. "Without any . . . passion?"

Clearly, he was a son of France and *not* a member of the ton.

"It would be of great benefit to us both," Verbena said. "Your standing would only rise in the eyes of society—a tailor marrying a gentlewoman. And I, of course, would be free of my parents, who I think are ready to auction me off to the highest bidder any day now." She smiled at him, hoping her desperation did not show too badly. "I'd much rather have you, whose company I find enjoyable, than a roll of the dice."

"Sensible as always, Mademoiselle Montrose," Étienne murmured.

"Please. Verbena." *Careful,* she reminded herself. Desperation could leak through even the smallest syllable.

"Verbena," he agreed, and then lapsed into a sort of dazed silence. His eyes focused on something in the middle distance. It must be quite a shock, beginning one's day in the grip of terrible heartache and ending it with a marriage proposal. Carriage passengers whose ill-trained horses came to a sudden, jerking stop often reported a similar sensation in their necks.

Étienne's neck, while physically unharmed, was nonetheless turning a bright pink under Verbena's watchful gaze.

Verbena tried not to stare as she waited for his answer. She feigned great interest in the fall of her skirts, rearranging them about her ankles.

If this conference bore no fruit, she would need to continue circulating at balls and parties, hoping to ensnare some silly man with more money than sense. Yet the season was nearing its end, and her chances of success had dwindled terribly. She had not been jesting about her parents' desperation to broker a match. Her mother was increasingly adamant that she use "all her wiles" to secure a proposal, which amounted to flirting with scandal more than Verbena was willing to. Her father had mentioned just the other day that he meant to sell the pianoforte, despite the fact that its loss would mean no music in the parlor should a suitor come calling. How was a woman supposed to be wooed in a silent tomb? Verbena could not produce loaves and fishes (and husbands) from thin air.

She dreaded the possibility of failure. If she did not marry by the year's end, she would be plunged into spinsterhood. And unlike Diedre Hollyhock, who still had her family's fortune to comfort her in her long, lonely days, Verbena would be penniless.

It was unfair that she had been born into a certain life, molded into a certain shape, and told that if she only played the game by its prescribed rules, she would be rewarded with a comfortable existence. Her talents were mere party pieces; she had no skills from which to earn a living. Now, due to her father's incompetence, she teetered on the brink of disaster through no fault of her own.

Well, that might not be entirely true. Verbena shut her eyes with the shame of it. Only yesterday her mother had chided her—while directing her lady's maid to tighten her corset strings until her bosom practically overspilled the confines of London, never mind her neckline—that Verbena had no one to blame but herself.

"You debuted to plenty of interest from eligible bachelors and entertained many suits," she'd said. "How could you squander your every chance?"

Verbena had ignored the barb. At the end of her debut season, flush with success and with no reason to believe her family's finances were about to crumble, Verbena had been in no rush to choose. If a gentleman third in line for an earldom wished to be on her dance card, she'd wonder if perhaps she might catch the eye of a gentleman next in line for a dukedom. When she had accomplished that, well, why not aim for a future prince? A *current* prince? A king from the Continent? What was the limit when she had her beauty, wit, and reputation? Verbena had even induced a scarcity of her attention, claiming a disinclination to dance so that her admirers were forced to attend her away from the dance floor, ensuring that no other woman had their eye during a grand ball.

That was how the game was played, Verbena had thought: learn the rules, bend them slightly in your favor, and reap the winnings. And for a while, it seemed to work.

How quickly one's luck could turn. Now her hopes hung on an Achillean tailor.

She glanced over at his thoughtful visage. She could only pray he was as desperate as she.

At last Étienne straightened his spine, the corner of his mouth lifting in kind. "Verbena," he repeated, his native French caressing the syllables. "I should become accustomed to calling my wife by her Christian name when we are alone, I suppose."

Verbena could not help her yelp of joy as relief surged through her. She clapped her hands together. "Then we are agreed? We will marry?"

Étienne ran a hand through his wild curls and surveyed the nearly empty bedroom. "I think so," he said. "I–I think we must."

She hesitated. His voice held the high, frantic note that Verbena often heard in ballrooms late at night when someone was about to make a rash decision. Étienne was her friend. He had only recently been discarded by a longtime lover, and in the worst possible manner; his thoughts were scattered, surely, and his spirit unmoored. As much as she wanted the matter settled, Verbena thought perhaps a decision like this should not be made in haste.

She opened her mouth to suggest that Étienne first settle into the house, then take some time before committing to her scheme.

Étienne, however, spoke first. "I never dreamed I would be married," he said with a helpless laugh. "My brothers will be very surprised. Oh, I must insist that I make our wedding clothes. I may be known for my coats, but I have been aching to try my hand at a gown. You would look very becoming in a manteau." He brightened. "When should we announce the banns, do you think? It is quite a process, I hear. Shall we begin tomorrow?"

"Hold on a moment," Verbena said. "Don't you think we should . . . ?" She trailed off. It was on the tip of her tongue to tell Étienne he should proceed with open eyes and a clear head, but her damned instinct for self-preservation kept her from forming the words.

"Do I think we should what?" Étienne prompted.

Verbena lifted her gaze to him. She could not afford to place her friend's well-being above her own. Not at this critical moment.

"We should go about this at a reasonable pace," she said. "You are still unknown to the ton except as their tailor. It will be a delicate operation, introducing you as an eligible bachelor looking for a well-bred wife. Let us lay the groundwork first: a courtship now, followed by an engagement in a few months' time. Any faster and we might invite rumors of an entirely different sort."

Étienne frowned. "But what scandal could there possibly be in two lovers rushing to the altar? It would merely seem a true romance, no?"

Verbena had to remind herself that her future husband, while knowledgeable about winter wools, knew little of women. "People might think we had . . . enjoyed each other's company far ahead of the wedding date," she said.

"Yes, a true romance! And anyway, I do enjoy your company."

"No, Étienne," she said. "I mean, it would appear as if I were with child."

"Oh." He thought a bit, then opened his mouth in a wide, surprised circle. "Oh!"

Verbena waved the thought away. "Not the worst gossip one might weather; Lady Brackport gave birth to her eldest about three months after her wedding day, and I daresay even a fool can work out those timings. Still, best to do this correctly."

Étienne leaned heavily on the chaise's curved back, looking dazed. "Yes, I believe you are right."

Verbena tugged her gloves back on. Now began the task of briskly issuing her orders. "Tomorrow you and I will meet in St. James's. If the weather is fair, everyone who is anyone will be promenading. You will escort me round the pond. My maid will accompany me as chaperone; you remember Betsy, yes? If your clients ask later, you will tell the truth: that we were introduced by a mutual friend and you find me quite witty. That is the truth, is it not?"

"Your wit, my dear, it is unmatched," said Étienne.

"Good." She buttoned her gloves at her wrists, slipping the

mother-of-pearl into place. "Two o'clock. By the fountain. Don't be late."

"I would not dare. Shall I walk you out?"

Verbena inclined her head, listening to the sounds of the workmen still hauling in the boxes downstairs. "I believe I will slip out the back."

"Until tomorrow, then." He took her gloved hand and pressed a kiss to the back of it. His dark eyes glittered as he looked up at her, and for a moment, Verbena wished that either of them could find any interest in the other's person.

Alas, she would need to settle for having a kind husband and an empty bed. It was more than most women could hope for, at least.

"Tomorrow," she said, and took her leave.

Chapter 4

Verbena bustled through London with a smile on her face and a noticeable spring in her step. What a difference a fortnight could make. In that short span of time, she and Étienne had successfully established their roles as young lovers embarking on a very proper courtship in keeping with her plan.

Their "chance" meeting in St. James's had gone well, with Étienne loudly exclaiming for the benefit of all passersby that it had been far too long since they'd seen each other, and had she received any word from their mutual friend Lord Eden? How fortuitous that His Lordship had introduced them all those months ago, he said, and how lovely it was to see her on such an excellent day in the park, and hopefully it wouldn't be too bold to say he'd only yesterday been thinking of her and their infamous misadventure. She'd held his well-dressed arm and chatted amiably as they took a turn around the pond, Betsy following at their heels like an anxious crow. Heads turned in their direction constantly. Their intimacy had been noticed by no fewer than four peers of the realm and a dozen ladies.

"I like how he speaks to you, miss," Betsy told her afterward. "Respectful-like. Not like some of your old callers, if you pardon my saying so."

Verbena was quietly pleased to have the approval of her maid and constant companion. Even if the marriage was a false one, it meant she was correct in her predictions that Étienne would be welcomed into his new role by all manner of people. And anyway, Betsy's opinion was more precious to Verbena than most.

Yes, the outing had gone flawlessly, as had the three other public appearances they'd managed since. Verbena had, of course, ushered everything along with a few well-placed comments in passing to Miss Hollyhock and her ilk. She simply noted that Étienne's good fortune suited him well, and had they ever seen a man dressed so fashionably? All of which was true.

"You wouldn't actually entertain a suit from a tailor?" one impertinent lady asked Verbena while they took tea at Miss Hollyhock's one afternoon.

Verbena pretended to think about it. "I suppose it would depend on the tailor," she said at last. "A well-mannered one, comfortably situated, who might support a wife and family would be infinitely more attractive than, say, a third son living on fifty pounds a year." A not-so-subtle reference to the girl's current beau. "Times do change, and so too must we. Wouldn't you agree?"

The tea, when Verbena sipped it in the ensuing silence, was scalding.

Once it was established that Étienne was pursuing her, and that Verbena was amenable, the whispers of the ton made their way right back to her. Most people, it seemed, approved of the match as entirely sensible, even romantic, given Étienne's humble origins. A few detractors sneered, thinking Verbena was too calculating in entertaining a newly rich man. Others expressed faux concern that she would be marrying beneath her station, but there would always be such reactions regardless of her choice in suitor. As long as the reception was generally favorable, Verbena considered her efforts to be a success.

Her sprightly walk took her to Marylebone for her afternoon appointment. She arrived at a modest home with a lovely crop of ivy just beginning to train up the facade. A smiling maid received her at the door and ushered her into the parlor, where her friend Belinda Chesterfield rose to greet her.

"It is so good to see you," said Belinda, clasping her close.

"It was good of you to invite me." Verbena returned her

embrace before seating herself on a handsome wingback chair. "You look wonderful. Married life agrees with you."

It had been nearly a year since Verbena had assisted Belinda in her midnight elopement, and in the intervening months, they had seen more of each other than they ever had during the seasons. Initially, Verbena had known Belinda only as a sad girl, forever in a state of near mourning, as her sister had mysteriously disappeared years ago. Now Verbena found Belinda an excellent companion and a good source of unvarnished information. Both Chesterfields were poets, and less concerned with their noble families than with each other; therefore, Belinda did not represent a threat to Verbena in any way. One might even say they were friends.

Belinda touched a hand to her white mob cap as she sat on the divan opposite. "Thank you. I must become accustomed to entertaining at home, I think. At least for the next few months." She placed a hand meaningfully on her middle, her cheeks aflame.

"Oh!" Verbena's hands flew to cover her mouth, then dropped when she realized she could smile freely here. "Congratulations, truly. Does Mr. Chesterfield know?"

"Yes, Horace is already panicking, but first-time fathers are allowed a little panic. I daresay he'll produce some excellent poetry in the state he's in," Belinda said with a laugh. "Men can be so emotional, don't you find?"

Verbena allowed herself a snort of laughter. "They've not been taught even a modicum of self-control, as far as I can tell." Then, remembering her wonderful ruse, she added, "Of course, there is the odd gentleman who might prove himself in that regard." She didn't wish to lie to Belinda, but she and Étienne had made a pact: they would not tell a soul the truth of their arrangement. Allowing her friend to form her own conclusions would only help their cause.

After a lifetime in high society, Verbena could make herself blush on command. All she had to do was think of pretty girls bathing in the Mediterranean. She did so now, infusing her cheeks with a pinkish glow.

Belinda hummed. "And how is Monsieur Charbonneau these days?"

Before Verbena could answer, the maid came in with the tea tray, and intimate conversation paused. Verbena took hers black with a little sugar, while Belinda loaded up her own teacup with enough to sustain an army, and plenty of milk besides.

"I'm ravenous," she confessed once the maid had gone and such sensitive topics could be revisited. "I could honestly polish off this entire tray of cakes and sandwiches on my own."

"Oh, please do. I won't mind!" Verbena nudged the tiered stand closer to Belinda. She had her eye on some iced biscuits, but she could practice restraint.

Belinda put a refusing hand in the air. "No, we have more important things to do than eat cake."

"Well, that sounds dire." Verbena sipped her tea. "What could possibly be more important than cake? Especially in your condition."

Belinda placed her cup in its saucer with an ominous click. She looked to the door as if trying to determine whether the maid was listening at the keyhole, then leaned closer to whisper, "Have you read any new poetry recently?"

Verbena paused to think.

You, dear reader, already know the answer: Verbena was much too busy to bother with poetry. Yet she did not wish to offend her hostess, who wrote poems, she'd heard it said, far surpassing those of her husband.

"Not recently, no," Verbena finally stated. "I have been most . . . preoccupied of late." She let the words work their magic on her friend's imagination. With the proper coy inflection, her intentions were obvious. It was a fine line between truth and lies, but she walked it as best she could. "I admit I've enjoyed Monsieur Charbonneau's company these past few weeks. I would not mind enjoying more of it in the future."

"That is what I had heard," said Belinda, "and then I read this." She produced a small sheaf of paper from behind one of the divan cushions and held it out to Verbena.

Verbena felt a chill go through her. She took hold of the little pamphlet, which was brittle and bound in cheap twine. The front cover declared:

More Poems to Amuse and Delight
by the Poetess Flora Witcombe

"Read the first one," Belinda told her.

Verbena flicked to the first page and confronted the words. There, in an unassuming and somewhat uneven typeface, was the following poem:

There dwells in Mayfair a maiden fair
Her head as red as flame
Though her coffers are sadly bare,
Filled to bursting is her brain.
Her love, they say, takes such care
His swordspoint sharp agleam
And upon her loveliness will stare
Yet this is but a dream.
For our sakes they seem a pair
Yet when night falls pitch-black
A man might tread upon his stair
Whilst in bed, he *waits–on his back.*

Verbena rose slowly to her feet. She clutched so hard at the pamphlet that its coarse paper became irretrievably wrinkled at the edges. A fury unlike any she'd ever known–even the one inspired by Lord Newham–overtook her.

She was obviously the unnamed Mayfair woman with no money to her name. The allusion to a sword must have been poetic license in referring to Étienne's needle. Or perhaps his manhood. Not that it mattered.

This was about them, clearly.

Who was this–this *poetess*? How dare she? Gossip was Verbena's purview. This hackneyed writer was putting all of Verbena's work at risk. It didn't matter that what she'd written was true–except perhaps the part about Étienne's preferences in bed; Verbena had no knowledge of that, nor did she want it. And anyway, they had both agreed: no affairs until after they were married. She was certain he had no men creeping up to his bedroom in secret. He was too intelligent for such a misstep.

Regardless! It was poor form for this poetess to air that dirty linen to all of London. Verbena didn't even know this woman! Why was she trying to ruin Verbena's prospects in this cruel manner?

If I were a man, Verbena thought grimly, *it would be pistols at dawn. No, swords.* An insult of this magnitude deserved a slow and painful punishment.

She realized she was making quite a scene in her friend's sitting room, huffing and puffing at the crinkling pamphlet in her grip. The urge for vengeance was at once overtaken by embarrassment at her outburst. She looked apologetically to her companion.

Belinda took a slow, meaningful sip of her tea, her eyes fixed on Verbena over the rim.

Verbena retook her seat, closed the shabby little pamphlet, and placed it on the low table with a calculated air of derision.

"What nonsense," she said, clipped. She did not relish lying outright to her friend, of course, but she had made a promise to Étienne. "What tawdry nonsense."

Belinda gave a delicate cough. "I agree completely," she said. "If it is meant to allude to you and Mr. Charbonneau–well! It's patently absurd." She glanced at her, then glanced away.

A little tension leeched out of Verbena's body. It appeared Belinda was willing to dance around the truth to spare Verbena's feelings, even if she suspected the poem was a faithful account of the facts. For the moment, that was all the security Verbena could hope for.

"Who is this–this Flora Witcombe?" she asked, glaring at the pamphlet's cover. "What have I done to inspire such wrath in her? *If* the silly passage is referring to me, I mean."

Belinda shook her head. "I doubt Miss Witcombe has any

quarrel with you. This is her bread and butter, you see: poetry that makes some subtle allusion to the gossip of the day. I would call it a terrible use of that art, but . . ." Here she hesitated, seemingly interested in the iced biscuits all of a sudden.

"But?" Verbena pressed.

Belinda let a biscuit clatter back onto the bone china. "It's exceedingly popular. Her tracts sell out with every printing." Her brow furrowed in sympathy. "This one has likely been read by hundreds of people already."

Shock stiffened Verbena's spine all over again. "What! But—how did she reach such heights of popularity without my notice?"

"Her 'society verses,' as she calls them, only reached prominence at the beginning of this year, when the royal funeral provided her with so much fodder," Belinda said. "I suspect that is why you were not familiar with her work."

Ah. Verbena gritted her teeth. Now it made sense. Verbena had been completely overwhelmed with social commitments surrounding the funeral, which, even in the dead of winter, had drawn all the ton back to London from their country estates. Moreover, over half her family's staff had been released before February. No wonder Verbena had not heard of this poetess. Lighthearted poems had been the farthest thing from her mind.

Belinda refreshed her teacup with a graceful pour from the silver pot. "That is why I sent you a note asking you to come round. I wanted to inform you before you heard of it from someone else."

"Still," Verbena murmured darkly, "I should have known about this, even if it was happening somewhat outside of my province." It was her business to know things, especially things that would be useful to her.

"Well, with your recent foray into romance, it's only natural that your attention was diverted," Belinda said.

That gave Verbena pause. Belinda was correct, in a roundabout way; this mad dash to find a husband had occupied Verbena's thoughts to the exclusion of all else. Very foolish of her. She knew better. She had to keep her ear to the ground, even—no, *especially* when she was busy securing a match.

Verbena was furious at herself. She craved satisfaction. If she could not achieve it with a blade, she would have to use her wits.

"Where might I find Miss Witcombe?" she asked. "I must congratulate her on her success and inquire as to whom this poem refers. And if I am the subject, then I must correct her error."

Belinda's lips thinned into a neat line. "Do you feel that's wise?"

"I have never felt wiser," Verbena said. Her teacup was in danger of exploding into shards, so tight was her grip on the dainty thing. Yes, she would confront this woman and take her apart just as she had Lord Newham. Everyone had their secrets, even poetesses. Verbena would pluck her like a pheasant.

Belinda relented with a sigh. "I am only somewhat acquainted with her, so I cannot tell you to which address you might send a strongly worded note. But I do know she frequents the Calliope Club. Horace and I are members."

"Both of you?" Verbena was taken aback. She knew many so-called secret clubs proliferated in London, catering to every sort of membership under the sun, yet those members were always constrained to one sex or the other, as far as she knew. "This club admits men *and* women?"

"One of the few that do. I've been a member for years," Belinda said. "Being the daughter of a duke has its advantages, I suppose."

Verbena leaned forward eagerly. "Where is this Calliope Club located?"

"In Curzon Street," Belinda said, "though it may not be so simple as appearing at the doorstep and demanding entrance. It's meant for writers and poets only. A lone woman with no standing in the arts would be turned away."

"You can accompany me, surely," Verbena said. "Tell the porter I'm also a poetess, and we'll be inside in no time." What was another lie when there were pheasants that needed to be laid bare?

"You forget: I cannot appear at the club for the next few months. Or at public gatherings of any kind." Belinda placed her hand on the slight roundness of her belly. "Even in that informal crowd, I would not be welcome in this state."

Verbena closed her eyes in frustration. God forbid a nobleman ever catch a glimpse of a lady with child! Not for the first time, the absurdity of society's rules made Verbena grind her teeth, but she set all that aside. One might as well shake a fist at clouds for covering the sun for all the good it would do.

"Apologies, of course you're right. Is there another way I might manage an invitation?" she asked.

Belinda thought for a moment, then motioned in the direction of a handsome writing desk in the corner of the room. "If you fetch some note paper and ink, I could write a letter of introduction. That might serve."

Verbena shot up from her seat. "Brilliant!" Tea abandoned, she collected the necessary supplies, including a lovely lap desk, and brought everything to the divan for Belinda's use.

Her friend crafted the letter with impeccable penmanship, leaving no doubt as to the quality of tutors she must have had as a child.

"There." Belinda signed her mark with a flourish and set about blotting the ink. "If anyone asks, you are an eager, unpublished poetess with a penchant for woodland verse. Everyone is fascinated with woodland verse these days, so you'll fit right in." She folded the note and sealed it with her husband's family crest.

Once the sealing wax was set, Verbena took the letter and secreted it into her reticule with all due care. "You truly don't mind aiding me in this subterfuge?" Her friend's reputation, while not as pressing as her own, should be spared a thought, she felt.

Yet Belinda only smiled. "When you have risked my father's pistol shots to aid me in mine? I owe you this favor." She placed a hand over the swell of her stomach again. "Gracious, more than one! I should probably name the child after you when it comes! Verbena Chesterfield, it's got a ring to it, don't you find?"

"And if it's a boy?"

"Verbenjamin," Belinda said without pause, causing the two women to collapse into laughter.

Chapter 5

Flora Witcombe arrived at the Calliope late, but as she was always late, she did not think much of it. Luncheon had come and gone, which was bothersome. The cook they employed at the club was quite talented. She hoped she could wheedle a sandwich from him later. First, she needed a drink and some fresh gossip.

As she handed her bonnet, gloves, and reticule over to the porter's tender care, she could hear the booming voices of her fellow members in the Blue Room discussing the latest news from Venice. There was always a good quantity of gossip coming out of Venice, or Paris, or any number of continental cities. Every so often, someone in the region even found time to create some art.

Flora turned to the oval mirror placed just behind the porter's station and checked the fall of her chestnut curls. They were behaving for the moment, though the summer humidity would surely ruin their careful arrangement before the day was done. Fortunately, unlike most ladies, Flora could simply remove her hair when it needed brushing.

She floated into the Blue Room, so named for its various settees upholstered in robin's egg velvet. A portrait of their society's founder hung above the mantelpiece, done in the most lurid style. "Society" was perhaps a generous way to define the little enclave; membership was not strictly regulated to the upper classes. The artists and poets who found refuge in this club were both famous and unknown, highborn and low, talented and–

Well, suffice to say, the club welcomed all types. So long as a person's artistic credentials were apparent or could be vouched for, they had a place at the Calliope Club. The lax atmosphere allowed women such as Flora to appear alone, unchaperoned, and without fear.

"Miss Witcombe!"

Perhaps one fear.

Flora turned to watch a man rise from his supine sprawl on a nearby armchair. His rosebud mouth stretched into a sardonic sort of smile. His gait as he crossed the room was a tad stilted, his limp barely noticeable in his specially designed boots. He was instantly familiar to Flora, though she could scarcely believe her eyes.

"How lovely to see you, Miss Witcombe," Lord Byron said. "It's been far too long." He took her hand and kissed it, his lips warm on the skin of her knuckles.

Flora's mouth thinned. "My lord," she said severely, retracting her hand, "what on earth are you doing here? Last I'd heard, you were in Rome."

"It was Ravenna, actually. Rome was ages ago." He tossed his head, his hair touched by candlelight. Several of the assembled guests—men and women alike—paused their conversations to stare. "A wonderful part of the world. God spared no expense when he crafted it." He feigned some interest in a trinket on a nearby sideboard, thereby noting the people all around the room who were taking note of him. He was the sort of man who was awfully impressed with himself, and always had been.

Flora was wholly immune to Byron's charms, however. She was lucky that she did not feel any pull toward the great planet of his personality, though she did admire his work. Some of it, at least. His latest cantos were not as pleasing, in her opinion, as his earlier ones.

"And you've decided to return to England at last?" His departure some years ago had caused a stir, preceded as it had been by a string of scandals so lengthy that Flora could not keep them all straight.

Suffice to say, Lady Byron was probably correct to be furious.

Byron winked. "Don't tell my creditors I popped back for the summer," he said. "One longs for one's homeland after so much time abroad." He paused to take a glass of sherry from a passing manservant. "And I may have made some small trouble for myself in Ravenna, which desires time and distance to smooth over."

Flora resisted the urge to roll her eyes, instead attempting to catch the servant's notice so that she might also have a drink. She failed to do so. "I assume you must not be too fearful of your creditors, your wife, or whatever you've escaped in Ravenna if you are telling me all this," she said.

Byron gave her a knowing look. "Your assumptions, as always, are practically fact. A little fodder for your poems, perhaps, to be published well after I depart." He handed his glass of sherry over to her, eyes bright.

Flora accepted it and took a sip. "Yes, a few coins in my purse and as much attention for your 'clandestine' visit to England as you can stomach," she said with dry amusement. "Honestly, my lord, will you ever be capable of doing anything without drawing every eye to you?"

"God, I hope not," he said, and held out his hand to accept another glass from a different manservant. "Shall we seek out some privacy to test your theory? You could see for yourself how capable I am with only your eyes upon me." His gaze remained firmly on hers, the leer unmistakable.

Flora's rejoinder came easily. "I believe I'll stick to collecting rumors. I have no desire to be at the center of them."

"Please do inform me if you ever change your mind." Byron sipped his drink in his self-satisfied manner until a slight buzz of conversation near the door caught his attention.

Flora followed his gaze and saw, standing in the doorway, clutching a fine reticule, a woman with the most beautiful red hair. It spilled like licks of flame from its arrangement atop her head, a style that suggested careless abandon but that Flora knew from experience needed careful work to achieve. Her cream gown was tasteful without being too ostentatious, cleverly trimmed to look expensive without actually being so. Flora's trained eye could tell.

The men of the club—and the afternoon's gathering was almost entirely men, as usual—whispered to one another, casting glances at the strange woman. The few women feigned boredom, though their furtive glances spoke the opposite. The porter appeared beside the new woman, puffing as if he'd been delayed by some other task.

"Miss Verbena Montrose," he announced, "bearing a letter of introduction from longtime members Mr. and Mrs. Horace Chesterfield, who vouch for the quality of the lady's pastoral poetry."

The whispers turned approving. Flora wondered how many of the men were recalling, as she was now, the tale of the midnight chase that had captured the collective imagination last year. This was the same Verbena Montrose who had been at the center of that, and all for the benefit, Flora was certain, of ensuring the Chesterfields' elopement was a success. Then, of course, there were the more recent dealings with that tailor that had reached Flora's ears. How interesting that she was now here. Flora hadn't known her to be involved in the arts. She wondered if Miss Montrose had read her latest pamphlet.

Miss Montrose scanned the room with a keen, intelligent eye. Then her sharp gaze settled on Flora's face and stayed there, unblinking and filled with ire.

Ah. So she *had* read the pamphlet.

Flora weighed the value of an undignified escape through the window, but it was no use. Miss Montrose bustled across the room, hurtling toward Flora like a cannonball.

Lord Byron strode ahead to meet her. "Miss Montrose, how wonderful to know you. I am Lord Byron, though you are likely already aware."

Miss Montrose made no answer and met his gaze not at all, which flustered Byron more than anything else. Flora would have enjoyed it if Miss Montrose wasn't still marching toward her with steely purpose.

Byron nearly tripped over his own feet as he pantomimed guidance toward Flora. "May I introduce you to one of our most commercially successful woman poets, Miss Flora Witcombe?"

Before Flora could even open her mouth to offer a polite greeting, Miss Montrose snapped, "Miss Witcombe, I would speak to you."

In the months that Flora had been publishing her "society verses," as she'd come to call them, never had a subject of her poems confronted her. Most were too embarrassed. A handful had sent letters, dancing around the intent but with sums of money enclosed that she could only imagine constituted a bribe. Those sums were returned to sender with haste, accompanied by a brief note saying there must have been some error, and she had no need for such payment. As Flora had told her fellow club members many times, if she had wanted to amass a fortune, she wouldn't have ever picked up a pen. It wasn't about money; it was her art. And anyway, the sales of her tracts supplemented by patronage supported her comfortably enough.

It had not occurred to her that some subjects might leap directly to fisticuffs without first attempting to pay her. At least, judging by Miss Montrose's stormy face, that was her desire.

Lord Byron cleared his throat and offered some measure of protection. "Ladies, perhaps we might all adjourn to the Green Room. I've been toying with some paltry lines of late, and I would be most obliged if a feminine eye cast a glance over them."

"I should like to speak to Miss Witcombe alone," Miss Montrose said, staring only at her, "if she is not otherwise engaged." Her regal chin tipped up into the air.

It was a lovely chin. Quite strong and ending in a sharp point. It put Flora in mind of daggers.

She steadied herself against the sudden and unwelcome urge to do something truly foolish. Part of her had always fostered an interest in the gothic, and the thought of kissing the point of a dagger was, to her, resoundingly attractive. Yet there was no time for such things when one was about to be ripped to shreds in the middle of the Blue Room.

"By all means," Flora said, though her voice was in tatters, "allow me." She lifted an arm to direct Miss Montrose and hoped her smile did not appear as watery as her insides felt.

Miss Montrose swept by with a sniff. The lavender scent of her hair caressed Flora as she went by. Flora took a shuddering breath, her eyes meeting Byron's briefly. He looked equal parts pitying and jealous. She glowered at him in return.

The Green Room was smaller than the Blue, used primarily by the club's members to discuss their nascent works. It was arranged to facilitate intimate conversation: a handful of wingback chairs stood in a tight semicircle, all upholstered in an array of green shades. Flora chose the sage chair nearest the grate, which she soon realized might be a misstep, as Miss Montrose was providing all the necessary heat with her incensed gaze.

Flora decided to feign ignorance. "Please," she said, indicating the verdant lime chair opposite. "How may I be of service to you, Miss Montrose?"

Miss Montrose sat primly on the very edge of the cushion, her reticule clasped in her lap. "Regarding a poem of yours I chanced to see the other day—" she began, then stopped. Her delicate nostrils flared. Flora felt it very unfair that Miss Montrose possessed nostrils so fine, and that she was being forced to notice anyone's nostrils at all. This woman was too dangerous by half, she decided.

"Yes?" she prompted, voice still scratchy. "I'm afraid you'll need to be specific. I publish dozens of little ditties every month." Flora injected as much apology as she could into her tone. Nobody liked a braggart. "One must make a living somehow."

A pink flush overtook Miss Montrose's pale cheeks. Flora watched in fascination as it spread down her throat. She unclasped her reticule and removed a folded pamphlet that Flora instantly recognized. "This . . . *obscenity*," Miss Montrose said, flattening its creases, "was brought to my attention by a good friend. I am exceedingly lucky to have many good friends in this world, Miss Witcombe." Her gaze whipped back to Flora.

Flora felt the force of her stare like a cat-o'-nine-tails. "Oh?" she managed, swallowing. Her throat was so dry.

"These friends understand my situation," Miss Montrose said. "I'm surprised you don't seem to. You are also a woman, making her way in the world. How must we do this, Miss Witcombe? What can we actually claim as our own?" She rolled the pamphlet into a sort of bludgeon, tapping the point of it against her knee with every word she said. "Our wit. Our charm. And our reputations. That is all." She ceased her tapping and pointed the bludgeon in the direction of Flora's chest, which tightened at the gesture. "When someone seeks to destroy one-third of that small collection of assets, it should come as no surprise that I would destroy theirs in turn. If you were a man I would not speak so boldly, but as we are two women, I see no sense in employing coyness."

"Miss Montrose, I can see I have caused you some distress—" Flora tried to say.

"What you have done is endanger my prospects by composing your 'little ditty,'" Miss Montrose said with fiery scorn. "You have tried to sully my name and that of Monsieur Charbonneau with tawdry, baseless accusations! And for what? Is this some sort of, of—blackmail? Is it money you're after? Because I am not in the mood to reward vipers and their poison tongues!" She flung the pamphlet at Flora, though it only fluttered harmlessly to the carpet.

Flora flinched anyway, feeling each word as a blade in her ribs. She stared at Miss Montrose, at her slight frame trembling in rage, her fine-boned hands clutching the arms of her chair. Not on the verge of sobbing, but poised to strike. This was not some meek society lady wrapped in silks and fine linen, stored away from life's trials. This woman was terrifying.

And Flora was helplessly smitten by her.

"Well?" Miss Montrose demanded. "Don't you have anything to say to me?"

Flora jolted in her chair. "I—yes. My goodness, yes," she said in a rush. "I am very sorry, Miss Montrose. It was never my intention—that is, my poetry is not a means of extortion." She accepted the cool look this earned her, then stooped to retrieve her pamphlet from the floor. She smoothed it out in her lap, uncurling the cheap paper as best she could. "Of course, if anyone were to think that particular poem referred to you or Monsieur Charbonneau, I would not allow them to continue laboring under such a gross misapprehension." Her eyes flicked up to meet Miss Montrose's, then lowered back to her lap. "I do not mean to denigrate the friend who brought my poem to your attention, but I doubt that most readers would be able to form such an . . . injudicious conclusion. Clearly your friend only worries for your stature and read between the lines some unintended meaning."

It was a gamble, but a calculated one. Flora watched the woman across from her carefully and hoped Miss Montrose understood. *Obviously, the poem is about you, but most people aren't clever. They won't see. You're clever, though, aren't you? You may be the cleverest girl in all of London. Please don't murder me. Or do–but slowly, so that I may at least enjoy your touch.*

Well, maybe it would be best if she didn't understand *all* of it.

Miss Montrose cleared her pretty throat. "If they do not refer to me, then who do your verses describe?" Her eyes were sharp as swords.

Flora was certain what she meant: *Who shall we name as the victim, if not me?*

"No one, Miss Montrose," Flora said. "My subjects are purely hypothetical. I only write about the things that . . . interest me."

The people, she would have more accurately said. The people who interested her, with their comings and goings, their adventures in love, their petty dramas and wonderful lives. Flora found it endlessly fascinating, these movements of the heart. It was no wonder the whispers of a budding romance, combined with Flora's established knowledge of the French tailor, had resulted in a poem.

Her gaze was drawn inexorably back to Miss Montrose's lips, which had ceased to quiver and were now pinkly parted. Flora had a notion that they could inspire many more poems.

"Well." Miss Montrose did not relax, as such, but a little of her anger seemed to slip away, her voice losing its hard edge. "I suppose if you tell that to your audience, then we have no quarrel."

Flora wriggled in her chair in eagerness. "Of course! I would say it a thousand times if it pleased you." *Careful,* she told herself. She subsided back into the plush upholstery. "Yet I fear announcing the fact unprompted will cause you even more grief. 'The lady doth protest too much,' et cetera. One must be careful not to inflame the public further."

Miss Montrose was miles ahead of Flora's point, shaking her finger thoughtfully in the air. "What I need is something more sensational to be revealed to the populace. Give the people something else to look at, and you can pass unmolested through any gauntlet. It is a tactic I have seen bear fruit time and again." She spoke this to herself as an aside, as if Flora's presence was merely incidental.

Flora wanted her desperately.

What a mind. What a spirit. Indomitable and unapologetic in her ambitions—Flora had never seen the like. Even in these artistic halls, Miss Montrose was a masterpiece.

She brought herself up short with a mental scolding. Miss Montrose may have been a uniquely spirited woman, but her circumstances were as common as could be. She needed to marry; everyone knew that. The Frenchman, the gentleman tailor, would take her as his wife. Her very appearance here at the Calliope was meant to protect this arrangement, false though Flora suspected—knew—it to be. Miss Montrose was fighting like a wildcat for the kind of life every woman was expected to have. Her desires did not align with Flora's, much as Flora wanted them to.

Still, she owed the woman recompense. "I could provide such a distraction," she said. "Lord Byron, for instance."

"Who?" Miss Montrose said vaguely. She was preoccupied with staring into the distance.

How delightful to find perhaps the only woman in England who didn't care about Byron's movements. "Lord Byron," Flora repeated. "The poet? You met him when you arrived."

"Oh, yes. I nearly forgot. Didn't he flee the country several years ago? It made quite the splash." Miss Montrose arose from her contemplative state and locked eyes with Flora. "If I recall, details of his exploits were my entrée into carnal happenings."

"You and most of Britain, I'd wager," Flora said, fighting off a blush unsuccessfully. "Anyway, he has asked me to publish a few lines alluding to his scandalous return to our shores. I had half a mind to withhold my pen, but in light of your situation, I am happy to oblige you both."

Miss Montrose's head whipped toward her. "You would do that?" Her eyes narrowed. "I had expected solicitors to become involved at the very least. Why are you being so accommodating?"

"It is no hardship, truly." Flora chanced a weak smile, knowing she would accommodate much more when it came to Miss Montrose. "Such a stir will likely pay for the next few months' rent on my rooms. And anyway, His Lordship relishes the attention." Byron had wanted her to withhold publishing until he'd left, but would he *really* mind? Flora suspected he was hoping to be caught out, prancing around in broad daylight as he was.

But that was not the detail that arrested her companion's imagination. "You keep rooms?" Miss Montrose asked. The suspicious tone in her voice faded away. "Of your own?"

"Well–yes," Flora said. "They're nothing grand, but . . ." She trailed off, knowing that any further discussion of her domicile in Covent Garden might invite further questions. It was already exceedingly strange for an unattached woman to secure lodgings without the aid of a male relative. She could not explain how she'd managed it without touching on intimate details–and Flora could not share those with anyone, no matter how beautiful they were.

"I'm very impressed. I cannot even imagine having such a luxury," said Miss Montrose, her soft voice suffused with wistfulness. She seemed genuinely in awe of Flora for her accomplishment of renting two rooms with their winter drafts and summer vermin.

Flora forced herself to exhale. As a child, she had once seen a traveling acrobat performing on a tightrope high above the heads of an awestruck crowd. She was poised on such a rope now, knowing that any misstep might send her tumbling to her doom. The only reason she could fathom for the abrupt shift in Miss Montrose's attitude was a desire for something that could not be won with anger. She'd already secured Flora's promise to print a more sensational poem; perhaps she now wanted guidance in her own poetry. It was not too unusual for other poetesses to seek Flora out for such purposes.

"My rooms are small and dreary, to be honest, which is why I joined this club." She kept her words steady and measured, like that funambulist's footsteps. "It provides a much more comfortable place to work and socialize. Perhaps you could bring your poetry here sometime? I would like to read it, if you would permit me." She watched Miss Montrose closely, and therefore detected in the downturn of her mouth some distress. Flora immediately reversed course, flailing on her high line. "But if you'd rather not–"

Miss Montrose spoke at the same time. "I'm afraid my poetry is still in its early stages," she said. "It would be such an embarrassment to show it to anyone. I must hone my craft further before inflicting it on some poor soul." She looked away from Flora, as if the corner of the room was the most interesting spot she'd ever encountered.

Flora attempted to overcome the awkwardness with a smile. "I understand, Miss Montrose. Forgive me. One's work is such a private thing in its early stages."

"Please," Miss Montrose said, "call me Verbena. Everyone does. At least, those with whom I am on intimate terms." Her eyes flashed as they met Flora's.

Flora found herself filled with such an incandescent joy that she could rival the fire in the Green Room's grate. "Verbena." She cradled the word in her mouth like a precious morsel. "In that case, I insist you call me by my given name as well."

"It would be my pleasure, Flora," said Verbena, and the confluence of their two names, twined together in the warm air of the cozy room, made Flora's head spin.

"My name sounds so much like music when you say it," she murmured. She did not intend to speak the thought aloud, but she did all the same.

There was, for a moment, naught but silence.

Verbena stood abruptly. "I–I should be going."

Flora stood as well, flustered and unable to conceal it. The pamphlet she still held in her hand fluttered as she worried it. "Are you sure you wouldn't like to stay for a glass of sherry?"

"I must return home." Verbena clutched her reticule. "Perhaps we can continue our conversation some other time, though. Might you like to visit me in Mayfair?" Her gaze took on an earnest cast.

Flora could scarcely believe it. How great a change a mere half hour could witness! From near murder to issuing invitations–Verbena certainly was a marvel. "I would like that very much," she said.

Verbena smiled and removed a card from her reticule. "My address. Visiting hours are open to you, should you want to make use of them."

Flora stared at the dainty typeface on the card, the silvered ink shining in the candlelight. "I will," she promised.

"Well." Verbena nodded primly. "I will say good-bye, then." With a smile, she swept out of the Green Room.

Flora waited until the door shut behind her, then turned and pitched the creased pamphlet into the grate, where it bloomed into a curl of ash. What had possessed her to write such a poem, anyway? Whatever crass amusement it had inspired in her before now made her feel sour with shame.

Though she could not hate herself too much; if she hadn't written the damn thing, she might have never met Miss Montrose–Verbena–at all.

Flora wrung her sore hands–the writer's affliction–as she thought. Verbena Montrose was an unforeseen complication in an already complicated life. But who could have envisioned that Flora's idle curiosity about the lives of the monied and infamous would produce such results? She had only collected what clues were available and pieced them together to form a picture, same as she always had as she searched for inspiration for her poetry.

Flora wondered at the strangeness of the world. That she should be placed in the same orbit as that angry, lovely woman! And that she should find in her such a kindred spirit . . .

The odds seemed impossible, and yet, here they were.

Tomorrow she would pay a social call to the Montrose house, she decided. If for no other reason than to be once more in Verbena's fascinating company.

Chapter 6

The following afternoon was bright and clear, the rain having abated for once. Verbena picked at her embroidery hoop in the front sitting room of the house on Barrett Street where she had lived with her mother and father all her life. The bay window afforded an excellent view of the street, and it was through this that Verbena spied Flora Witcombe turning off the pavement to glide up the house's front steps. At the soft tap of the door knocker, Verbena bent back over her embroidery and smiled. She had been hoping Flora would visit soon.

Verbena stabbed her embroidery needle through her work—a complicated piece depicting a sprawling tangle of flowers and birds that Verbena had been stitching away at for months—and tossed the hoop into a wicker basket at her feet. She could hear Stevens, the butler, opening the door to Flora's soft greeting.

Verbena stood, taking stock of the sitting room. The space where the now-sold pianoforte once sat was still empty and made the whole room look terribly lopsided; she should have asked the staff to rearrange the furniture to better hide the loss. Everything else, though, was cheery and clean, a light repast of cake arranged on the serving cart along with tea. Verbena had no idea why she was so nervous; she'd had many lady friends call in her time. Perhaps it was the novelty of a new acquaintance, and one with whom she fervently wished to make a good impression, that set her nerves jangling.

For she did want to impress Flora Witcombe. The woman

had proven to be not only reasonable in the face of Verbena's demands, but intelligent as well. When one was surrounded by dull people as Verbena was, meeting someone with a swift mind was a balm. And while she didn't want anyone to know the truth of her relationship with Étienne, Verbena was glad the person who'd deduced it was Flora and not a more sinister individual.

Stevens announced the visitor, then Flora swept into the room. Her brown eyes lit up when she saw Verbena, her entire visage softening wonderfully. Stevens, as was his purview, melted away.

Verbena could not help herself; she rushed forward and clasped Flora's hands in hers like they were old friends. "So good of you to come," she said, casting an eye over Flora's form. "And in such an exquisite gown!"

Flora blushed at the compliment, but it was no less than her raiment deserved. High-necked and lusciously decorated with frogging and braids, the lavender visiting dress tastefully set off her slim figure. She was a tall woman, Verbena thought, for Verbena was herself quite tall, and she needed to tilt her head back a bit to meet Flora's shy gaze. This was such a novelty with women that Verbena noted it giddily.

"Thank you, I confess it is a favorite of mine," Flora said. She nodded at Verbena's white muslin day gown with its tiered lace hem. "Though yours is far more fashionable and becomes you perfectly."

Verbena squeezed their hands together and smiled. "Let us agree that we both make very pretty pictures. Please, sit, be comfortable!"

A maid scuttled by to pour the tea and scuttled back out again. The two ladies were left, at last, wonderfully alone. They sat side-by-side on the divan, nibbling at the repast and sipping their tea.

"What a lovely home," said Flora. Her gaze floated over the sitting room, coming to rest, Verbena noticed, on the empty space where the piano had once stood. Verbena braced herself for the question—*Whatever is missing from here?*—but Flora merely held her tongue and stirred more milk into her cup. "Please tell Mrs. Montrose I find her tastes very refined."

Verbena allowed herself to breathe. Clever, but also kind. Flora was proving herself to be a rare sort, indeed.

"I will let my mother know you said so. I'm sure that will please her." She toyed with the handle of her teacup. In truth, Verbena had been the one who'd picked out all the furnishings several years ago. And anyway, Mrs. Montrose was never pleased by anything, but there was no need to burden Flora with that fact. She was only being polite. "Miss Witcombe Flora," she corrected herself, "I have heard from others how you came to be a successful poetess, but as we both know, others are often incorrect." She lifted a teasing brow.

Flora laughed brightly, hiding her mouth behind a delicate hand. "As I am justifiably counted amongst that number, yes, what you say has merit."

Verbena smiled, happy that her jest had been taken in the intended spirit. "So tell me yourself: How did you manage such a thing? I've never heard of a lady making a life for herself with a pen." She sipped at her black tea.

"I've been exceedingly lucky," Flora said, selecting a seedcake. "When I published my first poems, it was as a lark. Or rather, something I felt compelled to try. I had no idea people would want to read them." She looked down at her lap demurely, her dark lashes making fans against her cheeks.

Verbena leaned in closer. "But what did you do before you wrote poems? Where did you come from? Who is your family?"

"So many questions!" A red flush overtook Flora's pale face. "You cannot possibly find me so interesting."

Verbena saw no reason not to be forthright. "I do not believe there is another alive who is as interesting to me as you."

Flora inhaled sharply and regarded Verbena with a pleased look. "Well–" she said, but was interrupted by the entrance of Verbena's mother.

Verbena had it on good authority that Mrs. Montrose had once been a very pretty girl, with the same looks and coloring as Verbena herself. Even now in her middle age, Mrs. Montrose was still a great beauty. Yet the severity of her bearing and her tendency to scowl at anything that moved had turned her into something wholly unlovely. At the moment Mrs. Montrose was squinting–in the direction of Flora, at the small selection of cakes, at Verbena's dress, and then back again at Flora.

"You are entertaining?" she said to Verbena, sounding accusatory.

"Yes, Mother." Verbena stood and gestured at Flora, who stood as well, still clutching her teacup. "Mother, this is Miss Flora Witcombe, a poetess of great success and notable wit. We chanced to meet yesterday and I invited her to visit."

"A pleasure, Mrs. Montrose," said Flora, giving a sort of abbreviated curtsy. "You have a beautifully appointed home."

Mrs. Montrose did not budge from her place in the doorway, nor did she react to Flora's introduction. "Verbena," she said, crooking her finger. "A word."

Verbena cast an apologetic look at Flora before going to meet her mother. Mrs. Montrose turned and moved several paces down the hall, out of sight of the sitting room. Having no choice, Verbena followed, coming to a stop where her mother stopped at the foot of the back stair.

"A poetess," Mrs. Montrose intoned. She said no more, only gazed at Verbena with the most hateful fire in her eyes. She didn't need to speak; after a lifetime of living under her mother's thumb, Verbena could intuit the source of her ire. It wasn't difficult when everything Verbena did in some way provoked it.

Being brought up in such a situation was humbling to the spirit, but Verbena had made the decision around the time of her debut that she would not–could not–allow her mother's foul moods to affect her future. She had worked hard to cultivate a bearing that would not wilt in the face of a sneer, that could stand up to the vicious opinions of anyone in the ton, her mother included. There was no alternative, not if she wanted to escape. Her father was no help at all. He was more like a ghost than a parent to her, flitting only at the edges of her vision. When he did deign to include himself in family dealings, it was to mete out withering pronouncements that inevitably made Verbena's life at home even more hellish.

"Miss Witcombe is well-connected," Verbena said, aiming for an air of unconcern.

"To whom? Other poets?" Mrs. Montrose heaved a sigh and looked heavenwards. "Really, Verbena, at this critical juncture, I expected a little more seriousness from you."

Verbena plastered her best smile onto her face. "I assure you, Mother, I am quite serious."

"How serious can you be, whiling away your hours in the company of—of *artistic* women?" Mrs. Montrose said, filling the word with derision. "Did you not pay a visit to Mrs. Chesterfield very recently as well? What you need is a husband. Nothing miraculous—at this late date, any passable man with breath in his body would do. But instead of focusing on such a simple task, you waste your time socializing with ladies and filling your empty head with romantic notions!"

Verbena winced at her mother's increased volume. She spared a glance behind her, but the hall was empty. "Mother, please," she whispered, "if you must excoriate me, do it quietly."

That made Mrs. Montrose turn red. "Do not tell me how to speak to my own daughter!" Then, dropping her voice into a hiss anyway: "If you are not married soon, we will be ruined. Has that fact failed to penetrate your dull mind?"

Such unfounded jabs at Verbena's intelligence were so common that she had ceased to argue the point. Her mother believed what she believed, and nothing would ever change that.

"I am well aware," Verbena said. "And though it may not appear so at this minute, as I cannot be engaged in the process of husband hunting every waking moment, I promise you that I am making excellent connections and should have certain news for you shortly."

No one could know of her secret arrangement with Étienne, least of all her parents, who would surely throw a fit if they knew Verbena had agreed to a match without their input. Mr. and Mrs. Montrose would almost certainly find some fault in her choice of husband. Best to wait until the last possible moment to tell them of the engagement.

Her pronouncement seemed to mollify her mother only a little.

"For your sake, you'd better," she said. Her eyes flicked over Verbena's person. "And for the love of all that's holy, do something about your dresses. I've never seen such a shabby girl."

With that, she swept back down the hall, turning into the study and slamming the door closed.

Verbena sighed. The study was directly opposite the sitting room. Her mother clearly wanted to eavesdrop on Flora's visit. An annoyance, but hardly surprising. Under this roof, Verbena was under constant scrutiny. Oh, she could not wait to live with Étienne, who would not care about the company she kept! And who would, hopefully, have nice things to say about her dresses.

Verbena plucked at the trim on her cuff, recently replaced by her own hand with expert care. *Shabby,* indeed.

She returned to the sitting room to find Flora on her feet with her bonnet and gloves clasped in her hands. The apology for her absence died on Verbena's lips. Had her new friend overheard the argument? Was she preparing to leave already?

Verbena was overcome by embarrassment, an emotion that she normally took pains to avoid.

Yet Flora spoke before she could beg her to stay. "The day is so fine, don't you think?" she said, eyes tracing Verbena's face with liquid concern. "May I propose an afternoon stroll?"

There was nothing Verbena wanted more than to be out of that wretched house. She let out a grateful breath. "Give me but a moment, and I will be ready to leave directly."

Bonnet. Gloves. Parasol. Reticule. Sturdier shoes. A quick check of her hair–it looked fine, despite her mother's feelings on the subject–and Verbena was out the door, her arm looped through Flora's.

They walked down the bustling Mayfair streets, chatting idly about bits of gossip they'd picked up, Verbena in the world of the ton and Flora in artistic circles. Though their territories only overlapped a little, and shared few characters, for Verbena it was a fascinating look behind a curtain she hadn't known existed. The things people got up to that she'd never heard about, simply because they hadn't been born into a barony! She had previously only considered the practice of collecting secrets and rumors to be a practical one, but listening to Flora's story of how an unnamed poet was attempting to juggle three mistresses and a forgery ring besides delighted her to no end. It was amazing, the joy one could get from hearing the exploits of complete strangers. Perhaps, Verbena thought, that was what drew so many young women of her set to novels.

When that avenue of conversation was finished, they pointed out to each other amusing tableaus as they passed by. Two horse-cart drivers engaged in a spirited discussion of who had been at fault in a collision; small boys, barely in breeches, chasing each other along the pavement with sticks; a rangy dog with doleful eyes watching a lady walk by with a steaming meat pie in her hands.

Verbena giggled at this last one, especially when Flora said, "He reminds me of myself when dinner is very late."

It was approaching scandalous for a lady to admit, even in intimate company, that she hungered. Verbena's mother had once sent her to bed without supper for daring to inquire when the meal would be served. Girls, she'd said, should take pains to never appear ravenous. Verbena had learned from a young age, then, to hide her desires like carbuncles in a velvet-lined box, secreted away from sight. They were so hidden, in fact, that she herself often lost track of them, and could not say what they were.

Yet instead of relating all this to Flora, she only said, "You are so very amusing."

"Good. I like to see you amused," Flora replied. Her arm tightened companionably around Verbena's. "I hate to think that you aren't, sometimes." Her voice dropped to a softer register.

Verbena took stock of their surroundings. They had wandered around a corner and into a quieter lane with fewer fellow pedestrians and no carriages to speak of. The calm made Verbena slightly less anxious about sharing the facts of her home life. One never knew who might overhear a conversation in passing, after all.

"It shouldn't surprise you to learn my mother has always been a forceful woman," Verbena said, picking her words carefully.

She did not bother apologizing for the change in topic, as Flora certainly understood how the two connected. “I am sorry if you overheard her unpleasant reminders to me.”

“I tried not to,” Flora confessed, “but the sound carried. Oh–how can you stand it? She spoke as if you were nothing. Does she not know you?”

Verbena gave Flora a thin smile. “Do you?”

“Enough that I can say you do not deserve to be spoken to like that,” Flora said. She returned Verbena’s smile, though hers faded after they’d walked a few more yards. “I couldn’t bear it if you thought, even for a moment, that what your mother said about you was in any way true.”

Verbena looked over at Flora and was met by the most lovely, widened look in those dark eyes. It had been some time since she’d been the object of real concern.

“I know my mother is a fool,” Verbena said. “I arrived at the conclusion years ago. My only alternative was to agree with her assessment of me, and if I cannot rely on myself, then I am lost. Do you see now why I was so anxious to correct any misapprehensions that might arise from your poetry?”

“Yes, it’s perfectly clear.” Flora looked down at the pavement as it passed beneath their feet. “You must marry, if only to leave that awful place.” She sounded troubled. Verbena thought it likely that her new friend did not approve of her fictional courtship with Étienne, but was too polite to say so.

“It is my only recourse,” Verbena said evenly, “unless I want to remain trapped with my parents, watching them sell all that we own. Can you picture me as a spinster, sitting on a crate in an empty sitting room? Believe me, I am willing to do anything to avoid that. Judge me if you must, but it’s the truth.”

Flora stopped walking abruptly, bringing them both to a halt on the pavement. Verbena noted that all was quiet around them, no others about in the small side street. Flora’s arm unwound from hers, but only so that she could take Verbena’s hands.

“I want you to know,” she said, “that to be buffeted as you have been, and to still stand tall as you do–I would never judge you for any of it. I think you are the strongest soul I've ever encountered. Before meeting you, I had heard rumors of your wit and grace, but they do not do you justice. You are unparalleled, Verbena."

"Me!" Verbena laughed. "Who is speaking? Surely not the wildly popular poetess with a room of her own."

Flora took on a pink hue. "It isn't that impressive."

"Where is it?" Verbena asked, suddenly curious beyond politeness. "Perhaps I might visit you."

"Oh, no, you mustn't. It's in Maiden Lane," Flora said with a chagrined wince.

"Maiden Lane!" Verbena rifled through her memories. "Was there not a ghastly murder in a paintbrush factory there a few years ago?" She recalled the papers making much of the affair, which involved a decapitated body hidden among some barrels. Lurid details like that always stuck out to Verbena.

"It kept the prices down," Flora said with a shrug. "But how do you know about that?"

Verbena's lifelong fascination with the morbid was not, of course, the most ladylike trait she might have cultivated. She hesitated to tell the truth of it to such a new friend, and one she so desperately did not want to frighten away.

"I must have overheard the servants gossiping. But why should it make any difference to me that you live in Maiden Lane?" she said cheerfully. "I'm sure my mother would be happy to hear that someone had taken me off her hands, one way or another. A murder would be just as judicious as a marriage."

"Please do not make a joke of that," Flora said.

Verbena rolled her eyes. "After all these years, the murderer is surely long gone. Where is the harm in joking?"

"Not about that, about your mother." She tightened her hold on Verbena's hands. "You deserve only the best. If happiness could be found hoarded somewhere, I would steal as much as I could carry and lay it at your feet."

Verbena blinked, dazed. "That is . . . very poetic of you."

Flora smiled and ducked her head. "Sorry."

"No, no. I—" *Loved it.* Verbena loved it with her whole being.

She could picture so clearly Flora hauling a bucket—for was happiness not liquid?—and sloshing it heavily across her slippers, where it would soak like honey into the hem of her silk pelisse. She utterly loved that.

How strange. How wonderfully odd.

This had to be the mythical kinship that reportedly existed between women. Having been on guard for backstabbing from her feminine contemporaries her entire adult life, Verbena had doubted the veracity of such friendships. It was disconcerting yet exhilarating to be proven wrong by Flora Witcombe, who spoke so kindly and without an ounce of insincerity.

Verbena released an exhale. "I find it a very pleasing notion," she said. Her voice was quiet in the small street: "A very pleasing notion, indeed."

Flora smiled, then tipped her head back to regard the sky. "It will be evening shortly," she said. "We should get you home."

"And yourself as well," Verbena noted. A lone woman, even a self-sufficient poetess, could not safely wander the streets after nightfall.

"You first," Flora said. "Yours is closer. Then I will take a hackney back to Covent Garden." She took Verbena's arm once more and led her back up the street.

Verbena allowed herself to lay her head on her friend's shoulder as they walked. Flora smelled of ink and rosewater, a heady combination. She wished someone could bottle it.

"Thank you for this," Verbena said. "I needed to be free for a moment."

"Yes," said Flora. She patted Verbena's hand where it lay in the crook of her elbow. "At least for a moment."

Chapter 7

Flora let herself into her rented rooms and took in the state of them. A man's hat sat on a small table in the vestibule, a walking stick in the corner. Through the open bedroom door, one could see a small vanity situated under the window, where the last of the day's sunlight poured through the lace curtains. Pots of creams and rouge were scattered on the vanity's surface, the cosmetics mixed in with hair tonics and shaving soap. A fine shawl was draped over the brass bedstead, its tasseled points caressing the faded rug on the floor below. Next to it were a pair of highly polished Hessian boots. Though fastidious in her dress and person, Flora had always tended to neglect her surroundings.

At least it's mine, Flora thought with a sigh. Untidiness aside, Flora did love her little rooms. At fifty-five guineas a year, they were not the cheapest furnished rooms in London, but they boasted an extremely incurious landlady. Verbena had been correct to remind her of their rarity.

Flora went to the vanity, unpinning her bonnet and hairpieces as she did so. The curls—cleverly arranged on combs—were set aside in a toast rack she kept close at hand to maintain their shape. She sat at the vanity and took up a pot of cold cream. After being buffeted by a whirlwind like Verbena Montrose, it was only prudent to have a quiet night in, and so there was no reason for Flora to maintain her face.

Some nights, alone in these rooms, Flora remained Flora. She possessed several nightgowns of good quality and a long dressing gown embroidered with delicate vines that she might wear while sipping something in front of the fire. Today, however, she longed for the comfort of retiring completely, and so one face was removed in favor of another.

William emerged from the soft towel he'd used to wipe the remnants of cream from his skin, gazing out the lace-curtained window as he did so. His rooms faced the brick wall of the adjoining building, affording him the privacy he required. He completed his toilette, ran his hands through his cropped cherubim curls, and rose to change out of his gown.

He slipped into his unadorned nightshirt and silk banyan, then poured himself a glass of brandy. His lap desk was exactly where he'd left it earlier in the day, leaning haphazardly against an armchair. The timepiece on the mantel chimed, then continued its soft *click-click*, counting out the moments in the quiet room.

William retrieved the papers inside the lap desk's drawer with a sigh, ensconcing himself in his armchair to read over that morning's work. It wasn't much. *The Woman in the Window,* said his flowing script, beneath which was scrawled, again in his cramped, left-handed style, *by William Forsyth.* It was always a relief to have a title before he began writing the damn thing, even if said title left much to be desired. The women in these sorts of novels were constantly appearing in windows, or in swiftly passing carriages, or in deep shadows on the moors. He sipped his drink and read the few sentences he'd managed to complete, knowing that, however polished he might make them, very few eyes would ever pass over their final form.

Unlike Flora, the lauded poetess, William struggled to find his readers. His career had heretofore been relegated to tawdry mysteries and gothic stories of middling success. In a fit of pique, William had tried his hand at poetry. Yet when he'd put the nib of his pen to the page, the most curious thing had happened: the words that poured out of him were not his, not entirely. They belonged, he sensed, to someone else, or rather some part of himself that was not himself. He found it difficult to explain, and so allowed the verses to speak as closely to that secret flowering as best he could. Those early poems, rife with longing and romantic imagery, described the soul of a woman who wanted desperately to live, with all the tumult and strife that life offered.

Privately—for there could be no other way—William concluded that this soul resided inside him alongside his own, sometimes quite apart, more often so entwined that he could not fathom where he ended and Flora began.

For Flora was unmistakably a living, breathing person, not a mere pseudonymous creation. It hadn't even occurred to William, all those months ago, to attribute the poetry to anyone but her; she was the one who had written the lines, and so her name—which had come to William as easily as knowing how to breathe—had been the one typed on the frontispiece. It was quite the shock when that first chapbook published under her name sold better than all of William's previous works combined. He would never complain, though. Being the sixth son of a minor noble family, William was entitled to only twenty pounds a year, and was required to make his own way in the world. Flora's success meant they could both live a comfortable, if not extravagant, life in their private rooms in Maiden Lane above the paintbrush factory.

About a month after the first chapbook had sold through three reprintings, it became clear that Flora would not be content to live only on the page. William had gone about the thing with care, though he quickly discovered that people tended not to ask too many questions when there was coin to be made. He'd purchased the necessary clothing and feminine items as "gifts" for fictional sisters and beloveds, paying for an entire wardrobe with the money Flora had rightly earned for herself. He'd located a maid working in his eldest brother's house whose hair was the same chestnut shade as his own and held just the right amount of curl, and he'd induced her to part with several inches for a handsome payment. If the maid wondered at his reason for collecting her hair, she did not give voice to any questions. William was certain the poor girl thought him some kind of morbid collector. Better than the truth, he supposed.

While it was not precisely clear what would happen if William and Flora were discovered to be one and the same, it couldn't be good. William had seen men put in the stocks for the supposed crime of wearing gowns at masquerade balls; his double life, if exposed, would no doubt earn him worse than that from the constabulary. And in the court of public opinion (which, in London, was the one that truly mattered) he would be branded a devil in human shape, regardless of official judgment.

He shook his head and retrieved the lap desk. It would do him no good ruminating on such dire possibilities. His current ghost story needed attention, and he endeavored to give it some.

He scratched at the page, crossing out more lines than he kept. Inkblots bloomed on the paper where he paused too long, wracking his brain for the correct words. Writing with his left hand meant curving his wrist into an awkward angle and taking care that the sleeve of his banyan was kept well away from the wet ink. It caused terrible cramping in William's arm, but he'd adopted the style when it became clear that Flora needed a hand of her own distinct from his. It was fitting for her to keep a precise, elegant script, so like the gentleman he was, William had ceded the use of his right hand to her. Now, however, he regretted it terribly, as pain radiated from his wrist all the way to his elbow.

After a fruitless quarter of an hour of jagged scrawling, William scrapped the page entirely and tossed it in the general direction of the ashen fireplace. He was doing nothing but wasting ink at this rate.

He stared up at the flaking ceiling, flexing his left hand open and shut to dispel the ache, and wondered whether Miss Verbena Montrose ever experienced days like this, when the world seemed to hold all the proper words just out of reach. No, her poetry was likely as striking as she was. She probably wrote beautifully, never at a loss, as she was in conversation. A woman like that could only ever say exactly what she wished to say. William closed his eyes with a sigh.

Flora opened hers. The urge to communicate her deepest desires was overwhelming. Verbena was not the only woman capable of such things. She took up the pen and dipped it into the lap desk's recessed inkwell, then began to write in her tidy, flowing hand.

Dearest Verbena–

It is not an hour since we last spoke on our stroll, yet I am compelled to write to you now. Our earlier conversation feels like a dream that haunts my thoughts, if a haunting can be a gentle comfort. Thank you for your candor, and for accepting mine in turn, such as it was. In that selfsame spirit, I must tell you of my most ardent desire to see our friendship blossom. If my boldness shocks you, that is only fair; I am shocking myself, to be sure. Do you understand me now as you seemed to understand me so readily today? Perhaps I am alone in this, but I do not think I am. For the first time in my relatively short life, I think I have found a kindred spirit. Truthfully, I want–

Flora halted, the nib of her pen striking across the fine paper as if refusing to be party to such folly. What was she doing, committing these sentiments to the page? It was too scandalous to be borne. While her heart told her that Verbena could perhaps be trusted with her secret, what of everyone else? That horrible mother of hers was certainly capable of peeping at Verbena's correspondence. Then there were all the maids and the delivery boy, the dozens of people who would touch the letter as it passed between them–if anyone read those words and caught their meaning, it would spell disaster. Even the most independent poetess in London couldn't survive the assault on her reputation should anyone discover her attempts to woo a lady of excellent standing. How stupid to think for even a moment that such a thing was possible.

The shame of it all was enough to cause Flora to recede and William to return to the forefront. He tore the page from the desk and knelt by the grate, lighting a fire to burn the accursed thing. His other half possessed great talent, but not always great sense. They were lucky to have each other for balance.

William sat back on his haunches on the worn Turkish rug in front of the fireplace, watching the flames engulf the ill-conceived missive. The paper blackened and curled until nothing but ash remained, yet still William kept an eye out for any remaining scrap that might have escaped.

And anyway, Verbena Montrose was as good as engaged to that gentleman tailor, Charbonneau. William had never met the man, but even so it was obvious to anyone with an ear for rumors and half a brain that he was a lover of men. The inevitable marriage was clearly a farce, but weren't they all, to some extent? William rarely encountered a married pair who tolerated each other's presence, let alone delighted in it. His own parents, god rest their souls, had only ever achieved a vague politeness toward each other before succumbing to consumption, which William supposed was the best most English households could hope for.

Cynic, Flora whispered in the back of his mind.

"Romantic," he murmured back, but he knew the accusation did not sting her. If anything, he felt her pride at the appellation, a warm preening deep in their shared chest. He rested his forehead on his kneecaps with a groan.

The line between himself and his feminine half was so blurred as to be utterly useless. If he was cynical, so, in some ways, was she. If she was doomed to romantic leanings, so, in turn, was he. They were the same person, after all. The only difference was that William's sex allowed him to conduct personal affairs with ease—or any other sort of affairs, should he so desire. Which, given his unique situation, he did not.

Though he was at an age when most young men of means, paltry though they may be, were encouraged to sow their oats, William's oats were distinctly unstrewn. He had never taken anyone to bed, or, as Flora, been taken. He had never met anyone compelling enough to put the thought in his mind. Until Verbena.

Oh, Verbena! If only he could press his suit with her, things might be different.

William lifted his head, staring sightlessly into the crackling grate.

There was an idea.

Could he not, as William Forsyth, court the lady properly? There was no barrier to it, save her supposed attachment to the Frenchman, but that was easily dealt with. Surely she only meant to marry him for the sake of convenience. William was not a rich man, but he was far from destitute. With the sums Flora earned from her poetry, he might even be able to procure a suitable house in a respectable neighborhood at some future date. He was just as fine a marriage prospect as Étienne Charbonneau–better, if one cared to add William's family line to the equation.

Yes. Yes, why not? Why shouldn't he win Verbena's hand?

"I could," he whispered to himself. The flames in the grate gave a loud pop. William sat up stick straight. "I can. I shall! But first–" This last was said in Flora's soft voice, slightly higher but no less warm. She turned and reached for the abandoned lap desk, fixing a fresh sheet of paper upon its slant. "Let us tell London, in our own enigmatic fashion, that Lord Byron has returned from abroad."

After all, she had made Verbena a promise.

Chapter 8

Verbena watched Étienne's face furrow into a series of frowns as he glanced over the chapbook. The carriage–Étienne had commissioned a most luxurious one, as befit his new status–jolted on the pockmarked road, jostling their shoulders together.

"Much of the meaning escapes me, Miss Montrose," he said, closing the small pamphlet. Flora Witcombe's name was splashed on its front along with the title: *On His Unexpected (And Secretive) Return.* "It is a poem about . . . another poet?"

Flora's latest was deftly done, a set of rhyming couplets that alluded to a tragic hero, beloved by many, loathed by more, who had been cast out of the country in a confusing conflagration of scandalous circumstances. Yet the hero had very recently returned, Flora wrote, under cover of night. Such a "clever child" (a coy reference to Lord Byron's most popular work) should be closely watched, the poem said, for his next movements would prove most entertaining.

It was perfect. Verbena found herself in awe of Flora's skill and wit in a way she rarely experienced. It made her flush from her cheeks to her throat, the thought of all that intelligence supporting her cause. She was such an interesting woman, Verbena mused, both in mind and body. Stately, with a perfect spill of hair and the most exquisite taste in dress. The most interesting assemblage of nose and mouth and chin, both soft and strong. Many women in Verbena's circle were great beauties, but none made the impression Flora did. How fortuitous that she could call her a friend!

The carriage jolted over a rock, and Verbena was shaken from her fancies. She focused squarely on the little chapbook, giving it a pleased smile. Even the most ignorant reader would be able to glean the hidden meaning–if the reader was acquainted with the basic facts of that romantic world of British poets. Étienne, through no fault of his own, was not.

Verbena leaned closer so she could speak into his ear. "It alludes to a poet, yes, a famous one. Isn't it exciting?"

He regarded her with a wary eye. "More exciting than other sorts of gossip?" he asked. *About us, specifically,* went unsaid.

Verbena nodded. "He is *very* famous. Do not let it slip but–" She lowered her voice even more. "It's Lord Byron."

Étienne merely gave her a blank look.

Verbena stared back. Even she, who never picked up a volume of poetry unless forced, knew of the man. Of course, as he was a baron and the most scandalous one in recent memory, she could not help but know of him. "Childe Harold? Don Juan? No?"

"What are these? Noms de guerre?"

"Well, I suppose in a *sense* . . ."

Étienne shook his head. "I am not a reader of English poems." He smiled in his good-natured way. "Why would I when French poetry exists? It is, for all its faults, the superior tongue."

If Verbena did not know him as well as she did, she might suspect he meant this remark to be bawdier than it was. She laughed. "If you say so, Monsieur Charbonneau."

A loud throat-clearing came from the seat across the carriage. Verbena looked over at Miss Hollyhock, who sat primly with her hands in her lap, glaring in their direction. At her side, Mr. Chesterfield chattered amiably about the weather. Ah yes, Verbena had nearly forgotten the other members of their little party. Miss Hollyhock and Belinda's husband had been invited to share Étienne's carriage not only to act as chaperones, but to provide an audience for their playacting. They seemed to be succeeding in the latter ambition, at least. Miss Hollyhock looked very cross at Verbena for what she must have perceived as shameless flirtation. Wasn't it strange, how chaste friendship could be mistaken so easily for intimacy of another sort?

Verbena plucked the chapbook of Flora's poetry from Étienne's hand and secreted it away in one of her costume's many pockets. "A perfect day for some archery," she said to Miss Hollyhock. "Thank you again for securing our invitations."

"It was no trouble," said Miss Hollyhock. She cast an eye over Étienne. "Have you done much shooting, monsieur?"

"Non, I have not yet had the pleasure. Today will be my first foray." Étienne smoothed a hand down his elaborately adorned waistcoat. "Already I can tell I will enjoy it. The ensembles alone!"

Verbena had to agree; the whimsical outfits were unmatched. Her archery dress was a deep emerald with slashes of aquamarine along its puffed shoulders. The high waist and fitted bodice showed off her figure to great effect. Étienne had constructed his flamboyant costume himself, with soft trousers in a shade of complimentary blue. He seemed to be enjoying the sartorial aspects of their courtship to the utmost. Verbena hoped he took to the sporting portion of their fakery with the same ardor.

"No need to worry," she told Étienne. "Nobody attends these outings for the sport. The archery itself is an afterthought to the mingling."

"Here we are!" cried Mr. Chesterfield as the carriage rattled to a halt.

Verbena alighted with a helping hand from Étienne. Surveying the grounds, she found a cleared patch of grass where a handful of other guests were already milling about. Targets were arranged near the end of the lawn at the prescribed feminine distance of fifty yards. Servants in black coats stood by with polished longbows and the other accoutrements of the sport, while others bore salvers of drink.

The soft breeze rustled the large white ostrich feather in Verbena's wide-brimmed hat. She placed a hand atop it to keep it steady in the breeze, watching as Mr. Chesterfield escorted Miss Hollyhock to greet Lady Croydon, who was once more the hostess.

"Now remember what we discussed," Verbena said to Étienne in a whisper. She hooked their arms together. "Keep your head up, look them directly in the eye, and do not be cowed if someone tries to score a point off you. You are a rich man. You belong here, just like any other invited guest."

"Yes, yes, I remember," Étienne said. His eyes darted about, taking in many of the male members of the party. "Mon dieu, half my clientele must be here today."

"Do not worry about that. Greet them as you would an equal." Verbena paused. "Well, perhaps a bit more formally than your . . . usual equals."

He groaned. "You really think I can play this role? I have never once feigned love for a woman. I have never needed to!" Étienne looked back at his carriage, which was pulling away to make room for new arrivals. "This was a terrible idea. They will take one look at me and think I am afflicted with the French vice. And they will be perfectly correct. We should leave before–ah!"

Verbena had not wanted to pinch him on the arm, but she was also not about to apologize for it. Someone had to pinch some sense into the man before he ran like a panicked horse.

"Keep your toes in your pumps, monsieur," she hissed from the corner of her mouth. "Simply follow my lead and it will be simplicity itself. The ton sees what the ton expects to see–and they shall see an eligible young lady making a match with a handsome man of means. Oui?"

"Yes, my dear," said Étienne.

She tugged him toward Lady Croydon, and he went obediently. The dowager countess welcomed Étienne as if he were the most interesting specimen she had seen all season. Her clear delight in making his acquaintance set the stage for the rest of the archery party, which greeted him with enough politeness to appease their hostess. Verbena drifted from Étienne's side as he conversed with an older gentleman about their carriages; there were some topics even she could not pretend interest in.

She had only taken a few steps in the direction of the refreshment table when she heard someone call her name.

"Miss Montrose?"

The Scots brogue could only belong to one person.

She turned to find Miles McDonald loping across the grass toward her with easy strides. "You have no idea how relieved I am to see you," he said with a broad smile. The sun glinted off his eyeglasses. "How I managed an invitation, I've no idea, and now I'm like a babe in the woods. I don't know a single soul here."

"Nonsense! You've met Miss Hollyhock, have you not?" Verbena indicated Miss Hollyhock, who was also at the table, nibbling at cheeses.

Mr. McDonald lit up with genuine delight. "I have, yes! At the picnic."

"Wonderful to see you again," Miss Hollyhock said as she shook his hand in greeting. "Did you arrive very early?" Her eyes darted about, doubtlessly trying to see if Mr. McDonald had come in a hired hack again, or if he had learned his lesson.

"I arrived exactly on time. When you Londoners say two o'clock, I stupidly think you mean two o'clock. As it turns out, you mean something closer to three or half past."

He wasn't wrong. Not only was it fashionable to arrive somewhat later than planned, but it was polite. No hostess was ever ready at the appointed time.

Introductions were needed. Verbena conducted the social dance between the passing Mr. Chesterfield and Mr. McDonald; they apparently knew some of the same people in Glasgow and chatted for a moment about them. Then Verbena drew Étienne forward with a subtle guiding touch to his arm, presenting him to the newcomer.

"And this is my very, very dear friend, Monsieur Étienne Charbonneau," she said. They had agreed to such language as the preface to a formal engagement. It carried enough weight that even the most naïve country bumpkin could catch their meaning.

Miles McDonald turned from his conversation with Mr. Chesterfield, his grin still on his face. Then he and Étienne laid eyes on each other, and Verbena saw that grin slip into something filled with awe.

Étienne seemed just as frozen. It took a gentle prod of Verbena's elbow to get him in motion once more. "A pleasure, Mr. McDonald." He held out his hand to shake.

Mr. McDonald took it. "Your coat is exquisite, monsieur," he said. He took in Étienne's ensemble with unabashed interest. "You must tell me who your tailor is."

"Oh!" Verbena gave a high laugh. This had also been rehearsed. "Monsieur Charbonneau is actually the proprietor of a well-regarded–"

"I am," Étienne said, abandoning their carefully prepared script. "That is, I am my tailor. *A* tailor. For myself, as well as others." He was staring at Mr. McDonald like he'd never seen a Scotsman before.

Mr. McDonald had not, Verbena noticed, released Étienne's hand yet and was indeed cradling it in his own. "And could you be mine?" he asked.

Verbena was relieved that Miss Hollyhock and Mr. Chesterfield had already floated off to join the rest of the archers in sizing up their bows. Otherwise, overhearing such a bold statement, even if it was meant innocently, could raise eyebrows. Hers were certainly climbing skyward.

Mr. McDonald seemed to realize belatedly the implications of what he'd said. "What I mean to say is–! Forgive me, I'm new in town and I've been looking high and low for a reputable tailor such as yourself." He grimaced in apology. "I've gotten a few remarks on the . . . quaintness of my dress and would remedy that, if I can."

Étienne's eyes shone with delight. "Certainly, Mr. McDonald. It would be my honor. You can find me in Savile Row anytime." He paused, frowning at the archery targets some yards distant. "When I am not playacting the Robin Hood, I suppose. Let us hope I can figure out where to aim the pointy end, hm?"

"You know, I hunted with bow and arrow when I was a lad. Not so much lately, as you can probably guess." Mr. McDonald pointed to the black lens of his spectacles. "But I can show you the basics. If you'd like."

They were *still* holding each other's hand. For the good of their ruse, Verbena had to intervene. "Perhaps later! Shall we choose our bows now, monsieur?" she said, practically dragging Étienne away from Mr. McDonald and toward the archery field.

Étienne looked dazed, like he'd been hit over the head with a skillet. "Yes, of course. Later," he said, looking over his shoulder at Mr. McDonald for far longer than was necessary.

When they were some yards away and there was no danger of being overheard, Verbena murmured under her breath, "Careful, Étienne."

"Hm?" His head snapped back to face her. Finally. "What do you mean?"

"You and Mr. McDonald, making fast friends. Much too fast."

"I was only doing as you said! Head up, meeting the eye." He made a V with his fingers, jabbing them toward his blue ones.

"Yes, and well done, but you'll recall I said nothing about salivating over some Scottish dandy."

"I do not *salivate,*" Étienne said, "and I think 'dandy' is not quite the right word for Mr. McDonald." He shook his head. "That *coat.* Beautifully made, of course, but did you note the color? Woefully out of season. My hands are itching to clothe him."

"And unclothe him," Verbena said dryly.

Étienne looked at her askance. "I am not a fool, mon amie. He is handsome, yes, but it is not as if I can fall into his arms. I am going to marry you." He patted her hand where it lay on his arm, then his eyes took on a gloomy cast. "And anyway, after Bernard . . . no, it is too soon to be thinking of any man's arms." He said this with such deep sadness that Verbena felt almost guilty for teasing him.

"Quite right," she said. "Let us forget all that now. Pick out a suitable bow."

Étienne looked dolefully at the array of longbows in their polished stand, presided over by Lady Croydon's gamekeeper. The male guests were clustered around, arguing over how tight one should make the string and the best manner of stance.

"How will I know what is suitable?" he asked.

"Don't worry. Someone will tell you." And with that, she

unleashed Étienne on the men of the party. While he was occupied with all their advice—some sensible, most not—she made her way to the knot of ladies, who were clustered around another rack of shorter bows, more suited to their delicate frames.

Verbena selected one that seemed decent enough. She wasn't a terribly gifted archer, but that was all right; it would be unseemly for the ladies of the party to distinguish themselves too much, anyway. One or two arrows might find their way dead center, but most would be loosed in less successful ways.

Accordingly, the targets were set up first for the ladies at a distance of only fifty yards. Once the ladies finished their round, the men would shoot at a hundred yards. Verbena took her place among the other women gathered about one end of the lawn, all chatting pleasantly. She spotted Miss Hollyhock deep in conversation with Lady Jane Bell. Verbena caught Miss Hollyhock's hushed whispers as she approached.

"—as intimate in the carriage ride here as if they were already married. Mark my words, the match is inevitable," Miss Hollyhock was saying. "He must be quite financially solvent if she's entertaining his suit. Her standards have never been low. Why, she once rebuffed—"

Lady Jane's wide eyes caught sight of Verbena over Miss Hollyhock's shoulder. "Oh, Miss Montrose! We were just speaking of you."

Verbena smiled. For once, she was very pleased to be the subject of rumors—so long as they were the rumors she herself sought to sow. "All good things, I hope?"

Miss Hollyhock turned, not looking the least abashed at being caught gossiping. "The difference between good and ill, I find, is less important than that which is interesting or not. You, my dear, are currently very interesting. I believe this pleases you, though of course you'll never admit it."

"Of course! I deny it completely," Verbena said, though her wide smile showed her companions that she was in on the joke. As she'd hoped, the two other women laughed delicately behind their lace fans.

"May I ask what is so funny, Lady Jane?" came a pleasant voice from behind Verbena. "I confess I have a weakness for a good laugh."

Verbena turned to find a man about her own age dressed in a serviceable archery costume in shades of rich brown. He was on the short side for a man, with delicate features capped by a rosebud mouth. His chestnut hair was arranged, like many young rakes' that season, in a cherubic halo of curls about his head. When his eyes met Verbena's, there seemed to be a flash of something–surely not recognition, for she didn't know him at all. Perhaps eagerness.

"Ah," said Lady Jane, "I'm afraid Miss Montrose's clever witticism cannot be re-created. You would need to have heard the last quarter hour's conversation before it made any sense." A polite way to avoid any embarrassment. If men found out how women spoke about them and their prospects when they weren't in earshot, they would surely pass some law prohibiting it. "But let me introduce you," Lady Jane said smoothly. "Miss Hollyhock, Miss Montrose: this is Mr. William Forsyth. He is a great friend of my father's. Have you met before?"

"I have not yet had the pleasure." Mr. Forsyth stepped closer to shake first Miss Hollyhock's hand, then Verbena's. His hand was slim and warm, calloused in several spots. He held her hand a moment longer than was strictly necessary, his honey eyes staring at her. "I should tell you now, Lady Jane does me a great service in naming me a friend of Lord Cheff. He is a reader of my little books, for which I am very grateful."

Verbena pulled her hand from his gentle grip. "Oh? What is it you write, Mr. Forsyth?"

Lady Jane, meanwhile, feigned some need to absent herself from the conversation, gesturing vaguely. Verbena watched her go, wondering if she did not approve of whatever it was that Mr. Forsyth produced.

"The gothic, mostly," said Mr. Forsyth. Ah, yes. Quite controversial in some circles. "Ghosts, banshees, anything that might haunt a manor house. Lately, though, I have tended toward stories of, erm, criminal mischief and mayhem."

Verbena perked up. "Murder?" she asked, trying not to sound *too* interested in the subject. As much as she was fascinated by morbid stories in the London broadsheets, it did her no good to flaunt the fact in mixed company.

"Well, yes," said Mr. Forsyth. He eyed her curiously. "Amongst other salacious things that are not fit for the eyes of young ladies. At least, that is what my critics say."

Hm. Hm! Verbena looked at him anew. He *was* a rather attractive man, now that she thought of it. What he lacked in physical presence, he more than made up with wit. Her gaze lingered on his mouth, which, she observed, was pink as a kitten's nose.

What an extraordinary thought to have. And about a man. That had never really happened to Verbena before. She blinked hard.

"These are novels?" Miss Hollyhock said with a note of reproach in her voice. "And you publish under your own name, not anonymously?"

Mr. Forsyth shifted on his feet. "Yes, that's correct."

Miss Hollyhock turned to Verbena with wide, disbelieving eyes. In recent years, the novel had become a battleground in the court of public opinion. Many successful novelists were ladies, and that alone was cause for concern. Men often looked down their noses at such things, and if they dabbled in fiction at all, they were apt to do so secretly.

Verbena, having no time for novels, had no opinion on the subject. Although a man like Mr. Forsyth might persuade her to form one.

They were interrupted by a group of broad and strapping men in a range of ages. They all cavorted in a youthful way, however, sloshing their cups of wine so that their waistcoats smelled strongly of the stuff. Verbena was surprised when the tallest and perhaps eldest slung a meaty arm over William Forsyth's slight shoulders, nearly causing him to buckle under the weight.

"Ralph, please," Mr. Forsyth grumbled.

"Is Little Wee Willy boring you fine ladies?" said the interloper.

Verbena had no notion how one might answer such a question.

Mr. Forsyth pursed his lips and closed his eyes as if digging for some inner strength. He then looked to Verbena and Miss Hollyhock, saying, "May I introduce my brother, Lord Formouth."

Verbena placed the family now. The eldest brother was a viscount of some repute. No great fortune, though a respectable name. William Forsyth was the baby of the family, then. His novels were surely successful, if he was supporting himself thusly and not relying on a military career or business venture as the youngest sons of large families usually did.

"Don't forget us, Willy," another pack member crowed.

William Forsyth sighed. He gestured to each man in turn. "And my other brothers, Mr. Robert Forsyth, Mr. Reginald Forsyth, Mr. Rollo Forsyth, and Mr. Richard Forsyth." Each Forsyth lifted his hand to cheerily claim his name as it was listed. "Gentlemen, please meet Miss Hollyhock and Miss Montrose."

Verbena frowned in confusion. Though the men all shared the same shade of chestnut hair and fine cheekbones, their builds and, indeed, manners appeared so unlike William's as to be shocking. How strange that such different creatures could be related by blood.

Miss Hollyhock, luckily, was quicker to get the conversation back to a socially acceptable place. "Mr. Forsyth—that is, Mr. *William* Forsyth—was just telling us about his writings," she said.

The Forsyth brothers brayed at the sky. Lord Formouth's drink would have stained William's coat had he not jerked away from his brother's hold.

"Isn't it all so embarrassing?" said Lord Formouth. "I do hope you two don't go in for that sort of thing." He leaned closer, wine spilling. "So many respectable ladies these days do, unfortunately!"

Despite being no devotee of the art, Verbena bristled at the notion. It was not William Forsyth's fault that men hated the feminine realm and would denigrate any writings aligned with it. Poetry—now that was where men still acted as kings, dominating their conquered lands. With the rare exception of poetesses like Flora, the most widely read cantos were all penned by the masculine hand.

Flora. How dearly Verbena wished she could be here. Not only would she surely wield a bow with the skill of Artemis herself, but she'd know exactly what to say to these boors.

A thought struck Verbena then: she could say whatever she liked, even something cutting. She was practically engaged to Étienne; there was no need to simper for some wine-soaked viscount's favor.

Emboldened, she drew herself up to full height.

"I admit, I have not made a habit of reading novels in the past, but you have convinced me otherwise, Lord Formouth. I shall visit a bookshop tomorrow and inquire after Mr. Forsyth's latest." She nodded to the author in question. "If the tastes of ladies lean so heavily in favor of the novel, then surely there must be something to it."

William Forsyth stared at her with parted lips. His assorted brothers paused in their carousing. The eldest merely sputtered.

"But one cannot deny that ladies' tastes tend toward the frivolous and unserious," he said.

"Do they?" Verbena tipped her head in thought. "Yes, I'm sure that is true. Otherwise, the vast majority of men would remain bachelors, would they not?"

The brothers Forsyth seemed confused by this assertion, save for William, who laughed into his sleeve. Verbena gifted him with a knowing look. At least one man knew wit when he heard it.

William Forsyth caught her look and straightened, his mouth curving into a smile.

"Miss Montrose, something just occurred to me," he said. "My brothers will tell you that I am a miserable shot. I haven't so much as touched a bow since I was a boy."

"That's true," said one of the middle brothers. Rollo? It was difficult to keep them all straight. "Back then, Willy couldn't hit a target for any price."

"Perhaps," Mr. Forsyth said to Verbena, "you might show me the proper stance."

Verbena watched as the assorted brothers opened their mouths, no doubt to mock their youngest sibling for seeking assistance from a lady.

She was swifter. "Of course. I am a decent enough archer.

Come with me–we might be able to concentrate better beneath that shade tree." She indicated the spot with the tip of her bow, some yards distant, yet still close to the final set of targets.

They left the conversation to the mumbled jeers of William's brothers.

Jackasses.

Her irritation was only somewhat mollified by Mr. William Forsyth's bashful, pinked-cheek look. "I am sorry about them," he said once they had walked some distance. "They're awful, I know. You really don't have to show me how to shoot; it is enough to have escaped their company."

"Not at all, Mr. Forsyth. You cannot be held to account for your brothers' rudeness."

"Nor my lack of archery skills?" He squinted in the bright sunlight at the targets that had been placed on the grass. "I don't remember the distance being quite so great. You'd think because I was smaller then, the yardage would seem to shrink, but it's the opposite."

Verbena laughed despite herself. "Well, the distance will increase when the men take their turns. Right now the field is set for the ladies at half what you'll be expected to cover."

"Truly?" His cheeks puffed out while he surveyed the grass with a shake of his head. "Maybe I can convince Lady Croydon to split the difference for me. Seventy-five yards, right in the middle of the gentlemen and the ladies." He looked over at her with a soft smile.

Verbena tried to hide her mirth. Never in her life had she heard a man suggest he might be anything but a wholly masculine specimen. It was somewhat refreshing.

"I would not advise that, Mr. Forsyth," she said, covering her mouth with her hand. "Lady Croydon would not find it the least amusing."

Mr. Forsyth grinned. "Someone might. The only person I care to amuse, in fact."

Verbena desperately tried to recover her poise. "You might need to amuse more than one person, Mr. Forsyth. It is a party, after all."

The teasing admonishment seemed to miss its mark, for the man veered terribly into yet more familiarity. "Please, Miss Montrose, with all my brothers in attendance here today, there are too many Mr. Forsyths gallivanting about." He gestured to the small stand of men in the distance, laughing and clapping one another on the back. "Do you think you might call me William?"

It was on the tip of Verbena's tongue to point out that, abundance of Forsyths notwithstanding, he was the only one in front of her, so there should be no confusion as to whom she was addressing. Yet the look on his flushed face—beseeching and tender—gave her pause. There was something familiar about him, though she couldn't place her finger on exactly what. Something about his fine-boned hands; his willowy figure; his eyes—it was as if she knew him already, and knew him to be good company.

Yet they had been introduced only moments before, and he had given no indication that they had ever met previously. Surely he would if they had. He seemed so eager to know her; there would be no reason for coyness.

"I believe I could," she said, then recklessly added, "William." It was not the first time Verbena had engaged in bold flirtation, but never before had it given her a thrill in the depths of her belly. It sent a tingling all the way to her toes.

William's smile was as radiant as the sun itself, though it did not beat down at her the way the sun did now. It was a gentle thing. "Oh," he said. "Thank you for that." The relief in his voice was in no way disguised. Verbena had never met a person of such openness. How strange, that he had lived twenty-some years and had not yet hidden away the most vulnerable parts of himself. Everyone in society did, to some degree, Verbena included.

It almost made her want to invite him to use her own Christian name in conversation. Almost. The implications should she allow such an intimacy, however, were not favorable.

Perhaps her hesitation showed on her face, for William said, "I would never, of course, expect you to reciprocate. If there were a handful of Miss Montroses strolling the grounds, that would be another matter."

Verbena relaxed a fraction. It was an unusual sensation, being able to relax, even a little, in a man's company. "Naturally," she said. "I suppose I should be thankful that Miss Montroses are a rare thing of late."

William did not laugh at her small display of wit. He merely looked at her—not as some of the other men of the party were looking at the ladies' figures as they tested their bowstrings, she noted. His gray eyes passed over her face and lingered there as if he could see into her soul.

"I'm sure a Miss Montrose is more than rare," he said in a quiet murmur. "She is, I think, unique." He regarded her from beneath the fall of his thick lashes. "Would it be terribly forward of me to ask if I might read your poetry sometime?"

"My—what?" Verbena had told only Flora and, she supposed, a few members of the Calliope Club that white lie. "Where did you hear that I write poetry?"

"I, erm—" William glanced back at Mr. Chesterfield, who was busy stringing his bow. "Is that not Horace Chesterfield with whom you arrived? I suppose I assumed that if you were friends with him, you must at least have some passing interest in his art."

Verbena's shoulders unwound. It was annoying, but she supposed her cover story of being an aspiring poetess would need to be kept up for William's benefit in addition to Flora's.

"I confess I have not yet the courage to show my work to anyone. It needs so much more time before it's ready," she said.

"Perhaps when it's nearing completion, you might like someone to run an eye over it," William suggested. "I would volunteer, if you think it useful."

Verbena played at embarrassment. "I couldn't ask that of you. Why, you would be forced to rip it to pieces, I'm sure! My heart would be quite crushed."

Careful, she told herself.

"I would do all I could to avoid that," he said with a gravity the light conversation did not warrant. "Believe me when I say I desire only to keep your heart safe from harm."

Verbena pinched the inside of her cheek between her back teeth. What on earth was she doing, engaging in this bizarre flirtation with a veritable stranger? This was not at all what she had planned. She was supposed to be enraptured with Étienne, not the youngest son of a large family, and a novelist at that. It was the height of absurdity, to be lusting after anyone—especially when she had never done so before! Rage engulfed her, at herself, yes, but also at William Forsyth, who had the temerity to appear at this late date, when she could not allow him in her orbit. She glanced about for some escape.

Her eyes landed on Étienne—who was currently speaking with Miles McDonald under the shade of an oak. Their heads were bowed close in conference while they gesticulated to each other like excitable peacocks.

"Where are my manners?" she said, injecting crackling coldness into her voice. "You simply must meet my very dear friend, Monsieur Charbonneau."

After all, the whole point of her attendance was to solidify her supposed connection to Étienne. That fact did nothing to lessen the hurt Verbena could see flashing across William's unguarded face.

"Must I?" he said faintly.

"Oh, yes." Verbena viciously forged ahead. "He and I have been friends for a long time, but recently—you may have heard—he's come into something of a fortune."

"I had heard that, but—"

She felt it necessary to speak over him, lest he make some inquiry into the details. "Not that he wasn't already a *very* successful man of business, but now that he is positioned somewhat higher in society, well. Let us say I have been fortunate to enjoy Étienne's attentions of late." She glanced back at William to see how he was taking it. Right in the chest, if his pallor was anything to go by. Time to twist the knife. "But you must not care for standing at all. You seem perfectly content with your lack of it."

That caused William to gasp, soft and pained. His hand lifted to his chest as if the wound was a physical one.

Verbena actually felt sorry for him. He was handsome, and

kind, and seemed not to share his brothers' unfortunately common opinion of the fairer sex. And he laughed at her jokes.

Verbena hardened her heart. She did not need laughter; she needed stability. This was a necessary cruelty.

"I see." William mustered a smile, though it looked terribly sad. Verbena thought he seemed even more handsome in his torment, which probably made her an evil person. "Well. How wonderful for you both."

"Yes, it is." Verbena attempted to look the part of an eager bride-to-be. She turned back to where Étienne had been speaking to Mr. McDonald, and found that Mr. McDonald was now surrounded, worryingly, by the brothers Forsyth. No doubt discussing politics if their droning, overlapping voices were anything to go by. Poor Mr. McDonald looked dreadfully uncomfortable. But more importantly, Étienne was striding toward Verbena with a spring in his step.

"Mr. McDonald has kindly shown me the way around this bit of wood." He held his borrowed longbow aloft. "My hope is that I land my arrows on the target and not in the dirt. Anything better than that will be cause for celebration." His eyes bounced between Verbena and her conversation partner. "I am sorry, have we been introduced?" he asked William with perfect politeness.

Verbena did the necessaries, watching the men shake hands. Étienne did not seem to note the distress in William, instead engaging in easy conversation about their shared desire to make their archery outing a good one. William dredged up the same jest regarding a shooting distance of seventy-five feet, which made Étienne laugh in delight.

"Do you think our hostess would begrudge us a few practice shots?" Étienne asked furtively. "It seems unfair to let us loose without at least that."

But William demurred, saying, "I think, sadly, this heat has gotten to me. I'm not feeling well at all." He passed a hand through his curls, casting Verbena a rueful glance. "Perhaps it's best if I make my excuses now. Lady Croydon would be aghast if I ended up fainting in the middle of her exhibition."

"My word, Mr. Forsyth, why have you suffered in silence?" Étienne grasped his lithe arm. Verbena's husband-to-be really was a kind, considerate man. "Shall I fetch you something cool to drink? Miss Montrose, do you know where I might find such a thing?"

Before Verbena could direct him to one of the many footmen, Miles McDonald joined their small knot. His face was bright red and his lips pursed.

"These Forsyths are some of the most vulgar specimens I have ever met," he seethed. His brogue became more pronounced as he spoke, though he kept his voice to a low murmur. "If I were a different sort of man, I would be employing my glove for a hearty slapping."

"Mr. McDonald, have you yet had the pleasure of meeting Mr. William Forsyth?" Verbena asked, mortified at the lack of decorum among the gentlemen.

"Ah. Good to know you." He gave William a perfunctory handshake that somehow incorporated a small bow, like the man couldn't decide which was more proper and so split the difference. "Sorry that I've just insulted your kin," he said, "but as they insulted me first, I think I'm within my rights."

"I count none of my brothers as friends, sir," William said, barely lifting his gaze from the ground. "And despite our shared surname, I feel no obligation to defend them."

Mr. McDonald eyed him closely. "Do you harbor any ridiculous notions of Scotland as well, Mr. Forsyth?"

"I don't think I do," said William. He raised his head at last.

"You're not laboring under the misapprehension that we all live in holes in the ground?"

"No."

"You're aware that inventions such as the wheel have indeed reached that far north?"

"I should hope so."

"Then we two are friends." Mr. McDonald slapped a hand to his narrow shoulder. Verbena feared William would be knocked to the ground, slight as he was, but he managed to sway back upright.

"At least one good thing has come of this outing," William said, half to himself.

At Mr. McDonald's questioning look, Verbena supplied, "Mr. Forsyth is feeling poorly."

Mr. McDonald looked genuinely concerned at that. "Oh, no. It's this damn heat, isn't it?"

"Did you want something to drink?" Étienne asked once more.

William waved them all off. "Thank you, but I should take my leave. Would you explain my absence to Lady Croydon, Miss Montrose? I fear I haven't the stomach to do it myself."

Not waiting for further protests, William disappeared into the clutch of waiting carriages some distance away. Verbena watched him go, thoroughly and inexplicably morose at the sight of his retreat. She should have felt accomplished after dispatching him so quickly, yet she found she hated herself for doing so. How had he inspired such feeling in her in the span of less than an hour?

There is something odd about that man, she thought, but lord only knew what it was.

Chapter 9

"Of all the foolish things you could have done, Forsyth," William muttered to himself as he hurried away from the archery grounds. "As if she could ever want you—either of you."

What reason could a creature as exquisite as Verbena Montrose have to cast aside a perfectly lovely suitor in favor of him? William was, in her eyes, nothing more than a struggling writer from a minor family with little to recommend him. Étienne Charbonneau had a newfound fortune as well as a thriving business, an enviable address, impeccable taste in clothing, wonderful diction (for a Frenchman), an excellent bearing, a jaw most men would commit murder to possess, and, worst of all, a truly pleasant disposition. William could have hated him if not for that last bit.

William didn't stand a chance. He never had.

The sound of footsteps rushing to catch up with him gave William's heart the cruelest modicum of hope. He turned, wishing for Verbena, but received only Miles McDonald, who had his hand clapped to the top of his head to keep his hat in place.

"Listen, Forsyth," he said, "if you're leaving, I'm coming with you."

William despaired. "You really don't have to do that." Mr. McDonald would have been a welcome companion on any other day—he was witty and unpretentious, which was a rare combination at these sorts of gatherings—but William wanted no companionship at all. "I can find my way home on my own power, I assure you. Already I'm feeling improved."

Mr. McDonald waved a hand through the air and took William's elbow, guiding him along a path that cut through the waiting carriages and landaus. "It's not concern for your health that's moved me. I simply cannot abide the rest of the archery party for one minute more. What am I to do, waste a perfectly decent afternoon listening to those boors?"

"Miss Montrose is not a boor," William felt compelled to point out. And then, because it would be unfair if he neglected him: "Monsieur Charbonneau as well. They are good company."

"For each other." Mr. McDonald let loose a riotous groan. "They are to be engaged soon. Do you know that?"

William felt his heart sink. "I may have heard something to that effect."

Mr. McDonald merely gave a mirthless laugh. "Which carriage is yours?"

"I came in a hackney."

"As did I. Damn. Well, no sense in letting these go to waste." Mr. McDonald tugged at William's arm, directing him to the most ostentatious carriage of the lot, adorned in gold trim with tasseled velvet curtains in the windows. The Croydon crest was painted on the door in a riot of yellows and purples.

William's eyes went wide. "What are you doing?"

"You'll see. I say, driver! Driver?"

A top-hatted head popped from around the carriage. "Sir?"

Mr. McDonald smiled with all the boyish charm William envied in a gentleman. "My friend Lord Simperly here is feeling poorly," he said. "Lady Croydon informs me that yours is the fastest carriage in all of London. She was adamant that we make use of it to see His Lordship home safely."

The driver gave a sharp whistle, and soon a swarm of footmen were ushering them into the cool dark of the carriage interior.

"Lady Croydon will not be pleased when she finds out we've stolen her means of transportation," William hissed.

"It will be back before she even knows it's gone. If anyone asks, I'll feign ignorance. I'm new in town, remember?" Mr. McDonald grinned widely, showing off perfect teeth.

No one could argue with teeth like that.

The carriage ride to William's rooms did not take long. More's the pity, he felt. It wasn't often he entertained, for obvious reasons. He felt some anxiety over having a visitor to his home, but as much as he wracked his memory, he couldn't recall a single hairpiece or gown being carelessly left about.

When he showed Mr. McDonald into the sitting room, everything was blessedly in the proper place with the bedroom door firmly shut.

"I have a little sherry," William offered. He actually had a lot of sherry, and some wine, and some rum, but sherry seemed the most suitable offering for a new acquaintance.

Mr. McDonald removed an embossed silver flask from the depths of his archery costume and waggled it in the air. "Whisky," he countered. "And before you make any comments about my countrymen and our supposed addiction to the stuff, remember that I had to gird myself for an afternoon of English twaddle. Any man would need a stiff one." He unscrewed the cap and offered it up.

"I do not judge you at all." William took the proffered flask and went to the sideboard to scrounge up a couple of glasses. "I'm rather jealous of your forethought, to be honest. I should have had a drink or two before showing my face at the archery grounds. It might have taken some of the sting out of it."

Mr. McDonald threw himself on the small yellow divan, his long legs stretching toward the unlit grate. "Miss Montrose," he said knowingly. "She's quite a lady."

William paused his pouring. He looked up sharply at the insouciant lounge of his guest. "Did you also attend today's festivities in order to see her?" One rival was already plenty; he did not particularly want another.

Mr. McDonald laughed, his eyes crinkling merrily at the corners. "Yes, but not how you think," he said. "Truly, I have no designs on her. She's simply the first person in this damned town who's treated me with any decency. Naturally I was happy to see her again."

William frowned. "But you are not happy about her imminent engagement. You said so before we absconded with that carriage." He crossed the room and handed Mr. McDonald a glass of amber liquid. "Why?"

"That would require certain confessions." Mr. McDonald flicked his gaze up at William, then touched the arm of his spectacles. "Would you mind if I removed these for a moment? They're apt to give me headaches if I wear them for too long."

"Of course, make yourself comfortable," William said, not understanding why his permission was needed. Once Mr. McDonald's face was bare, he understood a bit better. "Oh. Your eye."

"Or lack thereof." Mr. McDonald gestured at the right side of his face normally hidden by the blacked-out lens, where a thick, shiny scar resided. "The result of a childhood affliction. It doesn't bother me at all. Unless I'm expected to shoot an arrow."

William thought, then lifted his glass of whisky. "To taking our shots only metaphorically."

Mr. McDonald looked at him for a moment, then smiled. He raised his glass in return. "That, I'll drink to."

William was not a practiced drinker, having only sipped sparingly in public so that he might always keep his head. Yet the failure he'd endured earlier was so disheartening, and the company of Miles McDonald was so pleasant, that the afternoon stretched into evening. William replenished their glasses many times over with his reserves, as needed. Conversation meandered from light topics to a complete rehashing of their families. They had both lost their parents within the last two years, they discovered, and so had much in common.

The sunlight was fading from the room as Miles slouched on the divan, cradling his glass in one hand.

"Étienne Charbonneau," he said apropos of nothing William could discern.

William groaned, flinging his head against his chairback. The name reminded him of his misfortune at the man's hands. "Monsieur Charbonneau. Damn him!"

"Yes, damn him," Miles agreed, sighing.

"He is entirely too decent. And so good-looking on top of it all!"

"Very unfair."

"Exactly." William felt strengthened by the fact that his new friend seemed to share his ire. He lolled his head to the side to gaze at Miles. "How can I compete?"

Miles gave him a confused squint. "Compete?"

"For Miss Montrose," William clarified.

"Ah, yes." Miles relaxed a bit. "Sorry, I forgot about her."

"Impossible. Who can forget her?"

"I can, apparently."

"Well, I cannot. Damn him."

"Damn who?"

"Charbonneau! Don't tell me you've forgotten him, too?" William waved a drunken finger in his direction.

"Of course not. What I am trying to tell you is–damn this seat," Miles said as he wriggled on the cushions, trying to lean closer though impeded by inebriation. "What I am trying to tell you, because you are a good man, as far as I can tell, and because I hear you writers are not scandalized by these sorts of things, knowing your Greek and so forth–"

"My Latin is better."

"I am trying to confess, if you'd let me." Miles's doleful gaze fell to his glass. "Will you let me?"

William instantly sobered. His mind caught up with Miles's slightly slurred words. Sitting straighter in his chair, he put out his hand, palm down, in a gesture meant to stop a disaster. "You're drunk," he said. "We both are. You needn't–"

"I was sent down to London, at my great-uncle's urging, to find a wife," Miles said. "He lives abroad but his letters were very numerous and very clear. He will not rest until I wed a proper lady." His misery was a living thing that curled up on the floor in front of the grate. "Yet my attentions lie elsewhere. You understand?"

William gave his friend–new yet already so trusting, and therefore, he felt, trustworthy–a fond look. "I do." He turned his glass in his hand, pondering the golden liquid. "Monsieur Charbonneau?" he said, lightly enough that they could pretend the mention of the man was unrelated, if Miles lost his nerve.

He lost only his composure. Miles groaned throatily, a hand pressed to his breast. "Étienne. Even his name makes my heart prance like a show horse. Have you ever met a man who could, within the span of an hour, arrest your senses so completely?"

William thought of Verbena. Of her fiery wit in the cloistered room of the club, firelight painting her radiant. "Not a man, no," he said, soft and low. "But someone."

"You refer to Miss Montrose?" Miles asked, surprised. "After only meeting her for the first time today? Not that I have a leg to stand on there."

William shaped a few words with his mouth before deciding on something that was not quite a lie. "It seems we've known each other much longer."

"Yes, but I thought we both might–that is, sometimes a man says one thing for the sake of–" Miles's face took on a brick hue. "But you're not like me at all. I'm a fool. I've scandalized you."

"Do I look scandalized?" William pointed at his own face. If he was flushed it was only a little, and only with drink. "Mr. McDonald, you said it yourself: we writers are a different breed. Why, half the Calliope Club is composed of men of your leanings. If I were to faint every time I heard a man sigh longingly for want of another man, I would never get anything done."

Miles did not seem convinced. His eyes darted from William to the door. "I've been a fool. Getting drunk, speaking much too freely. You could have me hanged. Do they still hang us here in London? I can never keep up with all your absurd laws."

"I think it's more often the stocks." It was a thoughtless thing to say. Miles's pitiful moan made William wince. "But that is reserved almost entirely for the lower classes," he rushed to add. "And anyway, I won't tell a soul what you've told me. I'll swear on anything you like."

"It's not a question of your discretion, Mr. Forsyth," Miles said with a shaky smile. "It's the fact that I have no friends in this place, and I fear I have ruined the one I found in you with my foolish mouth. I would understand if you snub me outright the next time we cross paths."

"Snub you! I would never–" William bolted to his feet, swaying a bit. A thought occurred to him. In the glow of good drink, it seemed like the best thought he'd had in a while. "I have secrets as well," he said.

Miles's eyes widened in vague distress. "Well, for god's sake, don't tell me. We needn't barter confidences back and forth just because I can't hold my tongue."

"I can't tell you," William said. He was warming to his idea. "I must show you. Will you stay there a moment?" He put his drink down on a side table and held both palms up toward Miles as if he might keep him in place.

"Really, William–"

"I'll return shortly," he said, then bustled into his bedroom, shutting the door securely out of habit.

Was it merely liquor that emboldened him so? Or was it the rare amity he felt being in the presence of a somewhat kindred spirit? It was impossible to parse, so intertwined as they were, so William did not attempt it.

Changing from one persona was, after all this time, a task that could be accomplished with alacrity, but that night, Flora was quick, even for her. What had been second nature to her was now simply nature. Her hair and paint fell into place, as did her muslin walking dress, high-waisted to flatter her slim figure. One final primp before her small mirror, and she left the bedroom, her silken slippers a quiet shush on the bare floorboards.

Miles, still sitting on the divan, turned to mark her entrance. He froze when he caught sight of her, his mouth hanging open. A miasma of discomfort settled over the room, making Flora tremble with nerves.

Perhaps this wasn't the best idea after all.

Miles popped to his feet. He seemed not to know what to do with his hands. They dangled at his sides, then clasped his opposite elbows. "Is Forsyth–?" His gaze drifted over her shoulder into the small bedroom. "Apologies. I thought we were alone." He squinted at her in abject confusion. "We haven't been introduced. Miles McDonald." He stuck out a hand for her to shake.

Flora felt a thrill trace up her spine. Miles was the first person to whom she had revealed her secret in the flesh. And here he was, not even recognizing her! It filled her with a sense of great accomplishment for some reason.

"We have," she managed to say with a calm that was fast becoming real as opposed to forced. "Though you know me by another name."

He came around the divan and took a few steps toward her, almost crouching as he moved, his head swaying side to side on his long neck. He was trying to examine her face from another angle, she realized. She obliged him by standing still, hands clasped demurely in front of her.

"William?" Miles asked.

She smiled, a tentative thing. "Only some of the time."

Miles's face took on a cast of awe and wonder. "And now?"

"Now I am Flora Witcombe."

"Not–! The poetess?"

"The very same."

"But you're famous!"

"Only some of the time," she repeated, laughing.

"My maiden aunt adores your work," Miles said. "I confess I have not read any myself, but I have been meaning to." He reached out and took her hands in his, marveling at her dress, her hair, her dainty shoes. "Come, sit, sit! I have–oh, but will you have a glass of sherry? That's what a lady drinks, is it not?"

"This lady should probably drink no more tonight," Flora said, allowing him to lead her gallantly back to her chair. She regarded him as they sat, his face a strange mixture of confusion and cheerfulness. "But please, help yourself to more if you wish. I know this is all a bit . . . unusual."

"We are all of us a bit unusual," Miles said, "or else what would be the point of living?"

Flora felt the warmth of true friendship flow through her. "Thank you. For your understanding."

"Of course." Miles glanced at her dress, then seemed to force himself to look back at her face. "May I ask how . . . ?" He trailed off, using his hand to indicate the whole of her person. His hand fell back into his lap. "No, curiosity should not outweigh good manners, should it? I would not ask a bird how she flies or the moon how she glows."

Flora smiled sweetly. "I do not mind telling you. It is a novelty to me, too. Having someone to tell, that is."

"Really?" Miles leaned in, all eagerness. "Then I will endeavor to be the best possible audience."

It was difficult to know where to begin. Flora picked at the fine stitching of her gown. "Do you recall the year without a summer?" she asked.

"Yes, three–no, four years ago, now, wasn't it?" Miles stared at the ceiling in thought. "Lord, has it really been that long? It feels both eons ago and yesterday. In Edinburgh, they rioted when the food ran out–at least, those who were not struck down by that awful fever did. I can only imagine what it was like here in London."

"It was awful," Flora said. She shuddered to recall that wretched time, when the freezing winter refused to give way to spring, lingering unnaturally. Crops had shriveled; people had starved; everywhere one looked was suffused with misery. Even the ton could not escape the ramifications of that summerless year, much as they tried to pretend all was well in their corner of the world. Flora recalled picnics with the guests wrapped in their fur stoles, eating the small selection of whatever frigid morsels had been hunted down. It was a fruitless exercise, but one good thing had come of it–at least for Flora.

"No one knew when the warmth would return, or if it ever could. When the world seems to be at an end," she explained, "one can hardly worry about little things like consequences. I thought, why not go to the dressmaker and make a few purchases? Why not wear what I like and live as I wish? Why not write new poetry in a voice that was also wholly new? It seemed as if all was lost, anyway."

"So it is only in the last four years that you have–" Miles

gestured once more to her person, grimacing apologetically. "Done so?" he finally finished.

"Four years in the act itself," Flora said, "though I suppose in spirit, it began earlier."

She explained while Miles listened with rapt attention: in a family as large as the Forsyths, and with so many brothers, William–for Flora referred to him thusly–was able to cultivate his interests with very little oversight. Their beleaguered nursemaid could not be in two places at once, after all. Art and writing were havens, providing him with his only comforts: myths and legends; stories of the strange and wonderful; and later, poems that opened doors to worlds previously unimaginable. As a young man, thinking he might participate in the opening of such doors in his own small way, William had carved out the most modest of livings writing gothic novels. His middling poetry found no audience in that crowded arena, Flora related quite frankly.

The work underwent a bewildering transformation when she herself wrote in William's stead. Of course, Flora could not be confined to the page. She described it to Miles almost like a trance.

"I would find myself moving through the world, thinking, this is not my body, these are not my thoughts. This is certainly not my clothing. I thought I might be going mad, but eventually I realized the only real madness would be to bury such a thing and feign complete ignorance of it. If the mind is desperate to convey a thought, that thought will not be ignored. So I experimented in private. The clothing I felt I needed, the posture. I felt myself becoming someone else." She licked her lips, pausing to collect her words. "Not that I wasn't William, but I was also myself, and perhaps more besides. There was no William without me, and vice versa. Do you follow?"

Miles inclined his head. "I cannot say a woman dwells within me, if that's what you're asking, but surely I can understand containing a hidden facet within oneself. To me, it seems perfectly natural."

Flora brightened. She'd known Miles was the correct person to confide in. He had, she suspected, a poet's soul. "Exactly right.

Once I became more comfortable with my dual nature, I was soothed. I cannot tell you how stark the difference has been. It is like breathing for the first time, having never gulped a mouthful of sweet air."

"You have rescued yourself from a terrible suffocation," Miles observed. "And become quite the successful poetess, to boot. Even a country squire like me has heard of Flora Witcombe, and I almost never venture outside of the papers' sporting news in terms of reading material."

Flora felt her face warm. She never knew how to respond to such praise. "Whatever small achievements I have made have been born of pure luck, I assure you."

"Miss Witcombe," said Miles, leaning across the arm of the divan to hold her slim hand in his. His eyes were kind as he looked upon her. "Given the extraordinary circumstances of your birth, bursting forth fully formed like Athena, I wager the odds were against you. Take your laurels when they're offered, would you? Lord knows a man would."

A gentle smile crossed Flora's lips. She squeezed her friend's palm in hers. "Thank you, Mr. McDonald. Never mind what those boors say; you're a true gentleman." Then, remembering the source of her earlier despair, she sighed and dropped his hand. "Now that you understand my situation, you see my dilemma. I am stupidly, wretchedly enchanted with Miss Montrose. While she seems to hold Flora Witcombe in some sort of esteem, she did not seem at all charmed by William Forsyth, who is the only one of us allowed to actually woo her. What am I to do?"

The stresses of the day, combined with the whisky and the late hour, took their toll. Flora put her head in her hands and cried, allowing her tears to wash down her cheeks and patter in her skirted lap.

"Oh, dear lord. Oh, she's crying. Oh, erm, come now." Miles moved to stand beside her chair, his hand landing atop her shoulder to rub lightly. "There, there," he said. "There, there."

"Is that all you can say?" Flora said between sobs. "'There, there'?"

"Believe me, I am grasping for something better. Give me a moment." His hand rubbed harder. "Well, look, she's only just met William today, yes? So she didn't cleave to him as quickly as she did Flora! That's not so strange; you are, in a sense, different people. Perhaps she needs time to get to know him. See all his fine qualities."

Flora picked up her head to stare at him, a tear dripping from her chin. "Do you really think so?"

"I do. Knowing you for even this short time, I can definitively say your other half is a good man, just as you're a fine lady. Anyone with sense in her head will agree, eventually."

"I suppose," Flora said, dashing away her tears.

"And what's more," Miles said, "I pledge to you any assistance I might offer. Simply say the word and I will sing your praises, or deliver your letters, or contrive a meeting, or—" He stopped, his eyes taking on that glassy, faraway look of a man who's just had a reckless thought enter his mind.

"What is it?" said Flora, feeling reckless herself.

"I don't know why this didn't occur to me earlier. It's so obvious." Miles grinned down at her. "I shall invite William, along with Étienne and Verbena, to Plas Tân manor."

"Plas Tân . . . ?" Flora realized her mouth was hanging open. She shut it with a click, her thoughts racing.

"Lovely spot on the Welsh coast," Miles said.

"I know it. I could hardly be ignorant of the most famous artists' residence in the kingdom."

The members of her club often spoke of Plas Tân, where a pair of older women, having scandalously escaped their betrotheds in Scotland, lived and wrote and painted and collected art in perfect solitude. Having no husbands and no income from their families, the ladies hit upon an excellent scheme: they opened their home to fellow writers and artists in exchange for some small recompense. The visitors could stay a week or a month, ostensibly to work on their art, though the papers reported that the social aspect of the place was far more enticing. It was a sought-after invitation, as only the most accomplished artists were chosen to occupy the dozen or so guest rooms. Lord Byron himself had boasted about his last visit to the ladies of Plas Tân to anyone at the Calliope who would listen.

"But how in the world would you ever manage a visit to Plas Tân?" she asked Miles. She did not mean to be insulting, but her new friend had shown no great artistic inclination nor connections to the sort of people who could rate such an invitation.

Miles made a frivolous gesture with one hand. "One of the ladies is my maiden aunt."

"This is a jest, surely."

"I swear to you, it's not. Aunt Bette and her lifelong companion, Anne, have often said their home is always open to me and my friends. I could write to them tomorrow and arrange the whole thing." He clapped a hand to Flora's arm. "Think of it: it's a very pretty spot, far from this filthy, rigid city. There are woods for long, contemplative walks, and the sea for bathing, and all sorts of leisure in between. William and Verbena could become very close, indeed, in such ideal environs."

Flora narrowed her eyes at him. "As might you and Étienne."

Miles merely shrugged. "I don't deny how appealing that would be, should it happen." His eyes sparkled with boyish devilry.

Flora chewed her lip. "I am certain they plan to marry in name only, but does that mean we should endeavor to ruin their imminent engagement? Even a couple that isn't suited has a right to be wrong, don't they?"

"Miss Witcombe, I think if all it takes to halt a courtship is putting yourself in the line of sight, then that's fair play." Miles nodded to himself. "If we two should offer them a more palatable option, then that is their choice. We'd actually be doing them a favor, if you think about it."

"I fear we are being very selfish," Flora said. A sullen malaise threatened to overtake her. Who was she—who was William—to interfere with a woman's prospects?

"Surely when you published your first folio, you had your detractors," Miles said. "Did they not call you selfish and a fool for sharing your talent with the world? Did you listen to them then?"

He scoffed. "God forbid a woman–or a sometimes woman–do anything that might bring her happiness!"

His words hit Flora like an arrow to the heart. Perhaps she was only hearing what she wished, but there was some sense in it. Verbena might be her life's great love. If there was a chance to win her, Flora had to try. She would forever wonder what might have been if she didn't.

"All right," she heard herself say, flush with drink and determination. "To Wales, then." She would need to pack a trunk. Only William's best clothes, of course. "Verbena will be so thrilled. She was just telling me how dearly she wanted more time to work on her poetry."

Chapter 10

"Betsy?" Verbena removed her bonnet, shaking her red curls. She wanted to be out of her visiting gown as quickly as her maid could manage it. Several invitations had been issued following the conclusion of the archery outing, and she'd diligently seen them all through that very morning and into the afternoon. She couldn't let any opportunity to bolster her supposed romance with Étienne slip away.

"Betsy, are you in?" she called once more. The words echoed around the foyer and up the staircase, but Verbena received no reply.

At least, not the one she wanted.

Her mother swept in from the study wearing a light cream day dress and her usual cross look.

"Where have you been?" Mrs. Montrose demanded.

"Visiting acquaintances. I told you." She stripped off her left glove and placed it on the side table next to the doffed bonnet before going to work on the fingers of the right one. "Where is Betsy? I should like to dress for dinner."

"We have more important things to think of," Mrs. Montrose said. "What's this I hear about you and a French tailor?"

Verbena dropped her other glove on the pile. "Mother, surely you don't listen to gossip." She was aware of her mother's opinions on ladies and sarcasm, namely that one should never wield the other, but she could not help the acid that laced her words. Mrs. Montrose had trained Verbena from a tender age to keep her ears open, her whispers continuous, and her chess pieces all ordered in her mind. And yet the word "gossip" inspired in Mrs. Montrose a virulent protest. It wasn't gossip, she had always said, to merely communicate information from one person to another for the purposes of better understanding and moving through one's world. Verbena, on the other hand, had no qualms about calling a spade a spade.

Right on cue, her mother's face darkened with a sour look. "Mrs. Albee and Lady Key told me today at tea–separately, mind you–that they'd heard from Mrs. Watts that you're being courted by some–some upstart!"

"Oh, Mother." Verbena sighed. This was rather earlier than she'd planned to inform her parents of her imminent engagement. So inconvenient, when things did not go to schedule. She lifted her gaze to the main staircase that sliced through the house's foyer. "Betsy!" she called. Why didn't her maid come? She lifted her skirts and started up the stairs.

Mrs. Montrose followed at her heels. "They say he runs a *shop*. That he makes a living sewing *coats* together. Are you really allowing such a man to press his suit with you? We can do better than that."

Verbena paused on the landing, not turning even when she felt her mother being caught up short behind her. "Can we really?" she asked the staircase. "For the last few months, you have been urging me to find a husband. 'Any man with breath in his body would do,' I believe you said."

"Well, I meant any man with breath in his body *and* a known family," said Mrs. Montrose. "Even a dull girl like you should know that goes without saying."

Perhaps at one time, the hurled epithets had caused Verbena great pain and engendered in her a desire to prove her mother and father wrong. Now, though, they were only a tiresome feature of her home life, like the faded portraits of Montroses past that lined the walls.

She turned to face her mother on the landing, one hand propped on the banister. In this position, she was a full head taller than Mrs. Montrose and was not above using it to loom.

"Étienne Charbonneau is a good man," she said evenly. "He has recently come into a fortune. His address is excellent. His manners and bearing are beyond reproach. And he is, most pressingly, eager to be in my company. I believe he means to propose. And when he does, I mean to accept."

"But his origins—" Mrs. Montrose protested.

"—are humble, and therefore worthy of admiration, given how far he's come." Verbena turned on her heel and stalked up the staircase to the first story. "Be reasonable for once in your life, Mother. There is no duke waiting in the wings to be our savior. There is only Monsieur Charbonneau, and he is perfectly adequate." She continued up the stairs, her mother following.

There was a long stretch of silence punctuated only by their two sets of footfalls. Finally, as they reached the door of Verbena's room, Mrs. Montrose said in a low whisper, "You are certain his finances are in order?"

"And more robust than half the gentry can claim," Verbena said. She flung open her door, hoping to find her maid occupied with some task that had kept her from coming when summoned, but the bedroom was empty. Not only was Betsy absent, but there was no dinner gown draped over the bed in preparation for Verbena's return. That was very unlike Betsy; her stalwart companion always had such things readied far in advance.

Verbena turned to her mother, who stood in the hall with her hands clasped tight. "Where has Betsy gone?" she asked.

Her mother dropped her hands to her sides and lifted her chin. "Your maid," Mrs. Montrose said, "has been dismissed."

Verbena could hardly form a response for several moments. "Whatever could you mean?" Betsy had been with the Montrose family since she was a little girl, her mother having been one of their chambermaids before being taken by a ravaging fever. Verbena and Betsy had grown up together, played together. Betsy had been a fixture in every one of Verbena's adventures. They were, if not friends, then something closer to sisters, if one sister paid the other's wages. "She can't have been dismissed."

A loud thump came from the floor below them. Both women

glanced down toward the sound. Another thump, followed by what sounded like glass breaking and muffled curses.

Mrs. Montrose sighed.

"Your father made the decision early this afternoon," she said, regarding Verbena coolly. "Though I doubt you would have been consulted even if you had been here."

"But . . . why?" Verbena groped for a seat before her knees gave way, perching on the edge of her featherbed. "Betsy has been nothing but excellent. And given how long she has served our household—"

"Your father can no longer afford her services." Mrs. Montrose strode into the room and plucked the most minuscule piece of lint from Verbena's skirts. "You know our situation. Your father looked over the ledger this morning and saw there was nothing that could be done. Sacrifices must be made if this family is to survive." She flicked the lint to the floor.

Verbena wondered wildly if it would ever be cleaned up, if any maids still remained. First the footmen, now this? "Did she—was there no note from her? To say good-bye, at least?"

All those years together, from girlhood on, and now they were to be strangers.

Mrs. Montrose sniffed. "I don't believe there was any time for her to put pen to paper, if she was even capable of doing so."

"She is more than capable," Verbena said, seething. All those years, and her mother hadn't even bothered to know the girl who was Verbena's constant companion.

"Be that as it may." Mrs. Montrose waved a hand. "Once a servant is dismissed, it's best to allow them only enough time to collect their meager belongings and depart. All under the watchful eye of your father, of course. Can't have these people stealing the silver."

As if Betsy had ever stolen a thing in her life! If anyone was a thief, Verbena mused, it was the Montrose family, stealing away a young person's best years in exchange for a pittance of a salary.

"Your father furnished her with a reference, of course," Mrs. Montrose added. As if that made up for all the rest.

Verbena stared at the lint on the rug. Her mother and father would probably never find it in their selfish hearts to feel outright sympathy for Betsy's plight—a good, solid worker dismissed for no reason but her employer's own faults—but there were also the more practical pitfalls of such a rash decision to consider.

"I wonder," she said lowly, "how on earth you expected me to win the heart of a noble gentleman without Betsy to assist me in dressing, arranging my hair, and presenting me to the world as an elegant young lady? You should be knocking on Monsieur Charbonneau's door with invitations to dinner; you should be kissing the hem of his coat. How dare you question my acceptance of his suit when you have hamstrung me so terribly?"

Mrs. Montrose's cheeks went scarlet at this insolence. "You—!"

A loud banging echoed from downstairs. The iron knocker on the front door was being put through its paces. Verbena waited a moment in the cold silence that followed.

"Are there any servants left to answer that?" she asked. "Or shall I go see who it is?"

"Oh, don't be silly. We didn't dismiss anyone else today, only Betsy."

So her parents had retained their own maid and valet. Of course. Sacrifices were for Verbena to bear, not them.

Someone indeed answered the door; she heard the thing creak open and a quiet exchange of murmurs, followed by a tread upon the stair. It seemed that Mrs. Montrose did not wish to be seen arguing with her daughter, leaving off their conversation to instead fuss with the brushes and tonics on Verbena's vanity table. She was ruining the careful order of everything when Stevens arrived.

"A letter for Miss Montrose," he said.

"I'll take that." Her mother crossed the room in two strides and plucked the creamy missive from him. "That will be all."

Stevens gave Verbena a single fathomless glance before departing, shutting the door as he went.

Verbena resigned herself to her mother's company as she undressed, starting with the many buttons on her calfskin boots. She was used to her parents reading the letters that came addressed to her; there was no expectation of privacy for her in the household and never had been. She hoped the letter was from Flora yet also wished it wasn't–not that Flora had ever written anything scandalous in their correspondence, but Verbena liked to pretend the words were for her only. Something intimate and sacred.

Mrs. Montrose scanned the letter with a bemused scoff. "Who on earth is Miles McDonald?" she asked. "Is he a better prospect than the Frenchman?"

Verbena calmly removed her delicate necklace and placed it on the vanity. "He has no money," she said.

"Pity." Her mother finally held the letter out for her. "He's invited you to some artistic–something. Why does he seem to think you write poetry? You've never written a line, have you?"

"He must be mistaken." Verbena took the letter and scanned it.

My dear Miss Montrose–

I wish to extend an invitation to you to my maiden aunt's home in Wales, where she is known to entertain the artistically inclined. A party composed of myself and some close friends will be accommodated at their house in Plas Tân. I have no doubt you will find the setting an excellent place to write your poetry. We will likely stay for a fortnight, if that is convenient for you. Please say you'll come; the retreat will be poorer without your company. Of course I have also invited Monsieur Charbonneau. As he is French, I suspect he has at least one artistic bone in his body. At any rate, I eagerly await your reply.

Yours, etc.–Mr. Miles McDonald

So Mr. McDonald had also learned about Verbena's supposed poetic soul somehow. This ruse of hers was becoming ungainly.

"Well?" her mother prompted, pulling her from her thoughts. "How shall you reply?"

Verbena stared down at the note. "I should love to attend," she said. "Monsieur Charbonneau will be there, apparently." Perhaps there they could more firmly cement their romantic lie; Étienne's flamboyant nature would surely raise no eyebrows if the gathering was composed of more eccentric souls than he.

"And how shall you travel?" Her mother snatched the note from her hands. "An unmarried woman, alone! With two men!"

"Naturally I will have a chaperone," Verbena said.

"Oh?" Mrs. Montrose asked. "Who?"

Verbena opened her mouth, then closed it. Her mother knew very well that Betsy, when she had been employed as Verbena's maid, was her usual companion for such situations. The thought of asking her waspish mother to accompany her on the journey turned her stomach. Not that her mother would ever deign to leave London; she detested the countryside.

"Perhaps you could spare Helen," Verbena said, naming her mother's own maid, a white-haired crone who had been with them for ages. She was harmless enough. And she dozed soundly during carriage rides.

Mrs. Montrose regarded Verbena with outright contempt. "Ridiculous. I have a life of my own, you know. I can't possibly do without Helen for an entire fortnight."

"It would be a great help to me," Verbena said, pushing down the rage she felt at Mrs. Montrose for denying her this one simple thing. "If all goes well on this excursion, perhaps Monsieur Charbonneau will propose." Their plan called for the announcement at a much later date, but never mind that. "Do you not think that a bird in hand is worth two in the bush? Once we are wed, my future will be secure. You and Father needn't worry about yourselves. Monsieur Charbonneau will provide for us."

Her mother's expression soured, her lips thin and unpleasant as she considered Verbena's words. Yet before she could answer, the sound of the front door knocker came once again. This time, it was a genteel tapping of metal against wood, almost musical.

"Oh, what now?" Mrs. Montrose charged from the room, only to be met in the hall by the butler.

"Miss Flora Witcombe to see Miss Montrose, Mrs. Montrose," he informed her.

Verbena's middle went tight and warm. "Tell her I'll be down momentarily, Stevens," she called. And she shut her bedroom door in her mother's face before she could protest.

It took much longer to change into a fresh gown—a pale mint with seed pearls along the neckline—without Betsy's help, but Verbena managed. She was eager not only to see her good friend but, as her thoughts marched into neat rows while she was occupied with rearranging her hair, to find a solution to her problems.

By the time she was dressed and rushing down the stairs, her cheeks were flushed with the excitement of yet another excellent plan forming in her mind.

Flora had been shown to the sitting room to wait. She was perched on the peach-colored divan, staring at the peachy wallpaper. At Verbena's entrance, she stood, a smile on her lips.

"I hope I'm not keeping you from some appointment—" Flora began.

Verbena shushed her, catching her in an embrace. Flora's dress was soft against her cheek where she laid it upon her shoulder. "You could not have come at a better time," she murmured.

"Oh, good." Flora gave her one excellent squeeze about her middle before pulling back to hold Verbena at arm's length. "How was the archery party?"

"Forget the archery party. Strike it from your mind," Verbena said. "Do you have any plans for the next fortnight?"

"Erm—I don't think so," Flora said, puzzled. "Why?"

Verbena cupped her palms under Flora's elbows. "I'd like you to come to Wales with me."

It was as if she'd requested Flora accompany her to the stars, so great was the effect on her dear friend. Flora's eyes went wide and her face paled. "Wales?" she said faintly.

"Yes, you've heard of it, surely? It's over on the right, if you're facing the Channel. An acquaintance of mine, Mr. McDonald, is taking a party to visit his maiden aunt. There is to be an artistic retreat, lasting a fortnight or so. Won't that be lovely? Étienne will be there, too. You could take the time to work on your poetry—we both could." The lie was quite easy by now. "Besides, getting away from London at the hottest part of summer is always an excellent proposition." She searched Flora's visage for the excitement she was hoping the invitation would bring, yet she only saw despair. "Flora? Whatever is the matter? Doesn't this appeal?"

"I—well, I would love to go with you, of course—" She appeared truly distraught, her brow furrowed deep as carriage ruts.

Verbena caught up Flora's hands in hers. "Then say you will. Please. I'm . . . a bit desperate, actually." She soothed her thumbs into the tense skin of Flora's hands, massaging away the aches that she knew must come with hours spent writing. "I need to be away from here." She lifted her gaze to the ceiling. In the ensuing quiet, the sound of her father stomping his way across the floor above was readily apparent, though blessedly his curses were muffled.

"Has there been some trouble?" Flora asked in a horrified whisper.

Verbena sighed. "Only the usual sort." She leaned in closer, dropping her voice to nearly nothing. "My parents think me foolish for entertaining Étienne's suit. They want me to marry someone from a known family instead."

Flora's whole face pinched. "I—that's, that's terrible."

"Even more terrible, my parents have dismissed my maid. I am quite alone." Verbena worried at her lower lip with her teeth. "Sometimes I think they must want me to fail, if only to have yet another reason to castigate me."

Flora shook her head. "You must go to Wales, then. Anything to get you out of this house, even if it is only for a fortnight."

"Yet without a chaperone, I won't be permitted to go." Verbena held Flora's hands tightly. "Please, can't you help me? I need you."

Flora blinked rapidly. "Of course I would help you in any way I can."

"So you'll come?" Verbena felt her cheeks heat. "You and I and Miles and Étienne—all of us will go together?"

There was a flicker of determination in Flora's eyes. "Of

course, if it will help you improve your circumstances. A marriage to an upstanding gentleman would be the solution to all your woes. That is perfectly clear." She stood straighter. "When do we leave?"

A happy yelp bubbled up from Verbena's throat. She threw her arms around Flora, squeezing her tight. "I will write to Mr. McDonald at once. We will have such fun together, I know it! Ah, I'll need to pack my own trunk, won't I?" She would include William Forsyth's novel in her luggage, she decided; she'd started reading it as she'd threatened at the archery party. It was too intriguing to leave behind for a fortnight.

"Oh, yes, packing," Flora murmured. Her eyes were fastened on the carpet, where the toes of their slippers nearly touched. "I have . . . so much to pack."

"You should get started right away," Verbena urged. "I will send word as soon as I know the shape of our plans. We can take Étienne's new carriage. It's quite comfortable." Verbena escorted Flora to the door, still holding her hands.

Flora released their joined hold to let herself out the door, not bothering to wait for Stevens. Before she left, she gave Verbena a long, lingering look.

"I hope you know what you're doing," she said. "I hope we all do."

"How odd you are!" Verbena placed a friendly kiss on Flora's cheek. She smelled of sweetness. "Take care getting home."

"Take care," Flora returned, and left.

Verbena stood on the doorstep and waved farewell, calling out last-minute advice to pack for seaside weather. She watched as Flora's beautiful bonnet disappeared into the thick London crowds, a perfect gemstone lost among pebbles.

Verbena stood there a moment with her arms wrapped about her middle, lost in thought. Some women, upon entering a marriage, neglected their old friends, too busy managing a household and—Verbena shivered a little—preparing for children. But Verbena did not plan to be such a woman, not at all. She hoped her friendship with Flora would be allowed to flourish, and that Flora did not feel abandoned by the changes in Verbena's life.

What Flora really needed, Verbena thought, was a husband of her own. Not a real one, mind—a false one, like Étienne. Someone who could provide for her all the comforts and security of a marriage without the usual obligations. Then the two of them could do exactly as they pleased. Their friendship could continue as it was, which was an exceedingly normal thing to desire. (Verbena had never had a true bosom friend before, so she assumed this was the case with all women who had them.)

Yes, she realized with a jolt. Why couldn't she procure a suitable husband for Flora? She'd already done it for herself; how difficult could it be? Perhaps Étienne could recommend one.

Or perhaps this trip to Wales might unearth the man they needed.

Verbena smiled to herself, watching the tide of London rush by her front door. It was all falling into place.

Chapter 11

"I still do not understand," said Étienne. "Can you explain it again?"

Verbena huffed, swaying side to side as their carriage trundled over the London cobblestones. They were traveling that morning to Flora's home in Covent Garden and then, she presumed, to wherever Mr. McDonald was lodging so that they might all begin their journey to Wales. Verbena had lied to her mother before leaving, saying that Étienne's waiting carriage was empty. It afforded her some time to speak with her future husband in private, time that was not unlimited. It frustrated her to waste it by repeating herself.

"It's perfectly simple," she said. "I must find a husband for Flora so that she might enjoy the same sort of arrangement you and I will have. A man like yourself would be ideal, don't you agree?"

Étienne sat primly on the carriage seat opposite her, his legs crossed at the knee. He wore an impeccable forest green greatcoat and a slight frown. "But what need does Miss Witcombe have for a husband? She is already a successful poetess, as you tell it. Didn't you say she keeps rooms of her own? A woman like that would not need a man."

"Not for money, no," Verbena said, "but as a shield against rumors of impropriety. After all, I anticipate she and I will be spending most of our time together after I am married. At least, that is my hope." Verbena stared dreamily out the open carriage window as she considered all its benefits. Long, leisurely mornings spent in each other's company, followed by long, leisurely afternoons. Flora could write her poems while Verbena tended to her correspondence; they could exchange the latest gossip, go on long walks together. Married life would be more than tolerable with her beloved friend Flora by her side.

Étienne made a considering noise. "My dear, there is no need to prevaricate around me. I do not mind if you plan to take her as your lover."

"What!" She whipped her head about to face him once more. "Why would you say that?"

"Oh, my mistake. You have already?"

"No!" Verbena slammed the carriage window shut once more lest any passersby overhear.

He frowned. "Well, why not?"

"Why–? For one thing, Étienne, we have agreed not to conduct any affairs before we are safely married," she said in a low whisper, tick-tocking a finger between them. "And for another, there isn't–That is, I'm not–"

"Like me?" Étienne gazed at her tenderly.

All the air seemed to dissipate. The carriage rocked them in the ensuing silence.

"Please understand," Verbena said once her breath had returned, "I do not think it such a terrible thing to be. But, as you likely are not aware, women are different. It is not unusual in the least for a lady to develop certain strong feelings for another lady. We are creatures of the heart, you see, and men are not an appropriate object for the more delicate emotions. It doesn't signify anything out of the ordinary!"

"I agree that it is somewhat common, what you describe," said Étienne, "but, my dear–you are aware that there are many women in the world who do love men? Who want to be in their arms and in their beds? You have heard more gossip than I; you must know that such things happen."

"I suppose, but–"

"And you must know," he continued, "that there are ladies who develop, as you say, strong feelings for other ladies. And these feelings can lead, again, into their arms and their beds?"

"Yes, I *know,* but I'm not–"

"And do you not think"–Étienne's voice rose over hers–"that you could be one of these ladies? You are already so exceptional, my dear. Why can you not admit what to me is so obvious?"

"And what is that?" Verbena said waspishly.

"That you want Miss Witcombe as a man might want a woman. That you want her the way I have wanted men." Étienne sat back in his seat, his hands held out palm up. "None of this is shameful. You said so yourself."

"It's not." That much, Verbena could say, and quickly. The rest? "For other people. As for myself, I . . ." She sealed her lips and looked out the window. Carts full of fruits and vegetables passed them by; soon they would be at Flora's address. "I suppose I have never had cause to consider it with any real seriousness," she said. "What would be the point when I am meant to make a tactically beneficial match? When the option is so outlandishly unavailable, why would one waste time thinking on it?"

"Ah." Étienne held up one finger. "But now the option is yours, should you desire it. When I am your husband, I will not stop you from pursuing any lover. Do you want Miss Witcombe in that role? Or do you plan to dance around it until Judgment Day?"

Verbena considered the London streets as they passed them by, the crowds that filled the air with their voices, their bodies. A teeming cauldron of hardship and song and smells. She had never considered there to be room in such a world for the thing Étienne described. Oh, Verbena was no innocent; she had heard every sort of rumor under the sun. Yet while there were words aplenty for men like Étienne–none of them flattering–she knew none for women who conducted affairs with other women. They had to exist, but Verbena could not name a single one. Even the famous ladies of Plas Tân, who were to be their hostesses–though they lived together without husbands, Verbena understood their devotion to be entirely chaste. They were the most famous virgins in the isles, reportedly without an ounce of passion in their souls. She supposed that was the sort of arrangement she had expected in her own future with Flora, though she had not grasped why until Étienne questioned it.

What did Verbena want, in the end? To be with Flora, of course. But how? Was the intimacy of close friendship not enough to sustain her? Wasn't Verbena's desire to bury her face in those soft chestnut curls a mere girlish whim? Had there not been consequences, dire ones, for pressing one's lips to those of a woman many years ago . . . ?

And could she not mitigate those dangers, now that she had secured her good fortune?

"You truly would not care?" she asked Étienne in a quiet whisper. "You would not think me foolish or–indecent?"

Étienne grinned. "Having been foolish and indecent for my entire life, I could not possibly care," he said. Then, more soberly, "I am sorry, truly, if I spoke out of turn. If I am wrong about the shape of your friendship with Miss Witcombe–"

"I do not think you are," Verbena said. She surprised herself with her own honesty. To want Flora as a man might want a woman . . . if she had to name these feelings roiling in her breast, she supposed that might be near enough. Her face and fingertips tingled as she allowed her thoughts to dwell on that name. "In fact, I think you might be entirely correct."

"Bien! And so?" Étienne leaned forward, a hand on her knee. "Do you believe Miss Witcombe feels similarly?"

"Quite possibly." Although she had no real experience in such matters, she had to believe the connection between them was a mutual affection. There would be time to persuade Flora into her bed; first, she needed to find her friend a false husband. Protection before pleasure.

Yes, best to sequester these new, tumultuous desires as best she could for the moment. There would be time to explore them later, if Verbena succeeded in her aims.

The carriage arrived in Maiden Lane well within the appointed time. Flora was already standing on the stoop, her violet pelisse whipping about her legs in the breeze. At her feet were three large trunks, one stacked atop another. The bottommost one was of a gargantuan size, nearly an armoire in its own right.

"Bonjour, monsieur!" Flora called to Étienne. "I am sorry about all this." She indicated the trunks with a bob of her bonneted head. "Believe me, I wish I could contain my raiment to a single trunk, but . . ."

Verbena opened the carriage door and hung halfway over the pavement. "How on earth did you get those downstairs alone?" she asked in lieu of a greeting. It was all she could do not to explode into sparks at the sight of Flora. She was lovely as always, but now that the veil was somewhat lifted from Verbena's eyes, she could allow herself to appreciate her friend as more than a friend.

"I was not alone, thankfully," Flora said. "And only two belong to me."

Before Verbena could ask what she meant, the door at the top of the stoop was flung open and Miles McDonald appeared lugging a lap desk. His cravat was coming loose from its knot and there was sweat upon his brow.

When he looked up and saw the carriage, he beamed. "I think that's the last of it," he said, his brogue more pronounced than usual as he panted for air. "Shall we?"

That was unexpected. As the driver and Étienne alighted to secure the luggage to the roof of the carriage, Verbena ventured forth. She met Flora on the pavement and kissed her cheek in greeting, one eye still warily on Mr. McDonald.

"I know I'm bringing much too much for a couple of weeks in the country," Flora began apologetically, "but luckily Mr. McDonald was kind enough to carry it down for me."

"Then you two know each other?" Verbena asked without a care for decorum. "*How* do you two know each other?" She whirled toward the carriage to await Mr. McDonald's response. Her instincts told her that he was not as quick-witted as Flora and would give Verbena an idea of what was really going on here.

Flora was an unmarried woman living alone, after all, and for Mr. McDonald to call upon her like this was highly suspect.

"Oh! Erm." Mr. McDonald paused in fastening the leather straps that held the luggage, looking to Flora with wide eyes.

Flora merely smiled and patted Mr. McDonald on his shoulder. "Miles and I are good friends," she said. "We share a mutual acquaintance, you see."

Mutual acquaintance? Verbena could scratch out the eyes of this mutual acquaintance, if indeed one existed at all. As if men and women could ever be friends! Verbena was, of course, forgetting her own friendship with Étienne at that moment, and Lord Eden before him, not to mention Mr. Chesterfield and a host of other perfectly acceptable gentlemen–but when one is in the throes of rage, little things like facts do not signify.

"Well," she managed to say through gritted teeth, raking her eyes over *Miles*. Christian names all around, she felt. What's good for the goose, et cetera. "Isn't that wonderful."

Étienne spoke a few words to their driver, then leapt down to the ground, dusting off his hands. "Is everyone ready to depart?"

Miles, Verbena noticed, was quick to offer Flora a hand in ascending into the carriage. An innocent gesture, and fairly unremarkable, but Verbena knew that innocent gestures could belie prurient aims. The grateful smile Flora aimed in his direction was too familiar. Verbena stood seething on the pavement as she watched the two of them share a laugh over something Miles said.

They had private jokes? Unacceptable.

"My dear?"

Verbena nearly jumped out of her skin at Étienne's whisper. A glance at Miles and Flora proved they were still laughing and arranging themselves, not paying any attention to the world outside the carriage.

"Yes?" Verbena whispered back. She feigned securing the button at the wrist of her glove.

Étienne lifted his brows. "If Flora needs a husband, perhaps–"

"No," she said.

"No?"

"Absolutely not."

"He might be amenable."

"Yet I am not." Verbena leaned in closer to speak into Étienne's ear. "I need you to be a distraction to Miles whilst we are in Wales. Corner him in conversation. Invite him on excursions. Whatever it takes to keep him apart from Flora."

Étienne looked wildly pleased at this request. "As my dearest wishes," he said, bowing to her.

Soon they were all seated, with the driver and his horses taking them out of London.

Verbena sat next to Étienne, sullenly watching Miles and Flora's lively conversation–apparently Miles wanted to show off the new coat Étienne had made for the occasion. Flora cooed as she felt the soft fabric of his sleeve, complimenting Étienne on his skill. Verbena's eyes narrowed at the picture the two made. They were sitting, in her opinion, much too close–never mind that the confines of the coach's interior did not allow for anything else.

Miles McDonald, Verbena surmised, was not a good candidate for Flora's future husband. While he possessed certain qualities that Verbena sought in a match for her friend–respectable, but not overly powerful; easygoing enough to be persuaded into a sham marriage; the ability to be molded for Verbena's purposes–Miles would not do. He was too attached to Flora already, and a marriage could not be false in the face of such affection.

Verbena's resolve strengthened. There was much to do in Plas Tân: establish her courtship with Étienne for whatever audience awaited them; keep Miles at bay from the woman she wanted; gently coax Flora into wanting her in return; and, most importantly, find another gentleman who would suit her beloved–and her own needs.

Chapter 12

Verbena stuck her bonneted head out of the carriage window and took in the sight that greeted their arrival. The grounds of Plas Tân were beautifully situated on a slice of land surrounded on three sides by dense forests, making it a cool respite in the midst of the summer heat. In the distance, behind the house, the sounds and smells of the Welsh coastline were readily apparent: seabirds and the shush of waves, the sharpness of salt in the air.

As the carriage drew closer, Verbena spied a dozen or so people, men and women both, engaged in an afternoon's painting session. They were arranged near a small pond in a loose knot of easels, canvases, and stools upon which the artists perched. Their subject was a nude man who stood upon a plinth, which was shocking in and of itself.

What was even more shocking was the model's identity. Once the carriage halted, Verbena saw it was Lord Byron himself. He was standing with one hip hitched higher than the other, a large grin on his face.

"Oh, heavens," Flora said, groaning behind her unfurled lace fan. She clustered close against Verbena's back, hooking her chin on her shoulder to get her own eyeful. "What is *he* doing here?"

"Standing naked, it seems," said Miles, poking his head out of another window.

He was soon joined by Étienne, who seemed unhurried to get his own peek. "Very continental," he said. "I feel right at home."

Byron must have heard their voices on the wind, for he turned and gave them a cheery wave. The group of painters looked in their direction accordingly. One of them, an older woman, rose to make her way toward them. Verbena perceived this to be one of the ladies of Plas Tân she had heard so much about. She wore the strangest costume Verbena had ever seen: a man's riding jacket, all in black, paired with a voluminous black skirt. Perched on her head of silver hair was a black top hat.

Verbena exited the carriage with the help of Miles and Étienne, gazing up at the house's facade in surprise as she did so. She had expected a modest cottage, but this was something more akin to a manor. The Gothic structure was built of hewn stone with windows of intricate stained glass. Sunlight gleamed across the patterns of blue and green and purple, calling to mind a fairy-tale castle. The windows did not depict the usual biblical scenes, but rather classical ones: Hercules with his lion skin. A ship beset by long-haired Sirens. The siege of Troy, clever wooden horse included.

A woman sitting on a rocky shore with scores of other girls arrayed before her, listening intently as she pontificated.

This one, Verbena stared at harder than the rest. It strummed a familiar chord somewhere in her breast.

"Sappho," came a reverent whisper from behind her. Verbena turned to see Flora, now also descended from the carriage, her own awed gaze fixed on the same window. "She's beautiful, isn't she?"

Before Verbena could admit her own ignorance—for she really couldn't remember that myth for the life of her—the woman in the man's coat reached the gravel drive.

"Miles, my dear!" She gathered her huge black skirts and rushed to greet him. Her age was difficult to pinpoint, given the lack of usual markers in clothing and bearing Verbena would expect, but the wrinkles adorning her pale face, especially around her smile, spoke of a long life.

"Aunt Bette," Miles said, elated. He paused in unloading the baggage to catch her in a warm embrace. "Lord, it's been ages."

"I'm the one who should be saying so! Look at you." Said aunt, whose voice shared Miles's gentle brogue, held him at arm's length to study his person. "And how fares Peeblewick? Tell me everything."

"It is much changed since you last saw it," Miles said. "For the better, I hope. When will you come visit me there? That is what I want to know."

During this happy reunion, Verbena noticed another woman exit the manor and approach at a more sedate pace, leaning on a cane carved into a sort of swirl. She had a light brown complexion and wore a man's tailcoat like Bette's along with a pair of breeches. Her head was scandalously without a hat or bonnet, and her jet hair, shot through with strands of silver, flowed unencumbered down her back.

"You must be the ladies Miles told us so much about in his last letter," she said as she came within speaking distance. "Which of you is Lily and which is Rose?"

"Oh! Erm, I am Verbena, Verbena Montrose, and this is Flora Witcombe." Verbena gestured as Flora raised a hand in greeting. She would have expected Miles to make these introductions (and hopefully dispel the awkwardness that came with their hostess misplacing their names), but he seemed too wrapped up in speaking with his beloved aunt.

The other woman's dark eyes sparkled with mischief. "I'm only teasing. Of course I know you, Miss Witcombe. We have a standing appointment with the bookseller in the nearest village. He provides your latest poetry like clockwork, albeit several weeks behind London."

"That's very kind of you," said Flora. A pretty blush painted her cheeks.

Their hostess turned to Verbena. "And Miles tells us you, Miss Montrose, are eager to delve into your work! Well, you won't find a better place to write than Plas Tân. I'm Anne, by the way. Miss Kirkwell, if you crave formality. I hope you won't." She reached out a hand and shook Verbena's limp one.

Verbena forced herself out of her shock and put some vigor

into the handshake. This woman was opening her home to her and her friends. She could not be rude, as much as she wanted to stare. She'd never met anyone like Anne Kirkwell, or Bette McDonald, for that matter. In matters of dress and comportment, they were more akin to bachelors than elderly ladies.

"I am certain I will find creative energies in this place," Verbena said. "Already I feel suffused with–well, I'm not even sure. A wonderful zeal, perhaps." Her gaze darted to Flora as she spoke the last, but Flora was turned the other way, taking in the sprawling grounds with wide eyes.

As Anne moved on to introduce herself to Étienne, greet Miles, and direct them to the appropriate rooms, Verbena edged closer to Flora.

"I hope you do not regret accompanying me," she whispered.

Flora looked at her with wide eyes. "How could I? Look at this place. It's heaven on earth." She smiled, a soft thing.

Verbena's breath caught. She ached to form a reply, but their hostesses bustled over before she could.

"All right, girls," said Aunt Bette. "Let the gentlemen get your things all settled. Here, let me give you the tour." She led them across the grounds, following a winding stone path that badly needed weeding.

The fifteen or so acres of property were crammed full of everything the ladies needed to sustain themselves. There was a vegetable patch laid out in neat rows, ringed with a lopsided wooden fence. Chickens roamed in gangs, their fat brown and white bodies bobbling along the ground as they pecked for sustenance. In the distance, Verbena spied a small shed around which a number of goats and two black cows were grazing. As she watched, a woman in a simple dress emerged from what must have been the kitchen door, carrying a bucket of scraps. This she toted into the shed for the animals to feast upon.

"Our dairy," said Anne. "That's Penny, our cherished maid who dreamed it up. Milk, butter, cheese–enough to feed us and a little extra to sell besides."

"You'd be shocked at the prices people are willing to pay for our cheese," put in Bette. "Genuine virgin cheddar! Made with the most untainted of pious hands." She folded her palms, prayer-like, against her chest, a gesture Anne immediately copied. The two women caught each other's gaze and giggled. A shared joke, then, possibly a long-running one.

Verbena was astonished to see them transform, only for a moment, from two aging spinsters into ladies barely out of their girlhood, their mirth stripping years from their faces.

"It's good cheddar," Penny said with mock sternness as she passed by on her way to the house.

Verbena was taken aback by the comment, and most of all by Penny's lack of "madam" or "my lady" when speaking to their hostesses. Anne must have noticed her surprise, for she said, "Penny has been with us since the beginning. She is devoted as can be. We owe her a great debt for that, and so have long since agreed not to stand on ceremony."

"Yes, could you tell me about that beginning?" Flora asked. "I have heard stories–well, rumors–but I would love to know how two ladies such as yourselves came to be here."

Verbena hummed in agreement. She, too, was eager to know whether the gossip was true or mere speculation.

"You tell it, Anne," Bette said as they ambled by a greenhouse bursting with life, great waxy leaves pressed against the glass panes amid the fog of condensation. "It's so much better when you tell it."

Anne smiled at her companion before spinning to face Verbena and Flora, walking backward with the utmost confidence that her step would not falter. Her cane clacked along the rocky ground as they rounded the back of the house, closer to the crash of waves.

"Bette and I have known each other from girlhood," she said, "growing up in the Scottish moors. Her brother, Miles's father, even courted me for a moment."

"A very brief moment," Bette said with a snap in her voice.

Anne narrowed her eyes at her. "Am I telling it or aren't I?" She returned her attention to her audience. Verbena was rapt, and so was Flora, her arm stiff in Verbena's grip. "Where was I? Right. As you may have noticed, I am the child of an Indian mother and a Scots father. I was sent to be raised by his family in Scotland, and the question of my future hung over my head like that sword. You know the one. And Bette here, she was up to her ears in suitors!"

"She's being modest," Bette said, also spinning around to walk in perfect tandem beside Anne. "She had dozens more than I did. There are at least three different sonnets devoted to her eyes alone."

"Written by whom, I wonder?" Anne said with a coy glance at her companion.

"So you were both to be married?" Flora interrupted. "To the winning suitors, I mean."

"Yes, it was all arranged. Mine was a doughy little man named Lord Gant. Bette's was a viscount, I think?"

"Baron," Bette said dryly.

"At any rate, we couldn't countenance it. We ran," Anne said. "Snuck from our houses in the dead of night, aided by Penny. We dressed as boys and made our way to England. By the time our families found us in a boardinghouse in Cornwall, awaiting passage to the Continent, the story of our escape had become quite the talk of London."

"Sonnets were written about that, too," Bette put in.

Anne grinned widely. "It's astonishing what can be done when the regent himself and half of Parliament think you a sort of folk hero. A few generous donations and a high-placed barrister speaking to our parents on our behalf, and here we are, caretakers of what was once a derelict ruin, now a center of the arts."

The sea came into view now as the ladies found themselves at the edge of the grounds, where the earth gave way to the sandy beach below in a steep incline. The gray-blue waves stretched as far as the eye could see. They all paused there to take it in, along with the conclusion of the ladies' story.

"What a marvelous tale!" Flora's incandescent joy was a wonder to behold. Verbena watched her closely as her pinked cheeks turned ever more rosy. "And if you pardon my curiosity—your manner of dress. Was that adopted before coming here or . . . ?"

It was unlike her to trail off like that. Verbena wondered why the women's clothing had caused such a wild blush in her.

Bette glanced down at her own shirted torso, laughing. "I don't recall when exactly we took on this affectation. Was it a decade or so ago, Anne?"

"Something like that, I think."

"It's exceedingly comfortable," Bette said. "Much more conducive to the management of an artists' residence than gowns."

"I do wish I could dress that way," Flora said with a mournful note in her voice. Verbena knew jealousy when she heard it.

"What's stopping you?" Anne asked.

Bette gave her arm a gentle smack. "You know what," she said. "It's the same thing that's keeping every woman from wearing trousers if they like, or refusing to take a husband. You forget, sometimes, the expectations that exist outside our corner of the world."

"Oh, yes." Anne's nose crinkled with faint distaste. "*Expectations.*" Said with all the vitriol of a curse.

Verbena felt a frisson of displeasure, aware of how she must look standing beside these two eccentric women. How perfect her posture was, how fashionable and flattering her mode of dress. How she planned to marry and live, if not the expected, normal life, a perfectly acceptable facsimile. Close enough that her acquaintances would never know the difference.

"Sometimes one must do what one is expected to do," she said. "No shame in that, is there?"

Anne and Bette shared a look. If their hostesses were to argue, they were stopped by the sudden appearance of Miles and Étienne, who rounded the greenhouse to join their group.

"Everything's stowed," Miles announced. "Thank you again, Aunt, for having us."

"Anything for my favorite nephew. Well, my only nephew." She patted him on his pale cheek. "When should we expect your other friend? What was his name . . . Forsyth?"

Verbena gave a jolt. "William Forsyth is coming here?" She barely registered Étienne's presence, his hand resting at the small of her back in a subtly possessive gesture.

"Oh yes," Miles said vaguely. "Did I not mention? He wasn't able to travel with us from London, some pressing piece of business, but he should arrive later today."

This was certainly news to Verbena. She would have thought William Forsyth's attendance warranted a passing mention on the long drive from London. Would he avoid her, she wondered, after the cutting remark she'd made last they met?

Verbena regarded Flora, who seemed intently interested in a nearby shrub. "Are you acquainted with the gentleman?" she asked.

"Hm?" Flora lifted her head, her face a drawn blank. "Oh, yes, Forsyth," she said, nodding. "I know him in passing. He frequents my club. Why?"

"No reason," Verbena said quickly. Their visit to Plas Tân was to be a carefully orchestrated one–certainly there was too much work to be done to be distracted by anything, even the mysterious, handsome writer of gothic novels. Oh, what did Verbena care for his handsomeness when she had just made peace with her desires for Flora? Surely she was the worst kind of wretch; she'd fallen once, and so perhaps would now fall for every breathing person who came into view!

"Is that Miss Witcombe I see?" came a booming voice. "And the rest of the party from London?"

Or perhaps not.

Verbena turned to find Lord Byron approaching with a slight limp, hair windblown in that fashionable way of the Romantics. He wore a Turkish robe tied loosely about his waist, which gaped at the chest in the most daring way. Verbena averted her eyes; someone had to maintain a sense of propriety, and it certainly was not going to be His Lordship.

"Ah, George, come and meet our new guests," said Bette. Her arm extended toward the eminent poet, ready to make introductions.

"George was one of our very first patrons here at Plas Tân," said Anne. "Our little enterprise would not be the success it is today if not for him."

By this time, Byron had moved into their circle. "The ladies and I are already acquainted, my dear Anne. We poets all know one another." He extended a hand to shake that of Miles, then Étienne, as Bette introduced them. Verbena noted how Byron eyed both men with the sort of look that might begin a journey of lifelong depravity. Then he turned to Flora and scooped up her hands, pressing a kiss to her knuckles. "Miss Witcombe! How fortuitous. It is because of you that I find myself here in Plas Tân."

"You have read my latest?" said Flora, not appearing at all apologetic about the thing.

"Every word," said Byron. "I had hoped for your pen to stay still until I'd returned to Europe, but I suppose it all worked out in the end. I so enjoy visiting this place; escaping the scrutiny of the London crowds merely provided a fine excuse."

Flora smiled. "I am glad you're not too enraged with me."

"Not at all. Ah, before I forget!" Byron produced a packet from his robe's pocket and pressed it into Anne's hands. The thing jingled as it went. "A little something for my deserving hostesses," he said.

"George, honestly!" Anne huffed. Verbena wondered if there was another person on earth who referred to His Lordship by his Christian name. "There's no need. You've already given us so much." She tried to hand the packet of coins back to him, but Byron shot his hands into the air and refused to touch it.

"As long as I have a guinea to my name, it belongs to you ladies," he said. "I only wish I had as fine a head for finances as I do for verse. Then I could keep you in the lap of luxury, as you deserve."

Bette put a hand on Anne's arm with a sigh. "It does no good to argue with him, you know." Anne demurred, but with a fond glare in Byron's direction.

"Excellent! Now." Byron lowered his hands in a happy clap. "Would anyone care to join me in bathing?" He fiddled with the tie of his robe.

Miles and Étienne both raised their brows in perfect tandem.

Verbena saw an exit and took it, along with Flora's arm. "We will leave you gentlemen to enjoy the sea. Perhaps we could be shown to our rooms?"

Their hostesses ushered Verbena and Flora into the manor, which proved to be eccentrically appointed as well. The walls were lined with tapestries and artwork, and every alcove and shelf was bursting with sculpture. Verbena and Flora were installed in their respective rooms and told not to rush in their ablutions.

"Dinner is whenever Penny decrees it to be," Bette said over her shoulder as she followed Anne down the stairs. "No formality here!"

Verbena's assigned bedroom was small and cheerful, with a narrow bed under a stained-glass window. Flora's was much the same. Their rooms were right next to each other and connected through the wall via a door, which Verbena assumed was originally meant for servants shuffling from task to task. Flora expressed her delight with the connection by giving a happy cry and flinging the door wide open.

"How wonderful," she said. "If any ghosts or ghouls come upon us in the night, we can simply run to each other for safety."

Verbena laughed as she unlatched her traveling case to retrieve her many vials of tonics. "I'm not sure how much safety I could provide. Not that I believe in such fancies, but if I was ever confronted with a ghost, I would likely do nothing more than tremble to pieces."

"Your trembling itself would be a balm to me." Flora smiled at her, then dropped her gaze to the pretty, if threadbare, carpet.

Verbena licked her dry lips. Perhaps now was the time to tell her friend about the notion she'd had, to convince Flora to marry a husband of convenience so that they could—do as they pleased. Whatever form of pleasure that might take.

Yet before she could broach the subject, Flora was at her side, peering down into Verbena's trunk. "You have the loveliest gowns," she said, reaching toward the ruffled hem of the topmost. "I envy your taste in dress. I can never seem to—"

"Don't!" Before Flora's finely tapered fingers could even brush the fabric, Verbena had arrested them. Images of ripped seams and slashed muslin whirled through her mind's eye. She clutched Flora's hand in hers, a vise tightening.

Flora's eyes went wide and her whole body still.

Verbena, ashamed at her sudden outburst, softened her tone for her next words. "I wish you wouldn't–Oh, it's very silly but I can't bear anyone touching my things."

"I had no idea," Flora said. Her voice matched Verbena's now-quiet one. "I'm sorry."

"It's no fault of yours." She was still holding on to Flora's hand, crushing her fingers in her grip. She released her swiftly and rubbed her palm up and down the length of her thigh as if she could rub away the guilt in that appendage. "You would never do anything cruel, I know that."

She turned and sat heavily on the edge of the narrow bed, all spirit draining from her. This was meant to be a lark of a country visit, and here Verbena was, turning her thoughts and deeds to awful memories.

Flora sat on the bed as well, not so close that any part of them touched, but close enough for Verbena to feel the warmth of her body across the few inches of distance. "You speak as if cruelty is expected from others." It was not a question, but rather an invitation. Quite an elegant one, Verbena thought, that could just as easily be answered as it could be discarded.

Verbena, after a moment's consideration, chose to answer. "I'm afraid I have some small, lingering fear about the state of my wardrobe," she said. "There was an incident. Years ago." Lord, she had been little more than a child, preparing to make her debut at sixteen. How could something that had happened so long ago still have the power to cause her limbs to shiver?

Flora, sweet Flora, put her hand on Verbena's arm, no doubt in a bid to calm her. Verbena wriggled closer so that their thighs and hips were perfectly aligned, and she brought Flora's arm about her waist. The comfort of her was immense, allowing the shivers to subside and the story to be told.

"It was nothing, really," Verbena insisted. "I had this friend—Winifred Stassel. We were playmates from childhood, as our parents deemed it convenient. As we grew older, we were quite inseparable." She frowned down at her lap. "Inseparable" seemed a paltry word for it.

Did Flora know the heady rush of a girlhood friendship forged in secrets and shared language? Did she also have, in her murky past, a girl who had at one time held the keys to her lockbox heart? Verbena did not dare ask, though she was certain Flora would answer honestly; she dreaded too much an answer in the negative, which would leave her in a state of loneliness she could not bear.

Winifred Stassel had been the empress of young Verbena's world, bending it to fit her whims. When such a whim turned, one fine afternoon at the Stassels' country estate in the privacy of a shaded glen, to the practice of kissing—only for practice—Verbena had been an enthusiastic participant. And when, some months later, their practice sessions ended abruptly so that they might, as Winifred said, focus on their upcoming introductions into London society, Verbena had not argued. Perhaps if she had, Winifred would not have become as cold toward her as she did. Then again, perhaps Winifred had always hated Verbena for reasons Verbena would never understand.

(It did not occur to Verbena, as it might to you, dear reader, that Winifred may have been enraged at the emotions that arose in her whenever her lips touched Verbena's, and unfairly placed the blame for such emotions at Verbena's doorstep.)

"We were to debut together," Verbena continued in what she hoped was a reasonable tone. "The day before the ball, Winifred paid me a visit, wanting to view my gown. It was a deep royal blue with silver embroidery—very fashionable that year. Winifred was always interested in what I was wearing, you see." Her face heated. The words felt imbued with unintended meaning, yet Flora did not waver.

She pressed her arm more firmly about Verbena's waist. "What happened?"

"Nothing that I could see at the time," said Verbena. "It was only later the following day, as I was readying myself, that my maid noticed a terrible slash through the back of the gown as if someone had drawn a penknife through it. Winifred must have ruined it whilst I was out of the room, fetching some jewels from my mother's collection." She could still feel the disbelief deep within her belly, where all her forgotten feelings were stored. The foolish theories she'd leapt to before she dared think of Winifred's betrayal—perhaps a rogue had come through the window in the night—perhaps a conflagration of moths—perhaps, perhaps, perhaps—

She shut her eyes, remembering. "I went to the Stassel residence with all due haste. Winifred did not deny it. She—she laughed. Said I would simply have to wear one of my old gowns, as I would have nothing else from the clothier until the following week. And so I did—I attended my debut in a most unsuitable gown. It was all very humiliating."

"I don't understand," Flora said. "Why would Miss Stassel do this to you?"

"Oh." Verbena looked to the stained-glass window, watching the way the light shifted through the bright colors. "There was a man."

"A man?"

"Yes. Lord Woolspeth, a young man. A boy, really, no older than we were. Winifred informed me before our debut that she was in love with him. She had never even met him, as far as I could tell."

"Why would she lie about something like that?" asked Flora.

Verbena hesitated. "I cannot know for certain." Though she could infer. One could not conduct kissing practice for as long as Winifred Stassel had without applying oneself to the stated goal of marrying well. "At any rate, I bumped into the man at a dinner party—my parents knew his aunt and uncle slightly. When I mentioned it to Winifred, she became convinced, for some reason, that I was trying to steal Woolspeth for myself." An unladylike snort left her. "The whole thing was absurd. I tried to tell her

I hardly spoke to the man. Winifred would not listen to reason, though." Verbena shrugged. "Less than a week later, my gown was in tatters." Along with any illusions that a bosom friend could be trusted.

Flora squeezed her tight about the waist once more, pressing her forehead to Verbena's shoulder. "How awful," she murmured. "How absolutely dreadful." The fall of her curls tickled Verbena's cheek.

Verbena turned her head slightly so that she might bury her nose in those curls. They smelled of sweet grass and sharp tonic. It was enough to make Verbena want to believe in illusions again.

"It was a long time ago," she said. "I should not be so tender about it still. And anyway, it's not as if I didn't manage the situation perfectly well."

Flora lifted her head and stared at her. "I thought you said you were forced to wear an old gown to your debut."

"Oh, yes. That could not be avoided," Verbena said. "I managed the Winifred situation, however. She ruined my gown; I ruined her prospects with Lord Woolspeth."

"You did what?"

Verbena lifted a hand palm up in the air, serving her story as one would a round of drinks. "Even then, I had some little talent at using gossip to suit my needs. A few well-placed tidbits and Woolspeth was engaged to the daughter of a viscount. I believe they have just had their third child. Everyone said he was too young to marry, but the dowry was extensive."

"You did all that to spite Winifred?" Flora asked.

"No, of course not." Verbena smoothed her skirts down her legs. "I also arranged for her to be married to a Russian diplomat."

Flora gaped at her.

"It was hardly an evil plot on my part," Verbena hastened to explain. "He was a kind man, well-off, with a good family. Winifred needed to marry someone, so why not someone who would remove her from England?" She laughed, remembering the look on Winifred's face at a subsequent ball that season, when the statesman had demanded two dances from her. "That way, our paths would not cross again. It was better for everyone involved, you see."

Best especially for Verbena, who could not stomach the sight of her former friend any longer, and so devised a way to ensure she would not have to. Simple. Elegant. Bloodless.

"I see." Only now that the story was told did Verbena notice Flora's pale face and parted lips. A frightened girl, indeed. "You are . . . a woman not to be crossed, aren't you?"

She looked like she had seen a ghost. Or a monster.

"She didn't *actually* love Woolspeth." The words tumbled out of Verbena. "Winifred didn't actually love anyone. She only wanted to marry well, and better than me, so I saw to it she did. Please believe that I would never harm—only when my hand is forced would I ever—oh, you probably think me an awful wretch!"

"Verbena." Flora gathered her wild hands in hers. "You have a talent, as you say. It makes me glad to hear of you wielding it."

Verbena's own lips parted. "It does?"

Flora shrugged. "When you first came to the Calliope, you terrified me. I think a woman should inspire a modicum of terror. It is her right, especially when the world would have her defanged and fawning in a sitting room somewhere."

"I am also capable of fawning in a sitting room," Verbena reminded her.

"Only because you are a woman of many talents." Flora grinned. "At any rate, I would never be so reckless with my own health and station as to sabotage your gowns." She quieted then, her face falling somewhat. "I would do well to remember to not be so reckless when it comes to you, I suppose."

Verbena was intimately aware of their hands, still clasped together. She drew in a breath. It would be the height of impertinence to suggest to Flora that they could stand to be a *little* reckless. She thought of kissing Flora as she had kissed Winifred all those years ago, but could not picture it. Those moments had been perfunctory, fumbling, almost cold at Winifred's insistence. Verbena distinctly remembered holding Winifred about the waist once, or attempting to, only to have her hands batted away. There had been rules, unspoken and perfectly rigid, which frustrated Verbena to no end.

Flora never frustrated her. She was like a cool spring flowing freely, never dammed, never running dry.

She swayed forward, thinking she might try, recklessness be damned, to press her suit with Flora.

Flora, however, was too preoccupied staring down at Verbena's wide-open trunk to notice her movement. "Is that yours?" she asked, pointing.

Verbena looked down into her traveling case. Amid the various items of clothing and underpinnings, there sat a copy of William Forsyth's novel *Colleen.*

"Oh, yes," Verbena said. The moment was gone, but no matter. There would be others at Plas Tân. She rose and picked up the cheaply bound book, its cardboard cover rough in her hands. "You said you know Mr. Forsyth, did you not?"

"Slightly, yes."

"I so rarely read novels, but curiosity caused me to seek out one of his."

"Really?" Flora stared at her with wide eyes. "And how are you finding it?"

"Well"—Verbena flushed with the excitement she usually felt when discussing morbid crimes—"it's about a murder, you see, and a ghost that—" She glanced up at Flora and saw, in her lovely face, a sort of queasiness that she perceived as politely quiet disgust. Verbena quickly replaced the book in her trunk, shoving it beneath some stays. "But of course, you don't go in for tawdry stories!" She tried to keep her voice light. "I suppose they're quite beneath you. Your artistic soul is too sophisticated for such things."

"No, no," Flora said, but with the sort of hesitation that made Verbena think she was not being entirely truthful. "It sounds like a very good book."

Verbena could not let Flora think her silly, or a fool, or anything less than a brilliant woman on par with a celebrated poetess, and so she did what many might do: she scorned the very thing she loved.

"It's not good at all," she said, burying a piece of herself within herself. "The writing is awful and the story laughable. I only found it amusing in a common sort of way." She affected a casual air as she continued her unpacking.

"I see," said Flora. She sat there as if she herself was a ghost, silent and pale.

Verbena cleared her throat. "Shall I help you unpack?" she asked.

That made Flora whip back into wakefulness. "What?"

"Once I'm done here." Verbena motioned to her trunk. "Shall I help you?"

"No! That is, I did not bring much."

Verbena cocked her head. "I recall you bringing two trunks, plus your lap desk."

"It's less unwieldy than it looks." Flora stood abruptly and moved toward the door between their rooms. "I think I will rest before dinner, actually. The journey has tired me more than I realized."

Verbena frowned at her retreating back. "Are you unwell? I can call for Penny if you—"

"No, thank you. A short repose is all I require." Flora gave her a watery smile. Her hand rested on the doorknob. "I'll close this, shall I?" She did so, shutting her room off from Verbena's once again.

Verbena heard the click of the latch, then returned to her unpacking with a shake of her head. She hoped Flora did not think less of her for reading *Colleen*. She retrieved the little volume and traced the author's name on its front. Mr. Forsyth really was a gifted writer, if he could capture her imagination so. Perhaps, when he arrived, there might be a chance to discuss the book with him.

No, Verbena told herself firmly. She tossed the novel onto the spindly nightstand. Mr. Forsyth might be entertaining, but there was no reason to waste time on him.

It was a shame she could not enjoy his company further. William could make someone a good husband.

Verbena paused in lifting a chemise out of her trunk. The gossamer fabric fluttered as she clutched it close to her chest, her mind too focused on other things to realize the wrinkles she was inflicting. Her gaze went to the stained-glass window, though the colorful shapes did not make an impression, as preoccupied as she was.

Yes, if a woman did not care much for rank or financial solvency–if, say, a woman was used to sustaining herself–then a woman might, under certain circumstances, be inclined to marry William Forsyth.

Chapter 13

Flora checked that the doors to her cozy guest room were locked—both the door to the hallway and the one that led to Verbena's room—before opening the first of her trunks. It was a clever piece of work: while several gowns were packed inside, overflowing in their riot of pretty colors, one could remove them and reveal the false bottom. Beneath that were William's best clothes. He would need to be in top form to catch Verbena's eye. She began to transform.

William was dealing with the buttons on his placket when he heard the door to Verbena's bedroom open into the hall, then shut again. The sound of Verbena descending the stairs in her sturdy walking boots alighted on his ear. William finished with his trousers, straightened the knot of his cravat, and studied himself in the looking glass. A fine gentleman stared back at him, albeit red-cheeked and trembling with nerves.

"Nothing to worry about," he muttered to himself. "She bought your novel, after all. She absolutely hates it, but she did buy it. That's a sale, at least." He groaned, covering his eyes with his hands. "Right. Don't mention the novel. Just—be charming."

William dropped his hands and gave the mirror his best smile. He looked like a deranged hyena. His face fell. This was impossible.

There was a stained-glass window in his little room facing the wood. From far below it came the sound of voices, Verbena's velvety tone among them. William crept to the window and, careful to keep himself hidden from view, swung open the colorful depiction of Athena in men's clothing so he could get a good look at the proceedings. Verbena, dressed in a fresh gown, was chatting with some of the artists who'd been painting Byron earlier. Their folded easels and boxes of paints were shoved under their arms. William had to hurry before someone else beat him to an invitation.

The house was thankfully quiet, and William crept through the empty hall and down the back stairs without meeting a soul. Penny was in the kitchen at the bottom of the stairs, but she hardly raised an eyebrow at his appearance.

"Did you just arrive, sir?" she asked while stoking the fire.

"Erm, yes," William said. "The ladies have already shown me to my room. All settled in nicely." He clacked his fists together, then edged toward the back door. "I'll just be going."

Penny was too busy with her work to pay him any mind. He slipped out back and nearly ran directly into Miles and his aunt.

"Oh!" said Aunt Bette, steadying William by the arm. "And who is this?"

Miles rushed to make introductions. "Aunt, please meet my good friend, Mr. William Forsyth."

"Your maid, Penny, gave me an excellent room," William said. An odd thing to say, but he felt it best to cover his tracks as swiftly as possible.

Bette frowned. "Oh? We are getting so full here. Which room did she–?"

"The one next to mine, I expect!" Miles looked meaningfully at William. "It was empty last I checked."

"Yes, of course. The room next to yours. That is where I am staying," William babbled.

"And now I'm sure Mr. Forsyth will want to partake in a walk through the beautiful woods," Miles said. "Long journey from London. Must stretch those legs."

"Exactly correct. Legs!" William laughed nervously. "Woods!"

Bette must have been inured to hosting a variety of odd people, for she gave William only a momentary look of concern before shrugging. "It's a perfect day for it. Have a wonderful time." She made her way past him and into the kitchen, greeting Penny as she opened the door.

Miles took a moment to clasp William by the shoulder. "Why don't you ask Verbena to join you?" With a sly grin, he followed his aunt inside and shut the door.

William made his way around the side of the house, tugging at his coat to erase the wrinkles. Once he rounded the corner, he caught sight of Verbena, still making conversation with some of the other guests. William paused and drew himself upright. He had to be brave. He'd come too far to fail now.

"Miss Montrose!" he called, striding forth from the house's shadow. "How good to see you again."

Verbena turned, a faint look of surprise on her features. Better than disgust, he supposed, considering how their last conversation had gone. The artists must have sensed William's desperation, for they made their excuses and departed for the front door.

At last, they were alone.

"Mr. Forsyth." Verbena nodded at him, a curious tilt to her mouth. "Did you only just arrive?"

"Yes," he said, "only just."

"I did not note the arrival of any coaches," Verbena said.

"Yes! Well. The driver was terribly quick; hardly came to a trot before I was shoved out. We made short work of getting here, though, I must say." William attempted a smile, then thought better of it. "And yourself?"

Verbena scanned the drive, no doubt already bored with this talk of routes and travel. "Our party came earlier this afternoon," she said, distracted.

William swallowed. It was now or never. "I met Mr. McDonald a moment ago. He suggested I take a stroll through the woods," he said.

"Sensible." Verbena turned and smiled serenely at him. She was as beautiful as a poem. "Would you be amenable to company? I should like to see more of the surroundings."

William's heart surged forward. "Exactly what I was about to suggest." He did not want to appear so eager as to be off-putting, but he could not help the excitement that colored his voice. He stuck out his arm. "Shall we?"

They walked across the grounds until they came upon a quaint, sandy path that led into the dense forest. In only a few steps, the world outside fell away. Close stands of oak and ash and sycamore trees flanked them on either side. Birds flitted between the branches, calling to each other in silky songs. Great green bushes with clusters of bright red berries bobbed in the pleasant breeze. William was comforted by the idea that Nature herself approved of his plans. She had provided him with the perfect setting in which to woo.

Verbena tipped her head back, one hand atop her bonnet, the other still grasping William's elbow. Her red hair escaped in wisps. It caught the sunlight that filtered through the trees and turned it to flame. William watched her in profile, entranced.

She looked over at him, and he quickly averted his eyes. "It's exquisite, don't you find?" she said.

William cleared his throat and stared at his feet. "It's not difficult to see why so many artists come here to find inspiration." He reminded himself that he would need to look Verbena in the face if he was to conduct any real sort of conversation. Oh, why was this so much easier when he was Flora? *She* was not so frightened of Verbena's grace and wit; she met it with her own, an accomplishment William could not hope to replicate.

Then Flora's voice came to him, whispering inside him as gently as the breeze itself: *There is nothing within me that is not already within you.*

The sentiment nearly made William stop in his tracks, so vital was its message of exquisite unity, yet he managed to compose himself. The air was crisp and clean, and he took it inside his lungs. Verbena was saying something. He forced himself to concentrate on her words.

". . . would not surprise me in the least if the assembled guests leave here with two or three great masterpieces," she said. "My good friend Flora Witcombe, for instance, will likely write a whole tome whilst we're here. She's extremely talented, you know."

That bolstered his spirit, even if the compliment was not wholly directed at him. William drew himself to his full height, which was only an inch or so more than Verbena's. "I would love to hear how your own work is progressing sometime," he said, "if you want to share it with me."

Verbena's mouth opened, then closed, pursed, then opened again. "I do not think I've written anything worth sharing. Not yet, anyway." Her cheeks pinked and her eyes darted to the wooded shade. She seemed embarrassed by his interest in her art, and that, he could not allow.

"I suspect that's not true." William steeled himself. *Boldness,* said his inner spirit, which sounded suspiciously like Flora again. *That is what we require.* "In fact–" He dared lift his free hand and place it atop hers where it lay on his arm. "I am certain of it."

She looked at him, startled.

He plunged ahead. How he managed to continue walking without stumbling over a rock or branch, he had no idea, but he did. "Perhaps it is only your skill that frustrates you. An untested and untalented poet is always content with what they produce. If you are not content, it only means you have an innate understanding of the work's potential. This is proof of your skill."

Verbena gave a surprised laugh. "So to be skilled in these arts is to be always discontented? That sounds to me like a terrible existence."

"Not at all!" He tightened his hand on hers, curling his fingers around her soft palm. She did not, he noticed, pull away from him. "It is the force behind all our efforts, the thing that keeps us alive. To be forever striving does not mean we are forever unhappy; it means we are afire with passion with every breath. The search for meaning has no end, I think, nor does our quest for improvement in our chosen arts. I myself–" William paused, biting his tongue to cease its prattling.

Verbena's wide-eyed look spoke volumes. This was all too much. He was speaking thoughts that rightly belonged to Flora the poetess, not William the novelist. Oh, if he could fuse the two halves of himself together, if only for a moment!

He released Verbena's warm hand, bringing his palm instead to his breast, where it rubbed against his pounding heart.

"Apologies, Miss Montrose," he said. "You probably think me a fool. A writer of tawdry novels, expounding on the nature of art and truth and the soul. What right do I have?"

Verbena made a sound of perfect sympathy, a little gasp that threaded through William's bones and settled in his chest. She stopped in her tracks, which meant William was obliged to stop as well. She clasped his hand in both of hers, creating a shield upon his breast where they were joined altogether. William nearly expired. She was *touching* him.

"You have every right," she said. "Truthfully, your writing is excellent." She looked up at him through her lashes. "I've been reading *Colleen*, you know."

William feigned a measure of surprise. "Have you?"

"I am absolutely rapt," she said. "Were I able to read whilst riding in a coach without feeling queasy, I would have spent the entire trip from London devouring it. As it is, I have your book to look forward to before I sleep tonight."

She sounded sincere enough . . . but Verbena's earlier condemnations of the book plagued William's memory. He swallowed. "There is no need to lie to me. I know my books do not appeal to a lady of your quality."

Verbena looked as taken aback as William had ever seen her. Her eyes widened and she dropped his hand to prop her fists on her hips. "Sir, I assure you, I could not conceive of a work more aligned with my very specific interests. Murder! Mayhem! A possible haunting! And that twist in the middle, with the servant girl?" She gave an impressed exhale. "I admit, I have not made a habit of reading fiction before now, but if your work is any indication, the appeal is obvious. I will read whatever you write."

"You will?" Either she was the most accomplished actress of the age, or she was being candid. William felt a thread of hope alight in his heart. "You don't think *Colleen* . . . silly? Common? It is not, I admit, a masterpiece of literature by any stretch."

Verbena scoffed. "Who needs a masterpiece? Is it not enough for a story to capture the imagination and bring some joy? If the only worthwhile writing is that which is destined for immortality, I fear we shall be poorer for it."

There are no sweeter words to a writer of a certain genre. William would have married her on the spot if he could.

Steady, his conscience told him. *This is a conversation, not a marriage proposal.* And anyway, his delight was tempered by the fact that Verbena must have been lying to Flora, who was supposed to be her bosom friend. That stung, though it was difficult to feel such stings when one has attained a reader for life.

He fell back, as he sometimes did, on modesty. "Not everyone would agree with you. I have received several strongly worded letters from gentlemen who worry my books are poisoning the minds of their wives and daughters."

"Ah, yes, Bowdler and his ilk." Verbena smiled. "Despite all the sermons on the subject, I assure you that women can and do indulge in popular literature without tumbling into disrepute. As if I cannot countenance a story of murder and intrigue whilst keeping my head—I read the broadsides, you know!" She bit her lip, then added, "Actually, I tend to linger over the more morbid details of the day's news."

William tried and failed to keep his expression blank. She was trusting him with something she had heretofore told perhaps only to Flora. "Is that so?"

"Mm. My mother says I am a ghoul." Was she blushing or was it merely a trick of the dappled sunlight? "I suppose she's right. Who but a ghoul would devour every printed word about murder and kidnapping?"

"Perhaps it is ghoulish to dwell on such things," William said, "but when one is fascinated by human nature, why should that fascination be constrained to light topics? There is so much to humanity; it is a—an overlong bolt of cloth that we will never finish unraveling."

Verbena lit up at his words. "Exactly! You understand." She peered at him with the same calculating look she often aimed at Flora. "How is it that you understand?"

William went cold all over. Was she making the connection in her mind, that William and his feminine half were one and the same? No, no, no, this would not do. He needed to bring her to the subject gently, and only after time and familiarity had softened her enough to accept his dual nature. If Verbena came to the truth on her own, he could only pray she did not hate him for it.

But the moment of suspicion morphed into happiness. Verbena smiled, wide and pleased. "You are a most uncommon sort of gentleman, aren't you?"

William felt the faint sheen of sweat overtake him beneath his clothes. Every iota of his body wished to protect his secret, but he calmed himself with the thought that Verbena couldn't be commenting on his hidden nature. She wouldn't be so cruel as to tease him about that; she was more likely to state her mind with no mincing of words.

Yet William could not accept the praise of his person; he instead grasped on to the praise of his work.

"Thank you for thinking my writing good. Very few people do, so it's gratifying to know at least one person enjoys it. And a fellow wordsmith at that!"

"About that." Verbena leaned in, her eyes bright. "Can you be trusted with a secret?"

William considered the question with all due seriousness. "Yes, I think so."

"I am no wordsmith," Verbena said. She lifted one elegant shoulder and let it drop. "I've never penned so much as a couplet in my life."

"Oh!" William stared at her, trying to make sense of her confession. "But–you–the club in Curzon Street, did you not–?"

She tossed her head, laughing with no remorse. "I lied to gain entrance. I needed to speak to–well, it's not important. The result, however, is that now everyone seems to think I'm an aspiring poetess. Really, I can't rhyme to save my life."

"And you've allowed . . . everyone . . . to continue thinking you write poetry?" William desperately wanted to ask why Flora in particular had not been taken into Verbena's confidence regarding this deception, but of course he could not. "Why maintain the charade?"

Verbena's smile faltered. "It is the nature of lies that one must sometimes cling to them. I'm sure I could come up with some excuse if pressed, but there are certain people I am loath to disappoint. Certain people who"—she cast her gaze to the side, into the shadows—"are under the impression that we have this thing in common. If I reveal that to be false, I wouldn't be surprised if I am cast aside."

William's heart was pounding fit to burst. *Oh, lord above, please tell me she means Flora.* Yet if she did mean Flora, then it was Flora whom she had so deftly deceived. Did Verbena's lies extend to more than poetry and literature? William wondered where the truth of her began, but then again, what did he care if she had lied, and about such a trivial thing? Didn't this world make liars of them all in some respect?

"I can't imagine anyone casting you aside," he said. "Not under any circumstances."

Verbena turned back to face him. "You are a forgiving man. Not everyone is." Her gaze drifted down to settle on his mouth. "It's so . . . convenient that we two find ourselves here at Plas Tân."

The sweat increased by a magnitude of at least ten. "Yes," he said, fighting off the urge to swoon. "Extremely, erm. Convenient."

"Are you staying long?" Her gaze snapped to his as if startled out of some contemplation.

"A fortnight, at least." Longer if Verbena wished. He would do, he felt, whatever Verbena wished, up to and including swallowing the sun.

"As am I. Excellent," said Verbena.

Excellent? Excellent! William did not usually give himself to hope, but how could he not when Verbena spoke such sweet words?

Verbena started to say something else, but a peal of laughter behind them made her turn around. William spied Miles and Monsieur Charbonneau strolling toward them. Their conversation was animated and their clothing disheveled. This was especially shocking for Charbonneau, whom William had never seen in anything but perfect dress. Now, however, he sported a twig in his hair and a smattering of dirt on the knees of his trousers. Miles, too, had the marks of the forest about him, with several leaves stuck to his coat hem. The two seemed so enamored with each other that they did not take note of William and Verbena at all.

At least Miles was proving lucky in love. William glanced over at Verbena to find her already looking at him. Her silent brow-raise spoke volumes. No doubt she, too, had noticed the twigs and leaves and had also concluded this was evidence of a woodland tryst. William was forced to think about trysts in general, which put into his mind what a tryst might entail with Verbena specifically, which meant he was now rather short of breath.

Miles and Charbonneau were still senseless of their audience. As William was a gentleman (at the moment, at least), he cleared his throat to announce to the pair that they were not alone. Miles at last noted him with a surprised yet pleasant smile. If he was ashamed at being caught out, he did not show it.

"Miss Montrose, Mr. Forsyth! Are you walking through the woods, too? Shall we all go together?" he offered.

"Splendid idea," Verbena said, and then said aside to William, "As my friend, I hope you will not tell anyone about what we've discussed. I would be mortified should the other guests discover my falsified artistic credentials."

"I would not dream of it," said William. He joined Verbena in meeting the men on the woodland path. Miles did not seem to notice as William discreetly brushed the leaves from his coat, too busy chattering away.

"Étienne–that is, Monsieur Charbonneau and I had the most extraordinary adventure just now," Miles said. "We were walking along the grounds when a tomcat streaked by with a hunk of cheese in its mouth! Penny the maid was yelling after him, and so we dove into the brush in an attempt to capture the poor beast."

"Unsuccessfully," Charbonneau put in, to which Verbena laughed.

"You would not believe how quick a cat can be!" Miles said before expounding further on the creature's movements. He created a sort of model of the supposed feline using his own hand to indicate how it had darted about in a madcap fashion, apparently bouncing off trees and fallen logs like a particularly wild billiard ball.

William did not believe their story for a moment, but they told it with such enthusiasm, he supposed he could forgive them. After all, it was their business. Amorous business, but theirs.

He watched Verbena from the corner of his eye. She had named him a friend. How magical, to have gone from an object of detestation to a friend in the span of a stroll. Even the sudden appearance of others could not diminish his elation.

If things continued in this vein, his success was assured. By the time they departed Wales, William was convinced he and Verbena would be, as the poets said, of one mind.

Chapter 14

Over the next week, Flora was forced to divide her time between appearing as herself and appearing as William. So much of her energies in the ensuing days were devoted to switching between her personas, rushing between the two bedrooms she was supposedly occupying, trying her damnedest not to be seen sneaking into William's room wearing a gown, and vice versa. At least Plas Tân was a beehive of activity with artists of all stripes buzzing about. It was not so strange for a guest to go missing in the middle of a writing session, for example, or for someone to slip away during mealtimes.

"I need to write something down before I forget," William would claim.

"I must rest my aching hand after all that work," Flora would say.

No one took note of these mundane things, especially not in such queer company. And although it caused Flora great distress to sneak about, it was worth it for the time both her sides were allowed to spend with Verbena. Intimate conversations, happy outings in nature, one delightful (and disastrous) afternoon where Verbena insisted they try their hand at milking the cows–Flora could not believe how close William and Verbena had grown, nor how strong the existing connection between herself and Verbena had become.

A little more than a week into her stay at Plas Tân, Flora came downstairs to join the others at breakfast. Verbena had saved her a spot on the long wooden bench, as had become their habit. (William had told Verbena and anyone else who asked that he never ate in the mornings due to some slight quirk of his constitution, and Flora had said she never ate at midday for the same reason. They traded suppers; Flora was keen to ensure both her personas enjoyed their time at Plas Tân—and with Verbena.) She took her seat, returning Verbena's warm smile.

After the eggs and toast had been demolished, Bette announced that there was to be a soiree on the grounds that evening complete with a bonfire.

"Such beautiful weather," she said. "We simply cannot waste the opportunity."

The assembled guests cheered at this. Flora could not help but think this was the perfect opportunity for William to at last make his feelings known. She glanced at Verbena, who was flushed with a happy glow.

"What does one wear to a firelight fête?" Verbena asked.

"Whatever one likes, I suppose," said Flora. In her own case, it would be William's finest raiment.

Once the breakfast things had been cleared away, Flora raced back to her room. She plucked a navy tailcoat with pewter buttons from her trunk's hidden compartment. It was an excellent coat. And a good thing, she thought, running her hands over the fine wool, as William would need to be his most charming, dapper self if he had any hope of persuading Verbena to accept his affections. Flora, of course, would need to absent herself from the soiree. She planned to excuse herself in the middle of dinner with complaints of a mild headache, then transform into William. He would have the entire evening to mingle with the other guests while Flora "recovered" in peace.

An entire evening to woo Verbena Montrose, capture her heart, confess William and Flora's shared secret, and make an agreement for all three of them to be joined in marriage.

It was a good plan, if William did not lose his nerve.

There was a tap at the door—the one that led to the hallway—and Flora quickly replaced the coat, rearranging the trunk so that the gowns covered the men's clothing. "Yes?" she called.

"I come to ask a favor from you." It was Anne's voice.

"One moment." Flora smoothed her hair and cast a glance about the room, finding no evidence of her dual nature anywhere about. She crossed to the door and opened it to her hostess. "What can I do for you?"

Anne smiled kindly. "So many of our guests are great lovers of your work, myself amongst them. Would you grace us with the pleasure of a reading tonight at the bonfire? We would love to hear the poetess in her own voice."

"Oh!"

Despite her carefully laid plan, Flora felt the seductive pull of the invitation deep inside her. (Poets are generally very susceptible to that sort of flattery; they leap at the chance to showcase their stanzas if given the slightest leeway.)

"I would be happy to–that is, I *would* be. Only, I seem to be developing such a headache." She pressed her hand to her forehead and tried to look pained. "I think I might rest in my room instead."

"Nonsense," Anne said. Being constantly surrounded by poets and their strange ways, she was apparently immune to such dramatics. "Directly after dinner, we will light the bonfire and have you regale us. If you still feel poorly after, of course you should rest then, but you wouldn't let a little thing like a headache keep you from your audience, would you?" She gave Flora a stern, auntlike look that would wilt even the most stalwart person.

"No," Flora found herself saying. "I would not."

"Good." Anne turned from the door. "I look forward to it!"

Dinner that evening was wildly informal as usual, men and women arranged around the long table in whatever higgledy-piggledy fashion they chose. Bette and Anne did not, as a rule, set out place cards. Flora successfully negotiated for a seat right next to Verbena, who did not hide her delight at the arrangement.

"I believe Penny is giving us lamb tonight. Isn't that exciting?" she murmured. Her delicate hand rested on Flora's thigh.

Flora very carefully did not think about it, or lamb. "Have you seen William Forsyth at all today?" she asked, knowing Verbena had not. She accepted a ladle of potato and leek soup from Miles, who was seated on her other side. They served each other instead of relying on staff, another novelty. "He was looking for you earlier. Told me you two had much to discuss."

"We will run into each other at the soiree, I'm sure. Are you changing into a new gown after dinner? I was considering something a bit more formal myself." Verbena's hand remained on Flora's leg, patting companionably. She chose a glistening piece of buttered trout from a platter presented by Étienne on her left.

Flora cast an eye over Verbena's costume, a gorgeous dress of shot silk, the dual colors of green and blue catching the light with her every movement. In the presence of a bonfire, she would appear as an immortal nymph, Flora was certain.

"Oh, please don't change a thing," she said. "You are beautiful as you are."

As soon as the words were out of her mouth, she knew she had miscalculated. William was supposed to be the one pressing his suit tonight, not she. It would only confuse the issue, speaking boldly like this.

Verbena, though, did not seem to mind. She looked over at Flora with a sparkle in her eye. "All right," she said. "But only if you also refrain from making any change. You could not be more radiant tonight." Her hand smoothed down the creamy taffeta of Flora's skirt.

Flora hid her grimace behind a bite of fish. She could make no such promise, not even in jest.

After the meal, the party moved outside to the lawn, where Penny had built a large pile of firewood in a circle of stones. Cushions and quilts ringed the nascent bonfire, and people took their places in the same informal way they had done at dinner.

"Here," Verbena said, taking a seat on one of the smaller cushions and patting the tiny slice of it left available. "Why don't we share?"

Flora was torn. She wanted to sit nestled against Verbena while the fire warmed them, but she needed to make her eventual escape so that William might return in her place. How could she ever get away if Verbena's attention remained wholly on her? It would be impossible to tear herself away from that.

Bette came up to Flora before she could decide how to respond. "Perhaps you could make your recitation now, Miss Witcombe?" Behind her, Lord Byron and several male painters were arguing about the best way to light the fire, as they'd apparently taken on the task for themselves. Bette gave them an aggrieved glance. "So that we might have some good entertainment as opposed to this farce?"

"I would be happy to," said Flora. With an apologetic smile at Verbena, she took her place atop a small marble bench that bordered the rose garden.

The assembled guests quieted their chatter as Bette clapped for their attention. "Miss Witcombe has agreed to perform some of her work for us! Miss Witcombe?"

Flora was not unused to reciting her poetry to an audience. It was a regular occurrence at the club, and her various patrons often trotted her out at gatherings to perform for their guests. She had several of her more popular verses memorized in toto, along with the cadence with which they were best delivered. Yet standing there in front of the unlit fire, dozens of eyes upon her, two of which belonged to a woman so cherished by her that she could not help but meet them and hold them—all memory of those poems left Flora's head.

The only thing that remained was the poem she had been toying with off and on since she'd met Verbena.

Flora prayed it wasn't too terrible.

"This has not yet been printed," she said, knowing it might never be. "Please excuse its roughness." She took a deep breath and began to recite:

How long hath I lived apart from love?
Separate from life entirely
Whose soft hand encased inside a glove
Never touching sweetness nor it—me.

Then!–she arrives with beauteous things
Her blazing sword striking down the dark
And for the first time my heart can sing
The life before and after laid stark.

Lay with me, whilst we still draw breath
Upon me, love, rest thy fiery head!
Allow thine lips to refuse sweet Death
And we two never leave this sweet bed.

There was a long stretch of silence as Flora spoke the final words. She stood on the marble bench and perceived, in the fading light of the setting sun, her audience's faces twisted in confusion. She could not know their thoughts, but she could guess: this was not Flora Witcombe's usual fare. This was not light society verse filled with bawdy innuendo and sharp witticisms. When confronted with a love poem, her first, no one knew how to take it.

Then Flora's gaze fell upon Verbena, who was situated on the edge of the crowd. Her expression was singular in its intensity; her eyes were wide, her mouth hanging open, her hands clasped to her breast. She was shocked, no doubt about that, but it was the sort of astonishment one might show when faced with a miracle, not a disaster.

That look, in Flora's view, made the entire exercise worthwhile.

The silence was shattered when Lord Byron, who had been fussing with candles and bits of paper, cried out in triumph. All eyes were pulled to the bonfire, which had finally caught and was growing ever brighter by the moment. Orange and red flames licked up the logs, reaching toward the darkening sky. The guests applauded—for Flora, yes, but for the fire as well. It was all a bit chaotic.

Flora stepped down from the marble bench with assistance from Miles.

"That was beautiful," he said in a whisper, "and very brave."

"It was nothing." She looked over to see Verbena rising to her feet, starting toward Flora with determination. There was little time. "William Forsyth is already late in arriving," she said to

Miles in a soft whisper. "Can you go to my room? You'll find hidden in the bottom of my trunk a navy suitcoat and fawn trousers. No, make it the black trousers."

"Navy coat, black trousers," Miles repeated.

Flora's heart swelled at the seriousness with which he took his charge; he was such a stalwart friend. She owed him a great debt.

She spoke in a rush as Verbena approached. "Meet me inside, in the cloakroom."

"Right. Good luck with your escape," Miles said, and took off toward the house.

Verbena replaced him at Flora's side. "That poem," she said, almost in a daze, "it was wonderful." Her eyes searched Flora's face as if all her secrets could be parsed there. "Have you–when did you have time to write such a gem?" Her smile was laced with the clever intelligence she always exhibited when digging for the truth in rumors.

"I couldn't say." Flora pressed a hand to her forehead and gave a small whimper. "I'm afraid all the excitement has emptied my head and put into it nothing but a pain. I should go lie down."

"What? Oh no." Verbena nudged Flora's hand from her forehead and replaced it with her own. "You don't have a fever, at least." Her touch lingered, fingertips tracing Flora's temple. "Perhaps if you sat for a moment–"

"No, I really must excuse myself before I swoon," Flora insisted. That, at least, was close to the truth. Swooning seemed more than possible when Verbena touched her with such easy intimacy.

Verbena's stubbornness, a trait Flora would normally adore, made itself known. "Then let me accompany you. I don't want you fainting on the stairs. I'll tuck you into bed and keep you company."

Flora hardened her heart. It was difficult, but she had no choice. "Please leave me be," she said, turning away from Verbena's touch. "I–I simply need a moment to myself."

Verbena, for all her practice in hiding her emotions, showed a flash of hurt in her eyes. "If you are certain," she said.

"I am. Good night." Flora lifted her skirts and rushed toward the house, wishing there was some other way to do what needed to be done. If all went as she hoped, though, Verbena would soon know the real reason behind Flora's actions tonight. They would laugh about it, she was certain.

Miles was in the cloakroom as promised, arms full of toggery and high country boots. He'd even thought to bring William's hair tonic.

"Oh, good man! If I weren't so in love with Verbena, I would have you in an instant," Flora said. She unpinned her hairpieces and placed them gently upon a wooden crate. The cloakroom seemed to function as Plas Tân's workaday cupboard: winter coats and woolen capes hung in crammed rows along with various things that needed storing. There wasn't much room to speak of.

"And if I weren't so enamored with Étienne, I would let you have me," Miles said. He clapped a hand over his eye while Flora unlaced herself from her gown. "Erm, I would help a man dress without a second thought, but I don't know what's proper in this case."

Flora yanked her bodice down to her waist, exposing her underclothes, all three layers of them, and the small amount of padding that lent her some semblance of curvature. "I don't care, damn you, just get me into a shirt!"

Miles's shyness abated as William emerged. It was still surprising, even after all these years, the speed with which he could step forward to take Flora's place and vice versa. He no longer made the change with great ceremony, yet he still felt a pang as he shed the skirts and underthings to make way for the masculine attire. He wished fervently that he might one day devise a manner of dress like that of Miles's aunt and her companion, piecing together clothing of each sex and wearing whatever pleased him. That, at least, would present to the world some of the joining of his two halves, or rather, the secret thing he sensed between them.

Soon Flora Witcombe was gone and William stood in her place, breathing heavily in the dark of the cloakroom.

"Am I decent?" he asked Miles.

Miles fussed with the buttons on his coat, the fall of his cravat. "As near to. Wait!" He shook some tonic into his palm and ruffled his fingers through William's hair, now loosed from its pins and hairpieces, so that it stood on end in the fashion of a startled owl. "There. Now go capture your lady's heart," he said, stuffing Flora's ensemble, underthings and all, into one of the many crates for safekeeping.

William pressed Miles's hand in his in a gesture of gratitude before spilling out of the cloakroom and making for the lawn.

Sadly, Verbena was not sitting alone, waiting for William to monopolize her attention. She was already monopolized by Lord Byron, who was seated next to her on the little marble bench where Flora had so recently given her recitation. As William approached, he could hear the man pontificating about poetry—or rather, gossiping about other well-known poets. Something about sisters, and his former lover, or perhaps all three mixed together.

Verbena had that look on her face that meant she was weary of Byron's forceful personality. When she caught sight of William, she seemed to perk up.

"Mr. Forsyth," she said. "How nice of you to join us."

"Yes, good to have you!" Byron got to his feet and squeezed his hand with great vigor instead of kissing it. There was a kind of genial aggression in the man's bearing that had been absent when dealing with Flora. One thing that didn't change was the leering calculation in Byron's eyes as he sized up William's form. No one, regardless of sex, was exempt from the Byronic inclination to abscond to the nearest bed for an hour or two.

"Miss Montrose was just telling me how much she enjoyed Miss Witcombe's little performance," he said, his gaze lingering at William's waist. (To be fair, William's waist was shown off to great effect in the navy coat, so he could hardly be blamed.) "What did you think of the piece, sir?"

"I'm afraid I didn't have the pleasure. I've just arrived," said William. He dropped Byron's hand and turned to Verbena, hoping without much hope to edge the man out of the conversation. "Was it Miss Witcombe's usual subject? I do so enjoy her society verses." A shamelessly leading question, but there it was.

"No, it was altogether a different sort," Verbena said. Her hands clasped in her lap, palm worrying against palm. "There was something quite unusual about it, I think. I was—quite moved."

Byron frowned at that. "It was a pretty piece of work, but as Miss Witcombe herself said, it was not complete. Could you not detect the places in which she must still smooth out the cadence?" He shook his head and grinned. "Then again, perhaps a poetess need not make the efforts that a poet would. The novelty of her sex is enough to intrigue the reader."

Verbena rose from the bench, her hands now clenched into fists at her sides. William could sympathize, incensed as he was himself. He could not stand idly aside while his other half was spoken of with such disrespect.

His blood boiled at the back of his throat, heating his words as he spoke. "You forget, my lord, that a woman's sex is no asset in her artistic and financial endeavors. Miss Witcombe has had to work twice as hard to earn half the respect that a man in her position would," he said. "What readership she has gained with her fair nature must be weighed on scales tipping heavily on the other side, where curiosity is drowned in sneering disbelief. The fact that there are not as many noteworthy poetesses as poets is not a mark against the entire sex; it is proof that yours has made it nearly impossible for theirs to succeed."

"Steady on," said Lord Byron, but William was just getting started.

"There are hundreds of ladies, thousands, perhaps, who could craft words that would bring you to tears if only they were allowed!" he said. "What masterpieces must be held silently in their heads whilst they raise children or work the fields! Can you imagine it, my lord, or is your own life's arc the only line to which your mind may bend?"

William stopped then, winded from his long speech. He breathed hard through his flared nostrils, sweating with the passion that had been stirred in him, but did not look away from Byron's shocked face.

"I agree entirely," Verbena said. William looked to her then, gratified to see her flushed with spirit. "You speak well and truthfully on the matter, Mr. Forsyth. If Miss Witcombe were here, she would be delighted to have such a defender."

"The lady needs no assistance from me," William said with creeping shame. Here he was collecting accolades for coming to the defense of—well, himself. "If she were here, I am certain she would have said much the same, albeit in prettier language than mine." He glanced uneasily at Lord Byron, who remained uncharacteristically silent. The man had no real hold over him, as he wasn't even supposed to be in the country at all, but he was still a baron, and a well-connected one. There was still the real threat of retaliation. "If I spoke too harshly, my lord—" he began.

"No, no." Byron waved an elegant hand through the air. "The greatest sin a poet can commit is to be careless with his words, as I was just now. It was an offhand remark I made, and you were right to correct me. I am a great admirer of Miss Witcombe's work, truly." He accepted a glass of something from a passing tray. "Perhaps," Byron said in that seductive drawl of his, "we might continue the conversation later? In my room?" His tone left no doubt as to the shape of his plans.

"I promised William a tour of the grounds," Verbena said, forcefully inserting herself into the tête-à-tête. She took a candle from a box that someone had placed on the ground for the guests' use and moved to the bonfire to light it. "He was not present when our fine hostesses showed my party about last week, and now is the perfect time."

William turned to her, not bothering to hide his relief. "Yes, Miss Montrose is to be my guide." An absurd falsehood, but as it was one of Verbena's making, he was obligated to follow along.

Byron narrowed his eyes at them both. "Is that so? An entire week here and you have not yet seen the grounds, Mr. Forsyth?"

"He's been so very busy, you see." Verbena looped her arm through William's, allowing herself to be held in its crook rather than the other way round, as she did when walking with Flora. Her candle glowed in her free hand. "Now, my lord, if you would excuse us?" And with that, she spirited William away.

As they left the circle of light cast by the bonfire, the heat of it at their backs, they bent their heads together to share a laugh.

"How ever do you think of such things on the spur of the moment? And with a straight face!" William asked, breathless. "How quick-witted you are."

"It is a skill anyone might foster," Verbena said breezily. "I felt it only fair to come to your rescue, as you had so gallantly come to the aid of my entire sex. I've never known a man to do so, not ever."

William hummed. "It helps not to be much of one, I suppose." The half-truth was intoxicating to say aloud, but he felt he must. He was in Verbena's good graces now–him, not merely Flora! A delicate introduction to the topic he wished to broach seemed prudent.

Yet Verbena took it as a jest. She slapped at his arm with a laugh. "Now, don't say that. You're twice the man His Lordship is."

"Closer to half," William murmured, but Verbena did not mark him. She was too busy pulling him farther into the dark. "Where are you taking me, Miss Montrose? Not that I will complain, even if the destination is hell itself, but are you sure we should venture this far from the fête?" The revelry was now a distant smudge of laughter and firelight behind them. A walk alone in the woods in broad daylight was one thing, but a shadowy assignation was quite another. William had no desire to ruin Verbena's reputation.

Verbena's eyes flashed in the candlelight, as did her lovely teeth. "Thank you for thinking of my honor, but I have observed the guests here at Plas Tân for days. There is a loosening of social etiquette here that I find quite freeing. By the by, have you any interest in horticulture, Mr. Forsyth?"

William perceived a building looming before them, its glazed panels reflecting the faint glow of the fire. The glass conservatory, brimming with plants and flowers, stood silent before them.

"I could be persuaded to cultivate some," he said, and melted at Verbena's answering laugh.

Chapter 15

The humid warmth was a balm to William's chilled skin after the short walk away from the bonfire. He closed the glass door behind them while Verbena forged ahead into the quiet dark of the hothouse.

"Such an improvement over our former company. Lord, what an ass he is," Verbena said, her voice echoing against the glass panes. She turned to William to smile wryly, her red hair ablaze from the light of her single candle. "Do you think His Lordship merely enjoys listening to himself talk, or does he actually believe all the nonsense that comes out of his mouth?"

Easy as it was to heap derision on Lord Byron, William felt it unsporting to do so when the man was not there to defend himself. And besides–"He isn't so terrible," he said. "He is only afflicted with the artist's disease: the selfish desire to capture attention, and the selfless drive to give the world something of ourselves. It's a struggle for all writers and poets, is it not?"

"Ah." It was difficult to tell in the shadows, but Verbena's face seemed to fall. She groped along a workbench until she found a chamberstick with a glass chimney–no doubt to protect the tender foliage from open flame–and used her own candle to light it. "I suppose I've never thought of it that way. As I am neither, it would not have occurred to me."

Now that they had two candles lit instead of one, William could see more of their surroundings. The hothouse was crammed so full of life, there remained only a narrow path down the center of the enclosure where a person might walk. On all sides, exotic plants that William had only seen in books pressed close: green palms, orchids with brilliant purple and yellow blooms, spiky pineapples rising from equally spiky plants in brass pots, and lush waxy leaves the size and shape of an elephant's ear. The full, wet scent of earth enveloped them, along with the cloying sweetness of some unknown flower. William wondered what it could be.

"Frangipani," Verbena whispered, as if she had divined William's thoughts. Her slim white hand reached out to caress a nearby branch, where a cluster of flowers bobbed. Their deep pink petals faded into yellow centers, looking more like a cake's decoration than a living plant. Verbena put her nose to one such center and inhaled. "Exquisite. It's enough to make one write sonnets. Here, you must try it yourself."

With great care, William picked his way over and sniffed at the offered bloom. It smelled a little like an almond pastry, but sweeter. "As you say," he said, lifting his eyes to meet Verbena's dancing ones. "Sonnets."

Verbena tossed her head back in a laugh, a movement that caused her feathered bonnet to catch on a low-hanging branch. "Oh!" She lifted a hand to bat ineffectually at the limb.

"I might be able to untangle you," William said. He reached for her, then stopped with his fingers hovering in midair, not wanting to breach any boundaries.

Yet Verbena seemed to have none, at least tonight. She smiled at him and undid the knot in her bonnet ribbon faster than William could blink. "This is simpler. It is so warm in here, after all." Her head of fiery curls ducked free of the trapped cap, and then she stood before him bare-headed.

William nearly expired. Flora had seen Verbena without a bonnet, of course, but the implications of such undress in these environs set his blood aflame. Verbena tugged the cap free of the branch, now that she could see enough to do so, and placed the thing on the workbench.

He attempted to keep the stammer out of his voice. "How

brave of you, to rescue yourself. Very admirable." It was a paltry jest, yet Verbena laughed again.

William hovered close to her side, ostensibly to remain in the small circle of light cast by the candles but wanting desperately to be near her. It was already too scandalous to be borne, the two of them unaccompanied in a darkened room while the merry party continued in the distance. The fact that Verbena was not protesting the situation, and indeed had engineered it herself, made William think that she was perhaps feeling quite tender toward him.

"You are a most unusual gentleman," she said. Her hand, the one not occupied with her candle, came to rest on his arm. Likely for balance in the dark, William told himself. The alternative was that Verbena wanted to touch him for the sake of touching him, an idea that made his head spin. "I don't know if I've ever met one quite like you. Have you always been sympathetic to the souls of women, or is it something you've learned by writing your tragic gothic heroines?"

"Oh, I've always been like this," William said breathlessly.

Verbena's gaze trailed up and down his figure as if taking stock of him. A slight smile quirked at the corner of her mouth. "That is very good to know." Her hand moved down his arm and touched the backs of his fingers. She did not even seem to realize she was doing it, except that William's hand twitched, causing her to inhale sharply. They shared a look, William's wide eyes finding Verbena's.

William knew he possessed a somewhat overactive imagination. It was this quality that allowed him to envision a life for himself that included Flora. Without his capacity for dreaming of a world that did not yet exist, William himself would not exist. So we must excuse him for wondering, despite the mounting evidence, whether Verbena truly felt affection for him now or whether he was just seeing what he wanted to see.

He took stock of the facts: she liked his writing, despite knowing most people would look down on her for doing so; she had complimented his staunch defense of women; she shared his interest in the macabre; she had confided in him the secret that even Flora was not privy to; and, perhaps most pressingly, she had brought him to a dark, deserted place far away from prying eyes so that they might talk—alone. It was not, he concluded, his imagination. Verbena felt as he did. She had to.

And so he had to tell her everything.

Heart thundering in his chest, William licked his dry lips. "Miss Montrose—" he began.

Miss Montrose, being Miss Montrose, must have assumed he had spoken a complete sentence, for she broke in with great cheer. "I would like to introduce you to someone," she said.

William froze in his confusion. He had not expected another party to be introduced at such a critical juncture. "Wha— Now?"

"Yes, tonight." Verbena practically glowed in the flickering candlelight. "Actually, I believe you are already somewhat acquainted. Do you know Flora Witcombe?"

Panic built in William's stomach, making him lightheaded. All around him, the thick walls of plants seemed to be drawing closer. Why had he not foreseen this possibility? Verbena was becoming fast friends with Flora; naturally she would want her companion to meet any potential suitor for the purpose of taking his measure. Perhaps he could imply this step be skipped?

"I am *very* friendly with Miss Witcombe. Yes, we have met previously. Many times."

Verbena's lips parted. "Really? Many times?"

"Well, we do belong to the same club," William said. It was true, after a fashion; William had joined the club prior to Flora's Athena-like appearance, but now that she was there, and the more successful writer between the two of them, he had neglected to pay the club's dues for his own membership for nearly a year. There was little sense in paying double for the privilege. "I fear I have not visited the place in months, but in the past we have had many long and productive—conversations."

"Strange that she hasn't mentioned that . . . ," Verbena said slowly. "She said only that you two were mere acquaintances. We were discussing your book, you see. I would have thought she would have said more, if there was more to say."

William forced a jovial laugh he did not feel. "Is that right? The excellent Miss Witcombe no doubt wished to see how you liked my writing before revealing our friendship. One cannot be too critical of one's friends. Awkward business."

"Then you are already quite close?" A strange look—eagerness and consternation both—overtook Verbena's visage for which William could not account.

"Yes, she would tell you the same, I believe. And, I hope, vouch for my character." Already he was composing Flora's lines in his head. Nothing lavish—he was all too aware of his own faults for that—but complimentary enough to nudge Verbena toward a courtship.

"That is good to hear," said Verbena. There was a coyness to her glance, eyes darting to William's form—not lecherously like some barons he knew, but coolly appraising. "You know, I have always adored matchmaking."

William wasn't sure what to do about this sudden change in topic. "Oh?" he floundered.

"Perhaps you've heard the amusing story of my midnight carriage ride whilst being hounded by the Duke of Rushford." She leaned in with a sly smile. "Do not tell anyone, but that was all in service to his daughter's love affair. If I can manage to assist in a union such as that, surely I can arrange for Miss Witcombe to find a suitable husband."

The pieces began to fall into place. Horror gripped William by the throat. He sputtered. "But—but I—"

"She is a wonderful woman, I'm sure you'll agree. Well, you already know." Verbena smiled tightly. "And the two of you have so much in common!"

"More than you might imagine," William muttered to himself.

"What was that?"

"Hm?" He blinked rapidly at her.

Her face was creased with curiosity. "I thought I heard you say something."

"No. Nothing." William's hopes were dashed upon the rocks of his hubris. This wasn't a midnight tryst with a woman who wanted him; it was a secret meeting conducted by someone who merely thought him a good match for a friend.

Everything William had worked toward tonight was exploding spectacularly in his face.

"I would like to be perfectly frank with you, Mr. Forsyth," Verbena said, though her voice sounded to William as if it came from the bottom of a deep well. "The arrangement I have in mind is a bit unorthodox, though I believe I know enough of your character to think you would be amenable to at least hearing me out."

William barely registered every other word she said. A hole was opening beneath his feet. Retreat was the only option, the hastier the better. He placed a hand to his temple. "I think I've developed an awful pain."

"Strange, Miss Witcombe is afflicted with the same sort of headache," Verbena said. She notably did not press her palm to his forehead to check for fever as she had with Flora, though she did look politely concerned. "Perhaps it's all this excitement."

"Yes, perhaps. I—I fear I must go lie down. Apologies."

Call him unmanly if you must, but William fled before he began to cry. As it was, he only made it a few steps from the greenhouse before a tear wended its way down his smooth cheek. He dashed it away, then stumbled over a rock. In his haste, he'd neglected to take the chamberstick.

He braved the dark until he was back in the orbit of the bonfire. The guests had been busy in his absence, and it seemed that all of them were at some stage of drunkenness. William spied Byron half naked and barefoot, his shirt and coat draped over a nearby statue, performing a kind of oration for the assembled. It took a moment of searching with craned neck before William caught sight of his lone ally.

Miles was in deep conversation with Étienne Charbonneau at the edge of the gathering. The two had eyes only for each other, their animated faces showing not a whit of interest in the rest of the party.

William needed two things in that moment: a friend to whom he might unburden himself and a hand in dressing in Flora's clothing in the dark of the cloakroom. He strode up to the men where they were seated on a split log–close enough that their knees kissed–and took Miles by the shoulder.

"Could I trouble you for a moment?" he asked.

Something in William's face must have shown his distress, for Miles peeled himself off the log with only a moment's hesitation and an apologetic look toward Étienne. "I will find you later," he said to the Frenchman.

"Of course." Lucky for William, Étienne was so infatuated with Miles's person that he did not seem to register William's misery. "I will wait for you." His tone, wistful and soft, implied he would do so under any circumstances, even if all the seas gang dry or whatever the hell the poet Burns had said.

William dragged Miles away before the statement caused him to prostrate himself right there on the ground. They wove their way through the staggering revelers and back to the little cloakroom.

"What on earth's the matter?" Miles asked, once they were safely ensconced. The scent of spirits on his breath was unmistakable, though not surprising. It was a party, after all.

"She wants me to marry Flora," William said. He was panting a bit from their energetic march indoors.

"Flora?" Based on his tone, Miles must have made a face, though William couldn't be sure in the dark. "That might be tricky, since you are her and she is you."

"Yes! I am aware!"

"You should tell her you can't," Miles said. "Explain the whole plot."

"It's not a plot, it's my life." William groaned, putting his face in his hands. "I want to tell her. I nearly did, thinking she was in love with me. But she's not in love with me at all. She only wants to foist me off on another woman!" His hands fell uselessly to his sides. "It's hopeless, anyway. I cannot say anything until I am certain that she is–sympathetic to my situation."

Miles rubbed his shoulder soothingly. "Bad luck, old boy," he said. Then, after a long moment: "Would you like me to lace you back into your corset?"

William sniffed. "If you would." Leaving this unloved man behind and returning to his alternate persona would be a comfort. A small one, but a comfort nonetheless.

"Come, then. Give me your coat." Miles scrabbled at the pewter buttons, but the drink combined with the darkness stymied him. His fingers simply could not get the job done.

"Here, let me," William said, joining the fray and succeeding only in tangling their hands together.

"No, I've got it."

"You haven't. Give it here."

"Would you—? Ha!" Miles at last unbuttoned William's tailcoat. He celebrated by shoving the thing off William's shoulders and diving for his cravat. "Stand still, would you?"

"I am still! You're the one who's swaying."

"Don't blame me, blame the Welsh. Did you know they make a decent whisky?"

William lifted his chin and allowed his cravat to be unwound. "Good. I'll need some after this," he said.

Just then, the cloakroom door opened, and light poured in.

William's head snapped to the side to stare at it, as did Miles's. There was an interloper in their midst, outlined in gold in the doorframe. One of the painters, a chap named Turner, stood there squinting at them.

It occurred to William that he was in a cloakroom with another man in the middle of being undressed by said man, both of them breathing hard, and that this innocent scene might be construed as something else entirely by their audience.

"Oh," Turner said, blessedly unperturbed. He appeared vastly more drunk than Miles was, his eyes bleary and his stance unsteady. "This isn't my room."

"No," Miles said helpfully. "It's the cloakroom."

"Not anyone's room, then," said Turner.

"True." William was glad that Flora's gown and underthings were still secreted away in the crate or else the situation would be much more dire. "Erm. Having a good evening?" he said, because it seemed polite.

"Decent, very decent." Turner nodded to himself. "Gentlemen."

And he shut the door, plunging William and Miles back into the cocooning dark.

"Well, fuck," Miles said astutely.

"Miles?" William said, hitting his head against the bulwark of coats behind him.

"Yes, William?"

"This night could not possibly get any worse."

These were, as you are likely aware, the most famous last words available.

Chapter 16

Verbena accepted a cup of something sweet and–she took a discreet sniff–wildly potent from a guest who was dishing the stuff out of a copper pot with a soup ladle. "The finest punch Wales can provide," the woman declared. Verbena had been introduced to her earlier in the week, but couldn't place her name, only the fact that she did watercolors.

"Thank you," Verbena said. She took a sip of the punch for show, not intending to drink much more than that.

Verbena did not abstain completely from drink, and indeed enjoyed a nightcap every so often, but she did not make a habit of indulging to excess at parties. She felt it always a good idea to keep one's wits about one.

Besides, being the only sober person in attendance often meant she was the sole proprietor of the knowledge of what had actually occurred, a position that she had often used to her advantage.

And she needed every advantage she could get.

Her meeting with William had, she thought, gone swimmingly up until the point where the man had feigned illness at the mere mention of courting Flora. Had he done so in the past and then decided against her as a prospect? If he was repelled by Flora, who was loveliness in human form, then he was an absolute fool. He usually spoke so sensibly, though, and with a great deal of veracity. Verbena considered alternate explanations for his behavior: perhaps William shared Étienne's nature? It seemed likely. How else could Verbena explain what a comfort it was to share a secluded, darkened room with William, despite the obvious danger in doing so? Then again, there were plenty of men, like Lord Byron, who admired both sexes, though of course that could never be acknowledged in polite company. She wondered if William was already in love with someone else. It would take a delicate touch to introduce to him the idea of marrying Flora for safety's sake alone, if that were the case.

She cradled her earthenware mug of punch in both hands and scanned the crowd. Lord Byron was holding court in a tight circle around the bonfire, regaling his audience with tales of the exotic pets he'd owned over the years.

"Every lad needs a leashed bear," Verbena heard him say, and she pointedly did not listen any further.

She considered, not for the first time since rejoining the party, that she might go inside and knock on Flora's door. But would Flora even wish to speak to her? She had been uncharacteristically short with Verbena before taking her leave. Oh, if only they could talk! Verbena wished dearly for the ear of her friend.

Then, as if some celestial being was bestowing blessings upon her, Verbena caught sight of Flora coming toward the bonfire, her pale skirts lifted to save the hem from the ground. Flora looked all about, craning her neck this way and that. The object of her search became obvious once her gaze settled on Verbena. She looked nowhere else.

Verbena met her just outside of the circle of firelight. "Flora? Are you feeling better?" She looked even worse than when she'd begged off an hour or so ago, citing an aching head. Her cheeks were violently flushed and her hair slightly disheveled, though Verbena only noted the latter because she had closely studied the neatness with which Flora's hair was normally arranged.

"Yes, I—" Flora pressed her lips together. Her distress was so obvious, yet Verbena could see no obvious cause. "I feel much improved. I thought it best to return before the festivities reached their end. I would never forgive myself if I missed all the entertainment."

Despite her cheery words, her fingers worried at her skirts in agitation.

Verbena offered her cup to Flora. "Would you like some? It's quite strong."

"Thank you." Flora had the cup to her lips before she was even finished speaking. She took a great gulp of the concoction, gave one small cough, then stretched her lips into a smile that her eyes did not reflect. "Have I missed anything interesting?"

Verbena gave the other revelers a glance. A man known for his sculpture was currently carrying the watercolorist on his shoulders, and the pair were taunting the crowd to form a worthy opponent. It was a marvel no one had yet fallen into the fire.

"Perhaps we should sit down." Verbena took Flora by the arm and led her gently to the marble bench, some distance from the rabble. "I have much to tell you," she whispered once they'd sat in close congress.

"Oh?" Flora's smile widened to a worrying degree. "I wasn't absent very long. What could have happened?"

A quick decision: it was often more prudent to keep all parties in the dark as one tested the waters. "I had an extremely interesting conversation with Mr. Forsyth," Verbena said. "Although I told him I would not divulge his secret, I cannot keep what was said from you, my dear friend." She leaned in closer so that her lips were at Flora's ear. "He wants nothing more than to court you."

Flora reared back, her face all pinched brows and slack lips. "What?"

"He intimated that he admired you and dearly sought your admiration in turn. Is that not wonderful?" Verbena clasped Flora's limp hands in hers, squeezing them in excitement. "I suspect he confided in me knowing I might tell you and urge you to consider his suit, and I certainly will."

Flora's lower lip trembled. "William Forsyth told you no such thing. He—he said nothing of the sort." She placed the earthenware cup on the ground at their feet. Verbena noted it was drained.

"Do you doubt your own charms?" she asked. "I assure you,

he is as captivated with you as a man could be. I think, perhaps, he might even be persuaded to approach this courtship in a less traditional manner." Verbena licked her lips. *A delicate touch,* she reminded herself. "You see–"

Flora jerked her hands from Verbena's grip. "You're lying to me. Why would you lie to me, Verbena?" A sheen of tears stood in her eyes, catching the dancing firelight in the distance.

Verbena struggled to form an argument. "I'm not lying. He said–"

"I know William Forsyth." Flora rose from the bench, her hands clasped over her middle like she was trying to hold a part of herself in check. "I know him very, very well. And I know for a fact that he would never say that."

What could Verbena do in the face of such passionate denial but smile and deny it in return? "Flora, sweet Flora. Men often claim to have no designs on a lady whilst harboring deep in their hearts that most tender of feelings. They cannot help it; they lack the language we have for it; they need encouragement before they can reveal themselves."

Flora shook her head, staring at Verbena like she had transformed into a knot of snakes. "You're unbelievable," she said.

That put Verbena's back up. She stood as well, bringing her nearly nose to nose with Flora, who was quite a tall woman. "I am doing you a kindness! If you would listen to me, I know a way to use this to our advantage."

"Our advantage!" Flora laughed loudly enough that several heads turned away from the firepit and toward their conversation. "You speak as if this is all a chess game or–or–or some war maneuver."

A flash of righteous anger flowed into Verbena. "It *is* war," she hissed, drawing Flora by the arm further into the shadows that might afford some privacy. "It is life and death." Étienne's, surely, and in a way, Verbena's own. "I am trying to keep all my friends as safe and happy as possible in the face of immense pressure. And if you would simply hear me out instead of calling me a rank liar, you might come to understand that."

"Tell me one thing," Flora said. "Does William Forsyth hold any interest for you?"

"Me?" Now it was Verbena who drew back. She dropped her hold on Flora's slight arm in shock. "What would I need with William Forsyth? Étienne and I—you know we have an understanding."

Verbena gave the group around the fire a glance to gauge whether their attention was still on the two of them, but thankfully someone had produced a set of long sticks that were being used to poke at the bonfire with the aim of encouraging its growth. The others were enraptured with the flames. She hoped it would keep them occupied for some time.

"And there is no chance of Mr. Forsyth replacing Étienne in your affections?" Flora's voice became small, her eyes falling meekly to the ground. "None whatsoever?"

Verbena had a great deal of practice in not looking cross, or befuddled, or anything but placidly appealing. She deployed this talent now to ensure her face remained uncreased. "I don't understand. Étienne is the only candidate for a husband in my mind." Even if she did find William Forsyth gentle and kind and pleasing to both her eye and touch, there was nothing to be done about it. Her agreement with Étienne took precedence. Surely Flora, who'd written an entire poem about the arrangement, could understand that.

Yet it seemed she did not. Flora appeared so agitated, in fact—pacing in a small circle, casting hurt glares in Verbena's direction—that Verbena was quite shocked.

"Flora?" She touched the back of her friend's shaking hand where it clenched in her skirts. "Why are you upset?"

"I cannot say." The tears in her voice made her sound very small. "I cannot speak of it."

That was promising. That was, at least, an admission that some secret stood between them—in addition to Verbena's, of course. It was Verbena's most fervent hope that Flora's secret mirrored her own: that she held for Verbena an affection that had no name.

"Not even to me?" Verbena curled her fingers around Flora's, feeling the rough patches of her quill calluses. "Whatever it is, I would keep it from the world. You know that, don't you? I would keep–anything you gave me." The art of dancing around the words. Verbena knew it well, so well that she suspected she might never be able to say in plain terms what it was she meant. She squeezed Flora's now-slack hand in hers and hoped the gesture imparted her intentions. "To my grave and beyond."

"You should not make such promises to me," Flora said, still in that leaden tone, her gaze fastened to their joined hands. "It's not prudent. Nor is it possible."

"I am an imprudent and impossible woman," Verbena said, "as, I think, are you." There was tremulous hope in her voice, that desperate need to find a kindred soul. "Aren't you?"

Flora raised her head then. The distant firelight charged the planes of her face in a riot of oranges and reds, shadows shifting in a way that made her appear like a different person altogether from one breath to the next. Verbena's heart swelled at the picture she made. Flora's berry-wine lips parted, slow. Verbena leaned in to catch her reply, their hands clasped to her bosom.

Then someone let out the most hair-raising screech.

Verbena whipped her head to the side, seeking out the cause. Already she was shielding Flora from whatever was in their midst, placing herself firmly between her friend and the rest of the party.

Flora, unfortunately, had the exact same reaction, and so the two of them battled to be the protector. They shoved at each other, their ankles and hands tangling in the process. It was a wonder they didn't stumble to the ground.

"What is it?" Verbena cried out. "What's happened?"

The gathering was coming apart at the seams. Men and women alike streamed in all directions, shouting, their inebriation making the mad dash even more chaotic. In the rush of petrified faces, Verbena caught sight of Étienne. His wild eyes lit upon her and Flora, and he struggled through the storm of bodies toward them.

"The fire!" he shouted above the din. "It is out of control!"

Only then did Verbena register the intense heat that was coming from the site of the bonfire, having previously mistaken it for her own excited flush. Through the gaps in the crowd, she spied the great conflagration, which had indeed escaped the bonds of the stone ring. Patches of grass were scorched or afire, as well as several wooden stumps that the artists had been using as stools. One of the painters beat at the flames ineffectually with his shed greatcoat, which served only to light the fabric, too.

Flora molded herself to Verbena's side, their hands still clasped. Verbena could feel her panicked breaths overtaking her body.

Étienne at last arrived at their sides and took them both by the arm. "Come," he said, "before it gets any worse."

But Flora tore herself from Étienne's grasp with a cry. Her wide eyes were pinned to something in the distance. "Miles!"

Verbena turned to look. Miles McDonald was standing close to the raging blaze, attempting to help a drunken reveler to his feet. He seemed not to realize his sleeve had caught, the fire licking its way along his arm. At Flora's cry, he first looked up, then at his sleeve. He tried to undo his coat buttons but seemed too overwhelmed with panic. Flora picked up her skirts and rushed toward him, a hotheaded display of valor that Verbena could neither understand nor approve of.

"Flora, don't!" She flew faster than she had ever moved before, catching Flora about the waist. Already the fire had grown taller than their heads, racing erratically across the grounds, no doubt fed by spilled whisky.

"Miles!" Flora shouted again.

Despite all the danger, Verbena still had time to consider that perhaps Flora had her eye on the destitute Scotsman. Was that why she had no interest in Verbena's plot to pair her with William? Rather silly, the things one might think when in the throes of a disaster. At least she was keeping Flora away from the blaze for now. Anyway, they were quite matched in strength, and it was anyone's guess who would flag first.

It all became a pointless exercise in the next moment, as Étienne leapt to Miles's aid. He grabbed a nearby quilt and draped it over his head, plunging through the inferno to reach

Miles. He wrested the burning coat off him and dragged him, wild-eyed, to a safe distance.

At this point a few of the more sober revelers had managed to organize a sort of human chain to pass along water. Pots of pond water were sloshed onto the fire, creating a curtain of hot steam that blanketed the scene. Verbena took Flora by the hand and fought through the confusion until they found Étienne and Miles lying in the grass beneath a tree, panting for air.

"Fools!" Étienne spat. "Why did they stoke the flames like that? Damn them!" Then, with an apologetic glance toward Verbena and Flora, still in a clinch: "Excuse my English, ladies."

Verbena relaxed her hold on Flora, but did not let go. "No apologies necessary, Monsieur Charbonneau," she said.

A handful of men were still beating back the worst of the flames, but for the most part, the conflagration was contained. Flora shrugged out of Verbena's grip and approached Miles, who looked quite pale and was cradling his arm close to his body.

"Mr. McDonald, are you injured?" she asked.

He gave her a bewildered look. His hair was in a state of total disarray, which was saying something, given the style he preferred. "I'm afraid I am. Slightly."

Verbena strode forward to help, but Étienne beat her to it. He took Miles's arm and unfolded it so that he could see the damage in the remaining firelight. The sleeve of Miles's shirt was burnt away in several places. Shiny red patches of burned skin showed through the holes.

"My god," Étienne murmured.

"It's nothing," Miles said, though he did not, Verbena noticed, look at his injured arm but instead kept his gaze fastened to Étienne's worried face.

"A burn is no small matter," Flora said, sticking close to him. "Even the smallest ones might fester."

Verbena narrowed her eyes at their closeness. "Yes," she said, "best have a doctor take a look. Don't you agree, Étienne?"

Étienne did not hesitate. "I shall take you myself," he said to Miles. "This ordeal has sobered me completely. We will leave at once."

Miles shifted on his feet. "Well. If you think it necessary . . ." He was staring rather boldly at Étienne's lips now. Verbena stifled a huff. What was the world coming to! Nobody seemed to be infatuated with the proper person tonight.

Étienne called for a horse and cart to be brought from the stables and for Penny to direct him to the nearest physician. The maid informed them that the ride would take most of the night and they likely wouldn't return until the following day. Verbena assisted in packing them a hamper for the journey while Flora ripped bandages from clean linen sheets and applied them to Miles's arm.

Before long, they were waving good-bye to the departing dogcart while the bonfire burned down to embers. The other guests had long since gone to bed.

Verbena ceased waving farewell when the cart went around a bend in the road. She looked at Flora, standing pale beside her, gaze still fastened to where Étienne and Miles had disappeared.

"Well," Verbena said, "say what you will about Plas Tân, but no one can claim that our evening was uneventful."

Flora did not so much as smile. She lifted a hand to her eyes, rubbing at them tiredly. "I suppose we should try and get some sleep," she said. "Though I don't know if I can."

Verbena swallowed. All night she had been dancing, not with partners, but around what she wanted to say. Perhaps, she thought, with dawn encroaching, just the two of them remaining on the grounds, she could do so.

"Share my bed," she said.

Flora's gaze snapped to meet hers. "What?"

"You're obviously shaken," Verbena said, hating how she reached so quickly for a plausible explanation that might soften her offer should it be unwelcome. "What happened tonight–it was frightening for everyone. Come to my room with me. We can sleep beside each other. If that would help." She raised two fingers, thinking to trace the back of Flora's hand, but then curled them into a fist. She must take care, she knew.

"That is kind–very kind," Flora murmured. Her gaze dropped, her chin sinking to her chest. "But I do not think it wise. I would not make good company. Good night." She hurried away, crossing the dewy lawn alone.

Verbena watched her go, a protest trapped in her throat. Perhaps she had only imagined the affection between them. Never in her life had she harbored tender feelings, and now that she did, were they destined to never be returned?

A hot dampness stung at Verbena's eyes. She wiped away the nascent tear in frustration.

Chapter 17

The following morning dawned bright and clear, which made Flora's foul mood all the fouler. She usually did not expect Nature herself to bend to human feelings, but in this case, the chirpiness of the birds and the clarity of the streaming sunlight were obscenely at odds with the general malaise that hung over Plas Tân and its guests. Flora encountered several specimens clutching at their aching heads when she ventured downstairs for breakfast. Most were only drinking cups of strong tea, but a few brave souls were picking at the toast and eggs.

The only person who appeared fresh and unaffected by the disastrous bonfire fête was Verbena. She sat at the long dining table, nibbling at a muffin and chatting with an ailing artist whom Flora recalled dabbled in portraiture.

"Ah!" Verbena lit up at Flora's appearance, her cheeks matching the pink walking dress she wore. "I was just telling Madame Le Brun here it's the perfect day to bathe in the sea. Anne says the waters are wonderfully bracing, and she's already sent for the local bathing machine. It should arrive before long! Would you care to take a dip, Flora?"

Flora caught a look from Madame Le Brun that seemed to indicate she, at least, would rather stuff her poor head under a pillow and sleep the remainder of the day away. Flora could sympathize. Though she had not overindulged in drink the night before as everyone else had, she was still feeling tender from the farcical in-and-out appearances as both William and herself.

Verbena clearly wished to act as if nothing had happened, but something *had.* Flora still couldn't believe that Verbena had tried to foist William on her when it was so obviously Verbena who needed to be with him. Her.

Oh, it was headache inducing, to say the least.

Flora rubbed her fingertips along her aching temples. "I'm not sure I could. I'm not myself today."

"All the more reason to take to the sea!" Verbena insisted. Beside her, Madame Le Brun flinched at her volume. Verbena continued, heedless of the pain she was inflicting. "It clears the mind and soothes the body. Most problems, I find, can be solved with the judicious application of water in some form." Her smile held a beseeching edge to it that, despite their argumentative conversation of the previous night, made Flora weak.

"I've never gone for a swim," Flora said. "I might not take to it at all." This was a slight dissembling. While it was true that Flora Witcombe had never been swimming, William certainly had. In rivers and lakes, he had swum naked as an otter with his brothers and university friends. Of course, that had been a boyhood lark, done in relative privacy. Bathing in the nude here was completely out of the question, as was being trapped in a tiny bathing machine with a gaggle of ladies. Flora couldn't imagine changing into a thin shift in front of anyone, save perhaps Miles.

Oh, poor Miles! She hadn't spared a thought for her friend's health that morning. She sat heavily on the bench opposite Verbena at the dining table. What sort of friend was she?

"The machine will only take us far enough for the water to come up to our necks," Verbena said, heedless of Flora's internal castigation. "And besides, the dipper will be there to assist if you need it. They're strong, these ladies. They won't let you drown."

Flora helped herself to a subdued piece of toast and began eating it dry. "Has there been any word from Miles? Perhaps I should go into town and see how he's faring."

There was a clatter as Verbena dropped her teaspoon against her saucer. Several guests groaned at the noise, clutching at their heads up and down the long table. Verbena had the grace to wince apologetically at the assembled before answering. "I'm sure he's all right," she said. "Étienne wouldn't allow anything to happen to him. There's no need to worry." Her words were clipped as she poured herself more tea.

How strange. Verbena seemed as upset as Flora was about Miles's injury, but in a different direction. Was she actually angry with the man for being burned? It wasn't as if he'd asked for it.

Flora tore her piece of toast into smaller and smaller pieces, letting them pile on her plate. Perhaps bathing in the sea with Verbena would do them both good—it would, at the very least, allow them a chance to speak within the private confines of the machine.

But what was she thinking! It was preposterous to even consider. She couldn't be in a state of undress in front of Verbena, not before she explained her dual nature. And she couldn't do that if Verbena failed to hold some sort of affection for both halves of her.

She flicked her gaze across the table. Verbena was stirring her tea with unnecessary vigor, the spoon clanging against the sides of the teacup in a way that made Madame Le Brun groan. The lady rose from the table with a hard look at Verbena.

"I am going back to bed," she announced. "I wish you luck, Miss Montrose, in trying to find anyone at Plas Tân who is amenable to your seaside scheme. Lord knows they'd have to be made of steel to stomach you." And with that, she took her leave, groping at the doorframe to support herself as she exited.

Flora stared at the doorway through which Madame Le Brun had left, then back at Verbena. Verbena laid her spoon quietly upon its saucer. The tea sat untouched.

"That was unaccountably rude of Madame Le Brun," Flora said to her. "You weren't the one pouring punch down her throat last night. She has no right to be angry with you."

Verbena managed a smile, though it was not at all happy. "She's quite correct, though. If even you will not accompany me, I doubt anyone else will." She sighed through her nose, gaze fixed on her cup. "That's all right. I should not bully you, or anyone else, into doing as I like."

A pang shot through Flora. She rose from the table. At first Verbena watched her with wide, betrayed eyes, no doubt thinking she was going to leave as well, but Flora only rounded the long table and took the spot so recently vacated next to her. She dropped her voice into the barest whisper. "Truthfully? I would love to go bathing today. It's only–I can be quite shy." She shrugged a shoulder. "And as I've said, I've never used a bathing machine. It fills me with anxiety to think of the mechanics of the thing."

She had only seen these machines from afar in Brighton. They were, in essence, wooden sheds that sat perched atop a set of carriage wheels. A folded canvas shade was fastened where a carriage driver would normally sit. Once loaded with bathers, they were driven into the water so that one might swim without the indignity of flopping about in plain view of everyone on the beach. Yet they seemed rickety and ripe for uncomfortable closeness.

Verbena's whole countenance blossomed. "Of course, I should have realized. If you are shy, I will turn my back when the time comes, and we two can change into our bathing costumes very quickly. The machine will give us the utmost privacy whilst we bathe, as well. It is an altogether civilized affair, I promise."

"And it will be just the two of us?" Flora asked. She could imagine nothing worse than another lady tagging along at the last moment and ruining any chance to speak of private matters. And Flora did want to speak of private matters–perhaps not the entire truth, as she had no desire to reveal herself to the woman she loved in untoward (and unclothed) circumstances, but she did want to press Verbena on the matter of William. There had been a spark between them, she was almost certain, if only Verbena would admit it.

Verbena grinned, wide and true. "You and I and no one else."

The bathing machine arrived as promised by midmorning. Flora stood at her window and watched the contraption trundle across the grounds, heading along a worn path that led down to the beach. She clutched a plain muslin shift in her hands. Anne had given it to her, saying it was the best sort of bathing costume a lady could have. It would cover Flora from throat to toe with hardly any flesh exposed. And yet, with only the one layer, which would soon be soaked with seawater, she would be more vulnerable than she ever had been. At least with Miles, the cloakroom had been dark and the final layer of underthings had remained in place.

Flora took a deep breath and stuffed the shift into a woven bag that already held a bath sheet and other necessities. She would be brave. There was no other path to happiness. She left the manor and walked toward the shore.

Verbena was already waiting at the appointed place where the rocky earth gave way to the black sand. She wore a beautiful bonnet with a clutch of fluffy white feathers pinned to one side, which swayed in the breeze like grasping fingers.

"The dipper says this is about the best weather one could hope for!" she said as Flora came nearer.

Flora shot a look toward the machine, which sat at the very edge of the water. A middle-aged woman wearing a headscarf stood up to her ankles in the surf, tending to the horse. Having finished her examination of the harness, she turned to them.

"All right, ladies," said the attendant in her Welsh drawl. "In you go. Calm seas today." Her gruff demeanor and strong, bulky physique put Flora in the mind of a champion pugilist, if pugilists assisted ladies up rickety steps with a firm hand.

Inside, the bathing machine was dark and cramped. There was only one small window at eye level set into the door they'd come through. Low wooden benches were built into either side with a high shelf near the ceiling.

"Put your finery up there so's it stays dry," advised the dipper, pointing at the shelf. "Once I shut this door"—she rapped her scarred knuckles on the wood at the back of the machine—"you'll have all the time you please to change. The horse is as calm as the water. Once we're out far enough, I'll open that for you." She pointed to the other door at the front end of the machine.

"Thank you," Flora said. She appreciated the short explanation, novice that she was.

The woman began closing the back door, then paused. "One

last thing," she said. "D'you want to be put in the water gentle-like? Or do you prefer to be tossed?"

Flora blinked politely. "Tossed?"

"The dippers in this area are renowned for their strength," Verbena said. "It's something of a tradition to be flung into the sea by them. Saves everyone a lot of tiptoeing in, I suppose."

The dipper puffed up with pride. "If I may say, I have a reputation as a champion flinger." She rolled her sleeve up to her shoulder and flexed her arm, demonstrating the impressive bulge of muscle there. "Name's Prudence," she said, putting her sleeve back in place. "Perhaps you've heard of me."

"No, but I am the poorer for it. I, for one, would love to be tossed!" Verbena said, her cheeks pink with excitement. "And you, Flora?"

"Well, I suppose–if it is traditional–" Flora could hardly construct a complete sentence, entranced with their dipper as she was. How wonderful to see all sorts of women in the world! And how wonderful to see a woman who was lauded for her physical capabilities, as divergent as they were from the usual willowy delicacy.

Prudence nodded approvingly. "Two tosses, then," she said, and clapped the back door shut, plunging them into shadow.

Verbena immediately sat and removed her slippers. "I am so glad you agreed to come," she said. "After all the fuss we endured last night, I wanted to speak to you. Alone."

Flora sat on the bench opposite and slowly unlaced her heeled boots. She heard the horse whicker, and then the machine jolted into motion, its wheels slowly churning through wet sand. Hooves splashed into the water. "I feel the same. After last night, we should clear the air." She concentrated very hard on her laces. "Why did you insist I turn my interest to William Forsyth?"

A quick glance showed Verbena occupied with the buttons of her short jacket. "Ah. That. I should explain." She shrugged off the jacket and stood, lifting the hem of her dress.

Flora bolted to her feet and turned around. "Don't forget, you promised," she said, hushed. "Back to back, yes?" She stared hard at the shadowed wall.

There was a long pause before Verbena, unseen behind Flora, laughed lightly. "Of course. Although . . ." Her stockinged feet shuffled against the floorboards as she turned, her voice now directed away. "If you are ever able to overcome your shyness, perhaps I could tempt you to swim in the nude. I hear it's excellent for the nerves."

"Not for mine," Flora mumbled to herself. Then, clearing her throat, she began undoing all the little mother-of-pearl buttons down the front of her walking dress. "To return to the topic of William—"

"Yes, I still maintain that he could be a fine match for you," Verbena said. There was a shush of fabric falling to the floor. Flora wished she could look Verbena in the eye right that moment; she couldn't imagine what the woman's face was doing. She sounded completely matter-of-fact about the whole ordeal.

"You . . . do not want him for yourself?" Flora asked. Perhaps there was something to facing away from each other for this conversation. It was somewhat easier to speak boldly. Flora shucked off her dress, then hurriedly pulled the long linen shift over her head. She kept her arms tucked into the voluminous thing and went to work on her stays with some level of safety.

Another laugh echoed from Verbena's side of the machine, this time more brittle. "Why would you ask me such a thing?"

"Why do *you* find the notion so amusing?" Flora shot back. She removed her stockings and smalls, not taking her usual care with the delicate garments. She balled them up and shoved them in her bag. "I do not need a husband. You, on the other hand . . ." She struggled out of her stays and flung them onto the high shelf to join her other clothes. The overlarge shift, she was relieved to see, hid the shape of her body well. "Forgive me for saying so, but all of London knows your father's financial plight. Why are you so obsessed with seeing me married off when I have no pressing reason to make a match?"

"Are you finished changing?" Verbena asked sharply. "I would like to say what it is I have to say to your face, if I am permitted."

Flora steeled herself, though privately she winced. "If you must."

Soft hands cupped her shoulders and turned her until Flora was looking into Verbena's eyes. Lovely though they were, they were stricken with the sort of pained determination that Flora had heretofore seen only in artists trapped in the fugue of creation.

"I–" Verbena began, and then stopped. The bathing machine stopped as well. The whole compartment swayed as they came to a standstill. The sea lapped at the bottom of the machine. A wave that must have been larger than the ones before sloshed its way under the front door, wetting their feet and the hems of their shifts with frigid water.

Flora gasped at the cold, but Verbena held her firm. Held her close. And placed her lips, slowly, sweetly, upon Flora's.

It took Flora a long moment to realize that she was being kissed. She had endured kisses before, but none like this. Verbena tasted of highly sugared tea and honeyed sweetness, yet after the first hesitant touch, she took Flora like a rake might, groaning into her mouth and wrapping her arms about her waist. Flora gasped as they pressed flush together, some latent fear clawing at her mind–Verbena would know, she would *feel* Flora's body and know–but she could also not resist. She succumbed to Verbena as the parched earth does to rain, opening to it and letting it inside.

Then it was over. Verbena pulled back, her mouth red from their kiss, her hands still clutching Flora tight.

"This is what I want," she said. "This alone, whatever you may call it."

Light dawned in Flora's soul. She was a terrible poet, she saw that now. Nothing she had ever written, no verse she had ever composed, had moved a heart the way Verbena's words moved her.

"It is the same with me," she said, unable to say anything more. She needed to, but where to start? She needed to tell Verbena about William, she needed–

A loud rap sounded at the front door of the bathing machine. Both of them startled badly, Verbena disentangling herself from Flora and leaping, in the span of an eyeblink, clear across the small space.

"You ladies ready to take to the water?" Prudence boomed through the door.

Flora looked wildly at Verbena. Her face was as red as Flora's own felt, her lips as tenderly used.

"We will raise suspicion if we do not," Verbena whispered.

"But . . ." Flora could not imagine pausing this world-changing conversation for any reason, least of all a swim.

Verbena stepped closer and pressed her hands around Flora's. "We can speak on the return trip. Yes?" Her eyes sought Flora's, despite Flora's inability to hold her gaze for more than a moment. It was all so overwhelming.

She nodded. "Yes."

Verbena went to the door and swung it open. Flora watched in a daze as Verbena chatted with Prudence, laughing about how much force the dipper would be using to toss her into the waves. As if everything were perfectly ordinary. As if the earth hadn't stopped turning the moment their lips had touched.

She watched Prudence heft Verbena in her strong arms, feeling a stab of inky jealousy. Verbena squealed in delight as she was flung, her lithe limbs flailing in the air, the white of her shift like a cloud against the summer-blue sky. She hit the water with a tremendous splash, resurfacing with her red hair plastered onto her head.

"Flora, come join me," she cried, holding out her arms. "It's amazing! Don't worry, your toes can touch the bottom."

Flora stepped out onto the small platform outside the machine door and blinked in the sudden sunlight. The canvas shade was rolled up against the mouth of the bathing machine, likely only put into service if other bathers were swimming in a separate party, so that they might be shielded from one another. Today, however, there was no need for it. She and Verbena were the only ones in the water. The only ones in the world, it seemed.

Well, except for their strong woman.

"Gently, if you could," Flora said as Prudence scooped her up. It was like being picked up by Artemis herself. She weighed as much as a sack of feathers in the dipper's grip. Then—weightlessness, the giddy freedom of flight, the sharp catch of Verbena's laughter on the wind, before the cold dark of the sea swallowed her.

Flora surfaced with a shocked gasp. Verbena had been correct; the water was not so very deep. Flora could touch her toes to the sandy bottom and stand with her head and shoulders above the waves, though it took a moment to find her footing. Verbena, meanwhile, was already sluicing through the waves like a nymph, circling Flora and splashing a great deal of water into the air. Droplets hung like diamonds in the morning light.

Prudence sat upon the bathing machine's board and watched them, presumably ready to dive in for a rescue if they showed any signs of fatigue. It was slightly disconcerting to be so closely watched. Yet when Flora caught Verbena's eye as they bobbed together in the water, she saw the same gleam there that glowed secretly in her middle: they would be alone again soon enough. In the meantime, they knew the taste of each other, and knew they wanted each other, and that notion was so buoyant, Flora could have floated all the way to Ireland.

They swam and laughed for a blissful hour or more, splashing each other and playing silly games. Flora, they soon found, could hold her breath underwater far longer than Verbena, a contest they repeated several times. Flora's anxieties faded the more time she spent in the ocean: her hair was wet, yes, but her clever pins held everything in place; her voluminous shift hid what could not yet be revealed; and anyway, soon they would be alone and Flora could tell all. She could hardly worry what Verbena might think of her revelation when Verbena herself had been so bold as to kiss a woman the way a man did. If that was not too scandalous for her, then surely the discovery that Flora was sometimes William and William was sometimes Flora wouldn't be so strange. It would even be a blessing, really, once Verbena understood that William could marry her, and wanted to. Very much.

Finally, when they had bathed as much as was expected, they called on Prudence to haul them back up the steps and into the bathing machine.

Once the door was shut, Flora took Verbena by her wet shoulders and kissed her salt-laced mouth. Verbena melted against her, the cool dampness of their shifts sticking together between their warm bodies. The horse, now hitched to the other end of the machine, began its plodding trek back to shore, causing the walls to shudder around them.

"I have something to tell you," Flora said when they parted. She pictured the myriad reactions Verbena might have to her secret once revealed, from the most horrid shock to the gentlest acceptance. One side of the scale seemed to weigh more than the other, but it still caused Flora's tender heart to race in her chest.

"No, I have something to tell *you,*" Verbena said. Her eyes held the fierce determination that characterized her so completely. "You must marry William Forsyth."

Flora blinked. "What?" she said. Her heart raced impossibly harder. "But why?"

"Hear me out. I've thought about it from every angle," Verbena said quickly. Her hands, just as quickly, fastened on Flora's trim waist. "As you have already guessed in your poem, I will marry Étienne in name only. You will do the same with William, if he can be convinced, and our dear husbands will allow us to do as we wish. Perhaps you and William could purchase one of the homes beside Étienne's, and we can live in such proximity that we'll be, for all purposes, together." She grinned, a wild stretch of her mouth that bordered on mania. "It is a flawless plan."

Flora could not think for how badly her head was spinning. "How long have you been plotting this?" she asked in a daze.

"Since you took me for a walk and told me I deserved happiness." Verbena smiled. Her eyes crinkled so much, they disappeared entirely. "Since the very beginning of you and me."

Flora tried to keep her thoughts in order, but it was difficult when their entire friendship was flashing through her mind, rearranging itself in light of this confession.

"But I do not want to be married to a man," Flora said. "Any man." Her voice sounded small in the confines of the machine, nearly drowned out by the sound of lapping waves.

Verbena snorted, unladylike. "Who does?"

The words shot through Flora like a poison-tipped arrow. She was, she supposed, a man at certain times, and therefore Verbena's quick disregard for the entire sex cut her to the quick. Perhaps the moment in the greenhouse really had meant nothing.

"It wouldn't be real," Verbena continued. "You wouldn't actually be his wife, not in any way that matters. This is the only way we can be together. Don't you see?"

It was on the tip of Flora's tongue, the whole truth–*I am William, and he is me, and we are something altogether strange; can you love me regardless?*–but how could she? How could she say the most dangerous of words without first being certain that Verbena could love her wholly–that she could love William? That she might accept William as her husband instead of a false one?

She struggled to concoct an argument in the face of Verbena's fiery conviction. "Would it not be better," Flora asked, "if your marriage could be a loving one?"

Verbena sighed impatiently. "I can count the number of 'loving marriages' in England on one hand," she said. "What good does it do to aspire to such impossibilities? No, I have bent my mind to the problem and *this* is the solution." Verbena stabbed a finger toward the shifting floor of the machine beneath their feet.

Flora could hear the combined sound of their heavy breathing in the silence that followed. It drowned out even the ocean. "And would you be happy?" she asked. "Married to another, seeking me out in stolen moments? An illicit affair would have us both looking over our shoulders and fearing every shadow."

Verbena sat heavily upon the bench, her hands bunched in the wet linen of her shift, clutching great heaps of it in her lap. "I would be happier than I am now, surely. What is your obsession with perfect happiness, anyway?" She scoffed, her gaze darting to the corner of the swaying room. "You may as well seek out the faeries."

Flora bristled. "The faeries might actually listen to me," she snapped. "You are not hearing what I'm saying. If you could be with me and only me, would you?"

"Of course I would!" The violence with which these words

exploded from Verbena seemed to propel her back to her feet. She stood, dripping saltwater, trembling in white-knuckled rage. "I would be riotously happy to be at your side always! If it were possible, I would wake beside you every morning in a little cottage with a funny thatched roof, with your lacework on the mantel and a large, sleepy cat dozing upon the windowsill, and there would be breakfasts and books and long strolls with no destination and no one would *ever* bother us." Her lips shook as she paused to breathe. Her gaze fastened to her skirts, which she plucked away from where they stuck like plaster to her legs. "But that is a child's dream. There is no sense in even thinking about it."

"Yes," Flora said slowly. "Clearly, you have not thought about it at all." It was not like her to speak so bitterly, but she couldn't help herself. It was the sort of conversation that had the power to change the world as she knew it, and for the worse. After this, she knew with creeping dread, nothing would be the same.

"I know you must marry for financial reasons," she said, gathering her shreds of courage, "but any husband would do, would he not? As long as he possessed some means."

"No, it must be Étienne," Verbena said. Her hands slipped around Flora's waist once more. "I've made a promise. You understand, don't you, the circumstances that might force a man in his position to marry as speedily as possible without arousing further suspicion?"

"I can understand your meaning, but not your logic," said Flora. Even if the rumors about Étienne were true, surely things were not so dire. It was not as if mobs of Londoners had stationed themselves outside his new home with flaming torches, demanding he be placed in the stocks. And besides—"Étienne could marry anyone. It does not have to be you." Flora took a step away, causing Verbena's hands to slide off her hips.

Verbena huffed, making fists at her sides. "It is too late in the race to change horses! For weeks we have cultivated this lie. Where are we supposed to find a new girl, willing and discreet, to take my place?"

"It could be done, if we tried," Flora said, though even to her own ears the protest was a weak one. Not a single name came to mind. "Surely we could at least *try*."

"Yes, of course we might. But where would *I* find a new false husband?" She gave Flora a wry look. "Do not forget, I am also ruined if I do not marry. And London is experiencing a dearth of suitable men. I should know; I've been searching for one long enough."

"Could you not marry William?" Flora blurted out.

Verbena boggled at her. "No! Because you're marrying William!" she said.

Flora shook her head. "I can't."

"Why? What's wrong with William?" Verbena placed her hands now on her own hips. "He's an excellent prospect."

"Then why not marry him yourself?" Flora retorted.

That brought Verbena up short for reasons Flora could not fathom. She watched the color drain from Verbena's pretty face and thought–hoped–she had hit upon a truth that Verbena had tried to keep hidden. That moment in the greenhouse, or when they walked through the woods–had it been real?

"Verbena–" she tried to say, but Verbena interrupted her.

"Truthfully, I do not find William to be pleasing company," said Verbena. Her gaze shot to the solitary window, giving Flora a view of her sharp profile.

"What?" Flora's voice quaked. "In what way does he displease you?"

"Several," said Verbena to the window. "He is, despite his good qualities, a novelist. As I told you before, I find such work laughable at best."

Flora sat heavily upon the seat, her wet clothes smacking against the wood. If a duelist's bullet had found its way into her heart, the damage would be minimal compared to hearing this pronouncement. Either Verbena was lying now, or she had been lying then, and why would she lie about this to the woman she claimed to love?

Oh, it was awful. Flora buried her face in her hands.

Verbena's voice sounded as if it were coming from the end of a long, dark tunnel: "I cannot conceive of a more uncomfortable life than to feign interest in his scribblings at every dinner party from now until my death. You have no such compunctions; therefore, you would make a fine match for him." She moved about the small machine, shaking out her dry clothes. "At least with Étienne, I find myself able to—to pretend at romance. I could not do the same with William. No, it would be impossible."

Flora lifted her head to stare at Verbena. "Impossible?"

"Yes." Verbena still did not meet her eyes, but picked at some loose thread along her dress's skirt. "Quite impossible. I am able to speak to him with courtesy, but only just."

Was Flora's dual nature so sundered that a woman could love one half of her yet loathe the other? William had always been, to her mind, the same set of stanzas, merely translated into a different language. If Verbena found him so abhorrent—if she could not even imagine pretending to love him—then she and Flora could find no happiness together. To do so would be to murder William Forsyth, who was innocent of all crimes save loving a woman who could not return his affections.

While these notions roiled inside Flora, her distress seemed to go completely unnoticed by Verbena. "So you see why I propose we follow the plan I have laid out. What do you say? Shall we attempt to secure a false husband for you as well?"

"No," Flora said dully.

"No?" Verbena reached for her, but Flora shrugged her arm out of reach. A tinge of admonishment colored Verbena's stare. "If William does not appeal, perhaps there is another? Not Miles, do not name him. He has told me he has no interest in marriage."

"He has?" Flora frowned. She knew this, too, to be a lie. The whole reason Miles had come to London in the first place was to find a wife, though he had admittedly not made much progress on that front.

"He has." Verbena's lips thinned to a tight line and she looked away.

Curious. Flora could not imagine such a conversation taking place without Miles informing her, but then again, a lot had happened since they'd arrived at Plas Tân. And why should Flora wish to marry Miles? He was hopelessly captivated by Étienne.

"It is not the candidate that causes concern," Flora said. Her cheeks heated with her growing rage. "Your entire scheme is anathema to me. I cannot imagine why you would ask me to follow you in this."

Verbena looked at her for a long moment, her head bent forward as if she was waiting for a flourish at the end of a jest. When none came, she reared back, her dry dress forgotten in her grip. It sagged to the floor of the machine, a dark, wet line soaking into its hem.

"I ask because we want each other," she said, "and this is how we can be together."

"Together! When you find it convenient, I suppose, and for brief moments, until such time—" Flora pressed her lips shut. She rose to her feet, wanting her full height for what she was about to say. "I do not think I could perform such acrobatics."

Verbena blinked once, her eyebrows rising to hide beneath her sweep of damp red hair. "You . . . are refusing?"

"I would always refuse such an accomplished liar."

A flash of hurt passed across Verbena's eyes, but it was swiftly dispatched. She nodded to herself a few times, then turned her back on Flora.

"I assume," she said, "that you wish to dress as we disrobed." She lifted the sodden fabric of her shift, not waiting for a reply.

Flora turned before she could see more than a glimpse of Verbena's bare calf. She bit back her habitual thank you for the consideration; a heavy silence had settled between them that could not be pierced, even by rote pleasantries. She dried herself with a bath sheet and dressed quickly, shoving her bonnet over the ruin of her hair and wishing for a piece of looking glass to check her pins. Though, given how wan and tired she felt, perhaps it was best not to see herself.

The machine rolled to a stop. They had returned to the land, leaving the sea behind.

Chapter 18

Verbena shivered as the bathing machine opened to release her and Flora. They stumbled like newborn foals onto the rocky shore, assisted wordlessly by Prudence. The moment her feet touched the ground, Flora walked straight toward the path that rose from the beach, leaving Verbena behind.

"Flora?" Verbena called to her retreating shape.

She did not pause even a moment at Verbena's cry.

Verbena tried to shove her feet into her slippers, but she gave up, instead stuffing them in her pocket bag alongside the damp sheet and shift. "Flora, wait for me, and we will walk together!"

Flora gave no sign of having heard. She climbed up the path to the manor grounds quite alone, her back straight as an arrow.

Prudence regarded Verbena with some concern. "Did your friend get seasick on the way back? I had the horse go as gentle as possible."

Verbena dredged up a smile for her. "I'm sure she doesn't blame the horse. Thank you for a lovely excursion." There was the matter of money to be paid for the service, which Verbena furnished with a pang. How few coins remained in her reticule. If only she could make Flora understand how dire her situation was—but she had explained perfectly, and the stubborn girl wouldn't budge! It made no sense.

Prudence paused in the middle of placing the bit in the horse's mouth in preparation for her journey back to town. "Would you like a ride back to the house? I can drop you on my way."

"No, thank you." Verbena clapped her hand atop her bonnet, lest the wind carry it off. Its strings dangled in the breeze, whipping along her cheeks. "I think I shall walk along the shore." What Verbena needed was time and space to think. Surely she could come up with some alternative plan that would make Flora see the light.

With a short directive to take care, Prudence led the horse to the path, the machine's wheels obliterating any trace of Flora's footprints in the sand. Verbena watched it happen, then turned and began walking down the beach, her pocket bag dangling from her fingers. The water shushed in and out in a way that proved a balm to her racing thoughts. A few times a wave arrived bolder than the ones before, washing over Verbena's bare feet and soaking the hem of her dress. She felt very alone, and very stupid, and not at all ready to face the other guests or her hostesses or anyone at all.

Especially not Flora.

Of all the results Verbena had steeled herself for, she had not expected this one. It would have been easier, she thought, if Flora had merely rejected her outright. If she had not kissed her in return. But she had, and despite this miraculous confluence of matched desires, they could not agree on the shape of their union. It seemed deeply cruel, to have been given a glimpse of Flora's sweetness only to have it wrenched away. And for what reason? Because Flora would have all of Verbena or none of her? What a perverse ultimatum!

Verbena kept her gaze on the press of her toes in the sand as she walked, watching the dampness etch out an echo of her form.

"Miss Montrose, is that you?"

Verbena shut her eyes and ground her teeth. The voice was among the least desirable sounds for her to hear at that moment: it belonged to Lord Byron. Still—she opened her eyes and lifted her head with a worn smile. No need to be rude.

Byron was seated on a flat, smooth rock that jutted out from an outcropping that met the sea. He wore no cravat nor hat, and his coat had been pressed into service as a blanket upon which he sat. His boots remained in place, however, which made sense given the rumors regarding his clubfoot.

Verbena was very aware, all of a sudden, of her own state of undress—her stockings and shoes stuffed into the dripping pocket bag, her feet scandalously naked. She dug her toes into the wet sand in a belated attempt at modesty. He gazed at her with those starkly blue eyes, not noticing her feet or not caring.

"I'm terribly sorry," he said, "but if you're looking to brood in this lonely spot, the position has already been filled."

"Pity, I have excellent references," Verbena said, grasping at jests where nothing else would serve. "Apologies. I will leave you to your brooding." She turned to go.

"Please don't." Byron rose with only a little struggle. "I daresay you won't find a better place for your own. Be my guest." He waved a hand at his crumpled suit coat.

"I couldn't steal your spot," said Verbena, hesitating.

"Well." Byron looked out over the sea. "It may be unorthodox but perhaps we could brood together." Verbena inhaled sharply at that, but he turned his gaze back to her and threw up his hands. "That was not an insinuation, for once! I only meant, if two people are burdened by the weight of their thoughts, and they wish to consider those thoughts in private, but there is no damn privacy to be found in a Welsh madhouse, for example, those two might . . . commiserate. In a way that does not imply anything untoward."

The distrust Verbena felt in her belly melted away in the face of Byron's pleading eyes. It went against her better judgment, being alone with a rake—*the* rake, the one to which all others were compared. Yet he seemed sincere enough. Furthermore, he had been very generous with Anne and Bette, so he couldn't be *all* bad.

While she hesitated, his gaze dropped to her bulging pocket bag. "If my behavior takes a turn for the worse, you may bash me in the head with that. Fill it with rocks first if it pleases you; here, there are plenty about." He stooped and began picking up stones and seashells that had collected in the nooks of the outcropping.

Verbena rolled her eyes. "Leave them," she said, and handed him her bag so that she might sit upon his spread-out coat, covering her feet as best she could with the hem of her dress.

Byron returned the bag to her with a wry look—"In case you need to defend yourself"—before sitting a foot or more away on the other side of the rock. They shared a somewhat awkward smile before Verbena turned to look out at the waves. For many long minutes, they sat in a silence that proved not entirely uncomfortable.

"Though you have no obligation to listen," Byron finally said, his voice nearly drowned out by the wind that whipped along the shore, "shall I tell you what I am brooding over?"

Verbena, being the sort of woman who hoarded information like a dragon does gems, could not let the opportunity pass her by. "It would be my pleasure," she said. "Tell me what weighs upon our great poet."

"What doesn't?" He sighed. "His wife has cast him out; his one daughter is a stranger whilst the other is in desperate need of proper schooling, which requires funds he does not have; he is in debt up to his ears; he must keep to the shadows whilst in his own homeland for the shame of it—"

Verbena made a sympathetic noise, but it made no difference. His Lordship wasn't done by half.

"—his Italian lover is likely about to cast him aside as well, at the behest of said lover's husband, who has quite inconveniently changed his mind regarding the entire arrangement; his writings are getting more hackneyed with every passing pen strike; and he cannot spend a single evening at an extremely accommodating house without unleashing bloody disaster on the poor inmates."

"Ah," Verbena said. "You were the one who stoked the fire."

Byron cut his eyes to her. "Yes. I stoked the fire. And I regret it terribly." He flicked a pebble over the water, where it skipped thrice on the waves before sinking. "I'll be lucky if Bette and Anne don't have me bundled into a carriage before luncheon. Not that I blame them; I am mad, bad, and altogether miserable. I'd hoped to stay until at least the end of the week, but—well, I'm fast running out of friends who will have me. There seems not a soul left in Britain who loves me any longer."

He pressed his face to his upturned knees and began to weep. Verbena was shocked by this naked display of emotion—poets were certainly a different breed. They were not like the other gentlemen of her acquaintance, who kept their loves and sorrows locked away behind a door marked PROPRIETY.

Say what you like about Lord Byron, but even the harshest critic had to admit he did not shy away from that which made him human.

Verbena was not sure how to react. Her lifetime of etiquette lessons had not touched on a situation like this. She lifted a hand, retracted it, then committed to placing it delicately atop Byron's shaking shoulder.

"There, there," she said, patting him. "It can't be as dire as all that."

This was, she knew almost right away, the wrong thing to say. Similar things had been said to her at her lowest points—a flash of how betrayal felt, even all these years later, like a poisoned blade in her spine—so she parroted them.

Foolish, she told herself. *Very foolish.*

Byron, though, was too polite to say so (perhaps for the first time in his life). He merely raised his head and gave her a watery smile through his tears. "Yes, I'm sure you're right," he said, though of course they both knew she wasn't. He dabbed at his wet face with his lacy shirt cuff. "Enough about my woes. Do you care to share your own?"

"No, thank you," Verbena said, swifter than she'd meant to. She tucked her hand back in her lap and faced the ocean, watching the waves roll in, then recede. There was no reason to share even the vaguest shape of her troubles with anyone, least of all a man well-known for his loose tongue and quick pen. Then again . . .

Was there anyone in the world less likely to bat an eye at her situation than Lord Byron? Compared to his own tribulations, hers was a tame affair. And what harm could he do? It wasn't as if he could reveal anything, lest he also reveal his clandestine return to Britain; in a perverse way, her secrets were safer with him than any other person.

While she considered all this, Byron began skipping stones. His first attempt was met with failure, the pebble sinking at the first touch of the water. "Rotten," he muttered, and scrounged around for another stone.

Verbena cleared her throat. "Have you ever loved someone you shouldn't?" she asked.

Byron gave her a look of frank disbelief. "Miss Montrose, you are familiar with my reputation, are you not? I am something of an expert on the subject."

"How do you avoid it?" Verbena asked. She rearranged the hem of her dress, tucking her toes into its soft fabric. "How do you–disengage yourself so that it does not ruin you?" Her carefully orchestrated life, her machinations and dealings: it was all on the verge of crumbling. Shameful tears pricked at her eyes, though she would not let them fall.

Byron sighed heavily and placed his own hand on Verbena's shoulder. He was a sight better at it than she'd been, his touch firm but gentle. "That," he said, "I know nothing about. All my life, I've only ever run headlong into ruin. I can tell you the exact dance steps, if you wish, but I have no experience in salvation." He scooted closer on the rock, whispering though there was no one else about. "I am not insensible to the terrible unfairness that exists between us. I have been allowed my dalliances and sins– have been celebrated and scorned for them in equal measure, but *allowed.* I was given the exquisite chance to fall, with open arms and a red, bursting heart, and damn the rest to hell. A woman, on the other hand . . ."

Verbena's jaw trembled as she withheld the pressing onslaught of tears. "I can only imagine my mother's face if I told her to damn anything to hell," she said, laughing wetly.

Byron smiled. "I do not have to imagine my own mother's reply. I heard it. Repeatedly."

A frisson of discomfort went through Verbena. It was a known fact that Byron's mother had died while he was abroad. A sad affair. Even those who despised him thought so. "I am sorry," she said.

"Well." He skipped another stone. It went quite far, four skips in toto. "We can climb all the mountains we like, or swim all the Hellesponts, but we can never be free of our mothers, can we? A mother's love and ire will follow us down into the grave. One may as well do as one pleases, as it will happen regardless."

"There is truth in what you say." Verbena peered across the ocean. "About this, and the allowances not afforded to a woman. She must, I think, walk on the knife edge all her life, terrified of the consequences should she fall."

"Yes, we cannot all take mysterious countesses as lovers to avoid paying our bills," Byron mused. He glanced in her direction, his eyes lingering on her face. "Though I know one or two countesses who would clamber to be introduced to you, Miss Montrose."

The comment was so shocking, Verbena could do nothing but laugh. "You are incorrigible!"

He schooled his face into mock offense. "I am only honest! These Italian women, their husbands are for show; it would be more shocking in that society if they didn't seek out affairs."

Verbena felt her face heat. "Is that so? How excessive." As if she herself had not devised that exact sort of plan.

"There is still, however, a strange expectation of loyalty." Byron seemed not to notice how flustered she'd become, too preoccupied with voicing his further thoughts on the subject. "Personally, I cannot countenance this Italian obsession with keeping one's lovers for one's exclusive use. Mark me, there will come a time when all societies will ask, 'For whom are we locking up our mistresses? Why all this base greed?' Love, in my opinion, can stand a little more freedom of movement."

"Careful, sir," Verbena said. "Once lovers possess the wherewithal to do as they please, they may find that what is most pleasing is not you at all."

She meant it as a jest, and Byron took it as intended. He had the look of a schoolboy about him, shrugging good-naturedly. "That is their right," he said. "As long as they'll have me, fleeting though it may be–well, I simply abhor being lonely." He quieted, staring out at the waves. Just as Verbena expected him to lapse into another round of sobs, he brightened. "Do you know what a brooding like this calls for?" he asked.

"I confess I do not."

"A ball," Byron said.

"A ball," Verbena repeated.

"A *masquerade* ball. It's just the thing. When I am banished back to London, I shall make the arrangements with speed." He tipped his head back and laughed. "I am telling you, Miss Montrose, you have not lived if you have not seen Venice at Carnevale. There is nothing so wonderful as being surrounded by masked figures, your own identity obscured, so that all may act without fear of their reputations. Put on a mask and the truth comes tumbling out!"

"And where do you propose to host this masquerade?" Verbena said. "You just told me you have worn out your welcome in nearly every corner of Britain."

Byron waved away this concern. "The Calliope has a ballroom; I am sure I can manage to negotiate its use, given that this will be *the* event of the season. Champagne from France. Caviar from Persia. Wine from Rome. Potatoes done several ways." (His Lordship worshipped potatoes, a fact that was well-known to Verbena and all others who followed such trends.) "I will invite a healthy mix of artists and the ton, and no one will be able to scoff at mixing when their identities are secret. You will be there, of course."

"Of course," Verbena said, though inwardly she prayed she might find some excuse not to attend once the invitations were sent. She wasn't sure how much more excitement she could take this season. "And the expense? Forgive me, but how do you propose to procure all this champagne and caviar and wine?" The potatoes, she felt, were the only sensible part of his plan, and so were not mentioned.

Byron paused, worrying his lip. "You make an excellent point. I doubt anyone would extend a loan to me, especially when I'm not supposed to be in the country."

For all his faults, it was depressing to see Byron stymied like this. Some men had bigger dreams than they did bank accounts, a situation Verbena also found herself in currently. That shared circumstance moved her to speak. "Lady Croydon has often said to me how dearly she wishes for more excitement. Perhaps you could make inquiries. She might wish to invest in your vision."

"The dowager countess? Yes." Byron stroked his singular chin. "That might just work. I will send some letters, see what can be done. Thank you, Miss Montrose." He smiled at her, though his face fell as he looked over her shoulder at something in the distance. "Damn. For a lonely spot, we're getting an awful lot of visitors."

Verbena frowned, turning to see Penny coming toward them. The maid drew close enough that she could shout without the wind whipping away her words.

"Miss Montrose, I must speak to you." Her eyes darted to Lord Byron. "And only you."

Verbena shot to her feet, pulse thrumming. "What is it? What's happened?" She worried for Flora, who might have returned to the manor in a state of terrible grief. If some awful fate had befallen her, and the last words between them had been said in anger . . .

Byron, still lounging on the rock, held up his palms defensively. "Penny, my dear, I'd like you to know that Miss Montrose and I have only been engaged in conversation and nothing else."

Penny ignored him. "Best come with me, Miss Montrose."

Verbena left Byron to his brooding without hesitation, following the maid down the beach. She waited until they were many yards distant before daring to speak. "What's wrong? Is it Flora?"

"Miss Witcombe?" Penny frowned in confusion. "Why should anything be wrong with her?"

Verbena chose to leave that question unanswered. Her mind raced to find another candidate for disaster. "Is it Mr. McDonald, then? What does the doctor say?" As much as she disliked the idea of Flora having tender feelings for the man, Verbena didn't wish him dead. She wasn't *that* cutthroat.

"Mr. McDonald is in good health," Penny said, keeping pace along the sand. "A note from the village doctor arrived whilst you were bathing; he's been bandaged up and is on his way back to Plas Tân."

"Then what's the matter?"

Penny's voice dropped to a whisper, even though Byron was but a speck in the distance and there wasn't another soul in sight. "I overheard some of the other guests outside the stable. I don't know who spoke; I didn't see. They were talking about that man

Charbonneau–about how he'd been doing lewd things in the cloakroom with another man last night."

Verbena stopped, her feet sinking into the wet sand. Penny obliged her by stopping as well.

"That is absurd," Verbena said. Étienne would not risk such a thing, not at this critical juncture! Would he?

Penny continued as Verbena's thoughts raced. "I know you and he are courting, which is why I thought to tell you right away." She shrugged. "Servants hear all sorts of things. And we know how fast a rumor can spread. The folks around here won't care, of course, but if it gets back to London . . ."

"Right. Yes, of course." Verbena picked up her skirts. What mattered now was preserving Étienne's reputation. Good lord, if he'd actually been so foolish as to make an assignation– "Penny, did you happen to overhear who the supposed second man in the cloakroom was?" She had a notion it had been Miles, though perhaps Étienne's lustful urges had guided him to some other man last night. A single romp in the woods could have been sufficient, she supposed, for those two.

Penny shook her head. "Whoever he was, miss, the whisperers either don't know or don't care."

Verbena gave Penny a nod of thanks and rushed back toward the manor.

The dogcart was pulling into the driveway when she at last made her way to the front of the house. Étienne was at the reins. Miles was laid out in the cart with a stark white bandage on his arm. He raised his good arm at Verbena's approach. "Miss Montrose, hello there!" His speech sounded somewhat slurred, as if the doctor had given him a draft that dulled his senses. "A lovely day, isn't it?"

"Mr. McDonald, I am glad to hear you're well," she called to him. Then, practically pulling Étienne down to the ground, she whispered, "I need to speak with you."

"My dear, you have no shoes," Étienne said.

"Never mind that," Verbena said, and tugged him bodily into the nearby rose garden, leaving a very confused Miles to navigate a one-armed dismount on his own.

Étienne twisted to watch him do so as he was frog-marched away. "Let me at least help him," he said.

"Miles will be fine. You, on the other hand . . ." Verbena manhandled Étienne behind a tall shrub cut into the shape of an overlarge corgi pup. It was quiet here, no one else about. Verbena lowered her voice anyway. "People are saying you were in the cloakroom last night."

Étienne frowned. "Oh?"

"With a man," Verbena added.

That made Étienne's eyes go wide and round. "As in—?"

"I'm afraid so."

"But that is ludicrous! I did nothing of the kind," Étienne cried. "I spent the entire bonfire night in the company of Mr. McDonald."

"Yes, that is what I am afraid of."

"Hold your tongue. All we did was talk!" He thought for a moment. "Excepting the few times Miles excused himself. Once or twice he left with that man, the writer—Forsyth. But he returned directly. I did not meet anyone in a cloak closet!"

"I believe you, I do," Verbena said. The man seemed genuinely offended by the accusation in a way she didn't think could be faked. "But it doesn't matter what I believe. It doesn't matter what is true. The only thing that matters is how others perceive you."

"Apparently I am perceived as a filthy little sodomite who will dally with a man when given the slightest chance." A beat. "It is normally true, but it was not last night!" he wailed.

Verbena glanced around the garden. "You mustn't shout so. The other guests here at Plas Tân tend toward the . . . artistic, yes? They have come to visit the ladies, who are themselves quite unusual and beloved for it. Perhaps this gossip is harmless."

Even as she said it, she did not trust in her words. Verbena had never met a harmless piece of gossip in her life. All scandal could be fashioned into a blade. It was only a matter of who wielded it.

Watching Étienne's face crumple into despair, she knew he shared this view. "And what happens when word reaches London?" he asked. "You know it will. These artists, their tongues have not stopped wagging since we arrived. They may not wish me ill for my penchants, but once the rumor leaves this circle of like-minded society, it will be over for me." His breathing became rapid and labored. "My brothers, our shop—my very neck!"

Verbena shushed him, taking him by the shoulders to give him a shake. "Keep your head. Think of everything Lord Byron has done and been accused of doing. He has survived, has he not?"

"I am not Lord Byron!" Étienne cried. "I do not have his title or his pretty words to shield me. I do not even have English blood, for god's sake! I will be ruined." He put his face in his hands and began to weep.

For the second time in the hour, Verbena found herself in the unenviable position of attempting to comfort a man in the throes of high emotion. At least with Étienne, she had no qualms in embracing him, and so she did.

"It's all right," she said, petting his curls. "It will be all right." What sort of monster was she, that she had been so distracted by her own troubles when this tragedy was playing out at her doorstep? What right had she to dream of a life with Flora at her side when there were more pressing matters? She had made a promise to her friend; she had placed him in this position and made him more vulnerable to scrutiny. It was her duty to see him safely through.

Verbena supposed if she was ever going to learn to be selfless, it was now.

"We are out of time," she murmured into Étienne's soft hair. "I had hoped for more, but we cannot linger."

Étienne lifted his wet face from her breast, where he had dampened the fabric of her dress. "What are you saying?"

"I'm saying—" Verbena closed her eyes and listened to the sound of the sea in the distance, forever heaving and moving. In and out, given and taken, calling to her. She would have to learn to ignore it. "I'm saying," she said quietly, "that we must announce our engagement today."

"Today!" Étienne squawked.

"Today," she confirmed. "And we must marry with all due haste." She sighed. "As unfashionable though it may be."

Chapter 19

"Do you think it might be wise to have the wedding outside of London?" Étienne asked from somewhere around the level of Verbena's knee. A pin sank into the soft flesh of her thigh.

"Prick!" Verbena cried through gritted teeth.

"Ah, sorry!" Étienne fought his way through the cloud of tulle currently strewn about Verbena's waist. His mouth was brimming with pins; it was only due to his great skill that he was able to speak without dropping any. "I hesitate to make any excuse, but you must realize I have not had much experience in this. Men's clothing tends to be much more . . . straightforward."

Verbena held back a sigh. "And yet you insist on making not only your own wedding clothes, but mine." The sting of the pinprick was fading, but the pain of the entire situation? That still lingered.

Étienne gestured with his tailor's chalk. "A gown like this is a work of art. How can I allow the opportunity to pass me by?" Her betrothed disappeared beneath her voluminous skirts once more. "Did you hear my earlier question, my dear?"

Verbena thought back. "You want to have the wedding outside of London? Where would we go?"

"To Market Eden," came the muffled reply. "Or rather, the Eden estate. Apparently, I have taken possession of the whole of Eden Abbey, according to my customers. Four have wished me a hearty congratulations already."

Verbena started, risking another jab. "How on earth did they get that idea?"

Étienne must have shrugged; the tulle heaved up and down. "Certainly not from me. Owning a house here in town is enough, in my opinion. I suppose, as the ton ponders how I came into such good fortune, they must inevitably come to silly conclusions. You would not believe the things I have heard secondhand." He resurfaced, red-faced, to whisper: "They say I am Lord Eden's long-lost half brother. Or I murdered him and forged his signature on various documents. Or I am the missing Lord Eden in disguise, and I am only playing at being a tailor and a Frenchman as a–how do you say? Lark?"

Verbena tipped her head back with a groan, staring up at the ceiling. It was much closer than most ceilings of her acquaintance, as the back room of Étienne's workshop was quite cozy. It was also stuffed to the gills with more bolts of fabric than seemed possible. (Étienne collected them, not trusting London drapers to have the exact shade or weave he required at the appropriate time.)

"I should have known the gossipmongers would be operating at full tilt, even after our announcement," she said.

They had cut their visit at Plas Tân short, returning to the city with Flora and Miles (bandaged arm and all) via an interminable carriage ride. No one spoke more than a handful of words for the entire journey. Where talk was rare, the glances were many and charged. Verbena could hardly keep track of how many times an intense look had passed between her and Flora, and her and Étienne, and Étienne and Miles, and, maddeningly, Miles and Flora. The final leg of travel brought them into London as night settled like a shroud over that great city. Verbena had felt it as she felt the pall cast over her heart. Flora was the first to disembark, and she had done so wordlessly, with only a solemn glance over her shoulder at the others. Verbena had tried to call out to her, but she had already disappeared into her building, leaving the driver to drag her trunks up behind her.

The day after the next, the notice appeared in the papers: Miss Montrose was destined to wed the successful man of business and fashion, Monsieur Charbonneau, lately of Savile Row. In the days that followed, Verbena received many letters wishing her well in her impending marriage. The veritable flood of sentiments lacked one distinct voice: she had not heard from nor seen Flora since that awful, silent carriage ride. Verbena had sent a short note round to Maiden Lane, a cordial message containing nothing but hope for a reply. There had been none.

It was difficult to play the chess game of high society when the bulk of Verbena's thoughts were occupied with Flora. Would she ever so much as see her friend again?

"My dear?" Étienne's hand rested on her ankle. "Do you have any preference? Here or Eden?"

Verbena shook herself from her stupor and smiled down at him. There was no need to burden her husband-to-be with her troubles; he had plenty of his own.

"I am thinking," she said, and then did so quickly. "It may behoove us to hold the wedding at Eden. Anything that removes us from the prying eyes of London." The ceremony itself would be a modest affair, as they always were; even among the ton, the engagement announcement held more importance than the act itself. If Étienne was already the subject of so many wild whispers, any distance from their audience would be to their benefit. Besides, Verbena could admit that the idea of being married on a sprawling country estate had its charms. There was only one problem. "You do not actually own the place, though. However would we manage such a thing?"

Étienne sunk more pins into the dress's hem. "Here is where it becomes rather strange," he said as he worked. "Truthfully, it would have never occurred to me at all, but I received an odd letter from Market Eden–the village, you see. Signed by several upstanding citizens: the postmistress, the farmers, the tavern master, a few shopkeepers. They seemed to slyly imply that I was their new landlord, as Christopher was absent, and that they were keen to welcome me to Eden Abbey–so long as I, like the absent Christopher, did not get it into my head to start assuming the usual duties of a landlord."

"I see," Verbena murmured. "It serves the village folk if everyone thinks you're the new master at Eden, and they are offering you a chance to claim that title though you have no legal standing—if, that is, you do not charge them rent."

"Provincial villagers," Étienne said, "are often very clever. I know; I used to be one myself."

"Well, you have no intention of charging them rent, do you?"

Étienne gave an affronted gasp. "Never! I would die before I joined the vile brotherhood of landlords; my brothers and I pay a criminal amount monthly for this very shop. If they wish me to pretend, I do not mind. I am already pretending at so many other things." He finished the hem of Verbena's gown, then sat back on his heels to regard his work. "Turn for me?" he asked, spinning his finger in the air in demonstration.

Verbena executed a turn, feeling the silky fabric swish about her. Now that all the layers were pinned in place, the dress took on a slimming silhouette with the bodice gathered tightly beneath her breasts. A silver manteau lined in blush-colored satin fell from her shoulders to cascade down her back. This, along with the dress itself, was trimmed in the finest embroidery, bursting with pink rosebuds, blue violets, and green vines.

"It's beautiful," she said, looking down at herself. Étienne had done exquisite work. For some strange reason, tears choked her throat. It didn't seem right that she should wear such a gorgeous thing while feeling so miserable.

"Only as beautiful as its owner." Étienne rose to his feet and gave her a peck on her cheek. He studied her face closely. "My dear, are you well?"

Verbena waved him away. "I'm fine. And so is this notion of yours about the wedding. We should go to Eden. It's strategically beneficial."

"How lucky I will be, to have such a strategic wife." Étienne gathered her hands in his. "I will make all the arrangements. I hear the Abbey has fallen into disuse; we will need servants to see to it and us, at least for a short while. Do not worry about a thing. My brothers are so happy that I am finally marrying, they will pay for whatever I need."

"That is good of them." Verbena managed a smile, though it felt weak on her lips. "I should get out of this dress and go. Can you imagine the rumors if we were discovered in the back room alone?"

Étienne rolled his eyes. "Quelle monstrueux. They would cast me as the Don Juan of Byron's verses, I suppose. I have been reading them. Quite amusing! For an Englishman."

That made Verbena's smile a little more real. Her life would not be so awful, she thought, married to this man. He was a sight better than most. Not to mention handy with a needle.

He helped her out of the gown and into her ordinary walking dress, taking care to position her bonnet on her head just so. She bid him good-bye and left the shop.

Verbena walked south on Savile Row, not wanting to return home just yet. As the engagement notice had already been printed in all the papers, there was little her parents could do to stop the proceedings, yet that did not curb their disappointment—nor their cruelty. Apparently, Mrs. Montrose had been holding out hope for a baron at the very least and was furious that Verbena had not consulted her before accepting Étienne. As punishment for Verbena's failings, she found herself ignored by everyone in the household. Even the servants had been instructed not to speak to her. It was like living in a tomb, playing the part of the ghost.

She chewed the inside of her cheek as she made her way along the crooked London streets. It wouldn't matter; soon she would be living with Étienne in Bloomsbury.

She hardly noticed that she'd been walking toward St. James's until she was inside the park, surrounded by the bustle of nannies and their wards out for their daily perambulation, along with gentlemen and ladies promenading. The weather was better than usual, and as she had no desire to rush home, she opened her lace-trimmed parasol and joined the throngs. She was one of the rare women walking alone in the park that afternoon, she noticed. Most were paired with men or strolling with one or two of their lady friends. One such threesome passed her by, laughing at something that had been said. Verbena watched them go with a maudlin twinge in her chest.

She missed Flora terribly. Their letters, their meandering conversations, their shared love of gossip—though Verbena would also be content simply sitting in her company. That seemed impossible, though, what with the impasse they had reached. Her slow stroll was punctuated with ruminations on how she could return Flora to her side. Was it even possible to transform from near lovers to arm's-length friends? Perhaps not. Perhaps that was for the best.

So consumed was she with these thoughts, she nearly walked headlong into another lone pedestrian. Only at the last possible moment did nimble hands fly to her shoulders to arrest her with a cry of "Careful, miss!"

She recognized the voice before she saw the face. William Forsyth stared back at her, wide-eyed. His eyes were a very charming shade of hazel, Verbena noted. Very similar to Flora's, now that she thought of it.

"Miss Montrose," he said.

"Mr. Forsyth."

They stared at each other some more before William released his grip on her shoulders, taking a full step backward and nearly knocking into a toddling baby in the process. A nursemaid, thankfully, grabbed the child by the arm and tugged it out of the way. Verbena saw all this, though William was too busy gaping at her to do the same. She was not sure why he was so affected by their chance meeting, but as for herself, she had not seen or spoken to him since that night in the hothouse, where things had been left in a quite unsatisfactory fashion.

"You are returned from Wales?" he finally asked.

"It would appear so." Verbena winced at the snap in her voice. She did not want to become bitter, though it seemed inevitable. Unloved women often did. "And yourself? Have you returned recently?"

"Yes, rather recently."

There was an awkward pause.

"What a wonderful place Plas Tân is," Verbena offered.

William grasped this thread of conversation like a sailor would a lifeline. "Yes! Most invigorating. And the scenery—"

"Oh, second to none," Verbena agreed.

They smiled at each other, as conversationalists do when they've managed a passable volley. Then the tension returned as they both realized they needed to continue somehow.

"Have you, erm, received a somewhat cryptic invitation to a ball at the Calliope Club?" William asked.

"I have!" Verbena had never been so relieved to have an invitation to discuss. The card had arrived the day prior, complete with embossed fleur-de-lis and the winged lion of Venice. Clearly Byron did not intend for anyone to ignore the masquerade theme. "Are you planning to attend?"

William's face took on a pained cast. "No, I think not. I find myself not in the mood for a masquerade." He looked down and away. "And yourself? Will you be attending?"

"Ah, probably not," said Verbena. "The wedding . . . there is much to do."

"Right. Yes. My most heartfelt felicitations, by the way. Monsieur Charbonneau is an exceedingly lucky man." Tragically, he sounded absolutely sincere.

"Thank you," said Verbena, attempting the same.

The conversation stalled once more. Verbena could not imagine continuing in this manner, with inane pleasantries and nothing of substance.

"Mr. Forsyth," she said, "I feel I must apologize."

His entire face fell. "If anyone is to apologize, Miss Montrose, surely I am the one—"

"No, no." Verbena held up her hand, then glanced about the park grounds. The crowds were so thick that some passersby were obliged to glance their way, if only to avoid a collision. Yet Verbena could not help but feel that the eyes lingered on the two of them specifically.

She was an engaged woman speaking with a single man. In broad daylight, of course, but the picture they made could be interpreted . . . not so kindly. If they stayed in this spot, they would only attract more looks.

William seemed as attuned to this as she was. "Shall we walk down to the canal?" he proposed. "It's such a lovely day."

"Yes," Verbena said, smiling nervously. "London only has so many."

It was an old joke, one that Londoners had been trotting out since before the Romans put up their walls, but William still laughed gamely. He did not, Verbena noticed, offer his arm, apparently preferring to keep his distance. Verbena feigned a need to fuss with her parasol, and so the awkwardness was sidestepped. She wondered at this attitude of William's; she knew she had behaved abominably at Plas Tân, but that should inspire confusion or disgust on his part, not—pain.

And he did appear pained, barely able to look her way, let alone hold her gaze. His face was drawn and pale even as he attempted to smile at acquaintances that passed or the ducks waddling across the lane. He flexed his right hand open and closed as they walked, making fists into starfish again and again. Verbena watched this movement with curiosity.

"Is your hand troubling you?" she asked.

"Hm?" William glanced down at his own arm as if surprised to find the appendage attached to him. His hand was splayed out, but he dropped it limply to his side. "A minor ache, that is all."

"The writer's affliction," Verbena said knowingly. "Our mutual friend Miss Witcombe suffers from the same injury."

"Does she?" William examined the ducks with renewed vigor. "I suppose she must."

Verbena cleared her throat and faced forward, pretending great interest in a flowering hedge of some kind. "Have you heard from Miss Witcombe lately?" she asked.

The man jolted as if he'd come into contact with a burning lump of coal sans tongs. "Erm, a little. Here and there. You know us writers," he said with a poorly executed chuckle, "always turning up at the same salons, the usual readings. Why do you ask?"

"I have unfortunately been out of touch with her since we returned from Wales," Verbena said. "I wonder if you might—that is, the next time you see her—" She stopped at the very edge of the canal, where the water lapped at the mud. Her throat was quite tight.

William hovered at her side. "Might I . . . ?" he prompted.

"Could you tell her I hope she is able to visit me sometime? As she used to do," Verbena said in a rush. "Or I could visit her if it is more convenient." She gazed into William's concerned face; he was short for a man, and so she didn't need to tip her head back quite so much.

It occurred to Verbena that William's height was very similar to Flora's. In fact, she mused, the two of them must be of a height if Verbena could face them on the same level. The thought tickled something in her mind, a thrilling sensation for one who enjoyed puzzles.

William, however, looked ill at her request. "I . . . will be certain to pass along your message," he said.

What a paltry thing the message would be! All polite nonsense when what Verbena truly wanted was to clasp Flora in her arms and cry, *I abhor the state of us! Please forgive me.*

She licked her trembling lips. William very gallantly looked away, she noticed. "Perhaps," she said, "it might be better if you could pass on a letter. I find I have much to say to our Miss Witcombe, and it would be unfair to expect you to memorize an entire essay."

William shifted on his feet, the point of his walking stick sinking deeper into the earth as it bore his weight. He peered at her like she was a specimen and he, one of the new scientists who made a study of such things. "You have that much information to impart?"

Verbena looked down at where the hem of her walking dress met the ground. She twirled her parasol for something to do. "I could fill a tome," she said with no sense of self-preservation. "Several, if I was not interrupted." She tried to smile, though it slipped from her face as she glanced up at William's serious visage. "Please, Mr. Forsyth. I have tried everything else to reach her. I would not make this request of you if it were not terribly important."

William placed both his hands, one stacked upon the other, atop the brass head of his walking stick and looked out over the canal. A pair of ducks, a drake and hen, splashed in the shallow gray water, and seemed to occupy the whole of his attention.

"Do you not agree," William said slowly, looking only at the ducks, "that heartbreak can be so painful, so horrid, that some things are best left unsaid? Wounds cannot heal if they are continually prodded, just as our writers' hands will always ache if we never cease in our work."

A cold chill ran down Verbena's spine. Perhaps Flora was once again on intimate terms with William; how else could William know the shape of their separation if Flora had not confided in him? She fought the feeling of betrayal and—yes, jealousy.

Flora had William with whom to share her secret burden, while Verbena had no one.

"A wound unchecked might also fester," she said. "The afflicted limb may never be the same, but with treatment, one might salvage something of its old use."

William closed his eyes, his face pinched as he rubbed at the bones of his left wrist. "You will be a married woman soon."

"Yes, under circumstances our dear friend understands quite well," Verbena snapped. "Or has she not seen fit to share those particulars with you? She seems to have shared everything else."

A strange sort of vacillation overtook William. He opened and closed his mouth several times. "Flora has not been gossiping with me, if that's what you mean. I have only . . . inferred certain points."

Inferred! Verbena glared at a couple passing by much too close. After they had moved on, she continued. "Will you help me or not? A letter delivered discreetly, that is all I ask."

He turned to her at last, and the agony in his eyes made her stifle a gasp. There was a sheen of tears there as well, the sight so familiar, Verbena felt the odd sensation of having this very conversation at some other date. But that was impossible. Everything William embodied, actually, was altogether impossible.

"I am sorry," he said. "I cannot be your messenger."

And here we must pause, dear reader.

Cleverness was to Verbena as natural as drawing breath, yet in that moment, she cursed herself as the worst kind of fool. What had once been muddied waters were now perfectly clear. We can forgive her, for how is anyone supposed to see the truth when the veil of lies has been draped atop every bowed head from the moment of our birth? But we digress, if only to enumerate what Verbena had at last come to realize.

Thing the first: William was in love with her. No man could look as he looked and sound as he sounded without being desperately, hopelessly in love. And she knew that look because–thing the second–she had so recently seen its twin on Flora's own face.

Verbena's gaze drifted down to William's fine-boned hands, which he was once more preoccupied with massaging. If Verbena were braver and more presumptuous, she could have taken his right hand in hers and felt the same calluses that Flora bore. She had done it before, had she not? In that dark greenhouse, the air thick with wet life, William's palm a contrast of soft and rough in her grasp. She had not made the connection at the time because it would be inconceivable for anyone to make such a leap, and yet–and yet–

Facts slipped into place like dinner guests at their assigned seats. He was her, and she was him, and the two were one. Simplicity itself.

What a relief it was to discover one's affections had not been cruelly divided, but rather delightfully fixed! What a joy, knowing one's heart recognized its mate before one's eye could. It was like something out of a fairy tale.

Except, of course, Verbena had never believed in fairy tales, rejecting them even in leading strings as frivolous nonsense. Reality impressed itself upon her like a marble slab. Even if she was correct in her assumptions, she could not make any move to indicate what she knew, or thought she knew, not while in St. James's surrounded by what seemed like half the population of London. Furthermore, the truth did not change her circumstances. She was promised to Étienne, and to dissolve that union now would be tantamount to throwing him to the wolves.

But surely William could understand that. Why did he not

confess to her so that they might be as Verbena had planned originally, outside the bonds of wedlock but together nonetheless? Did he not think her worth the trouble an affair might cause? If only she could persuade him without wielding her knowledge of his secret like a rapier—if only she could describe how welcome he would be in her bed, as himself, as Flora, as anyone he wished, so long as he touched her with those aching, callused hands.

"Miss Montrose?"

Verbena roused herself from her quiet ruminations. All these thoughts had flashed through her quick mind over the span of an eyeblink, yet her spirit felt them as if an eon had passed. She looked into William's sweet, sad eyes and saw in them the same soul that existed within Flora. It was like being shown a vision in angled mirrors, which projected the figure again and again into infinity.

"Yes?" she said, strangled.

"I was saying, I apologize that I cannot be of use to you in this matter," said William, "but I think it best if I abstain from any involvement."

Verbena looked about helplessly. The park teemed with witnesses. "Perhaps, Mr. Forsyth, we should adjourn elsewhere and discuss this matter more privately." She needed only to tell him what she suspected, and time to convince him she loved him regardless.

"Privately." William's voice was flat.

"Yes," Verbena said. She looked to him beseechingly, begging him silently to understand her meaning. "There is so much to discuss. You, and I, and our dear . . . friend, Miss Witcombe." *Oh, please understand me!*

Yet William would not. He shook his head, his voice dropping to the smallest whisper. "It would not be prudent," he said, "for any of us."

"But—" Verbena tried.

"You are affianced," William said, his eyes flashing with that stubborn fire Verbena knew so well. How silly she had been not to have noticed Flora in him before now. "You can no longer afford to meet with unmarried men in private. Simply speaking to me here is too dangerous. All your plans, all your machinations–it will all be for nothing if you persist."

"*William,*" she said, and spoke into those syllables all she could not say.

William reared back as if slapped. His eyes were large and damp. "Don't," he murmured. "Please."

Verbena cursed the hundreds of eyes that surrounded them. If not for their audience, if not for propriety, she would do more than simply say his name. How could she not wish to comfort the man when he was so clearly exposing his most vulnerable parts to her?

There was something of a poet in him, she thought. A laugh threatened to burble out of her; there was very literally a poet in him, or rather, a poetess.

She dared place a hand on his arm in sympathy, casting about for something to say that would not spell his ruin. "Will I see you again before the season ends?"

The final weeks were rapidly approaching. A few more balls, a handful of lavish events, and then the ton would disperse to the country until the following spring.

William shook his head. "I fear you won't."

"Perhaps I could persuade you to come to Lord Byron's masquerade," she said, casting about for some pretense to speak again. "Perhaps we might–"

"I am sorry," William said. "A worthier gentleman has earned his spot on your dance card."

Verbena flushed all over, her skin growing hot. It was only due to her legendary possession of self that she did not inform him of the truth: that she knew of none more worthy than he. "I do not dance," she said instead. "I am quite famous for it."

"Of course. I nearly forgot. Pointless, then, to argue about it." William took two steps away from her. With a determined jut of his jaw, he touched the brim of his hat. "Good-bye, Miss Montrose," he said, and disappeared into the crowd.

Verbena watched him leave the park, a mournful shape in a sea of color.

To any other woman, this would have been an ending. For Verbena, this was merely another variable. She might still succeed; she had to.

She strode back toward Mayfair, already composing the first of many letters in her head.

Chapter 20

Flora sighed as she waited her turn to enter the ballroom, her commedia dell'arte mask a heavy weight across her nose and cheeks. It was a handsome piece of work, painted in diamonds of green and blue, matching her gown to perfection. The half mask sported a frill of peacock feathers along the brow in a sort of plumed cap.

She wished she had opted for one of the full-face masks that covered their wearers from chin to hairline; it would have kept her frown concealed from the other guests. She had had no desire to attend this function whatsoever, not when her heart lay broken in pieces by the canal in St. James's. Yet when her acquaintance Belinda Chesterfield, another poetess from the Calliope Club, sent her a letter saying a mysterious patron wanted to meet with her at the ball for the purposes of commissioning a new set of works, what else could Flora do but agree? The season would be over shortly, after all, and the chances for patronage would be slim until the following year, when the ton began throwing their riches about once more. Flora supposed she should be grateful for the chance to earn a little more coin for her rented rooms, and even more grateful that Mrs. Chesterfield was willing to lend out her husband so that Flora could meet her potential benefactor at this infernal masquerade as proposed.

"Are you all right, Miss Witcombe?" Mr. Horace Chesterfield whispered at her elbow. He had apparently caught her miserable expression.

She attempted a smile, though the corners of her mouth barely lifted. "I'm fine." She patted his arm, which was looped gallantly through hers. "Thank you again for escorting me."

As much as they flouted the laws of etiquette, even the Calliope would not allow an unpartnered, unchaperoned woman to attend their ball. Normally the choice of Mr. Horace Chesterfield as a chaperone–married and in no way related to Flora by blood–would have been forbidden, yet the rules on the invitations demanded complete anonymity. Any man would do, and as Mr. Chesterfield had planned to attend anyway, it seemed more convenient than dragging Miles to this wretched event.

They at last reached the ballroom door and handed their invitation to the master of ceremonies, who had no reason to think they were anything but man and wife, or brother and sister, or any number of acceptable pairings. He merely ushered them inside the ballroom.

Byron had outdone himself. A gigantic chandelier of purple and gold paste gems had been hung from the center of the ceiling, ablaze with opulent candlelight. A troupe of musicians in half masks played against the far wall. Salvers of wineglasses were borne by servants dressed as harlequins and Pierrots, their masked faces doll-like and eerie. Several hundred revelers were decked out in all their masquerade finery: feathers and lace, flowers and satin, dripping in jewels both real and false. Some wore costumes that concealed their identities completely, but most had made only the barest gesture in that direction. Flora recognized several members of her club, alongside the dowager countess and her entourage.

It was an exhilarating scene, but Flora wanted nothing more than to be home.

But first, she had business to attend to. "Mrs. Chesterfield mentioned that this patron was quite eager to speak with me before supper is served," she said into Mr. Chesterfield's ear. "How will I know him?"

Mr. Chesterfield shrugged affably. "Belinda said he would know you by your mask and approach you directly."

Flora touched the feathered edge of her mask, a gift from Mrs.

Chesterfield herself. "It just all seems so needlessly cloak and dagger. Why couldn't this mystery patron write to me instead? Or meet me at the club during the day?"

"I have ceased to speculate on the motivations of rich men," said Mr. Chesterfield with a sigh.

"Mr. Chesterfield," Flora said, "you yourself are a rich man." Compared to most, at least.

"And I could not say why I do whatever it is I do, either. Unless, of course, it involves my excellent wife." His eyes twinkled behind his mask. "In that case, my reasons are clear. Why, I would even escort a lovely girl to a ball, if that is what's needed."

Flora inclined her head in thanks, though she wished to groan. Why had she let Belinda Chesterfield convince her to attend? Even the promise of a lucrative patronage did not seem so enticing, now that she was inside the hot, crowded ballroom. Everywhere she looked, she was only reminded of what she would never have. There wasn't a single person in attendance who was not paired man to woman, or at the very least, embroiled in a knot of conversation with an even number of each. Arms were wrapped around waists and shoulders, whispers being passed from lips to ears. Painted mouths stretched into smiles, laughing under the lines of half masks. Obviously the veneer of anonymity gave the guests leeway to be free with their attentions.

Mr. Chesterfield raised his voice to be heard above the buzz of the music and voices. "Would you like to dance once they start playing something suitable?" he asked.

"Oh, no, thank you," Flora said. "I would rather not."

"I wouldn't mind. Belinda says I'm a rather accomplished stepper. I know all the old country reels and even some of the new ones."

He was trying to cheer her up, she knew, and she wished she could tell him what a futile endeavor that was. Verbena Montrose was going to be married in a few days. There could be no cheer in Flora's soul with that wedding on the horizon.

"Perhaps later," she said, though she doubted she would change her mind.

Mr. Chesterfield might have smiled at her in reply, though it was impossible to tell with his mouth hidden behind his mask. Yet in the next instant, his whole spine went rigid and his eyes shifted in his mask holes as they tracked something across the room.

Flora didn't need to see his face to correctly interpret his consternation. The source of his agitation became clear when the thick crowd parted to admit Lord Byron into their midst.

"Pah!" said Mr. Chesterfield almost to himself. "Not that rake again. He still owes me three pounds from a card game."

"Hello, fellow strangers!" Byron said in an odd, gruff voice. He swept his tricorn hat from his head and executed a theatrical bow. His small mask, shaped like a cat's head complete with pointed ears and trembling wire whiskers, was not nearly enough of a disguise; his chin could be spotted leagues away.

"Good evening," said Mr. Chesterfield stiffly.

Byron righted himself with a grin aimed at Flora. "Might I steal the alluring gentleman away for a moment? I fear we have some business matters to discuss."

Mr. Chesterfield harrumphed. "Is the business the matter of the three pounds you owe me?"

"I owe you? We do not even know each other's true identities."

"Everyone knows it's you, Byron," Flora said, sighing.

Byron frowned. "Some people enjoy a little mystery, you know. But yes, all right, ruin it for us all." He turned to Mr. Chesterfield. "Please, Mr. Chesterfield, if you would be so kind?"

Mr. Chesterfield gave Flora an apologetic glance as he was enveloped by Byron's arm, along with his voluminous black cloak, and spirited away to some corner of the ballroom where the press of bodies hid them from Flora's sight.

She crossed her arms. A fine thing! Nothing like leaving a woman unattended at a ball that was no doubt brimming with rakes and scoundrels hiding behind masks. Her teeth ground together in frustration.

A servant swept by and deposited a glass of rich red wine in her hand without slowing down. Flora stared into the cup in confusion. This night was foisting all sorts of things upon her without her say-so. She was just about to scan the room, desperate for any knot of conversation she could reasonably insert herself into, when the ballroom doors opened. Flora watched with her heart in her mouth as a newcomer strode in.

He was the epitome of grace and masculine bearing, from the tips of his well-heeled pumps to the top of his jaunty tricorn hat. His stockings were a faultless silk, his breeches a light cream. His waistcoat, at least the part that was peeking out from beneath his black cutaway tailcoat, was a sumptuous brocade of midnight blue chased with silver. He sported a full harlequin mask over his face with black and blue diamonds painted across it, interrupted only by the sparkle of false gems that seemed to stand in for beauty marks.

The gentleman was handsome to the extreme, a dandy of impeccable taste, and all the more breathtaking because Flora knew him to be Verbena Montrose.

Even stuffed under the tricorn hat, Verbena's hair was unmistakable. The few errant curls that spilled between the confines of hat and mask were all Flora needed to identify her.

Flora, in her panic, turned fully around so her back was to the door. What in the world was Verbena doing here—dressed in *those* clothes—on the night before she was to leave for Eden?

The red wine that Flora had been clasping listlessly in her hand suddenly looked more attractive, and she quaffed a long swallow. With drink to steady her nerves, she attempted to glance over her shoulder to ascertain Verbena's progress, only to find that the Midnight Harlequin was now standing right behind her and staring fervently into her eyes.

"Why have you—?" Flora tried to ask, but Verbena—or rather, her alter ego—raised a single gloved finger to her porcelain lips. Flora's words died on her tongue. Her heart fluttered in her breast.

The band struck up a waltz.

This had the effect of causing all the other guests to cheer heartily, save for Verbena and Flora—who were silent and motionless in the great sea of bodies—and Lord Byron, whom Flora spied barreling in his distinct gait across the ballroom.

"No waltzes, I said!" he cried, but was intercepted by the master of ceremonies, who clearly disagreed with Byron's opinion on the German dance. An argument ensued, the musicians having subsided to await the result.

Despite the bizarre circumstances, Flora could not help but laugh. She sensed Verbena's eyes staring at her through the mask's holes and thought the look conveyed curiosity. She rushed to meet it—and fill the awful silence between them.

"His Lordship detests the waltz," she said, "not because of its scandalous intimacy, as so many of the older generation do, but because he cannot participate." She lifted one slippered foot in demonstration. "He can dance a reel or even a quadrille well enough when he may depend on the support of the other dancers, but his foot makes it impossible to lead in a two-person arrangement. If he cannot be involved in a sensual exhibition, I suppose he feels no one should."

Finally, across the ballroom, Byron raised his hands in defeat and bowed his head. The victorious master flicked a hand toward the conductor to indicate he should play on.

Another cheer erupted as the waltz began anew. Flora set her half-empty wineglass on a passing salver, worried she would drop it in the crush of dancers rushing toward the floor.

Then Verbena extended her hand.

Flora stared at the white calfskin that encased Verbena's palm. These were men's gloves. It was on the tip of her tongue to ask where Verbena had procured such a perfect pair, but there were more pressing matters. She was being asked to dance.

"I'm afraid I have only waltzed in quite informal settings," Flora said. If one could call being whirled around the club by tipsy poets waltzing. "I—I hardly know any of the steps."

Verbena said nothing, merely kept her tongue behind the impassive harlequin mask, and waited.

It would cause more of a scene to refuse than to simply accept. Flora took a shuddering breath and placed her hand in Verbena's waiting one. "All right," she said, "but do not mock me if I step on your toes."

It was impossible to tell what expression Verbena wore under her mask, but Flora imagined she could detect a slight wrinkle at the corners of her eyes that betrayed a smile. They swept onto the dance floor together just as the various couples were establishing their places in the concentric rings the waltz called for. Verbena led them to a spot quite in the middle of it all, which was a relief to Flora at first, as she assumed it meant they would be well hidden by the other couples. Yet she soon realized it only made them the center of attention, not the least because they made such a striking pair. Of all the men in attendance, her partner stood alone in matters of dress and comportment. Flora could feel the eyes of the guests lingering on them as they arranged themselves into the prescribed stance.

Flora swallowed hard. Verbena's hand wrapped around her waist, holding her close. Flora mirrored her, placing her own hand on the fine wool of Verbena's tailcoat. The faint swell of Verbena's hip was only apparent by this touch, dulled as it was through the layers of Flora's opera gloves and Verbena's many items of clothing.

Flora's mind was awhirl. It seemed too cruel to contemplate, but she feared this appearance in men's raiment might be her erstwhile friend's way of saying she knew the truth about William. It seemed a mockery of Flora's entire life. Why else would Verbena stare at her so silently, so intently? Surely it was a look of judgment.

"Are you the mysterious patron I'm supposed to meet tonight?" Flora asked, her voice quiet under the noise of the ballroom so that only Verbena might hear.

Verbena, maddeningly, did not answer. She did not need to. Her hard stare said all.

Flora set her jaw, lest the tremble in it betray her. The last thing she needed was to burst into sobs in front of hundreds of people.

The band swung into the waltz, and the dancers began to dance. Flora let herself be moved by the music and Verbena's firm hand. They were an excellent match, of equal height and similar builds. But beyond the physical, they seemed to be of one mind, at least when it came to the steps. Flora could feel how Verbena planned to move before she did, their feet carving out the patterns of give and take that made the waltz such a seductive and intimate prospect. Though its popularity had given way to a more English–and therefore less effusive–version of the original continental style, it still held within its movements more passion than Flora could bear.

For much of the beginning, they were side by side, their hips brushing as they went through the steps. Then the men–plus Verbena–spun the ladies about, large, strong hands clasped to dainty waists. Or, in their particular case, Verbena's small, strong hands clasped to Flora's fairly ordinary waist, which owed its slight curve to the judicious use of stays. They pressed close, chest to chest, so that Flora feared her heartbeat would be noticeable even through the thick brocade of Verbena's waistcoat. Another complicated spin and Flora found herself embraced in Verbena's arms, back to front. She could feel Verbena's metal coat buttons digging into her spine. Warm breath ghosted along her neck, and she closed her eyes against the sensation.

With the tattered threads of her composure gathered as best she could, Flora opened her eyes and saw, in the wall of faces that passed them by, approving glances and impressed moues. Tears pricked her eyes. Under any other circumstances, Flora would be thrilled to dance like this with Verbena, but now–with so much pain between them and even more left unsaid–she was bereft.

Thankfully Verbena spun her again, and Flora was able to stifle the first sob against her shoulder. Tears ran free of her mask and soaked into the dark wool there, her face hot as a coal.

"Flora?" It was the first word Verbena had said to her all evening. There was concern there, perhaps, but mostly surprise. "What's the matter?"

"You're very cruel," Flora mumbled into the soaked wool. She tore away and stumbled off the dance floor, nearly barreling into several couples before finding a break in the spectators.

"You see?" she heard Lord Byron hiss above the music. "I am not the only one who simply cannot abide the waltz."

Flora ignored him, instead darting through the nearest French door and onto the portico. The covered stone walkway was deserted, the columns as silent and empty as a deep forest. Flora took a huge gulp of the night air, feeling it cool her from within.

She collapsed on a bench seat formed into an elaborate U shape. There was a long tradition of wronged women weeping into their hands outside of masquerade balls. Why not join that illustrious number, was her feeling.

Flora slipped off her mask and dabbed at her wet eyes with her gloved wrist for want of anything better, staring sullenly down at the gray flagstones.

A handkerchief appeared before her. Flora sat straight up and stared at the owner of the hand that proffered it. Verbena had removed her tricorn hat and pushed her own mask up to her hairline, where it was held in place by its silken strap. Her eyes were pinched in worry, and her hair, now free, tumbled about her shoulders.

Flora's gaze returned to the handkerchief. The initials E.C. were embroidered on one lacy corner. That was one mystery solved, at least.

"Is Monsieur Charbonneau aware that you have absconded with his ensemble?" Flora asked. She took the handkerchief and wiped her eyes.

"Of course. He helped shove me into the damn thing." Verbena placed her hands on the upturns of the U that formed Flora's seat, leaning in close. "Flora–"

"You must replace your mask and hat," Flora interrupted, twisting the damp handkerchief in her hands. "Someone could come out here and see you. Do you have any idea what might happen if you were caught dressed like this?"

"I actually don't."

"Nor do I, though I shouldn't like to find out." She turned her head to stare at the French doors, her whole body taut as a bowstring. "An actress strutting upon the stage might be allowed her breeches, but this is no evening performance."

"Flora, if you'd just listen–"

"They might put you in the stocks. Or worse, in the papers." Flora sensed she was babbling, yet she could not stop herself. "Think of your reputation. Think of your impending marriage. All you hold dear would be ruined."

"*Not all.*" This was said so forcefully, so violently, that Flora flinched. Dropping her hat to the ground, Verbena lowered herself into an unladylike crouch so that she was in Flora's lowered line of sight. Their eyes met and held. "Not all," Verbena repeated, but gently.

Flora watched, frozen, as Verbena lifted one gloved hand and brought it to Flora's cheek. She fought her instinct to lean into the touch, her lashes fluttering.

"Why did you come here?" she asked. "And dressed like this? To mock me?"

"What?" Verbena reared back so violently her mask nearly toppled off her head. Her hand, so recently cupped to Flora's face, hovered in the air. "I came here to dance with you! How else was I to do that if not in men's raiment?"

This made no sense to Flora. "Why should you wish to dance with me?"

"Because tomorrow–" Verbena swallowed. Her hand came to rest on the arm of the bench. She looked down at the flagstones beneath her bent knees. "Tomorrow I leave for Eden. And I could not bear to be married without first confessing to you the whole of my feelings."

"Please don't," Flora said, but of course Verbena did not listen.

"My heart has but one occupant, and it is you," Verbena said. She stared desperately up at Flora, her face pinched. "No, wait, I should say my heart has–damn it all, you know I'm no poet."

Flora froze, her breath caught in her motionless chest. "I do not know that," she said, though it came out weakly.

"Yes, you do. Or rather, William does." Verbena gazed at her imploringly. "And so, then, do you."

There it was. The truth, no longer secret.

Flora steeled herself for the wave of panic that would surely overtake her, yet it did not come. A kind of peace washed through her in its place. The worst possible thing had happened–and still, the world turned. The dancers inside the ballroom still danced; the chatter of conversation did not abruptly stop; the musicians played on. And Verbena, crouched there at Flora's feet, did not have the look of a woman disgusted. She was, in fact, smiling carefully.

"You know," Flora said, breathing at last.

"Yes, and it's a good thing, too. I was having a devil of a time trying to understand how I could be in love with two different people when I had no real inclination to divide my affections," Verbena said. She reached slowly for Flora's slim hand, cradling it in her gloved one and rubbing her thumb in the center of her palm. "How lucky for me that you and William are one and the same."

"Lucky?" Flora did not allow her mouth to hang open in an uncouth manner, but it was a near thing.

"Of course," said Verbena. "Consider: as you are both man and woman, you can move unencumbered between the two halves of society. It really is remarkable. The things you must hear from both corners!" She nodded to herself. "No wonder you've been privy to the most comprehensive gossip in London. With your changeable nature, you can access both the masculine and feminine spheres. Why, you're practically unstoppable!"

Flora frowned up at the underside of the portico's overhang. "I've never thought of it like that. To be honest, most times I feel rather vulnerable."

"I think you're the most powerful creature in London," Verbena said. She reached out and clasped Flora's trembling hands in hers. "Powerful and clever."

Clever? Oh, no. Not I. "It is not some trick," Flora said, the words tumbling out of her. "You must understand, this is the very opposite of deceit. I was not trying to mislead you or anyone else, I only–"

"I understand." Verbena lifted their joined hands and placed Flora's palm to her own hot cheek. "It was perfectly clear to me, from the moment I arrived at the conclusion, that this could not be anything but your true nature. Why else would you risk yourself so?"

"Madness?" Flora suggested.

Verbena laughed. "If you are mad for donning a skirt, then so am I for wearing these breeches." She wriggled in place a bit, finally coming to sit on the flagstones with her legs crossed in a loose knot. "Actually, I quite like them. I might start wearing them at home. Étienne surely wouldn't mind." Her happy countenance slipped a bit. "You know I must marry him, don't you? That he requires a wife to ensure his safety? The same concern you have for me being discovered dressed like this—he must dodge those dangers daily."

"Yes, but—" Flora felt her eyes prick with tears again. "But must it be you?"

"Time works against us. He must marry before the whispers get any louder," Verbena said. Her words fell between them, matter-of-fact, dispassionate, completely levelheaded. "I made him a promise when the arrangement favored me. Now that he is the one with the greater need, I cannot abandon him, much as I'd like to. I would be—well, no better than the lowest rake."

Despite her misery, Flora felt a sense of pride in Verbena's decision. Only a few months ago, the woman might have done anything, abandoned any friend, in pursuit of her goals. Now, her noble nature shone through, damn it all.

Verbena hesitated. "You might still consider my original proposal," she said. "You could marry a man willing to masquerade as a loving husband, too. Perhaps Miles would please you." Even as she suggested it, her lips twisted. Odd.

Pieces began to fall into place. "You are jealous," Flora whispered. Her hand fell. "Of *Miles*?"

Verbena huffed. "You two are very close."

"Because he is my friend!"

"I feared he might be more besides." Verbena glanced up at her. "He is . . . handsome." This was said so grudgingly that Flora nearly smiled.

"Miles is captivated by Étienne alone," she said instead. "And even if he were amenable to your scheme, I would not marry him. I—" Flora wrung the handkerchief some more. "I'm afraid I have become accustomed to living my life as freely as I am able. To marry falsely would be to close doors I would rather keep propped open. Can you understand?"

Verbena regarded her with sympathetic eyes. "I will not lie and say I understand when I do not," she said, "but my love for you is beyond understanding, and so I hope you won't hold that against me."

Flora abandoned the ill-used handkerchief and tentatively held Verbena's hands in hers. "I couldn't. Although . . ." She struggled against the unfairness of it all. "It seems we are still at an impasse."

"I fear so. All my cleverness and none of it can be brought to bear when it matters most." Verbena blinked up at her, her own eyes damp. Or perhaps it was merely a trick of the flickering lamplight. "Flora, I am sorry."

"I almost wish you had not come," Flora blurted out. "To dance with you, to hear you speak like this—only the once and never again—is that why you arranged for us to meet here?"

"No, I came to ask if you would . . ." Verbena thinned her mouth into a taut line.

"What?" Flora asked. "What is it?"

What else was there to give?

Verbena's green eyes stared up at Flora imploringly. "Come to Eden with me?"

Flora nearly laughed, a hysterical catch in her throat. "Eden!"

Verbena rose onto her knees so that her gaze was nearly level with Flora's. "For no untoward purpose. Only, I am going to be very alone there. No one save Étienne and Miles will know the truth of the thing; my parents, Étienne's brothers, the servants, all the other wedding guests will require me to put on a false face. But you could attend. If you like."

"For what purpose?" Flora demanded. "Why should we prolong this agony?"

Verbena stared at her, bereft. "I do not think it agony to be in your presence. To be near you is–it is the only thing I care for. Will you blame me for wanting to eke out every last possible moment before I am wed?"

Flora looked away, unable to stomach the pain in that beloved face any longer. "You speak as if marriage will be the death of you."

"It will be," Verbena said. "A quiet one, a death of the spirit. For once I am married, you will refuse even my friendship, I think."

It was true. Flora felt her heart clench, a tendril of guilt tightening around it. "Once you are married, there will be no room for William in your life. He will not be allowed to take walks with you, or meet with you at the club, or pay you a visit. The best he could hope for is to see you briefly at some dinner party, or a dance, or an afternoon's entertainment, and exchange only banal pleasantries about the weather."

Verbena winced. "I do so hate talking about the weather."

"If only half of me is allowed your friendship," Flora continued, "then I fear I, too, would die a quiet death."

"No sense in both of us perishing," Verbena said, soft and resigned. She struggled to her feet. "This was a mistake. I should not have accosted you like this. Forget I ever came here; forget I ever asked anything of you. I've been tremendously selfish. Unforgivably foolish." She affixed her mask over her face once more, hiding her strife behind the expressionless porcelain. "Put me out of your mind. Act as if I was never here."

Flora retrieved Verbena's discarded hat from the ground and stood to hand it to her. She groped for something to say; it didn't seem right for everything to end like this. "You look very handsome, though," she said. Whatever jocularity might have existed in the words disappeared into wistfulness.

Verbena shoved her red hair beneath her hat with swift, jerky movements. "Well. At least there's that." She finished hiding her long tresses and then stayed there, breathing hard, mere inches from Flora. Her eyes drifted over Flora's face as if memorizing it.

Flora wished she could dash Verbena's damn mask to the ground so that she might do the same. It seemed inconceivably cruel to her that this was the end of their acquaintance. Her head pounded, her hands trembled. This could not be the end.

They moved in perfect tandem: Verbena lifting her mask so that only her lips were exposed, Flora swaying forward to meet her.

They kissed—hands gripping waists, breath stuttering. Verbena lifted one hand to cup the back of Flora's head, keeping her in place. Flora melted against her, letting the tears come.

Then it was over. They parted. Verbena replaced her mask, fitting it to her face.

"Good-bye, my love," Verbena said, and swept back into the ballroom as swiftly as she'd appeared.

Flora stood alone on the portico for a long moment, her shaking fingers brushing her recently kissed mouth. "Farewell," she said to no one.

Chapter 21

Flora returned to the ballroom with her mask clutched in her hand. She had stayed outside on the portico until the bells from the church across the street rang midnight. Enough time, surely, for Verbena to make her own escape. Now Flora's only desire was to find some quiet room where she would not be disturbed while her emotions overtook her.

She might never see Verbena Montrose ever again, in any guise. Flora was not so naïve as to think the world required justice to function, and yet this turn of events seemed unduly cruel.

As Flora pushed her way through the harlequins and Pierrots to reach the doors, she spared a thought for Mr. Chesterfield, who might want to know of her exit. She spotted him by a table of canapés, laughing with his fellow poets, and it occurred to her that Chesterfield had likely been in on the ploy from the start. Well, if he'd played a trick on her to ensure her attendance, she felt no compunction in playing a trick on him by disappearing.

And so she did—swiftly, moving down the unlit corridor of the Calliope Club, away from the heat and dazzling colors of the ballroom.

The rest of the club was quite abandoned, which suited Flora's purposes perfectly. She slipped into the Green Room—where she and Verbena had conducted their first verbal sparring match—and collapsed into a moss-colored armchair. There was no fire in the grate, and no candles lit. The only light came from a glimmering streetlamp that stood outside the window. The noise of the ball was distant enough that it could be from another realm entirely, a world where Flora did not fit at all.

She put a hand to her mouth to stifle her sob, then remembered she was totally alone and need not stifle anything. Her hand fell to her lap as she cried, the force of it wracking her frame. It made her feel so fragile, so weak, her breath gone somewhere beyond her reach. She'd read of heartache but never believed it to be a physical affliction as some insisted. How foolish she'd been—every iota of her body was revolting against the loss. Every jot of her wanted Verbena.

She pressed her chilled hands to her hot face. Oh, how she wished for a pair of trousers and a tailcoat in that moment! If William could be the one to struggle under the weight of misery, then Flora might find some small reprieve. Or perhaps not. Perhaps this was one of those burdens they shared with no alternative. Something whispered at the edges of Flora's mind—*Will you not consider me even now?*—but she had not the strength to listen to it.

She let loose a strangled wail in the silence of the room, a terrible sound from the depths of her many-faceted soul.

Over in the corner, a figure sat upright on the shadowy chaise lounge. "Mrpmh?" it said.

Flora, heartbroken or not, found the self-preservation to scream.

Fortunately, the creature leaned out of the shadow and into the slice of lamplight that fell through the window, showing itself to be a rather creased Lord Byron. "Why the devil are you screaming?" he said, a hand clapped to one ear.

"Why are you haunting dark rooms?" Flora demanded in return. She wilted in her armchair, her fright leaving her cold and shaky.

"I am not haunting anything! I was simply resting my eyes." He produced a flint box from his pocket and struck the included taper, then went about the room to light two mirrored wall sconces. "There. Now you may see I am merely a man, not a demon."

"You're missing your masquerade," Flora observed. She caught sight of the whiskered cat mask Byron had worn earlier hung by its silken cord on the globe stand in the corner.

Byron scoffed and tossed himself onto an emerald divan, where he lounged on his side with his chin propped on one fist. "Then I count myself lucky. Leave those braying boors to their waltzes." He shuddered, then lapsed into a brown study, his gaze surveying nothing but the floor. "I understand that times will change; it is the nature of time to do so. Yet I never considered that in changing, there would be no place for me in Britain any longer."

Flora dabbed at her eyes with Étienne's purloined handkerchief. She knew a thing or two about having no real place, but she'd thought Verbena might prove to be a sort of place. Could a person be a safe harbor?

It didn't matter now; she'd never have the chance to know. She muffled a sob into the handkerchief, her eyes squeezing shut.

Byron must have, at last, noticed her distress, for she heard him quit the chaise, his unique gait crossing the room. "Miss Witcombe, whatever is the matter? I know meeting me in a dark room would startle anyone, but surely now with the lamps lit—"

"No, it's not you, my lord." She raised her eyes to find him pulling a footstool closer to sit directly before her, his face a mask of concern. "It is another matter entirely. I—I've just suffered a great shock."

Byron's gaze narrowed. "Has someone accosted you? That ruffian you were waltzing with? I have no pistol at hand, but if you give me a moment, I'm sure I could find a gentleman in the ballroom who is not so ill prepared." He made as if to rise from his footstool.

"Sir!" Flora placed a hand on his knee, keeping him in place with that single touch. "Truly, my dance partner is not at fault." She hesitated, withdrawing her hand to clasp the handkerchief in her lap. "At least, not solely," she whispered.

"I see." There was a gentleness to his voice that Flora had not expected. She lifted her gaze and saw Byron staring at the handkerchief she held. Glancing down, she saw Étienne's embroidered initials were quite evident to anyone who cared to look.

"Oh!" She despaired at the awkwardness of it all. Byron couldn't possibly think she was heartbroken over Monsieur Charbonneau, could he? Many men might share the initials E.C. but only one had accompanied her party to Plas Tân less than a fortnight ago. She balled up the handkerchief in her fists, though the damage was already done. "It's not as it seems," she said weakly.

Now Byron was the one touching her knee, an indulgent pat that conveyed his sympathies. "You are not the first to fall in love with the wrong man," he said. "He is to marry our illustrious Miss Montrose soon, is he not?"

"Yes, but it really isn't–"

"Do you mind if I smoke?" He retrieved another case from his coat pocket, longer and flatter than his flint box. "Tales of heartbreak always make me crave a cigar." He opened the box, revealing a neat row of the things, each wrapped in dark brown leaf.

Flora sighed through her nose. Clearly Byron was not going to believe her even if she explained–not that she could explain that her disastrous love affair had actually involved Verbena, not Verbena's fiancé. She held out a hand. "As long as you allow me one as well."

Byron's brows rose high. It was considered very uncouth for a woman to smoke anything, at least in mixed company. Then again, it was frowned upon for an unmarried lady to sit in a darkened room with the maddest man in all of London. Byron eventually presented a cigar with a flourish. "Of course," he said, as if he gave cigars to ladies every day.

There was the usual ceremony of snipping the ends and getting a light from a lamp. Flora found it all quite soothing. She was not the most prodigious smoker, nor did she partake in snuff very often, but William was apt to find himself in men's clubs and in the company of his brothers, where a hookah or cigar might be pressed upon him. If Flora could not seek the comfort of William's clothing, she could at least indulge in his vice. She took the cigar between her lips and drew in a heady mouthful of tobacco.

For a long moment, the two puffed away in silence. Flora

was feeling more herself now—or more of someone, at least. She leaned back in her chair, stuffing the accursed handkerchief into the bodice of her dress, and enjoyed Byron's fine cigar. If she could only live in this fashion every day of her life, she would consider it bearable. Not necessarily a daily cigar, of course, but the combination of a masculine pursuit while wearing feminine garb, or vice versa, was so pleasing to her, she could almost forget the farewell she'd endured on the portico.

Almost.

"Do you think," she drawled as she smoked, "that love always ends in tragedy?"

"Yes," said Byron immediately. "Without a doubt." He formed his lips into a perfect *O* and sent a ring of smoke trembling toward the frescoed ceiling—cherubs and lambs. Flora had always detested the Green Room ceiling. "I think it must. Life always ends in death; there is no avoiding it. Even if one were fortunate enough to marry one's greatest love and remain together for decades, there is still the final parting."

Flora regarded him skeptically. "But if one dies of old age at the end of a long and happy union, that cannot be considered tragic, can it?" That was what she had dreamt of with Verbena, before all hope was dashed.

"Perhaps not to outsiders. But to the lover left behind to languish?" Byron considered the glowing orange end of his cigar. "What else is left to us but to embrace death? To make love to the tragic."

Flora tapped a measure of cigar ash into a convenient vase at her elbow. She had not planned to take Byron into her confidence even this much, but his words filled her with a reckless abandon. "I was issued an invitation tonight," she began.

"Whilst at *my* ball? The nerve," he muttered.

"I was invited," Flora continued, "to attend an event that will assuredly bring me grief and pain. No, that was but one invitation. I was also invited to be a mistress." She gazed coolly at Byron. "Now I wonder if to refuse both was a fool's choice."

"Do you want my advice?"

"Not particularly."

He ignored her. "You are speaking to a man who has given and accepted many such invitations. Although if the event you mention is your lover's wedding, I can't say I've gone so far as that. Wait–no." He paused and stared up at the ceiling, his lips twisted to one side. "Does it count if I've gone to bed with both bride and groom?"

"My lord," Flora said sternly.

"My point is"–Byron sat up from the slouch he'd adopted atop the footstool, his cigar tip flirting dangerously with some fringe on a nearby tablecloth–"to live your life in the avoidance of tragedy is a fool's errand. Misfortune will find you. That is the natural state of things. You may as well try to grasp what happiness you can alongside the pain."

Flora shook her head, smoking thoughtfully. "You speak as though there should be no thought for any consequences."

"Consequences! What are consequences?" He leaned forward, his eyes blazing through the haze of smoke. "We're poets, for god's sake. We are, all of us, at various speeds, descending into hell! When you get there, don't you want to have something amusing to tell the devil?"

That brought Flora up short. She was not certain she believed in hell or the devil, but she thought Byron might have a point somewhere in there. A dual soul like hers was not an easy one to bear; William was a balm to her, of course, but lately, perhaps because of the strength of her affection for Verbena, she found herself wanting more. It was as if, having for some years lived the two lives of her two halves, a third, somewhat more unified presence beat within her. This was not apart from that which was Flora and William, but some alchemy of them both. There was salt, and there was water, but then–the ocean. That was what she felt like at her core, an unknowable, blue-green world, the depths of which she could hardly fathom.

And each part of her did want to see Verbena again. Even if it hurt, even if it was all for nothing–could she not at least try? She–he–was as vast as the sea. Perhaps it would not bring her lasting peace and joy to be Verbena's secret lover, but her current circumstances were not much better.

Maybe Byron was right. Maybe there was nothing but tragedy to be had.

She might as well make it a good one.

She stood so abruptly her cigar dropped an inch of ash on her gown's skirts. "I must go to Eden," she said.

Byron frowned. "What, now?"

"Tomorrow. As soon as possible." She brushed the ash away. "A coach–I will need to hire a coach." The prospect of sharing one packed with strangers making the same slow journey filled her with dread. This grand gesture was going to be quite expensive.

"I have a coach," said Byron.

Flora stared down at his lounging form. "You do?"

"Well, I have the dowager countess's coach." He waved a hand through the air. "She gifted me its use so that I might complete the masquerade preparations with speed."

"Won't Lady Croydon expect it returned tomorrow?"

"Yes, but by that time"–Byron tapped his cigar ash into a silver dish–"we will already be on the road to Eden."

"We," Flora said flatly.

Byron smiled at her like the cherubs on the ceiling frescoes. "Oh yes," he said. "We."

Chapter 22

"Thank you, Mother, but I can manage on my own," Verbena said, practically marching Mrs. Montrose out of the drafty bedroom.

"But don't you want to hear my hard-earned wisdom?" Mrs. Montrose insisted. "Your wedding night–you should be prepared!"

"I know all I need to about what happens on a wedding night." Verbena assisted her mother another inch into the dark hall. The Abbey was in poor condition even here in the main wing, a thick layer of dust and debris along the edges and tucked into corners. Cobwebs draped lavishly along the neglected wall sconces and various pieces of framed artwork; the hired girls from the village had barely the time to clean the few rooms that would house the small wedding party, leaving the rest of the manor to its disrepair. Étienne and his elder brothers were staying at Market Eden's sole inn, while Verbena's parents were housed in the only other bedroom that could be whipped into shape, all the way across the Abbey in another wing.

It was not the grand wedding Verbena had envisioned, but perhaps it was fitting. It wasn't as if her marriage would be all that grand, either.

"What do you mean, you know what happens on a wedding night?" her mother demanded. "Where could you have learned such a thing?"

Verbena bit her tongue. She didn't need to remind Mrs. Montrose that gossip often involved a level of detail that made it difficult for a young lady to *not* know the particulars of the marriage act.

"Poetry," she said instead. "Now get some rest. I will see you in the morning."

"Oh, all right. Do try to arrange your hair more pleasingly than usual tomorrow. Just because this is a country wedding does not mean we should look like slouches."

"Good *night,* Mother." Verbena closed the door with a loud bang of finality, then rested her forehead against the musty wood.

One more night. She could survive one more night. Then her promise to Étienne would be fulfilled and everything would be as it should.

Verbena pushed away from the door and fiddled with the cuffs of her nightgown. She wasn't at all tired, even after the exhausting journey from London and the lukewarm bath she'd taken in the copper tub the village girls had dragged into her temporary boudoir.

Verbena went to the window, pushing aside the moth-bitten curtains so she could see the moon more clearly. The thin crescent showed starkly white in the black sky, surrounded by dots of stars. Somewhere in the distance, a bird cried. She was a creature of London and as such was discomfited by the abundant country quiet punctuated only by the occasional scream of nature and groan of the manor around her.

At least she would not need to stay more than a single night in this wretched place. She and Étienne were to embark directly on their honeymoon, with Étienne's carriage whisking them away as soon as the ceremony was finished. Their "wedding night" would be spent at a modest inn of good repute. Verbena wondered if Étienne had thought to bring a deck of cards with him; they would need *something* to pass the time.

She shivered. They had decades more stretching before them, and cards alone would not be enough to pass it happily.

A knock sounded at the door: three sharp raps with no hesitation. Verbena turned swiftly, a strand of her fiery red hair catching on her lip. "Mother," she said, swiping it away, "I told you I will see you in the morning."

"It's me," came a voice. Not Mrs. Montrose, but a beloved, dear voice. The mere sound of it made Verbena's heart leap into her mouth.

"William?" She flew to the door and tore it open. "Ah, apologies. Flora." (It had not been apparent to Verbena before, but their voices were nearly identical. How strange, the ways in which one's eyes dictated one's perception.)

There, in the shadowed hall, looking radiant among the dusty fixtures, was the voice's owner. A tentative smile, and Verbena's heart skipped a portion of its work. "Good evening," Flora said, her words and manner imbued with a strange formality.

That would not do.

"What are you thinking? Get in here before my parents see you." She took Flora by the arm and pulled her inside, shutting the door tight.

In Flora's hand was a heavy valise of dark leather, very much like a man's case. Her hair was characteristically arranged to perfection despite how long she must have been on the road, and her heather-gray dress was similarly unmarred by travel. She looked somehow different, however. Changed, as if her bearing and demeanor had undergone some kind of transformation. Her shoulders were thrown back and her head held proud, putting Verbena in mind of Artemis at the head of a hunt.

It took all of Verbena's not-inconsiderable willpower to say in a trembling voice, "You came." Not her most clever observation, but there it was.

"I did. Apologies, but I was unable to send you advance notice to expect me," Flora said, her gentle words at odds with the rest of her. "I knocked on the kitchen door and gave one of the serving girls a shilling, and she allowed me upstairs. I told her it was crucial I speak to you before the wedding, and that was not a lie."

"Well, it must be very important indeed if it warrants an entire shilling!" Verbena said bitterly.

Flora must not have detected any acid in the words, for she only forged ahead with complete earnestness. "I had to see you before you are married. I–" She stopped and placed the heavy valise on the floor with a thud. "I could not let it end as it did at the masquerade."

Verbena sat heavily on the edge of the featherbed, her arms crossed protectively over her middle. "How shall it end, then? Unless you have reconsidered my proposal, I do not think anything will change." She glanced up warily. "You, however, seem changed. Has something happened?"

Flora lifted her heavy black bag in answer. "I will tell you all, but first, would you mind very much if I . . . donned some fresh clothes?" She glanced over her shoulder at the decoupaged changing screen that stood in the corner, depicting a bizarre array of shirtless pugilists. (The erstwhile Lord Eden had had strange taste.) "It would bring me great comfort to wear trousers for this conversation."

"Oh! Of course, please." Verbena motioned toward the screen.

"Thank you." Flora offered her a shy smile, her cheeks glowing a faint pink as she ducked behind the panels. The shuffle and shush of fabric could be heard like faint birdsong in the quiet room.

Verbena sat on the bed, worrying at her dressing gown's belt and wondering what exactly would happen if her mother discovered a man–somewhat, at least–in her bedroom the night before her wedding. A whipping would be a kindness; more likely she would find herself choked to death under Mrs. Montrose's hands.

Yet she did not fear her mother's wrath as much as she despaired at losing this last chance to speak to the one she loved. If William wished to be present instead of Flora, she could hardly request he absent himself. She had meant what she'd said at Byron's masquerade: her heart did not distinguish between the two.

Verbena cleared her throat, trying and failing to ignore the shape of William's bared body silhouetted behind the paper screen. "You must have, erm, traveled mostly in trousers, I suppose?"

"Actually, I traveled as Flora for the duration," William said. His head popped over the top of the screen, his hair now cropped in its usual fashion. "Lord Byron kindly offered me the use of his coach. With the caveat, of course, that he come with me. He claimed a great desire to 'see this little town where so much drama is scheduled to take place.'"

Byron was *here*? In Eden? Surely he would not attempt to attend the wedding. Good lord, if he swanned in . . .

Verbena put the thought out of her mind; there were more pressing matters. "I admire the ways in which your nature allows you to flit from one world to another. I wish I could do so, but I fear without a mask to hide my face, no one would take me as a man." She lifted a hand to her hair, which hung in loose waves about her shoulders. It was difficult to imagine cutting it short; she'd always prized her hair.

William was once more out of sight behind the screen, the long lines of his legs apparent as he worked them into his trousers. "You'd be surprised. Most people see only what they expect to see." He stepped out from the protection of the screen, still arranging his clothing.

Verbena was awestruck. William was now barefoot, his trousers creased sharply down the center of each leg. He wore a woman's white chemisette atop these. A brightly colored shawl, embroidered with pink and blue flowers, draped across his shoulders. His cheeks and lips still held traces of Flora's rouge. He was altogether ethereal and lovely, a combination of both sexes without any shame as to the blurring between them.

"Miss Montrose?" Only William called her that, never Flora. Not since they'd become intimates.

Verbena's eyes snapped up to meet his. "Yes?"

He wrapped the shawl tighter about his frame. "You were staring."

"Oh, yes. I–I am sorry. You just look so . . . different." She bit her lip. "It startled me."

William glanced down at what little raiment he wore. "I thought I might take a page from the ladies of Plas Tân and invent a new style for myself. At least in private." He lifted his gaze, slow and careful, to Verbena's. "Does it disturb you to see me like this?"

Verbena considered it for a moment. It was difficult to think when those pink lips and soft, wild hair were so distracting, but she soldiered on. "You have a talent," she said at last, "and it gladdens me to watch you wield it."

William hummed at that. "It does not feel like a talent. You would not say the sun has a talent for shining, or the moon a knack for changing shape. They simply are as they are made."

Verbena eyed his strange—and strangely beautiful—mixed clothing. "Forgive my ignorance, dear William. Will you sit?" She gestured to the vanity bench across from her.

William gazed at her with that pained expression he wore when running across a mixed-up metaphor in prose, then very slowly lowered himself to perch on the bench. He gave the assorted balms and ointments on the vanity table an interested glance, the long, white line of his neck baring itself to Verbena's gaze as he looked over his shoulder. The candlelight played along the birdlike wing of his collarbone, exposed as it was in the thin chemisette. Verbena was possessed by the lecherous urge to bite it.

With great restraint, she cleared her throat. "Would you like to avail yourself?" She nodded at the vanity. "Or I suppose I should say, does Flora? If, indeed, the two of you do not always share the same desires."

A delicate thing, discussing desires, yet Verbena could not avoid it, not when William was here with her. In her room. Alone, together, the night before she was to be married.

"That is one of the things I needed to speak to you about tonight. You are, above all others, the one I would trust with this." He turned back to her and flushed a warm pink. "I confess I have lately considered calling myself a third name."

"Really?" Verbena tried to rein in her surprise.

"It was a long carriage ride from London."

"What is it?" Verbena asked. "The third name, I mean."

A moment's pause, but only a moment. Considering the weight of the thing, it was a miracle. "Willa," he said.

"Oh, as in . . . ?"

He shrugged ruefully. "In this, I am not very creative. But it fits, does it not? At least"—another shy smile—"I think so."

"And is Willa— That is, are you," Verbena ventured, "man or woman?"

"Both, perhaps. Neither. Or rather—" He sighed and looked up toward the cobwebbed ceiling. "I do not think my state a godlike one, but the nearest I can explain is existing as the trinity does, each part comprising the whole."

"But how shall I regard you?" Verbena asked.

"However you wish, I suppose. There is no error you can make, so long as you do not think me solely one thing or another." He touched her hand, fingertips trailing along her skin.

Verbena smiled encouragingly. Tears pricked at her eyes, the overwhelming emotion of seeing her beloved like this moving her like nothing else ever had. "Then I am extremely gratified," she said, "to make your acquaintance, my dear Willa."

Tension flooded out of the newly christened Willa, his shoulders dropping from where they had been cinched up to his red ears. A sigh of pure relief flowed from his lips, his eyes closing briefly. "I thought you would be," he murmured. "I thought, I hoped, yet I did not *know.*" His eyes opened, warm and searching on Verbena's face. "How wonderful it is, knowing."

Verbena dabbed subtly at her eyes with the cuff of her dressing gown. "What else?" she said.

"Hm?" Willa asked.

"You said that was one of the things you needed to tell me tonight." Verbena clasped her hands about her knees. She could barely stand her mounting excitement, though it was tinged with dread. Surely Willa had not appeared at Eden Abbey intending to share this part of himself, then say farewell forever? Surely there was hope. "Why are you here, sweet Willa?"

Willa licked his lips before forming the words. "I came because you asked me to."

Verbena waited, but there was nothing else. She cocked her head like a curious spaniel. "Simple as that?" she asked. "No other reason?"

"Reason and sense leave me where you are involved," Willa

said. He rose from the vanity seat and paced the room, his naked feet tracing a path from the bedside to the window, then back again. "I am powerless in this regard. Perhaps I shall always be powerless when it comes to you."

"Now, really!" Verbena had heard a lot of declarations in her time, but this was too much.

"No, no, it's quite true," Willa said. "I tried to stay away, to ignore my heartbreak, and yet here I stand. I think I shall always come when you call. I came to you tonight–and I will come again, once you are married, if you so desire it." He stopped pacing, his hands clasped behind his back, the dark window behind him showing the long stretch of night. "I would sunder myself for your sake. I would be solely Flora, should you deign to be seen with me in public. Bosom friends might promenade arm in respectable arm." He swallowed. "Or you might prefer William take the role of your lover. If we are ever discovered, it would be better to be accused of the usual sort of affair instead of an unnatural one. Then again–"

"Wait." Verbena held up a hand, pleased it did not tremble visibly. "You have reconsidered my proposal? You . . . have not come to ask me to forsake Étienne?"

Willa looked at her, bereft. "I would not ask you to treat a friend so cruelly. His life is at stake."

"But before, you said–though I did not know your reasons, which are now readily apparent–" She motioned at Willa's trousers, his shawl. "You told me you could not bear to live a half life with me. Yet now you say you will?"

"I will do whatever you require of me," Willa said softly. "I am, despite my best efforts, utterly devoted to you. And I do not foresee that ever changing."

"But it will," Verbena blurted out. "It would have to. If you did as I asked, if you cut yourself in two when you have only recently understood the unity that exists in your dual nature–"

"I could be myself when we are alone," Willa argued. "That, at least, will be a great comfort to me."

"I do not want you to be with me despite the misery it will

cause you. I do not wish misery upon you at all!" The tears, which had threatened throughout the evening, now swelled over the riverbanks of Verbena's eyes. She dashed them away with the sleeve of her dressing gown. "I could not bear it if the strain of a clandestine affair caused you to regard me with bitterness. Oh, why would you introduce me to your third, beautiful name only to tell me you would destroy it? I do not want it done, not ever! I–I want you whole." She covered her face with her hands and began to weep.

It was a strange sensation; tears normally only came to Verbena when she required them. To be sobbing without her own say-so was an awful thing.

"My darling girl." Soft, swift footfalls crossed the room. Verbena felt the air shift as Willa knelt at her feet, clutching at the fabric of the dressing gown that covered her thighs. "Please don't cry. You must understand that, even without an arrangement between us, I would still be required to hide this version of myself from the public eye. I cannot be destroyed by that, only forced to choose which persona would have the pleasure of your company in polite society."

Verbena lifted her wet face and pinned Willa with a look. "Yet doing this for my sake would bring you pain. Do you deny that?"

Willa's face pinched. He was no liar. "I do not," he said at last.

"Then I cannot allow it." Verbena could hardly believe the words pouring out from her. Here was the one she loved, offering himself up exactly as she had wanted, and she was refusing him? Where was the Machiavellian girl who devised ploys that could shape the royal court? Dead, perhaps, murdered by love. "Think practically," she said, sniffing hard. "You cannot tell even the simplest lie to save your own skin. How can you be expected to conduct an affair with me–as man or woman–without exposing yourself eventually? Not to mention your misery would likely cause you to make missteps that a more contented soul would not. You could be ruined."

"I do not care for my reputation," said Willa.

"*I* care for it," Verbena countered. She envisioned, terrifyingly,

William being discovered and losing what little support his family gave him. Worse—Flora being exposed as William's alter ego and losing all patronage. It was too terrible to contemplate the possible ramifications if either came under such scrutiny that their nature was discovered. "I care for your reputation; I care for your good health; I care for your safety and freedom; I care for *you*." She gave up all pretense. "I love you, dear Willa. I love you too much to keep you for myself."

Willa stared up at Verbena, his fingers twisting in the silk of her dressing gown. "All right," he said, though his voice was choked with tears. "Yes. All right. As you say. Pah!" He rose to his feet, giving Verbena his back. It shook under her gaze, a fine tremor in Willa's shoulders, making the embroidered flowers bob in some imaginary breeze. "Stars above. Even being rebuffed by you is sweet, if it means hearing you say those words."

Verbena stood without hesitation and placed her hand on Willa's quaking shoulder. That did not seem enough to hold her love in one piece, so she claimed his narrow waist with a cinch of her free arm. Her hot cheek pressed against the plane of his back, rising and falling with Willa's breath. "I am sorry," she said. "I would tell you every day, if I could."

"In a little cottage with a thatched roof," Willa said between sobs. "With a tabby cat on the window ledge."

Verbena pressed her forehead to the blade of Willa's shoulder. She could see the cat's fat tail swinging, a beam of sunlight slicing through the curtains. "But it's not to be."

"It's not fair," Willa whispered. His hands came up to clasp Verbena's, crossing his arms to do so, folding himself in a second embrace. "We have only just found each other. We had no time."

"We have tonight," Verbena said. She kept her eyes closed, listening to the hitch inside Willa's body as he gasped for air. She held him tighter and willed her words to find their mark. "If I ask you to stay, will you do so out of devotion? Or would you stay only because you truly wish to?"

"Honestly, I cannot parse the two," Willa said. Verbena wished she could see his face as he spoke. "All I know is my soul yearns for yours, even if it is only for tonight."

Verbena turned him in her arms and, after searching his pretty eyes for any hesitation, pressed her mouth to his with a boldness that surprised them both. Willa made a noise against her lips, a high whine of need. His body sagged against hers so that she took nearly all his weight. She took it gladly. And wanted more.

She deepened the kiss, tasting the plush softness of Willa's mouth, his tongue, the salt of tears. Verbena allowed her selfishness, which would be forever put aside after this night, to come to the fore. Her fingers lifted to the tousled hair at the back of Willa's head and clutched, holding him fast to her. Her arm tightened about his waist in a crushing grip. Even if he had the strength to move, he would not have been able to. He was hers, if only until daybreak.

He was hers and no one else's.

The thought startled Verbena enough that she pulled away. Willa, taking great gulps of air between his kiss-bruised lips, stared at her beseechingly.

"Why have you stopped?" he asked.

"I—I'm pawing at you like the worst rake." She took Willa by the shoulders and pushed so that there was a few inches' distance between them. It seemed a gulf, an ocean, but she could not think when they were nearer. "You are a man, at least some of the time," she continued. "You should be the one to . . . direct us tonight."

Willa stared at her like she'd spoken ancient Greek. No, he probably knew ancient Greek; Swedish, then. "By rights, I should be the one following your lead. It's not as if I've ever—not with anyone else," he said.

"Well, neither have I," Verbena said hotly.

"I didn't presume so."

"Good!"

"Lovely."

Verbena caught her lip between her teeth and looked down at their feet. "So we have no idea what we're doing." She shook her head. "What a pair."

"You seem to have some idea," ventured Willa. "I don't mind, you know. Why shouldn't a lady be the one who kisses instead of waiting to be kissed? Does it make me lesser to be the canvas for her affections? I cannot believe so; I do not feel lesser in your arms." He leaned in only the barest inch, which was all it took for Verbena to embrace him tightly about the hips once more.

"You don't?" Verbena asked. It was a grave question, and this close to Willa's expressive face, she could clearly see the sincerity in his eyes as he smiled.

"Not a bit," he said. "I feel adored."

Verbena resolved to adore him as best she could for however long she was allowed, and damn whatever roles they were expected to inhabit. She kissed him again, hard enough to make him squeak in surprise, before cupping his face in her hands.

"Come to bed with me," she said.

Willa nodded, eyes near shut in bliss, his shawl slipping from his shoulders to land in a puddle on the floor.

Verbena tried to undress him, but she was stymied by the unfamiliar fastenings of his trousers. They weren't at all like the breeches she'd briefly worn for the masquerade, and her frustration could not be hidden. Willa's callused palms caught hers, drawing her attention to his fond, amused expression.

"Shall I?" he asked. "I know my way around both sorts of clothing."

Verbena lifted her jaw. She would not be embarrassed by her lack of knowledge; they had already established that there was no shame in it. "You shall," she said, injecting some imperiousness into her words.

Willa shivered against her, his eyes fluttering closed for a moment. "You are very talented at giving instruction," he said.

Verbena winced, not wanting to remind her beloved of a schoolmaster. "I should couch my requests more gently, I know."

"Please don't. Not on my account." Willa lifted their joined hands and crushed his smooth cheek to her knuckles. His eyes were deep, black pools, reflecting the candlelight's flicker. "Direct me as you would, Verbena. I would be a tool for your pleasure."

A thrill shot through Verbena's middle. It was a lovely thing, to have permission. She stared at Willa in wonder, then allowed her lips to curve into a catlike smirk.

"Disrobe completely, then. I don't want to see a stitch of clothing on you," she said.

Willa complied with alacrity, shoving off his trousers and chemisette. There was not much else, his state of undress being what it was, so it all happened in an eyeblink. Verbena let her gaze travel over him: the soft lines of his body, the smattering of freckles and beauty spots, the tender expanse of his thighs, at the apex of which his sex waited, wreathed in dark curls. She did not allow her eyes to linger there, though it was a near thing, forcing herself to look instead at Willa's softly parted lips.

"Am I formed to your liking?" he asked. Clearly the question caused him no great anxiety. He knew how pleasing he was to Verbena—he must, the way he tipped his head coyly to the side to bare his pale throat, the way his hips tilted ever so slightly toward her gaze. His hands, far from covering himself in shame, instead trailed up his own ribs, a teasing touch that Verbena wanted for herself.

She took him in another bruising kiss, feeling his hands clasp her tight around the waist. Pulling back, she nipped at his plush lower lip. "On the bed," she said, not answering his bratty question.

Back when she'd thought her future meant the usual sort of marriage to the usual sort of gentleman, Verbena had had no interest in bedroom exercises. The thought of a man did nothing to excite her, and even her earlier imaginings about Flora, when she'd thought Flora a singular person, were tentative and unsure. Yet having her hands on a beautiful creature who was neither—who brought with him no expectations as to Verbena's desires—sparked something inside her that had never before ignited.

She fairly tossed Willa to the bed with a clever spin, though Willa obviously went willingly. Verbena crawled atop him, shedding the layers of her dressing gown, her nightgown; every blasted gown she'd ever worn, it was all torn away. Her bare skin—places of her body that had never felt touch, nor given it—lit up with the sensation of meeting Willa's. Her strong thighs astride his hips, arms tangled, their breasts pressed together. They breathed hard, hearts hammering, the air between them humid.

Verbena stared down at where their bodies met in a way that felt celestial. Surely this could be no earthly act, to join like this? As far as Verbena could fathom, they hadn't even *done* anything yet, so how could this touch feel so blissful?

She lifted her gaze to Willa's face, intending to ask if he felt similarly, but her words were crushed in her throat. A look was all she needed to know her beloved's feelings on the matter; his eyes were huge and damp, his mouth open as if to produce the first notes of a hymn. He felt, she was sure, the same pleasure.

And the same pain. Her heart broke to think it.

For after tonight, he would be hers no longer, and their days would stretch out in opposite, lonely directions. Verbena would never have this again with him; she would never even see him. Not in actuality, not as he was now–open to her, and so completely Willa. This was all there was. Her hand tangled in his hair, every iota of her desiring only to keep hold of him.

The realization must have struck Willa at the same moment, or else he read the truth of it in Verbena's face, for his eyes shone with thick tears.

"Pretend it is not the end," he said. "I cannot bear the weight of it."

She kissed him, pressing him into the featherbed, pinning him down with her hands on his slim shoulders. *Damn all poetry,* she thought. *Damn all words.* What good were they now? There was no word for Willa in all of English.

When she finally released him, his lips were ruby red, high spots of color on his cheeks that rivaled the color of Verbena's hair. He looked devastated, and devastatingly beautiful. If they made love like this, with her riding atop, she did not think she could countenance seeing his every emotion flit across his face.

Verbena wrestled him onto his side instead, placing herself in the curved symbol of his body, her back to his sweat-dappled chest. She reached behind herself to clamp a hand to his hip. He was ready for her; she could feel it. She urged him forward, wanting no air between them.

"W-wait," Willa said. "Not– Please not like–" He squirmed in a feeble attempt to get his hips away. "Not inside."

Verbena, despite it all, still had her wits about her. She caught Willa's meaning, his panic at the possible consequences should she demand that particular act. There was no reason to bring a potential child into this quagmire; it was painful enough already. But he would do it if she asked. She knew it like she knew the directions on a compass. It was a heady thing, having that sort of power over another soul, and Verbena was loath to abuse it.

"Like this, then." She reached her free hand between her own legs, fingertips brushing the sage-leaf skin of his sex. He gasped sharply against her ear as she brought it forth.

"Your thighs," he whispered. It sounded prayerful.

Verbena tried not to think too much about that, lest she be distracted forever. She needed something to ease his way.

She grabbed his hand instead and guided it to her own sex. "Touch me. Get yourself wet with it."

"Here?" His careful fingers brushed at the dampness already forming within her.

She bit down on a stifled groan. "Sweetly, now."

And he was. He was perfectly, achingly sweet. His fingertips gathered her slick and painted it along the satiny insides of her legs, where he was clasped tight. He fucked her thighs and kept one patient hand cupped over her sex, so that each thrust gave her something to savor. She arched her back and reached for him, one hand a brand on his snapping hip, the other tangled in the hair atop his head.

He drew closer, molding himself to her back. His thrusts changed to a lewd rubbing like the grind of a grist mill. Verbena was incandescent, hot all over and sweating in the close air of the room. He was working so hard, all for her pleasure.

The thought sent her spiraling to her end.

He spent only after her shaking subsided. The essence pulsed in the hot vise of her legs, searing heat against her skin.

"Oh," she said, panting. "Oh, you beautiful thing."

"The mess–" Willa said, breathless in her ear, already apologetic though he still pulsed against her.

"Will keep," Verbena said firmly. It was sticky as honey, but she did not hate it. She took his limp hands in hers and held them tight to her own chest. Some naïve part of her wanted to think she might feel him always, though she knew it was not to be. This, along with every other pleasure, would be washed away come morning. Before her wedding.

She felt Willa's forehead press hot and slick against her nape. His breathing was still uneven, though she could not tell if it was from their exertions or encroaching sorrow.

If only there could be a cottage with a thatched roof. If only a fat tabby existed on a mantel somewhere. If only they could enjoy slow and easy breakfasts seated across a table from each other . . .

No. They had only tonight. Perhaps, she reasoned, if they didn't stop, the night would never end.

She rolled over, turning Willa on his back as she went. He stared up at her from his spot on the mattress, his mouth parted, his whole body lax and willing.

"Let me satisfy you again," he begged.

She ducked her head and took one of his dusky nipples between her teeth. He hissed at her tug.

"Several more times, at least," she promised, kissing it.

Chapter 23

The following morning dawned overcast with the threat of rain heavy in the air. Verbena could see the storm clouds gathering on the horizon through the filthy windowpane. Even the sheep seemed to be holding their breath.

Quill-callused fingers alighted on Verbena's bare shoulders. She gave a sigh as Willa moved her hair aside so that she could press a kiss to the nape of her neck. (Even in the confines of her own thoughts, Verbena had resolved to honor her beloved's request, never regarding her as solely man or woman, but both by turns.)

"Would you like me to help you?" Willa asked. Her voice was as quiet as the rest of the manor.

Verbena caught her eye in the small mirror affixed to the inner lid of her rosewood vanity case. "It would be cruel to have you act as bridesmaid to me today."

Willa merely selected a silver comb from the case. "I don't want to leave you just yet."

A tremor ran through Verbena at the words. Willa would have to leave eventually, she knew. And when she did, they would likely never see each other again. It would be too painful, passing each other in the street, attending the same parties, all the while unable to embrace each other as they wished. At least they'd had one night—one passionate night. Verbena's eyes drifted shut at the first touch of Willa's hands in her mussed hair.

One night was not enough. How could she be without this touch forever after?

Verbena cleared her throat, determined not to weep; she didn't need a puffy face on top of everything else today. "My mother was adamant that I take care with my coiffure," she said. "It is her view that I do not arrange my hair at all pleasingly most days."

"Your mother has no taste," Willa said mildly. She drew the comb through Verbena's red tresses, gently working out a snarl. "Your hair is unmatched. I envy your hair. If I could shrink to the size of a mouse and make a nest in a handful of discarded strands, I should be very happy."

The picture was so absurd that Verbena could do naught but laugh. "A mouse?"

"The size of a mouse." Willa left off combing long enough to demonstrate an inch or two between thumb and forefinger, still communicating via the vanity case mirror. "You would hardly notice me. I would be very quiet."

Verbena's helpless smile gave way to sorrow. Forevermore, Willa would be more than quiet; she would be silent, and Verbena would never again hear her beloved voice. She watched in the mirror as her face fell and her eyes became wet. Willa *tsk*ed and held her by the shoulders.

"No, please don't cry," she said. Her soft, warm breath ghosted along the back of Verbena's neck.

Verbena cleared her throat and sat taller on the plush stool. "Perhaps," she said, striving for a normal tone, "you should take a lock of my hair as a memento."

Delicate fingers, the makers of poems, combed through Verbena's tresses. "I do not need a memento," Willa said. "What would it signify, to keep a piece of you locked away in some jewel box? That is not my Verbena. She could never be contained by something as common as that."

The wave of sadness returned. Verbena was so brittle, she felt she could break in two. She gave a little sob, covering her lips with her balled-up lace handkerchief before more could be heard.

"Please don't speak," she whispered into the lace. "Please, one more word and I might–"

Willa moved from behind the small stool to kneel on the floor beside it, pillowing her head in Verbena's lap. Her arms wound about Verbena's middle and held her tight. "No more words," she promised.

Verbena curled over Willa, pressing her hot face into the fine brocade of her gown, and allowed them both a moment of grief.

There was a knock at the door. "Mrs. Montrose says I am to fetch you for the procession, miss," called one of the serving girls. "Are you ready?"

Verbena lifted her head and took stock of her reflection. Despite her efforts, her face was pink and puffy, her eyes shot through with red. She had never looked worse. Her mother would not be pleased.

Well, in a mere hour or two, she wouldn't need to give a fig about what pleased her mother.

"I'll be downstairs directly," she called back. "Only a moment."

Willa released her, but stayed on her knees, gazing up at Verbena with the most lovely, sad eyes. "Shall I leave?"

Verbena considered this. Selfishly, she did not want to send Willa away just yet. It was foolish to prolong the agony, yet if she could steal a few more moments with the one she loved . . .

"Could you stay? Would you?" She cupped Willa's cheek in her palm and watched her lean into the touch.

"As long as I am able," Willa murmured against her wrist.

The wedding party made the short journey from the Abbey to the local church on foot. Étienne's fine carriage, loaded with the bride and groom's luggage, was to meet them immediately after the ceremony to spirit the newlyweds south, where they would board a boat bound for Calais the following morning. The honeymoon had been a gift of the brothers Charbonneau; Étienne and Verbena had been forced to accept it.

The procession to the village church was a small affair, composed only of Verbena and her parents; Willa (perceived by the assembled as Verbena's good friend Flora, who had unexpectedly been in the area and had decided to attend the wedding on a whim); Étienne and his brothers; and Miles, who was acting in the capacity of Étienne's witness. The weather was bleak as they made the short trek on foot from Eden Abbey across the rolling hills and country lanes. More than once raindrops pattered against the brim of Verbena's pearl-trimmed hat, but it abated before her father and Miles could deploy the umbrellas they had brought.

Silence reigned as the procession crested the final hill and the modest church came into view. Verbena glanced over to Willa, who was walking at her side. Willa was looking at her as well, and only looked away when their gazes met, a guilty flush climbing her neck. Verbena peeked over her shoulder at Étienne, but that sight was no better. Her groom was giving a longing look to Miles, whose single visible eye was filled with concern.

At least the misery of the occasion was evenly distributed, she reasoned. Verbena squared her shoulders and clutched her small posey of local wildflowers closer to her belly.

The vicar was waiting for them in the churchyard. Mr. Montrose shook his hand and mumbled a few words of thanks. The others began to file past the headstones and into the vestibule. Verbena moved to follow them, but Étienne bade her wait with a light touch to her arm.

"I need to speak to you," he whispered.

Miles and Willa both turned in the doorway to give them a questioning look, but Verbena waved them on. "We will only be a moment," she said.

Their two companions did as she asked. The family members and the vicar had already gone inside, not bothering to wait for the betrothed couple. The two of them were incidental to the proceedings. Weddings, as a rule, were not lavish affairs at the best of times, but Verbena could not help but feel hers would be even more perfunctory than most. It would take all of twenty minutes, perhaps less, to be concluded.

Her heart sank at the thought. So little time left to be in Willa's presence.

The heavy wooden door of the church shut, leaving Étienne and Verbena alone in the churchyard. The wind whipped about them, threatening to take Verbena's hat. Several yards distant, a flock of sparrows leapt into the air, then returned to their perches atop the headstones almost en masse, like a dance where half the participants were a step behind. Étienne uncharacteristically removed his tophat, baring his head under the roiling sky.

"What is it?" Verbena asked. "Étienne, what's wrong?"

He shook his naked head. "I cannot do this."

"What? Don't be silly." Verbena gestured to the church. "We're here. We're already—this is already being done."

"Marrying you is the most reasonable course." Étienne lifted his head. His eyes were wild. "Yet I do not think I am a reasonable man. I am in love, and that has sapped me of all reason."

Verbena frowned, squinting at him. "In love?"

Étienne's cheeks took on a pinkish hue. "Miles," he said simply.

A flailing confusion overtook Verbena. "Is that what you call taking a roll on the forest floor?"

"What forest?" Étienne frowned. "What are you talking about?"

"The woods! In Wales. You two had—" She gestured to her own head and knees, indicating the evidence they had displayed on their persons after their romp.

"When we chased the cat?"

"As if there ever was a cat!"

Étienne shook his head. "We never . . . Miles and I have not dared. We have been chaste as nuns, as you and Miss Witcombe have been."

Verbena puffed out her cheeks and looked away.

Étienne gasped. "You didn't!"

"Oh, leave me be," Verbena said. She could not take yet another insult heaped upon her this morning. "It was one night." Her face felt in turns both fiery and numb.

"One night! If only I could have one night with Miles." His yearning was palpable.

She threw her hands in the air. "Fine! So you're in love with him! You still need a wife and I still need a husband." She bit her tongue when it came to the latter; there had been a husband-and-wife on offer for her, if only she had abandoned Étienne. "What does it change?" she said in a low voice.

Étienne merely stared at her. "Everything, my dear. My heart belongs to that man"—he pointed at the church doors—"and I cannot pretend otherwise."

It took all of Verbena's iron will not to beat him about the head with her posey of flowers. As it was, she clutched the beribboned stems so tightly, and shook so violently, that several white petals fluttered to the ground.

"You are being absurd," she said in a low hiss, cognizant of the people waiting for them right inside. "Think of why we agreed to do this in the first place. What of your reputation! What of my security! What of our futures! All of London is expecting us to return as man and wife. What do you plan to do, walk away from society entirely?"

"Perhaps," Étienne said, challenging.

"Perhaps!" Verbena gave a single, mocking *ha!* "Would that I could be as bold as you, monsieur."

"You could be," he said. "You always have been. Why not now, Verbena? Where is your boldness when it truly matters?"

Her face went hot. "I am not bold," she said.

Now it was Étienne's turn to bark a *ha!* into the air. "There is not another woman in all of England as bold as you."

That brought Verbena up short. What Étienne was saying rang true; she had been bold enough to stage this false marriage and all its other myriad plots. She had stood firm against her parents when questioned about her decisions.

Why, then, could she not be bold now? Why, with all her cleverness and wit, had she thought herself unequal to the task of forging a different kind of life? Lord Eden had done it; the women at Plas Tân had done it; the dippers of the coast had done it; hell, even Lord Byron himself had done it. He'd embroiled himself in every conceivable type of scandal on the way, but the fact remained, he *had* done it.

Her entire life, Verbena had sidestepped scandal at any cost. It was the game forced upon everyone, so it had never occurred to her to do otherwise. Playing the game had gotten her to this point—standing in a graveyard with a groom who was ready to bolt.

Perhaps it was necessary to play by a new set of rules.

All this passed through Verbena's mind in the course of an eyeblink. It was only afterward that she realized Étienne was attempting to earnestly talk through their available options.

"I–I do not know what would happen if we were to call off the wedding," he said. "The consequences may be awful, but if we tell your parents and the vicar the truth of this sham–"

"No," Verbena said. "Truth is a luxury we cannot afford right now. We must do something else. Something unexpected." She felt, for the first time in days, her old strength return to her body. Her spine felt straighter, her shoulders prouder. "Go into the church. Fetch Miles and Willa."

Étienne frowned. "Willa?"

"I mean Flora," Verbena amended. She could explain her beloved's new appellation later, if Willa wished it. "Quickly! We have little time." She pushed at his arm, urging him toward the door.

"My dear," he said, "I do hope you know what you are doing."

Verbena gave him a smile and tossed her posey off into the graveyard. "When have I not?"

Chapter 24

After a short and bewildering consultation in the graveyard, Willa returned inside, her heart pounding in her breast. The church's interior was, as so many village churches are, ancient and minuscule. Willa counted only a handful of wooden pews on each side of the aisle that ran up the center of the nave. These were entirely empty, as the wedding party had gathered nearer the altar, which was situated behind an elaborate chancel arch. Willa's eyes lifted to take in the faded frescoes that had been painted there centuries ago: angels and saints, books and keys, a sallow-eyed Christ looking slightly annoyed by the whole affair.

She picked her way along the edge of the nave, past the narrow lancet windows that allowed only slivers of watery light into the church. Her footsteps might have echoed terribly, but the murmurs of the assembled group at the front offered blessed cover. The arch was supported by thick, elaborately carved columns, and Willa found she fit neatly behind one, where she could listen to and watch the proceedings.

"And where is our bride and groom?" said a voice at her elbow.

"Oh!" Willa nearly leapt a foot into the air, twisting to find a hunched woman dressed in ragged skirts with a tattered headscarf tied over her gray hair. In her hands she clutched a broomstick. "Oh, I am sorry. I did not see you there."

"That's quite all right. Most people do not see old women." Her country accent was thick as treacle. "Especially a charwoman going about her duties." Her eyes twinkled in a way that Willa found most familiar.

She bent her knees so that she might look directly into the woman's face. As adept with cosmetics as she was, Willa immediately noted the traces of pearl powder and India ink. She looked more closely, then stifled her gasp behind a palm.

"Come now," Lord Byron whispered in his own voice. "You would not deny a sweet granny a peek at the nuptials, would you?" He swept his broom along the church floor in a cursory manner, gaze darting around the arch to the altar.

Willa dropped her hand. "What the hell are you doing here?" she demanded, keeping her voice low for fear of the echo.

"Isn't it obvious? I've decided to do as my most infamous hero did and attend under a feminine guise." Byron gave a shrug, once more adopting a hunched posture. "After whisking you away from London in my own coach–"

"Lady Croydon's coach," Willa corrected.

"Six of one, half dozen of the other," he said. "Anyway, after going through all that trouble, you cannot possibly think I would miss my chance to watch you steal that French tailor away from Miss Montrose. It's not every day one sees true love triumph."

"I am not stealing–" Willa stopped and sighed through her nose, reminding herself of the part she had yet to play. "Fine. Stay for the wedding. But for god's sake, do not let anyone know who you are."

Byron gave her a rakish look, shaking his broom heartily. "In this flawless disguise? Impossible." He continued sweeping the floor, or at least miming so as he crossed the aisle.

Willa watched him go and prayed he would not disrupt her plans. She peered around the chancel arch once more to spy on the wedding party. Mrs. Montrose seemed the most agitated of the group, glaring at everything within seething distance: the altar candles, the silent vicar, his record book, the other members of the party. Even Christ on the cross was not immune. "Where is she?" she hissed into her husband's ear. Her words carried well in the empty church.

Mr. Montrose fished a watch from his fob pocket and consulted it, shaking his head.

"It is nearly noon by now, surely," said the eldest Charbonneau.

"The bride and groom have no reason to drag this out so long," muttered the next brother.

"Weddings should take no more than half an hour—any longer and it may as well be a coronation," said Mr. Montrose.

Willa looked back toward the vestibule, where her compatriots were hopefully positioning themselves. In short order, she saw Étienne pop his dark head into the nave and give her a questioning look. Willa beckoned him onward. He nodded and disappeared once more.

A glance at Byron showed he was wholly preoccupied watching the scene at the altar, which was lucky. Willa clutched at the marble arch and held her breath.

The overlapping voices of Étienne and Verbena began softly, barely audible over the remarks from the wedding party, but in time they rose to a level that could not be ignored. Mrs. Montrose was the first to hear, her head whipping around to stare down the center aisle. Soon, the rest of them, including the vicar, were craning their necks as the argument swelled. Willa plastered her back to the chancel arch to keep herself from view. Sweat beaded beneath her clothes.

"You cannot do this to me!" Verbena shouted. "You are a rake! The lowest rake!"

"If I am a rake," Étienne roared, just as loudly, "then at least I am an honest one! You, dear Verbena, are nothing but a liar!"

"A liar?" The screech made Willa want to laugh so badly, she was forced to cover her grinning mouth with her palm, lest she give away her position. "If that's the way you feel—!"

"Feeling has little to do with it! Not where you are concerned!"

"What on earth . . . ?" Mrs. Montrose bustled forward, no doubt intending to investigate the awful row, but before she could cross into the nave, Étienne burst from the vestibule.

His hair was a wild riot of curls, and his eyes bulged with emotion. He sported a flush of determination on his cheeks as he strode forward to meet the party.

Étienne paused at the threshold of the chancel arch and addressed everyone: "It brings me great pleasure to announce the wedding is off."

Gasps and protests erupted. Étienne ignored them.

"I cannot marry Miss Montrose," he continued, his voice echoing in the chamber, "not when my heart belongs to another."

"Who?" his brother demanded.

"Yes, who!" Mrs. Montrose cried.

That was Willa's cue. She stepped smoothly from behind the pillar to stand at Étienne's side. His sweaty hand clasped hers as he gifted her with a mischievous smirk. Then it was right back into his role. He faced the wedding party again.

"Miss Flora Witcombe," he declared. "I love her, and she loves me. I intend to elope with her immediately."

"Hurrah," said Willa. She was not much of an actress, but it did not seem to matter. Their audience was already frothing at the mouth in the face of this performance.

"What!"

"Sacre bleu . . ."

"Now see here–"

French and English voices fought for dominance, and in the confusion, the door to the vestibule clanged open. Verbena marched in, resplendent in her wedding clothes.

The hubbub died down as she pointed an accusing finger in Étienne's direction.

"I am not being left at the altar by an unrepentant worm like you," Verbena said. *She* was an excellent actress, of course, full of verve and emotion. Willa had to remind herself not to grin as she watched the masterful strutting. "*I* am leaving *you*! So that I may be with *my* true love."

Miles poked his head out of the vestibule and gave everyone a weak wave in greeting. "Erm, good morning."

Verbena motioned him forward with rapid movements of her hand until he was at last standing by her side. They, too, joined hands, with Verbena beaming sunnily at her supposed beau. For less than half a moment, her gaze fell on Willa, and they shared a truly happy look.

"I have been in love with Mr. McDonald this entire time," Verbena announced. "I cannot keep my heart from its match any longer. We are *also* eloping."

The ensuing uproar shook the stained glass in the church's window frames. Mr. Montrose said something quite insulting about both the French and the Scots, which set off Étienne's brothers in a shouting match that deafened every ear. The vicar seemed overcome with embarrassment and launched into a prayer. Mrs. Montrose remained frozen with the sourest look etched on her face.

In the confusion, Willa felt Verbena tug on her sleeve. "Come," she whispered. "Quick as you can."

Willa picked up her skirts, ready to run.

"Hold on, you!" cried Mrs. Montrose, rousing from her stupor. She barreled toward Willa, her arms outstretched.

Willa froze in fright, as still as a doe in the center of the aisle. Verbena had her by the arm, but even her insistent pulling could not make Willa move. Not in the face of such a frenzied attack by an enraged mother.

A broomstick appeared under Mrs. Montrose's charging feet. She tripped and fell quite spectacularly on the polished floor.

Willa looked up wildly to meet Lord Byron's smirk. Even dressed as a crone, his mirth was unmistakable.

Go, he mouthed, then launched into his false accent, piling apologies onto Verbena's mother. Of course, his fumbling attempts at helping her to her feet only served to keep her prone on the floor longer.

With one final nod of gratitude to His Lordship, Willa made for the churchyard. She did not spare a single look back at the wedding party, who may or may not have descended into blows by that point. She was flanked by Étienne and Verbena, with Miles right behind them. Together, all four tumbled out into the sunlight. Étienne's coach awaited them as planned, the driver giving them a worried look.

"What's going on in there?" he asked. "Sounds like fisticuffs."

"Never mind that," said Étienne. He wrenched open the carriage door and began assisting Willa inside. "Drive, man! Drive as if the devil himself is on our heels!"

"Close enough, seeing as it's my parents," Verbena muttered as she joined Willa in the carriage.

Willa clasped her in her arms, holding her trembling body in a tight embrace. "Oh, you were wonderful!"

"Do you think they believed it?" Verbena asked into the fall of her hair.

"Of course they did. It could not have been done more neatly."

Miles hoisted himself onto the seat across from them, tugging Étienne in by the hand. "Drive!" he shouted.

"To the coast as planned, sir?" asked the bewildered driver.

"Non! North! To Scotland!" cried Étienne.

The driver whipped the horses into a frenzy before the door was even shut.

Chapter 25

Their long journey north eventually drew to a close. Verbena could not help but keep her hand firmly ensconced within Willa's and her face turned toward the open carriage window. When she spotted a particularly pretty vista—which was often, in that part of Scotland—she would direct Willa's attention to the sight with giddy eagerness. As both Willa and Scotland would be home for the foreseeable future, she wished to familiarize herself with them as much as possible.

"I know it's the hundredth loch we've passed today," Verbena said as the carriage followed the curve of the water's edge, "but I think it's the loveliest yet." She squeezed Willa's hand in hers, her head whipping back and forth so she might take in the loch and Willa's pleased expression equally.

Willa gave the view a polite glance, then fastened her gaze on Verbena. "As lovely as a thing can be," she murmured. She squeezed Verbena's thigh through her pelisse.

Verbena was still unused to such attentions, and she glanced across the carriage to gauge their travel companions' reaction, only to find they were paying no mind. Miles lay across the seat with his head in Étienne's lap, napping. Étienne stroked his fingers through Miles's hair, humming to himself. Miles was, Verbena noticed, drooling a bit in his sleep.

Willa must have noted this too, for she smothered a giggle against Verbena's neck. Verbena tucked her lips to contain her happy squeal. It was still a novelty to love so freely. She could hardly wait to arrive at Miles's home so that she and Willa could finally be alone. The stolen nights at inns along the road were not enough; though they could share a bed, as ladies did in those establishments, the walls of such places were thin. Verbena had been forced to keep her touches brief and furtive with one palm clasped tight across Willa's mouth to stifle her whimpers. It would be wonderful to finally have the privacy to let those cries tumble from her lips.

But as Verbena thought about their new home, so close now, her mischievous smile slipped. She turned back to the window and contemplated the gentle, verdant hills that lined the roadway. Her plan, made in such haste in the churchyard, had its pitfalls. Heading to Scotland had a dual purpose: to convince those who cared about such rumors that both "couples" had absconded to Gretna Green to be wed, and to settle in Miles's hometown, far from London's whispers.

Yet Miles McDonald was not a rich man, and whatever lodgings he was to provide for her and Willa would surely be much less comfortable than Verbena's previous home. She needed to steel herself; however small or squalid the rooms turned out to be, they were still a generous gift from a man who had very little. Verbena would accept them with grace and good spirits so as not to offend.

Willa, as if sensing the encroaching worries, squeezed her warm hand around Verbena's. Verbena shot her a grateful look. They could have an entire conversation, it seemed, using no words whatsoever.

Willa was the first to look away. She nudged the toe of her Hessian boot against Miles's lax leg. "Wake up, Miles," she said. "Tell me how much farther we must go. Surely we are close?"

Miles roused just as the coach rattled along a bend in the road. He sat up and looked out the window, his hair sticking up in comical licks. Verbena suppressed a chuckle; the hours spent together in the carriage had improved her opinion of the man, who she now saw was kind and quite silly.

Of course, knowing that he was not her rival helped immensely.

"Nearly there, Willa," he announced. (The long journey had also given them all ample time to be properly reintroduced.) "See that rock? That's the boundary of my family's land." He pointed out the window at an outcropping that resembled a flat bench.

"Do you not think we should stop somewhere along the road before we arrive so that I might change into more suitable clothing?" Willa asked. She was dressed for travel in her trousers and waistcoat with a velvet pelisse for warmth. While their driver had been paid to keep his opinions of his passengers' dress to himself—a much better use of Étienne's honeymoon money than Calais—Verbena knew Willa felt a measure of anxiety that she would be deemed lewd by the people of Peeblewick.

"I don't think anyone will mind what you're wearing," Miles said, which was strange. "No one should bother us. Not where we're going."

Verbena's heart sank. Her friend, she reasoned, must be alluding to the fact that they would be living in such obscurity that no one would take note of them whatsoever. Still, better to wallow in obscurity than be placed in harm's way.

Her dour thoughts must have been apparent on her face, for Willa leaned close to whisper in her ear: "No matter what, as long as we are together, I shall be grateful."

"Yes," Verbena whispered in return. "Agreed." She pushed the sour imaginings from her mind.

Étienne hung half his body from the window, craning his neck for a view of Miles's property. "Ah!" he said. "Your home is just past this parcel, then?"

Miles stuck his head out as well, choosing to flank Étienne's body with his own instead of availing himself of the window opposite. Verbena rolled her eyes at the sight of their lower halves, which interrupted her own view. "No, this is it," Miles said.

Now Verbena's curiosity was aroused. She levered herself through the empty window and caught sight of the tract stretching out before them.

"This parcel?" she yelped. "Here?"

"Why, yes," said Miles, his voice carrying over the coach's roof. "Can you not see from that side?"

Verbena reached back and grabbed for Willa's arm to maneuver her through the window as well. She could hardly believe her eyes, and felt it prudent to have her beloved's confirmation that they did not deceive her. Willa obliged by releasing a shocked gasp, an entirely sensible reaction.

Because Miles's home was a fucking castle.

It loomed high into the sky, its ivory-colored stonework shining in the sun. Ramparts trimmed the roofline like orderly teeth while turrets thrust upward at appropriate intervals. The windows were many and as clear as the lochs Verbena had viewed on their long journey. Roses grew fat and red in the hedgerows that lined the lawn, and thick woods bordered the land on all sides.

"Miles," Willa said slowly, "this–this is where we are to live? Are you sure?"

Miles withdrew back into the coach to collapse on the seat. "I think I know it well enough. I've lived here since I was a boy, you know."

The rest of the party joined him, sprawling on the cushions with their wind-mussed hair.

"But dear Miles," Étienne said, "how is this possible?"

"Are you not impoverished?" Willa demanded.

"What?" Miles laughed. "No, not at all."

"So you are wealthy!" Étienne cried.

Miles shifted uneasily against the cushions. "I would call myself comfortably situated."

"You're not 'comfortable,'" Verbena said. "You're rich! Castle rich." She flapped a hand at the window. "Everyone in London thought you a pauper!"

"Did they?" Miles asked. "No one ever told me that."

"Why would they?" Verbena said. "It seemed–apparent."

"Oh. Golly." Miles grimaced.

"You could have *said,*" Étienne insisted.

"Well, I didn't want anyone thinking I was a braggart!"

Willa groaned into her hands. "You mean to say you let us all think we would be living in a ramshackle hovel out of *politeness*?"

Miles's eyes widened in alarm. "You thought–?" He softened. "And you decided to come with me anyway?"

"Of course we did. We thought there was no alternative." Verbena regarded him closely. "And, of course, there is no alternative to company so good as yours," she added.

Miles beamed at her. "Likewise, Miss Montrose."

Étienne's gaze had gone all dreamy. "I'm going to live in a castle," he murmured.

"More of a manor," Miles said apologetically. "And it's not as if I have a title or anything. My father purchased it from a noble family who'd fallen on hard times."

"If that's the main house," Willa said, "I can't wait to see the cottage you're giving us."

Verbena remembered then: Miles had described only vaguely the "outbuilding" she and Willa were to have. She had pictured something sad and dreary, but seeing the McDonald estate now, her spirits were much improved.

As the carriage made its way up the long, neatly maintained drive, a portcullis rose to admit it. Verbena boggled as they passed beneath the high archway and into a neatly tended courtyard. A veritable flood of onlookers surged forward to meet them, men and women in various costumes, some in their shirtsleeves or with their hair hanging loose down their backs, all smiling for reasons unknown.

Verbena pressed her arm protectively over Willa's chest to keep her in the shadow of the coach's interior. "Miles, who are all these people?"

"Why, the servants," he said. "Peeblewick is quite extensive, as you have noted, and it requires a large staff. They are–well, I probably should have told you earlier, but they are all, to a man, for want of a better phrase, exceedingly devoted to me."

An older gent with a wisp of white hair about his ears fought his way to the front, grinning widely. "Master McDonald! It is so good to have you back at Peeblewick," he called as the coach came to a halt.

"Good to be back, Silversmith," Miles said, flinging the coach door open. "And, as promised in my letter, I have brought more souls to populate the old pile." He held out his hand to Verbena, who took it after only a moment's hesitation. She could trust her friends, now that they'd come so far together. She allowed herself to be led out of the coach and into the sunlight. "Miss Verbena Montrose," Miles said to everyone, "lately of London."

"How do you do, miss," said Silversmith, shaking her hand with delightful informality. "I'm what you might call the head butler here at Peeblewick. At your service." She could perceive that the healthy blush on his cheek was actually rouge.

Miles's butler . . . was wearing rouge.

While Verbena gaped, Miles continued with the introductions, assisting Willa from the coach. "My good friend and compatriot, Willa Witcombe," he said, leaving off, Verbena noted, any honorific. The butler and assembled servants did not bat an eye at that nor her strange dress, welcoming Willa into the fold with the same warmth Verbena had enjoyed.

"And finally," Miles said, "Monsieur Étienne Charbonneau, my dear, dear companion." He helped Étienne down from the carriage as Étienne blinked in the bright light.

Silversmith kissed Étienne in the continental fashion on both cheeks. "Welcome, monsieur," he said. The rest of the staff echoed the sentiment with a loud cheer.

Étienne stood there, dazed. Verbena felt similarly. It was as if they had been transported to a fantastical realm where nothing was as it had been. She reached without looking and found Willa's hand reaching already for hers. They squeezed their fingers around each other's, a reminder that this was real.

"Miss Montrose and Willa will take the cottage by the burn," Miles informed Silversmith.

"Certainly. Sarah! Eleanor!" The butler ushered forth two cheery young maids. "Show our new residents to their lodgings, please."

"This way, miss," said one to Verbena. The girls led the way, shooting curious smiles over their shoulders as they walked. They left the courtyard, making their way down a garden path that led over a small footbridge and across a storybook sort of stream. One of the maids placed her hand on the small of the other's back, giggling softly at some whispered aside.

Willa held Verbena's hand tighter. "Are they all like us?" she said under her breath. "Can they really be . . . ?"

It seemed too wonderful to contemplate, yet here they were, being led by two girls younger than they through a stand of trees.

"Not too far now," called one lass up ahead.

The other nodded at the surrounding forest. "Gives you a bit of privacy, I reckon. Close enough to the big house if you need anything, apart enough to do as you please."

Verbena blinked at that. Her hand tightened in Willa's. "I think," she said, "we should get a house cat. Right away."

"A tabby?" Willa's smile was like the dawn, like dusk falling, like everything in between—just as she was.

Verbena nodded. "A fat one."

Epilogue

A mere eight months later, Verbena found herself at the writing desk in the front sitting room of the cottage. It fit perfectly beneath the window so that she could look out over Miles's fields and watch the dots of shaggy cows while she wrote. The scent of honeysuckle, which grew in thick vines around all the lower windows, wrapped her in its embrace. Verbena inhaled it deeply.

When she'd first occupied the cottage with Willa, Verbena had insisted that the desk was merely for her correspondence. While it was true that she maintained a robust flurry of letters back and forth with her friends in London, Wales, and abroad, she had, eventually, begun scribbling out some amusing bits of prose.

They were not novels, exactly, nor were they etiquette guides for young ladies. They could possibly be called memoirs; Verbena's writing was a sort of compendium of her life's work, which was collecting the most delectable tidbits of gossip and well-founded rumors. Her goal was to put down in writing every speck of dirt that she had ever uncovered on members of the ton. As their number was finite, and everyone was in some way related to everyone else, it became increasingly clear that anyone could be blackmailed by such a comprehensive accounting. Which was quite gratifying.

When Willa had read the first passage Verbena completed, she'd sat up in their cheery, warm bed with her toes tucked under Verbena's ankles, her mouth hanging open.

"Darling, do you mean to print this?"

"Shouldn't I?" Verbena asked, snuggling closer. Willa always smelled wonderful in the early morning, skin warm and soft all over.

"You mention everyone by name! It's all so very . . ."

"Scandalous, yes." Verbena put her head on Willa's slight shoulder, where it fit so well as to have been made for her. "I do not intend to publish it, not yet. Once it is all finished, I will make several copies for safekeeping. And if anyone should ever attempt to disturb our little enclave here, I will be ready."

Willa shivered against her. "You will ruin lives if this goes to print, you know."

"Only if anyone tries to ruin ours," Verbena said.

"My beautiful Boudica." Willa bussed her on the top of her head. "My warrior queen. But when you say 'anyone' . . . "

Verbena hummed in agreement. "It will take some time, I expect, to amass information on every single lord and lady. I am only recently arrived in Scotland, after all, and must familiarize myself with a whole new cast of characters. Every lady needs a hobby, though."

"I am so glad that you love me," Willa said. "Otherwise you would be quite terrifying."

Verbena raised a knowing brow in her direction. "I don't terrify you now? This must be rectified." And with Willa's happy yelp, Verbena tackled her into a more pleasing position.

Verbena smiled at the memory while at her tiny writing desk, then banished all thoughts from her head save the ones regarding Lord Dulwich and his extensive gambling debts. She completed the final paragraph of that entry before sitting back in her chair to stretch her arms luxuriously.

To her right was the fireplace, and above it on the mantel sat a fat tabby cat named Sappho. The animal had appeared at the back door of the cottage, mewling for attention. Verbena and Willa had obliged with a saucer of cream. Naturally, he–for they had named him before making a thorough investigation of his feline form, and once that was done, the name had already stuck–

opted to stay indefinitely. Currently Sappho was doing what he did best, which was nothing at all. He lay sprawled on the mantel with his tail swishing sleepily back and forth. Verbena followed its movements, a pleased smile on her lips.

The smile only grew when Willa came down the stairs, his Hessian boots tapping out a smart beat on the weathered boards. No doubt her dear heart had also been hard at work that morning at his own writing desk, which occupied much of the second bedroom upstairs. Willa had balked at dragging a "man's" desk up the stairs for his use, saying he would be content with a model like the one Verbena owned, but Verbena had rightly pointed out that Willa's desk needed to be properly large. It was, after all, servicing two writers—Flora Witcombe's poems were stored in the right-hand drawers while William Forsyth's gothic novels in progress were housed on the left.

Willa was even contemplating releasing some work under his own name, but had not yet decided what form it might take. "I might try my hand at joining the Romantics," he'd said just the night prior while cooking their simple dinner of chicken and vegetables stewed in wine. (Verbena was not as adept in the kitchen as Willa, but she could slice potatoes well enough.)

"Poetry?" Verbena had asked, cutting her potatoes into precise rounds.

"Novels, perhaps. Love stories, certainly." Willa's tiny smile had curved upward. It was startlingly similar to the one Sappho wore after he feasted on minced fish. "Now that I consider myself an expert on the subject."

Verbena fell a little more in love with him then.

She fell a little more in love every day, actually, and for the smallest reasons. The way he stood on the last stair, frowning at the letter in his hands, for instance, as he was doing right now. The sight of his inky wrist and wild curls. Every moment was cause to love him even more.

"I have to go down to London tomorrow," Willa announced with a sigh. "Some issue with the printers."

"Oh dear." It wouldn't be the first time they'd been apart, but it didn't make it any more palatable. She liked Willa in her bed and in this house. She liked it very much. Still, business was business. "Will you be traveling as Flora this time?" she asked. If so, they'd need to arrange for Étienne to accompany him. Willa's "husband" was normally very accommodating, as he enjoyed visiting London every few months to peruse the latest textiles, all brought directly to the Bloomsbury house by the best drapers. Of course, Willa and Étienne were not actually married, nor were Verbena and Miles, but outside of the estate, no one knew that. And Miles had paid the local magistrate a judicious sum never to divulge it.

Willa shook his head. "This is a job for William, I'm afraid. Paper prices, negotiations. As Flora's patron, they should know I am very displeased." He rolled his eyes. It was tiresome, Verbena knew, but necessary. He hopped off the step and drew close to press a kiss to the top of Verbena's head. "I will return as soon as I am able."

"Whilst you're there, you may as well look in on my parents," Verbena said.

Willa drew back, wide-eyed. "Are you serious?"

A few months into their stay at the McDonald estate, the two of them had dined with Étienne and Miles in the main house–a succulent dish of pheasant. Miles had brought up the subject of Mr. and Mrs. Montrose, who had apparently written to him, demanding to know what had become of their daughter and, more pressing in their estimation, how exactly Mr. McDonald proposed to compensate them for this outrageous breach of decorum.

"I could have my solicitor send them a strongly worded letter," he'd suggested.

Verbena had only laughed. "That would not deter them. The only thing they care about is money." She'd placed a hand on Willa's bouncing knee beneath the table, calming her nervous movements. "Offer them an annuity of–what do you think is fair? Twenty pounds? And tell them they shall receive this generous gift from you, a man who has received no dowry, by the way, only if they agree to never write or attempt to see us again."

"Twenty pounds is not very much," said Étienne. "It would not keep a respectable lady in comfort, let alone a couple."

"It is twice what I was given in a year as pin money, when I was given any at all," Verbena countered. "Therefore, it should suffice for their purposes."

Willa's knee bounced once more under her hand. "Oh, but Lovely," he said (he often called her Lovely), "would they really accept such a small sum in return for never again seeing their only child?" His big, dark eyes gazed at her with something like heartache. "I cannot imagine anyone allowing that, not at any price."

Verbena smiled and squeezed his knee. "You forget, my parents do not share your excellent taste. They will accept it," she said.

And she was proven correct. Mr. Montrose's response to Miles's proposal arrived swiftly, and the payment for his continued silence was dispatched with the same alacrity. Verbena was easy in the knowledge that she was free of her parents forever.

Willa's family was another matter entirely. As far as the Forsyths were aware, their brother William had absconded to the Continent with a new bride and was happily settled in an obscure Italian village. His letters arrived as if from a packet ship, with a few coins slipped to the local postmaster to protect the ruse. Verbena had worried that Willa would be bereft without his family, but he had assured her that it was a relief to no longer be expected to visit with his boisterous brothers except when he wished; his visits to London were his to manage.

As for Étienne, he had quickly become enamored of Highland dress and established a small but thriving shop of his own in town, which he staffed with trusted apprentices who shared his nature. His brothers thought him well situated with his new wife, and as long as no one told them otherwise, all was well.

Furthermore, there was no real danger of the brothers Charbonneau–or anyone else of their acquaintance–discovering the actual shape of their lives. The staff at Peeblewick respected Miles far too much to gossip about his affairs, not because he was a decent employer (though he was) but because he consistently opened his doors to anyone who sought safe harbor. Word must have spread through the secret channels that have always existed among certain populations, for the needful arrived with terrible regularity. Verbena had seen with her own eyes the queer sorts that came to their little enclave. It was Plas Tân on a grander scale, a place where those of their disposition could get back on their feet or find a home, far from the strictures of the outside world.

It was not a perfect haven; nothing was. Which was why Verbena had focused her energies on her memoir. Call it insurance, call it blackmail–she had no qualms in wielding this, her chosen weapon. Not if her preferred family was ever at risk.

"Lovely?" Willa's voice brought Verbena out of her reverie. "I said, are you serious? I would rather not pay your parents a visit, as I do not think I would be a welcome guest. Do they even know William?"

Verbena turned in her desk chair to smile up at him. "No, of course not. I only meant, perhaps you could stroll by their new address." An address in a less grand, though perfectly serviceable, part of town, as befit their reduced circumstances. "I want to make sure they are where they say they are. Always a good idea to know the locations of the pieces on the board."

"If my own heart sends me, I shall go," Willa said with a teasing glint in his eye.

"Well, I am not sending you away just now." Verbena hooked her fingers in Willa's skirts and tugged until he bent to meet her lips. "We have until tomorrow."

"I should pack a trunk." Willa kissed her, slow and sweet. "I should do a great many things."

Verbena opened her thighs in a wide V, the obscene movement made more so by the trousers she now favored. "You should have a seat here, I think," she told Willa quite seriously, "and relax a moment. Don't you agree?"

With a shy smile, Willa clambered into Verbena's lap, his skirts flowing over her legs. "How can I not," he said, "when you are the most agreeable?" He leaned down and gifted Verbena a kiss to her forehead. "The most lovely." Her nose. "The most–everything."

Verbena smiled up at him, her hand making its own journey up his leg. "Why, Willa," she said, "what poetry."

Acknowledgments

It is a truth universally acknowledged that a book is not, and never can be, the product of a single person, no matter how much of a control freak they are. My dearest thanks to:

- Dana, first and always
- Lauren, who gave me the idea for Willa in the first place
- Kaila, who was correct in saying I was missing a masquerade
- Jesse, for rescuing chunks of this manuscript from the jaws of my laptop
- Mom, for making me tea while I wrote chunks of this book that my brother Jesse then had to rescue from my laptop
- Larissa Melo Pienkowski, the most tireless agent in the biz, as we call it (we do not call it that)
- Anna Kaufman, the best enabler I could ask for and an even better editor
- Natalia Berry, for the amazing notes and flawless poetry

- The entire team at Vintage Books, including Nora Reichard, Amy Ryan, Mark Abrams, Steven Walker, Christine Hung, Nadia Blocker, and Demetri Papadimitropoulos.
- Jay Hulme, who kindly explained the Church of England to me on Bluesky
- The New York Public Library, which furnished me with many biographies on Lord Byron
- Lord Byron, for being so fucking weird that everything I wrote here is normal by comparison
- Authors Against Book Bans, for giving me a place to put my energy
- And finally, my wife, Kara, who makes this all possible.